F

FINAL

RECKONING

JEFFERY L CHENEY

CRAIG J CHENEY

JARED L CHENEY

Cheney

FINAL
RECKONING

Published by 7 Cs Books, LLC
P. O. Box 231
Vernonia, OR 97064
www.7CsBooks.com

DEDICATION

To Heinlein, Asimov, Clarke, Bradbury, Wells, Verne, Herbert, Niven, Adams and all the other great ones who set us on a path that we have greatly enjoyed.

Final Reckoning

PROLOGUE
Caspar Shipyards - Worth System
1 January 2787

"Happy New Year, Chet!" Srini said cheerily to the guard as she walked down the corridor, dimly lit while most of the space station's staff was asleep or at some party elsewhere in the station, towards the checkpoint outside Electronics Bay 20. She worked hard to keep her face still. The green Forrester Family uniform the young guard wore brought back all her anger at the situation she, and her planet, were in.

"Don't remind me," Chet grumped back, tipping his chair upright and slipping the reader back into his sleeve pocket. "If I never get assigned the graveyard shift on New Years' Eve again, I will still have had one time too many."

"Common problem last night, I'll bet—having one too many."

"Say, that's a good joke, Ms. Vasaulli. I'm gonna remember that one."

Srini smiled acknowledgment. "Can you buzz me in?"

Her smile made him want to say yes. Srini was a very attractive woman; not too tall, nice curves in all the right places, and with dusky skin several shades darker than you normally saw. Dark skin or fair skin was almost as rare as blonde hair — well, *naturally* blonde hair — these days. Chet didn't have much experience dealing with attractive women, especially attractive women who seemed to enjoy speaking with him.

He really didn't want to do anything to make her angry with him, but regulations were regulations. Instead of the yes he wanted to say, he answered, "It's four in the morning, ma'am. No one in until the shift starts at eight. You know that."

"Oh, I should be expected. I made prior arrangements with Admiral Epstein's office to come in early this morning to start running diagnostics on the piece of testing equipment we need to install later today, down in slip four." She pulled a data strip from her lab coat's pocket and held it up. "I still have my copy of the returned request, if you need to see it."

Chet hesitated, then reached out and collected the thin black piece. "It's not that I don't trust you, of course, but I'm going to have to log you in..."

"Oh, I understand. Don't worry about it."

Chet moved the few steps needed to enter the guard shack, where his strip reader was. Srini followed, removing her lab coat as she went. Her nerves were humming and her heart was pounding out of her chest. When Chet leaned forward to insert the strip, Srini drove the homemade taser, which had appeared in her right hand, under the base of his skull and triggered the device. Chet slumped forward bonelessly, unconscious before he could feel any pain. This was the first time she had needed to put her training into practice and she was pleased that things had proceeded exactly as she'd been told to expect.

Srini struggled to ease the young man's body down to the small floor, leaving the folded coat under his head. If only Chet had taken her word for it, it would have been better for both of them. She would have been in and out with no one the wiser. Now, she was certain the assault would have been witnessed by video pickup and a quick response force would be here in seconds to deal with her. She struggled to hold back the tears as she realized there was probably no time for her to complete her task before they arrived. The only thing left for her to do was to make sure she was killed in the fighting so she could not be made to reveal any secrets.

Eight months before, Forrest attack craft had come streaking in from out of nowhere and overwhelmed Granada's defenses. The takeover of her planet had been quick and brutal. Now, her homeworld was being held in thrall. She had, with many of her friends, joined a group that was fighting back. If she had failed in her mission to raise the alarm to the outside galaxy, at least she could protect the identities of the others who might still have a chance to succeed.

If she was to be killed, though, she would need to offer lethal resistance. Not her preferred option, but then, the outcome of this morning's operation would not be what she preferred either. She squatted next to Chet's unmoving form on the floor of the shack and took his two weapons, a fletchette pistol and an energy rifle. She didn't know the first thing about their specifications, she was an electronics engineer, not a soldier, but she could tell which end to point away from her and ten seconds was enough to locate and deactivate the safeties.

Ten seconds was more time than she should have had, but nearly a minute had gone by, and no one had come. Abruptly, she looked around the interior of the room and realized that there was no camera *inside* the shack, and nothing that had happened *outside* would have made anyone suspicious. Perhaps she had time after all.

Srini looked around to take stock of her situation. There was nothing she could do about Chet, more than she had already. He massed easily twice what Srini did. Chet would be discovered the next time someone came to this bay, but with the holiday celebration last night, maybe that wouldn't be until the next shift started. That should be plenty of time for her to be far away.

With that in mind, it was worth a few minutes to do what she could to slow pursuit and hide her identity. She tucked the pistol into the back of her waistband and leaned the energy weapon within easy reach. Chet had left his account at the terminal active, so she delved into the system menus, erased the last hour of visual logs, and put the surveillance gear into a diagnostic cycle that would keep it occupied for a quarter hour. Srini certainly was not a soldier, even though she'd been trained in some of the basics by Granada Unfettered, but computer systems were much closer to her expertise. This was not a permanent solution, obviously; Chet would identify his assailant when he came to, but if she could get a head start, maybe that would be enough to eventually leave the station and continue fighting back on the planet surface.

She glanced at the rifle, but left it where it was with some regret. She couldn't take it with her; once she left the surveillance area controlled from this station, she would be spotted immediately. Her resistance group could certainly make use of it, though.

The only other task left was to remove any signs that she had been here. In the second drawer she tried, she found a stack of napkins from the station's food court. These she used to wipe off her fingerprints from anything she had touched. The used napkins she stuffed in her pockets.

Next, she pulled the lab coat from under her victim where he laid. She was saddened again for the action she'd been forced into taking. She'd known this would be a possible outcome, and she'd steeled herself to do whatever it took, including killing him, but he really was a likeable young man, and she knew the Forrest Marines would deal harshly with him for letting himself be blindsided. It was only the anger at what his Family had done to hers that had made it possible for her to act. Covering her fingers with a napkin, she pressed the actuator that unlocked the door into the electronics bay and departed.

Once into the bay, she headed straight through the gowning area without stopping. Before the Forresters had come, this bay would never have been left idle, even on holidays. The invaders didn't have enough manpower to watch everything all the time, so work was shut down after one shift, and the slaves were herded back into their quarters. It had to end, and Srini would do what she could to see that happen. Although, with the way things had played out, she supposed there was a good chance she wouldn't live long enough to see it now.

She was not going to be defeatist, though. She wanted to finish her primary mission. To do that, she still needed to get what she came for and get it set up and transmitting before first shift started. She made her way through the processing equipment to bay 12N. There, halfway up on the right side, someone had left a ceramic wafer box sitting, as she'd been told to expect. She thumbed it open, retrieved the circuitry inside, and put it in her pocket.

This was the final component in the tightbeam transmitter that Srini's group had been constructing slowly over the last five months. Forrest had come to Worth with fire and destruction eight months before, and almost everyone had expected the Warner Navy to arrive within a week to release the planet from their captors. That hadn't happened.

When it was clear that help was not coming, it didn't take too long to deduce why. No one outside the system knew of the invasion. Forrest had been clever about moving the transshipment warehouses farther away from the planet, so that outside shipping never saw too much, and so could not report anything amiss when they got to their next stops.

With the tightbeam, Srini would transmit a message to the captain of the oblivious freight-hauler sitting at a warehouse near the jump point now, and the news would be out as soon as it could jump free. The Navy would finally arrive, and the filth that had killed her fiancé would get what was coming to them.

"Stand where you are," a harsh voice said to her as she came back out to the corridor. "Hands on your head."

Adrenalin slammed into Srini's bloodstream and it took an effort of will to move slowly and place her hands on her head. Three Forresters in light armor surrounded her with weapons leveled at her torso. "What's this about, officer?" she asked. She could not allow herself to be taken alive, she knew that. There were too many secrets, and the names of too many people who would also die if she were made to divulge them.

"One of our soldiers has been incapacitated, and we find you leaving the area he was guarding. What do you *think* this is about?" To the man on Srini's right the leader said, "Put her in cuffs. We'll take her down to C level to answer some questions."

The soldier addressed shouldered his weapon, but the other two kept theirs trained on Srini. She winced inwardly as she realized her mission was doomed after all. The frustration of the last several months threatened to overwhelm her but she fought it down. She only had one mission left. She had to make them kill her.

When the man reached out to grab her wrist, Srini moved as quickly as she could, pulling the arm out of reach, intentionally throwing herself off-balance and falling backward while drawing the pistol from her waistband. She pointed, rather than aimed, for the center of the man's chest and pulled the trigger. She'd known the flechettes would not penetrate the man's light armor, but that wasn't the point. She had no real desire to kill anyone, except maybe the leaders who had ordered the dismantling of her world. No, the object was simply to get the right reaction from the Forresters.

While that had been her intent, she hadn't considered the angle at which she was shooting. Her small stature and the fact that she was off-balance and falling meant her projectiles had a sharp upward angle when they hit. The armor didn't stop them, only deflected them up, where they savaged the man's chin and face. He bellowed in pain and released his grip on Srini to hold his wound.

Srini's concentration was on making her one shot look sufficiently serious before the other two weapons could reacquire her, so she hit the floor without protecting her head. A bright light flashed as it struck the hard flooring, and she heard several high-pitched staccato whines. She did her best to ignore the pain and shifted her aim toward the leader, on the assumption that if she wasn't yet dead, they needed more convincing.

Her eyes wouldn't focus, and when they did, the woman was not there. Srini sat up too fast, and nearly passed out. Knowing it was illogical, she rolled to one side, trying to evade the counter-attack she knew was coming. The spinning made her head hurt worse, so she stopped and tried again to take aim at the leader. She scanned left and right and finally located her on the decking, lying unmoving.

For a few panicked seconds, nothing made sense. Then the sound of hurried steps and familiar faces added to her confusion. "Auger?" she asked, giving the name its French pronunciation, so that it sounded like O. J. "What are you doing here?"

"Saving your skin, it would seem," the shorter woman said with a grin.

"But the plan was—"

"—More than what we told you. You had all the information you needed to have," Auger finished for her, squatting down and feeling the back of Srini's head. "Quite a goose egg you gave yourself. Just sit there for a few seconds while I get the rest of the team moving."

Srini did as directed, trying to get her mind a bit less fuzzy. By the time she felt she was able to stand, Auger had half of the new arrivals heading away again, carrying captured weapons, their own homemade rail guns, and dead bodies. Auger was directing a couple others to do a more thorough scrubbing of the area and then to disappear.

"You ready?" she asked Srini when she approached.

"Yes," Srini said at once, though she was less sure than she sounded. Time was not on their side, however, so there really was only one possible answer.

Srini led the way outward to 9th Ring and turned spinward. In Caspar, unlike other stations, the spin was not for the purpose of creating an artificial gravity, which the station provided via a Gravitas system, but to balance the heating received from Worth's rays.

Auger stayed right on Srini's heels for turn after turn. A man named Yorgason, thin, with brown hair and an angular face, whom she didn't know except by name, came next. He kept his hands in the pockets of a light jacket, where his flechette pistol was concealed. James, a dark-haired and muscular man a decade older than Srini, came last, leaving a good distance between himself and the other three. This man she knew well, having received hours of training and many bruises from him. James' eyes moved constantly, taking everything in.

There was almost no one visible in any of the hallways they traversed. They weren't far from G Spoke, which was primarily given to offices and smaller shops, so this was not surprising. Nothing out this way was open for business yet, and all the big parties had been closer to the central hub. Srini led the group unerringly through narrow passages and alleys, coming out into the open only once when they crossed the broad passage of 10th Ring. They moved casually to avoid standing out, weapons out of sight.

There wasn't much of the station left beyond 10th Ring, and another five minutes had the small group looking at the locker room and the airlock which would allow them to cross over to hull 198, more than halfway completed. Unfortunately, they were looking at something else as well; two Marines stood to either side of the airlock.

"Why can't the Forresters ever stick to our plan," Auger muttered, motioning everyone into the shadows.

"What do we do now?" Srini asked.

Auger muttered something else.

"What was that?" Yorgason asked.

"I'm thinking!" Auger whispered harshly.

James stood close enough to hear the conversation, but he kept his back to the others and watched everything else instead.

"We can't not go," Srini said, keeping her voice low to match the other woman's. "Once they discover they've lost some guards tonight, this station is going to be locked down tight for a long time."

"I know it," Auger agreed. "But we've already spent two months getting all the components built and in place. If we make a play for it now, and can't get it done, we may not ever have the chance to try again."

"If we don't make a play for it now, we still may not ever have the chance again," Srini urged.

Auger chewed her lower lip for a few seconds. "No. I'm calling it. All of you take different routes back to the rally point. Srini, you're burned, so we're going to have to find a way to smuggle you down to Granada." She looked at each face to make sure her instructions were understood. Each of the others nodded and turned to go different directions.

Srini's self-chosen direction was straight toward the locker room and its Forrester Marines.

James' solid arm shot out and grabbed her by the collar. He yanked her roughly around to stare at him. "You heard her," he said sharply. "Save your life to throw away when it will do some good."

Srini struggled to free herself from the grip, but once his vise-like hand got a second purchase around her wrist, she knew there was no way to get free unless James allowed it.

"All right," she said grudgingly. "I'll go."

James watched her pocket the lump and move off into the maze of alleys. Auger followed her, but not too closely. Yorgason stepped away next down a different path.

James took a last look at the guards. Though he agreed there was almost no chance they could have made it through, a part of him felt that Srini might have been right. There was no guarantee that another opportunity like this could be arranged in the future. For now, there was no help coming to the Worth System. No one knew what had happened here. By the time the rest of the galaxy found out, it might be too late.

CHAPTER 1
18 October
WNS *Pathfinder*

Lieutenant Monica Samuels pressed her face up against the transparent aluminum of the airlock's viewport and looked as far forward as she could manage. Inside the lock, there were three additional ports and through the forward one she could just see the suited form of Staff Sergeant Burton appearing.

Samuels took a deep, cleansing breath, thankful that she finally had a few moments of calmness to enjoy. Her list of tasks hadn't magically disappeared, but now that she was here to greet the returning sergeant, it made no sense to go start another task. If she did, she would only have to hurry right back in a few minutes, and so she indulged in a few blessed moments to herself, with no one bringing her new problems to solve.

She looked out on the endless black of the Worth system and thanked the Creator that she was still alive. Based on probabilities, there was no reason to expect she should have been. So she sent her gratitude out into the universe to whatever divine intervention had caused her insane plans to retake the stolen Warner Navy ship to result in both a successful recovery, and most importantly, in her continued existence.

She leaned closer to the hatch viewport and could see the sergeant had made only a little progress. The small figure in an

EVA suit was close enough now to see that she pulled two other suits behind her.

Samuels had asked Sergeant Burton to go out to her former hide-out in one of the outer holds and retrieve the last of the crew that had been taken captive during the long struggle to reclaim the ship. Burton was moving slowly and only using her left arm to pull herself along the guide rope.

"You should have let me go out and get these last two crewmen."

Samuels spun at the unexpected sound to find her friend, Amber Sullivan

"Amber, don't do that!"

"Do what?"

"Sneak up on me like that."

Sullivan grinned. "Not much fun in that."

Samuels grinned back and returned to watching the approaching Marine. She couldn't believe the difference in Sullivan. At the time Samuels had pulled her off the shuttle full of soon-to-be-exiles when Captain Brighton had sent her back aboard *Pathfinder*, Sullivan had been a whimpering, boneless heap that she had been trying to protect. Now, she was standing straight and looking at her with purpose and direction. Sullivan's blonde hair was now perfectly tied off in a pony tail and her uniform was clean and pressed. There was no remnant of the lost girl who had come back with her and cried for a week.

Now Samuels wondered if that lost girl had all been some elaborate act. It almost had to have been. Judging from the reputation her real unit had, they didn't employ people who would fall apart under pressure.

"I would have preferred sending you out to collect them, too," Samuels finally said. "I would have let Burton stay in the medbay and recover from the battle that re-injured her arm, but you know she doesn't trust you. And she considers this a security matter. She won't step aside and let anyone else take over security issues until Aichele is out of medbay."

"You're the captain. You could appoint me to be part of the security force. With his broken ribs and punctured lung, Aichele is not coming out of medbay soon, if Doctor Johnson has anything to say about it."

"No, Amber. For one thing, traditionally, only Marines are security and you are still navy. For another, Burton is not going to start trusting you just because I put you on her team. It's more likely to cause additional problems than solve anything. Plus, I have a feeling that Doctor Johnson will not have as much say about Aichele as she wants."

"Teach assigned fleet personnel to security."

"Well, I'm not going to follow his example in anything."

At that comment, Sullivan laughed.

"I guess that is understandable. I still think Burton should be in medbay right next to Aichele."

The young officer didn't answer her friend, but instead looked back out the hatch viewport at the sergeant, gauging how much time she would have to finish this topic before the subject arrived. Sullivan was right about where Burton belonged. Samuels was concerned for her as she continued forward. The effort seemed to be pushing her to her limits. The two suits tethered to her were floating free, but she kept going through a cycle of pulling them forward, making her best efforts to keep pace with them with her awkward movements, falling behind, and then having to yank them backward again.

Sergeant Burton and Gunny Aichele had risked everything to help her take back *Pathfinder* from the Forrester Marines and the mutineers who had taken control of the ship. Samuels had been working to sabotage the ship in order to keep the mutineers from leaving the Antoc system with their prize. It hadn't taken long to realize someone else must have had the same idea, but months had past before she identified that these two Marines and Sullivan were the ones doing the same thing. It wasn't until the four of them had managed to work together that they had been able to make a real dent in the pirates. Unfortunately, the mutineers had managed to move the ship out of the Antoc system anyway, here to the Worth system, where they had people waiting to take the ship from them.

She looked out the hatch again and noticed that Burton seemed to have stopped pulling herself along.

"Are you okay, Sergeant Burton?"

Samuels watched as Burton's helmet came up.

"Yes, ma'am. I'm almost back to the airlock."

"Yes, I can see you from the hatch. Did you have any problems picking up Young and McGough?"

Burton unlatched her safety clip, moved it across to the last run and pulled herself carefully along the cable toward the hatch.

"No, ma'am. I put them to sleep and got them into their suits without any problems. These are the last two crewmen that I had captured."

"Very well, if they agree to accept the amnesty, we can put them to work."

"Ma'am, I still think this is a bad idea."

Samuels laughed quickly.

"Yeah, Sergeant. I caught that the last dozen times you brought it up, but I don't see any other ideas that let us get *Pathfinder* fixed quickly enough to escape."

The problem was, Samuels could understand Burton's concerns with her solution. She had offered all the mutineers the possibility of amnesty if they were willing to help repair the ship enough to let them escape back into safe territory.

The Worth system belonged to the Warner Family. It should have been safe here, but the entire system had been taken over by Forrest Family Marines and it seemed the Forrest Family was in control on the planet and on the various space stations as well. They needed to get *Pathfinder* out of here and get back to Antoc to rescue Captain Brighton and the rest of the crew that were marooned with him before they died. In order to do that, she needed all the crew, whether they were former mutineers or not. Most had just been going along because their officers had taken the ship and they thought there was no choice. If they would swear to help, she would give them a chance. The fact that the Forrest Marines, who Leung had invited onboard to purchase the ship, had killed several of the mutineers while trying to double-cross them, had forced many of the crew to believe that Samuels' dubious offer was their only remaining option.

Not wanting to continue the debate over vocom, Burton slid a little further down the safety line. Young and McGough's momentum had kept them moving forward while she'd been stopped. Burton maneuvered smoothly to get them moving back toward her and headed directly for the airlock. When Burton finally reached the hatch, she stopped again and placed her helmet against the lock, waiting several moments before beginning the sequence that would allow her to enter with her two unconscious prisoners.

Finally, Burton pulled herself in. After she was in place, she slowly pulled the long tether that was tied to McGough and Young, who had drifted away while she maneuvered herself inside. Once that was complete, she cycled the lock and began the process to get them back aboard *Pathfinder*. This would put all the crew back together for the first time since Burton had escaped to the outer hold to hide from the mutineers.

As the pressure seal hissed open, Samuels nodded to Burton.

"Thank you, Sergeant. Amber and I can get them out of their suits and transferred to the holding cell. I know you'd like to check on Aichele. I think the doctor was just finishing surgery and he should be into recovery soon."

Burton had started to remove her EVA suit but she stiffened as Samuels finished. The captain wasn't sure if her words had made her angry because Burton's face was turned away from her.

"That's all right, ma'am. I'll take care of them and make sure there are no surprises."

Samuels nodded and pointed to the blood leaking from Burton's right shoulder as Burton finally turned to face her.

"I appreciate that, Sergeant, but there is no need. Sullivan and I can handle it. Your wounds should still have you in medbay after the damage you took in that last battle."

Burton stood a little straighter and slowly rubbed her head. Her blond hair had been cut near the scalp for her own surgery in the aftermath of the mutiny only a few months back and the new hair was plastered to her head with sweat from her exertions. She turned her grey eyes to the young officer and looked at her squarely. Her voice was calm and quiet.

"That's likely true, ma'am, but I am the one responsible for security until Aichele can recover, so I am not able to trust it to anyone else. I know that you think Sullivan is trustworthy, but I'm not able to make that assumption. I am forced to check everything myself." She finished her explanation as the last of her EVA suit dropped to the deck.

Samuels could feel the veiled challenge in the statement. She knew that Burton had only gone along with her promotion to lieutenant because Aichele told her that she had to, though she had agreed to that promotion at the time. Could she be rethinking it now?

"Staff Sergeant, I understand your need to feel that the ship is secure, but I am still in command of *Pathfinder* until I am relieved by a higher authority. I will leave as much of the security as possible to you, but understand that I am in command. Sullivan has been cleared by me, is that understood?"

The declaration made Samuels cringe internally as soon as she said it. Her father, the head of a minor family's operations, had taught her everything he knew about leading people. He would be embarrassed to see her telling a subordinate who was in charge. It was exactly the wrong way to go about taking command, but the whole situation had her flustered and frustrated.

Burton stood rigid, her EVA suit at her feet. She looked at Samuels again and blew out her breath.

"Yes, ma'am. I understand. Gunny Aichele and I have talked about this. I will not always agree with you, and on security matters I will always tell you when I don't agree, but I will follow your orders." Burton took another deep breath and continued, "Lieutenant Samuels, I do not agree with your course of action regarding Sullivan or the trusting of former mutineers. However, if you order me to do so, I will implement your plan. I would urge the utmost caution, however. The mutineers still outnumber us on this ship, and the more freedom they are allowed, the more chance they can retake the ship from us."

"Your reservations are noted, Sergeant. Leung has a permanent guard assigned to watch her whenever she leaves her quarters. Beyond that, we do not have the manpower to watch everyone. Do you have any further suggestions on security?"

"Have you changed all the command locks?"

"Yes. I took care of that immediately."

"I would lock this airlock with the EVA suits inside to your command code, as well as Gunny Aichele's and my own. With all the escape pods gone, that will eliminate any chance someone can leave the ship without authorization. As outgoing communications are still down, that limits the mutineer's ability to get any help."

"Agreed. I will take care of that now. You take Sullivan with you and clear these crewmen by whatever means you feel appropriate. If they pass, get them working on the engines with Leung. When that is taken care of, check on the Forresters in the brig and then report to medbay to see if Doctor Johnson needs any assistance."

"Yes, ma'am."

"I'll be on the bridge once I finish here, if you need me."

"Understood, ma'am. Let's go, Sullivan."

Without further comment, Burton pushed aside her EVA suit and left it lying on the deck inside the airlock. Picking up her blast rifle and slinging it across her back, she motioned to

Sullivan to grab the smaller McGough off the deck. She grabbed Young by the back of his collar and headed out into the main corridor, his feet dragging along the deck.

* * * * *

Burton made her way to the security suite at the forward end of the corridor and palmed the hatch open with her free right hand. She continued toward the back of the office and palmed another lock plate. The door opened into a short corridor with four locked cells.

Three of these were minimum-security, with carbon fiber bars set at fifteen-centimeter intervals. The fourth cell was high-security. It had a solid front with a small barred window near the top and a small food slot near the floor. The high-security cell contained three Forrest prisoners. They were the only surviving members of the twelve-man team that had double-crossed and killed several of those who had wanted nothing more than a payday.

Many within the crew had been active participants in the mutiny, while others had been pretending, like Samuels, and had just been trying to get through the ordeal and survive. These Forrest Marines had had no intention of letting anyone off the ship alive. This was a high-stakes game that allowed for no errors and no witnesses.

Unfortunately, Commander Leung and the other mutineers hadn't realized that until it was too late. They had thought they could come out of their adventure with a fortune and disappear. The truly sad part was that Leung had survived and others had paid her price for her.

The other cells held some Forrester civilians and the other crew members who had yet to be cleared. The last room, directly across from the high-security cell, was still empty, and it was there that Burton took her prisoner and unceremoniously dropped him to the floor. She reached up with her left hand and rubbed her right shoulder. It ached and her whole arm felt like it was on fire. She had tried not to use it on her EVA trip, but apparently she had used it more than she thought. Her hand came away red and she knew she had torn loose her surgical staples.

"It looks like Captain Kerritt got you after all," came the call from the compartment behind her as Sullivan deposited her burden on the floor beside Young.

"It serves you Warners right for trying to keep the riches of the galaxy from the rightful hands of the people. You've been getting rich off the sweat of the other Families for too long, but now you're going to pay for your arrogance."

Burton ignored the taunts. She knew from experience that it only made things worse to react.

Sullivan and Burton finished removing the EVA suits from their unmoving charges while the prisoners carried on issuing taunts. Burton continued to ignore them.

"You will never get away with this," the most vocal one shouted. "You've killed Forrest citizens in the performance of their duty. We have rights!"

Burton made her way to the outer brig door with the suit pieces, but stopped short when she heard the containment door unlock behind her. She froze for a split second and then reacted to what had to be a betrayal by Sullivan.

The impervious barrier swung inward and the three Forrest Marines moved with a speed that demonstrated there had been nothing wrong with their training. Sullivan followed the swinging door into the confined space and caught the first Marine squarely in the jaw with the butt of her blast rifle as he made a grab for her. The breaking bones were audible three meters away as Burton tried to get back into the detention block to prevent the escape she believed to be happening. The second Marine went down with Sullivan's return stroke as it connected with the side of his head. The third grabbed her by the shoulder and spun her back to face him. She went with the pull and slid the rifle to hold it with one hand on the butt and the other at the end of the barrel. As she came around, she pushed out with the stock to slam into the man's face. Blood sprayed from a broken nose and she flipped the stock to hit him with the butt end again, this time across the jaw. Teeth and blood flew again and hit Burton as she stepped across the threshold to the gruesome scene.

"You are murderers and war criminals," Sullivan said as the last Forrester fell to the floor.

Sullivan kicked the man in the chest and said, "Your rights are whatever I tell you they are."

She calmly walked past Burton without looking at her or the bleeding Marines.

Burton was stunned for several moments, but finally pulled the cell door closed and it locked into place. She sat down with her back against the door and tried to decide what to make of the situation. The fact that Sullivan clearly didn't like the Forresters made her feel some kind of kinship with the woman, and that in itself raised more red flags.

That was exactly the kind of trick an infiltrator would pull to try to gain the enemy's trust.

CHAPTER 2
18 October
WNS *Pathfinder*

Gunnery Sergeant Eric Aichele slowly felt his consciousness returning and tried fighting the pain that swept over him as it did. His thoughts were jumbled and for a time he could not place his surroundings.

The pain was still there, he thought, but the world was wrapped in fuzzy cloth and he could not swim his way through it to get where he was trying to go. The feeling was familiar. After nearly sixty years as a Marine, he had felt this way several times before. Those memories were comforting, keeping any fear or panic at bay. He knew that he must be coming out of a drugged state, but it did nothing to help him clarify his current situation. He thought about opening his eyes, but couldn't make his thoughts tell him whether that would help him in any way. It was too much effort anyway; he couldn't manage it just yet. He thought he heard voices, but he couldn't make out what was going on.

Suddenly, the pain in his side intensified and his eyes flew open of their own accord. His head swiveled to the side automatically, to take in his surroundings. The electric shock of the pain which shot through his body removed any residual grogginess. He immediately felt the throbbing pain in his side and chest that the medication he had received could only dull, not remove. He knew where he was. He was in a recovery room of a ship medbay.

Suddenly, he had an image of Burton lying in the very bed where he now lay and his memories came flooding back.

"Burton," he called out.

It came out as a croak as his throat tried to make sounds it wasn't ready for. The name caused his memory to focus on his partner. He saw her in his mind's eye being hit by a shot to the chest of her armor and thrown back into the debris of the boatbay to lie still. He had to find out if she survived.

He slowly sat up. Perhaps slowly wasn't the word he should have used. *Somewhat slower than a glacier*, he thought to himself. Each muscle contraction created agony in his abdomen and chest. *I am definitely too old for this flaming garbage.*

As he sat up, his intake of breath caused him to begin coughing, each one producing an accompanying stab of pain, and it took several minutes to be able to get his body under control enough to investigate the cause of his surprise. Behind the glass partition, inside the operating room, he saw three gurneys racked on the back side of the room and on top of each was a sealed body bag.

He ignored the light-headedness that swept over him as he put his feet on the deck; hanging onto the edge of his bed until his vision unblackened itself enough to see where he was going. He had made it three steps before he heard the door open behind him.

"What do you think you're doing! Get back into that bed immediately."

Aichele ignored the outburst. He knew as soon as he recognized the medbay that the doctor would be in to check on him; she would surely have monitors set to notify her as soon as he woke up. He had only gone another two steps before she caught him and held him. He still ignored her, trying to get to his partner, she needed him. He had failed to protect her. Who were the other two bodies? Samuels? Had he been right to mistrust Sullivan? Was this the result? Or was Sullivan the other body? He had to get to Burton. He owed her that much; to look at what his failure had caused.

"Gunnery Sergeant Aichele, stand at attention!" the doctor called in her best attempt at a command voice.

Aichele's body reacted of its own volition to the years of training and snapped to attention as well as it was able, but it was enough to break into his thoughts.

"Chin, get in here and help me."

At her call, a burly crewman came into the room and took one shocked look at the Marine before running to assist the doctor. The thin medbay gown Aichele wore was beginning to soak down the right side with blood. The dark patch was small but growing fast.

The Marine began to collapse and Doctor Johnson was forced to try to catch him before he could fall to the deck. She managed to get a knee under his backside and hold him momentarily but both were headed to the floor as Crewman Chin arrived to avert disaster.

"Help me get him back into his bed."

"Yes, ma'am,"

"I'm okay," Aichele mumbled. "Just give me a second."

"You are not okay," the doctor shouted back, her fear for her patient overriding her normally calm demeanor. "Now get back into that bed and let yourself heal. You're worse than Burton. She wouldn't even let me finish working on her before she took off."

"Burton is alive?"

Johnson looked at Aichele and wiped her head.

"As of an hour ago, though I wouldn't swear to anything now."

Aichele allowed Chin to help him back onto the bed as he tried to make sense of what the doctor was saying. The fog in his head wouldn't let him connect any meaning to the words. Burton's not dead?

"All right, now lie down and relax," the doctor said soothingly. "Let me take a look at your side."

"Doctor, I'm fine. If you could seal up whatever is bleeding, I need to be going."

"Marines!" the doctor sighed. "You are in no shape to be going anywhere and you don't know that you are needed anywhere. You don't have any idea what the situation is on this ship. I won't have you killing yourself for no reason."

"Ma'am, I beg your pardon, but I have a fairly good idea of the situation," he began now that his mind had cleared enough to begin putting words to his thoughts. "Burton was injured, possibly severely and yet she is not here in the medbay being treated. You said yourself that she left before you were satisfied with her treatment, so the need must have been great. As there are only the two of us, she has no back-up until I get there. Therefore, I need to leave immediately."

"You are in no shape to leave." Johnson repeated. "You can't even make it across the medbay."

"I could have made it if you didn't interfere and I am much stronger and more clearheaded than I was then."

"Right. But only because I forced you to be horizontal, so that what little blood you haven't leaked out could pool around what little brains you have in that jarhead of yours. Now lie still, or I will get a blunt instrument to induce a medical coma."

"Doctor. I do need to go."

"Gunnery Sergeant, you are staying right here until I can guarantee that you will not die in the next room."

The Marine closed his eyes and moved his head slightly from side to side.

"Ma'am, you don't have the choice. Under WFC, section VII, paragraph twelve, it states that 'no military nor civilian personnel shall interfere with fleet personnel in the performance of their duty during emergency or conflict; said emergency being declared by the duly authorized commanding authority or during a declared state of emergency or war.' I wouldn't want you to get into any trouble, ma'am."

Johnson looked at the Marine for several seconds before she began to laugh.

"Oh, you wouldn't want to get me into trouble, huh? Gunny, I don't know how you can even say that with a straight face. I could cite you four separate regs from the Fleet Code that *require* me to keep you here until I deem you capable of taking care of yourself. Don't quote regs at me."

She stood and stared at him for several moments.

"That being said," she began, "I also know that short of drugging you insensible, which I ought to do, there is no way to keep you here against your will, so if you are going to do this, it'll be my way.

"Chin, go find Burton and bring her here, if she isn't too busy," she said to the lingering crewman before turning back to the injured Marine.

"Now, let's see if we can put Humpty Dumpty back together again."

CHAPTER 3
18 October
WNS *Pathfinder*

Lieutenant Monica Samuels stood in front of the helm controls at the center of the bridge of WNS *Pathfinder*. She was a lieutenant by virtue of an order by her commanding officer, who was, at the time of the promotion, in rebellion against the Warner Family government. She doubted that she would retain the rank once she managed to get the ship back to Warner-controlled space. She laughed silently to herself at the thought, since keeping her rank was the least of her problems.

The bridge was eerily silent; like a scene from a dream just before it turns into a nightmare. It seemed hard to believe that this particular nightmare had started for her on this same spot only four months earlier. The helm controls in front of her were comforting and complete in a way that nothing else on this ship seemed to be. They represented a job that she knew well and could do with complete competence. They constituted a place of sanctuary when everything else in her life and world had been chaos. To her left, the scan and weapons consoles were still torn open; wiring and circuit boards exposed. Behind that, to the rear of the compartment, the astrogation computer was a mess of shattered components and blackened surfaces. Standing alone in this room, she was reminded again of the devastation that had been caused by both sides during the covert battle for control of this ship.

Pathfinder was a revolutionary leap forward in technology that would allow faster and unlimited transfer from system to system. The Family that controlled this marvel of physics and engineering would have a monumental advantage against all others. On one side of the battle, the Warner Family had been working on this project for nearly nine years, and had finally developed a working prototype. On the other, the Forrest Family had arranged to have the prototype stolen, and then had taken armed possession of her.

The ship's executive officer, Edward Teach, and chief engineer, Katherine Leung, had stolen the ship with the offer of a huge reward. Before being sent into exile on a planet of the Antoc binary system, Captain Brighton had sent Samuels back aboard the ship to try to restore the ship to Warner control. Whether he had any realistic hope that she could accomplish anything or not was debatable, but he did send her back. Most of her friends had not been so lucky. Ensigns Hayes, Mitchell and Roberts had all accompanied the captain to their unknown fate.

Whatever results Captain Brighton had expected from her, she had been instrumental in recovering the ship from the pirates. However, since the successful takeover of the ship from the mutineers, which she had managed with considerable help from three combat veterans, *Pathfinder* had become a ghost ship. It had felt empty after Captain Brighton had left with those loyal to him, but those left behind were almost all gone now as well. It seemed improbable in the extreme that two NCOs and a wet-behind-the-ears ensign only a few months removed from her academy graduation could successfully effect such a daring action against the people who had stolen the ship.

It had not been without its costs, however. Both Sergeant Burton and Gunny Aichele had been severely injured during the final action. Ensign Omundson, Samuels' classmate at the academy, had been critically injured in his own escape attempt and had subsequently died, despite the best efforts of the ship's surgeon.

Morrison's death had hit her hardest of all. He had died right in front of her, trying to carry out orders she had given him. She felt the weight of it was something she would never be able to bear, but every time it threatened to paralyze her, she wrenched her mind to those who were still counting on her, and it forced her back into motion. It seemed like a crushing thing to her but Gunny Aichele had said she did everything right. It certainly didn't feel that way to her.

She knew that her own best course of action at this point was fairly clear. How to accomplish it was not. She needed to get *Pathfinder* back to the Antoc system in an effort to rescue Captain Brighton and the others from their exile, but she did not have a clue how to do that without the astrogation computer.

As was becoming her habit, she took a few minutes to make sure all the command consoles were slaved to her personal code and then sat down in the captain's chair. She leaned back and mentally made a list of the things left to do. With Omundson dead, she was the only line officer left on *Pathfinder*, except for Leung, who was technically under arrest, but roaming, with a guard, in order to help repair the ship.

They had all the crew back inside the ship and repairs were underway on the communications array. They also had a team trying to close off the damaged hatch into the boatbay. "Team" seemed so much more impressive a term than the two people it represented. Dr. Johnson was working as quickly as possible to verify the loyalty of the remaining crew members through the use of truth drugs. That action was not legal, even if she claimed the far-reaching power of a ship's captain, but she had to be *sure* of everyone. There was no margin for error. So far, though, it seemed that most had been going along with their officers in an effort to stay alive rather than any commitment to the plan. Very few seemed to have been involved in the takeover from the beginning, and so far all had accepted her offer of potential amnesty.

It was fortunate that this was the case, because the list of tasks was growing out of hand. If it weren't, there was no way she would allow Leung even limited freedom.

Aichele, already up and mobile, as Samuels suspected he would be, was sure that the repair of the damage to the boatbay hatch would allow them to jettison the Forrest assault shuttle attached to the belly of the ship without loss of atmosphere if they needed to, but she was willing to hold onto it for now. They might need it to escape from *Pathfinder* if things got even worse. It also kept the Forresters from docking another parasite ship to that bay if they found out they had lost control of the ship.

She thought about the two Forrest Marines that had been overlooked during the takeover. They couldn't afford any more nearly fatal mistakes like that. She felt that old trickle of fear threaten to take over again. *You're too young to be a lieutenant, let alone a ship's captain,* it whispered in the back of her mind. Captain Brighton had told her to stay. She wondered if he would shake his head if he saw her now. She shook herself free of her thoughts as the comm erupted with noise.

"Unidentified ship, this is FFF *Hammer*. Cease all movement and prepare to be boarded."

Her head came up as she heard one of the Forrester ships identify itself for the first time. They had gotten the tracings of several of the destroyers on their scanners a few times but had never heard anything on the comm to confirm that they were, in fact Forrester ships.

"Unknown ship *Hammer*, this is Commodore William Brighton, commanding Task Force Ten of the Warner Space Navy. Stand down your weapons and prepare to give an explanation of your actions in this system."

Samuels sat bolt upright as she heard the name and recognized that rich baritone voice. *Captain Brighton is here! How was that possible? And calling himself a Commodore in charge of a Task Force?*

She sat there stunned for several moments before activating the toggle on her command chair to enable the ship-wide intercom.

"Burton and Aichele to the bridge, double-quick," she said simply before leaning back in her chair and letting out a long breath that she hadn't realized she was holding.

* * * * *

"Do you want these sandwiches?" Dr. Meghan Johnson asked, indicating a pile that she had just completed. Her light tone belied the dark circles under her eyes. "I could drop them off somewhere on my way back to the medbay. I really need to finish testing the rest of the crew."

"No ma'am. You go ahead with the crew. I'm going to take this bunch down to the brig," Sergeant Burton said indicating her own tray. "When I get back, I'll take those down to Engineering with me."

Burton made her way toward the galley door, carefully balancing the food tray in her left hand. Her right arm was again in a sling to immobilize it after the doctor saw what shape it was in after her EVA tasks. She hadn't quite reached the hatch before she heard Samuels' summons. The reinforcing phrase, 'double-quick,' made her drop the tray on the nearest table and sprint to the bridge with a quick apologetic glance at the exhausted doctor.

She turned up the corridor toward the bridge and continued her sprint. She reached over with her left hand and put pressure on her right arm, pushing it to her chest to try to minimize its movement and the subsequent pain, but she did not slow her stride. As she rounded the corner into the forward cross-corridor, she saw Aichele approaching at a much slower speed. The man still arrived at the hatch first and had entered his code into the bridge hatch by the time Burton reached his side. They went into the compartment together to see Samuels standing in front of the captain's chair. Her face was white and she looked unsteady.

"What is it, Captain?" Aichele asked as he charged onto the bridge. The lieutenant's composure was so shattered that she didn't object to the title Aichele gave her. Burton had never heard her let that pass before. She wasn't comfortable with her new rank or her new command.

"It's Captain Brighton, he's here."

"What?!" Burton and Aichele said in unison.

Their outburst seemed to calm Samuels and she sat back down in the command chair.

"We need to get busy. I need communications back right now. If the Forrest ships are distracted, we might be able to take advantage of the confusion to get out of the system, but I need to talk to the captain first. If he sees us trying to slip out and believes that Leung still has control, he may fire on us to keep us from getting away."

Burton felt herself go cold inside. The surge of excitement she had felt was dashed like a plunge into icy water. She looked at the young officer and nodded.

"Captain Brighton would not have been expecting Forrester warships here in a Warner system. He may get forced back to the jump point. If that happens, he may fire on *Pathfinder* before he jumps," Burton added.

Samuels sat forward in the command chair. "That was my thinking. If he can't get back to us and thinks it is still a lost ship, he will feel that security responsibilities override the need to recapture the ship. He will attempt to destroy her rather than let Forrester have the prototype engines. We need to be able to transmit."

Aichele leaned forward. "It won't be quick or easy. I've been working in the comm room. The explosion really did a number in there."

Samuels visibly winced at the reminder of the bomb she had been forced to detonate in an attempt to keep *Pathfinder* from jumping into this system.

She looked at Aichele. "Could we use the comm gear on that Forrest shuttle?"

He looked at her with a tired frown. "Not unless you can bypass their security lockout."

She shook her head back at him. "Not likely. At least not in the time we have. All right, Gunny, take Sullivan, Chin and anyone else you think you can trust and get to work fixing comms. I think Dr. Johnson has cleared Goodwin as trustworthy. These communications are our highest priority, even if we have to abandon all other repairs. Sergeant," Samuels continued, turning to Burton, "I hate to do this to you, but you're going to have to go EVA again and erect a replacement antenna from stores, since we don't currently have one."

Now it was Burton's turn to look embarrassed at the damage she had inflicted on her own ship.

"Yes, ma'am."

"Then I want all the Forresters off this ship immediately. Take someone to help you and get them into suits and, personally, make sure their suit beacons work before you put them out an airlock."

"Understood, ma'am," said the Marine as she also started for the hatch.

"Sergeant," Samuels called to the retreating NCO, "no accidents. Double check all the oxygen tanks and beacons. Only the Forresters, though, I'm sure Captain Brighton will have a few questions for our Warner prisoners, and keep the most senior Forrest prisoner, just in case the captain needs any information that Leung can't supply."

"Aye-aye, ma'am," Burton said with a nod for emphasis as she turned toward the hatch.

Lieutenant Samuels rubbed the ringed planet rank pin on her high collar with her thumb and forefinger while she thought franticly. The unwanted thought intruded again, reminding her that she still needed to replace this gold pin with the similarly shaped silver pin denoting her promotion in rank. As always, she dismissed the thought as quickly as it came; she still felt like an ensign and had no desire to appear before Captain Brighton as anything other than what she was. That thought brought her sharply back to her dilemma.

What more can I do?

CHAPTER 4
18 October
WNS *Pathfinder*

Lieutenant Samuels walked through the warped, half-open hatch into the communications room one hour after overhearing Commodore Brighton's call to the Forrest ships.

"...so even if we get this all re-coded, we still won't be able to transmit," Mark Goodwin was saying. Samuels slowed with a sense of guilt as she crossed the hatchway into the compartment. The room still evidenced the blackened scars on the wall that bore witness to the destructive power of the bomb that had gutted the compartment. A bomb that she had planted. A bomb that could have killed her shipmates, regardless of the fact that she had not intended that consequence. She stood frozen for several seconds before completely entering the room. All the consoles were in disarray and parts had obviously been scavenged from all the auxiliary boards to reconstruct the main board. Mark Goodwin and Gunny Aichele were positioned with their backs to her, which allowed her to regain her composure. Goodwin was seated at the only chair left in the room, directly in front of the main communications console. Aichele was standing to his right with his left arm on the high back of Goodwin's seat in support. He had changed back into his Marine uniform, despite the heavy bandages that she knew were wrapped to support his ribs. He seemed tired and foggy, as if he had still not recovered from the anesthesia of his surgeries. *He probably hasn't,* she thought and turned her attention back to the task at hand.

"Why not?" she asked, causing Goodwin and Aichele to turn to face her.

Aichele waved a hand at Goodwin, who nodded and answered.

"We're not getting a return from the transmit circuit. I don't think the new antenna is any good. Also, the targeting software seems to be bad."

Samuels looked at the piles of hardware stacked to the sides of the room.

"Do we have another replacement for the antenna?"

Goodwin shook his head.

"No, ma'am. There's nothing in stores and all of the back-ups on the hull were destroyed by Burton's rampage."

Aichele straightened and turned back to Goodwin.

"That's not fair, Goodwin. She was working to protect —"

"That's enough!" Samuels roared, trying her best to emulate the command tone that she had always heard from Brighton. Surprisingly, both quieted. Looking at her with varying expressions on their faces. Goodwin slightly shocked and Aichele embarrassed.

When she was sure she had their attention, she continued.

"Now then, what have we got that will work to transmit?"

Goodwin looked at Aichele before he answered in a soft voice.

"Nothing. The personal communication gear the Forresters brought on board is too short-ranged. It's possible that we might've been able to use it to reach Brighton when he entered the system, but he was out of range within minutes and is continuing on a course that will take him farther out of the system. I'm sorry, but we're just out of options. We've gotten all the weapons back online and we've even got the targeting emitter repaired, but we simply have nothing to work with here and I doubt the Forresters will let us requisition a new transmitting laser antenna anytime soon."

"Is there any way to boost the output of the personal gear?" Samuels began to ask, but she broke off her query when she looked at Aichele's face. He stood there with his head cocked to one side and his eyes slightly unfocussed.

"An idea, Gunny?" she finally asked.

"Um, maybe, ma'am," he began as his focus cleared and he turned his attention to his captain. "I was just thinking that the targeting emitter uses nearly the same laser as the communications gear and we might be able to adapt it to use as our antenna."

"Is this possible?" she asked her engineering tech.

"It might be," Goodwin replied hesitantly. "Gunny Aichele knows more about tactical systems than I do, but if the frequencies are a close match, we might be able to adapt it. We'll also need to adapt the targeting software to interface with the communications hardware, but it might be doable. I know all the tactical software is good because I just reloaded it from storage."

"Good job. Get to work on it."

She walked out of the compartment and tried to leave all of its ghosts behind.

She headed down the starboard corridor, past the medbay, and hesitated for a second in front of that hatchway before continuing on. Dr. Johnson was busy enough without her bothering the routine. She needed to stop there later, but it could wait. She continued aft until she reached the access into the boatbay. When she entered, she saw Chin and Burton moving the Forrest prisoners to the airlock. Or, more accurately, Chin was moving the prisoners and Burton was standing to the side with her rifle, covering all movement. Sergeant Burton had donned a fresh set of assault armor and was standing aloof and menacing behind her darkened visor. There was one pair of Forrest Marines on the deck with their feet pulled up underneath them while Chin moved the other two toward the access hatch halfway down the bay on the port side. He motioned them down the ladder and waited until they had cleared the access and then dropped quickly down behind them. They were clearly not up for a confrontation with their suited hands secured in front of them and the cumbersome suit interfering with movement. It was all they could do to manage the ladder in their encumbered state. Samuels could hear their footsteps retreating to the far end of the passageway and then Chin's footsteps returning alone for the last pair. Burton's helmet had turned toward her as she entered and, after a quick nod, she had continued to scan the prisoners and the boatbay in measured, regular sweeps.

Samuels made her way over to Burton when she was sure it wouldn't interfere, and she waved her hand at the nearest hold that had been converted to a temporary overflow brig for the prisoners. There was some faint pounding and screaming that could be heard through the walls even from here.

"Release Chin to help Aichele and Goodwin as soon as this is done. I want you to remain on duty here until I can release some more personnel to relieve you. I don't want any of those crewmen loose on the ship until they are cleared."

"Aye-aye, ma'am," came the response from Burton's speakers. "We're almost done with the Forresters now. Everything else is secure. Dr. Johnson just took Crowson back to his quarters. He passed the test, but he'll be out of it for a while and she came and took Green, the cook, to test next. She has Sullivan in there as security. That will probably be all she can get to for a while. If Green turns out to be trustworthy, at least she can stop working in the galley and concentrate on one job."

Samuels wanted to either laugh or cry at how helpless she felt. The ship was torn apart. They had no one to fix it until they could get them cleared by the doctor. If they had been in on the mutiny from the beginning, could she really trust them loose on the ship, even though she had offered them amnesty? And what about Leung? She had actually killed Commander Teach and maybe Lieutenant Lamont. Could she leave her loose at all?

"Where is Commander Leung?"

"I locked Leung in her room for now. Gunny said he needed to work on the comm room and I needed to take care of the prisoners, so there was no one to guard her. Your orders were that she needed to be guarded at all times while working. I thought this was correct."

Samuels noticed that Burton left off any rank for the mutineer. Rightly so, she supposed.

"Yes, I agree. We need her help, but we don't need any more death and destruction."

"Quite so, ma'am."

"All right, I'm headed back to the bridge. I'll be there if you need anything."

"Understood, ma'am."

Monica Samuels had just reached the hatch to the central corridor when the ship's proximity alarm sounded loudly, echoing in the empty spaces of the boatbay. She looked up at the speaker in momentary confusion and then she began to run.

CHAPTER 5
18 October
WNS *Yargus* / WNS *Pathfinder*

"Okay, listen up."

Major Sheli Chowdhury watched her troops as they moved down the central walkway to settle into their positions on Shuttle One. No one moved at her command, but she could tell they were all paying attention.

"As soon as we come out of jump, we are going to drop away from *Yargus* and head for pod three on the port side of the target. We will attach quickly and go in hot. Anyone not in 'Warner Black' is to be considered hostile whether they are in military uniform or civilian dress."

Several heads came up at this change from the normal rules of engagement.

"Any Warner that you encounter may be friendly, or they may be assisting the pirates, so take all precautions to ensure your safety. This is a possible hostage situation, but don't make any assumptions."

She looked down the double row of Marines, who had all reached their seats by this time. There were four groups of six in two facing columns. Most of the troops were sitting casually, looking up at her. A few were more rigid, and some were lounging, as much as it was possible to do while in full armor. Most had their helmets racked under their feet, but a few had them latched on their heads and a couple even had the face shields down. This was not a common practice, but each person prepared for combat in their own way. "I know that most of you don't know me, except possibly by reputation," Chowdhury continued, then had to wait while someone seemed to choke and then cough a few times. "...but I want to make something perfectly clear." She waited until every eye, or face shield, was turned her way. "No one takes unnecessary risks. I run a tight team, and I know I can be a real pain sometimes, but you have not experienced pain until you try to hotdog on a combat op that I run. There will be nothing left of you but a puddle that dribbles out when I pop your armor release. You are going to envy Humpty Dumpty. Hear me on this. Understood?"

"Ooh-rah!" they shouted back in unison.

"All right, Lieutenant Mdembe is going to be coming in opposite us with his team on the starboard side of the target, so watch your fields of fire. My team will head forward and take the bridge and Lieutenant Kelley's team will take and secure Weapons Control. Lieutenant Mdembe and his team will split and go aft to secure Engineering and also the attached shuttle. Any questions?"

As she spoke, she felt the slight nausea that indicated *Yargus* had jumped. She knew the plan and her two shuttle pilots had been informed, so she wasn't surprised to feel the vibration in her feet as the shuttle engines went hot. They were still in standby, so there was no appreciable noise to deal with, but they were ready as soon as Commodore Brighton gave them the 'go'.

"Saddle up, troops. We're going hot in about thirty seconds."

She made her way several steps forward to the side-facing jump seat that would be her perch for the flight in. To her right, she had a view of the flight deck and the two shuttle pilots. They looked young and nervous, and Chowdhury knew this was their first combat insertion, but they were competent and they hid their nerves in the routine of their flight checklists.

To her left, she could see her Marines doing their own final checks on their gear and many more helmets were being secured in place. This was the first combat for any of these Marines, she was sure. She remembered the first time she had gone into real combat instead of the training drills. A few would freeze. She would have to watch and make sure all moved with their teammates. She doubted there would be much of that. These were Marines. The drive to be seen as not letting their teammates down would keep them moving as it had done to combat Marines for centuries.

It was amazing how soothing the routine of preparation was. It calmed her at a time when she needed it most as she approached *Pathfinder*, her old home and last duty station. The memory of her exit from *Pathfinder* still stung. She couldn't believe she had let those idiots get the drop on her in the corridor; but even worse, she couldn't believe she hadn't seen the piracy coming. Brighton obviously had seen something, and was able to make some preparations, but she had been so concentrated on finding the mole that she had begun to relax after Jhonsruud had been captured. It had been inexcusable.

She knew her nerves were ramping up in anticipation of evening the score, but she fought down that feeling and concentrated on doing her job. Everyone needed to concentrate on doing today's job.

The pilot's strong soprano cut into her thoughts before she had time for any more self-recriminations.

"Drop in five, four, three, … Drop."

Chowdhury felt the release of the shuttle from its attachment points on *Yargus*. She could see the stars stream across the forward view plate in front of the pilot as the shuttle raced ahead to its rendezvous with her old ship. She watched the scan console on its mount across from her as it showed *Yargus* continue to accelerate toward Granada where they would use the planet to slingshot themselves at a faster velocity out away from the gate they had just used to reenter the system. She could imagine the consternation and surprise on the faces of the crew who probably thought they were jumping to safety, only to find themselves back in the inner system they had just jumped from. *Yargus* was now inside the fleet that had been chasing them and that fact had given them a chance to get onto *Pathfinder* without the Forresters intervening.

Brighton knew his primary mission was to get both *Pathfinder* and the fact that Forrest was holding this system back to Earth. He didn't need to fight those other Forrest destroyers in order to accomplish either.

Conscious of her previous thoughts, she dismissed *Yargus* and concentrated on her part of the mission.

The pilot was very good and was pushing through *Pathfinder's* weapons envelope at the shuttle's highest rate of acceleration. At the last possible second, she flipped the shuttle and began the reorientation that would put them next to the target in a position to attach and board. The pilot knew the most dangerous part of the mission was this one, when the enemy could detect them and fire on them before they got close enough to attach. She was using her high speed to minimize the time *Pathfinder* had available in which to engage them. The element of surprise appeared to be working in their favor, since the target's weapons remained inactive.

Major Chowdhury watched as her old ship's image grew until it nearly filled the screen in front of the pilot. The view had not changed, regardless of the orientation of the shuttle to the target. Still, there seemed to be no reaction from the old destroyer, which was not what she had been expecting. The pilot was excellent and the shuttle came to rest mere meters from the target hatch, well inside the range where *Pathfinder's* weapons could bear on the shuttle.

"Breach team to the airlock," Chowdhury called without moving. The four Marines in the front seats moved immediately and, grabbing their gear from the compartments around them, strode to the airlock between Chowdhury and the rest of the troops. A solid hatch came down just in front of Chowdhury, cutting her off from the flight deck. She looked back to see that all of her Marines had donned their helmets and closed the face shields. She closed her own.

"Seal check."

At her voice, twenty armored thumbs went in the air and she keyed her radio to the flight engineer.

"Vent the compartment."

She knew all the operational timing was in her hands now. Lieutenant Mdembe would not breach the inner door on hold ten, which was on the opposite side of her target airlock, until forty-five seconds after she entered the boatbay. She wanted to give the defenders plenty of time to focus on her before the other team came in at their backs. She would rather have had Bravo Team come in through the hull behind the bridge and work aft, but they needed to minimize the damage to the ship if they were going to be able to grab it and jump out before the Forrest fleet could return from the outer system and she didn't need an extra hole in the bridge.

Yargus would fight to keep the Forresters off their backs while they made whatever minor repairs were necessary, but they couldn't delay them indefinitely.

The breach team hit the override on the airlock and opened the inner door while she listened to the high whine of the massive pumps that were pulling all the air from the cargo area where her troops sat.

When the inner indicator light turned amber, her breach team hit the release on the outer lock and let the slight decompression carry them out into the void. Confident they knew their jobs, Sheli left them to it. She waited to a count of ninety, then she stood and moved to the outer hatch. A collapsible, temporary tube was now connected between her hatch and the outer hatch of the airlock on *Pathfinder*. Her team fell in behind her at a silent signal and Lieutenant Kelley with his team behind them. At her silent count of forty-three, she launched herself lightly out the hatch and moved through the tube, grabbing the occasional handhold to keep herself oriented properly. Just before she reached the end of the tube, she checked that the hatch was clear before she sailed, feet first, through the open hatch and into the cargo hold. As soon as she passed the threshold of *Pathfinder*, its gravity began to assert itself and she touched down easily in a maneuver that appeared graceful, but was truly one of the most difficult skills that she had ever been able to master. She moved forward to the inner door as the breach team sealed the tube behind the last member of Kelley's team. The air was quickly being replaced in the cargo pod from cylinders brought along for that purpose. She reached the inner hatch as the breach team attached their charges and, at their look, she signaled with a nod and the hatch blew inward. She checked behind her at the rest of her team, then primed her blast rifle and leapt through the hatch into the boatbay. She rolled, as well as you could roll in Marine PUMA armor, and came up tracking from aft to fore and saw no immediate resistance. She heard two more of her team land behind her and mirror her actions, each with their own zone of responsibility. She stopped dead and called to her team.

"Hold fire! Hold fire!"

She looked at the group in front of her and identified the four figures in rumpled Warner Fleet uniforms standing at attention by the forward bulkhead. The young Ensign Samuels, wearing new lieutenant's pins, took a slight step forward from Gunnery Sergeant Aichele, Staff Sergeant Burton and Dr. Johnson and then saluted smartly.

"Welcome home, Major. We were hoping the Commodore would send someone like you over to us. We could really use your help."

CHAPTER 6
18 October
WNS *Pathfinder*

Major Sheli Chowdhury marched toward the bridge access hatch with her armored helmet under her left arm. 'Lieutenant' Monica Samuels trailed in her wake like a copepod parasite following a great shark. She was followed, in turn, by the obviously injured Sergeant Burton in her rumpled dress blacks, her right arm in a sling and her blonde hair shaved close, and finally by Lieutenant Mdembe and Gunnery Sergeant Aichele bringing up the rear and watching all the group as if he were trying to protect the young officer from a devouring predator. Chowdhury did not slow her pace in the familiar surroundings as she retraced her steps in reverse from that fateful day in June when she had been captured and expelled from this ship. Passing through the scene of her humiliation forced her to recognize that, again, she had not fully prepared for all the possibilities; that, for the third time in her career, she had failed to prepare for the possibility of treachery. She forced her feelings down, brutally imposing her will upon her emotions, but the visible injuries to Burton's arm and shoulder were a renewed reminder of her failure. At least her failure had not cost Burton her life as Chowdhury had feared for the last several months it had done.

Chowdhury keyed the bridge hatch to open, yet the portal stubbornly stayed closed in her face. Samuels ran up, apologizing, as she keyed in the code that successfully opened the armored door.

"I'm sorry, ma'am, I cleared all the codes so that neither the pirates nor the Forresters could get back in once we took over."

Chowdhury maintained her silence as she strode past the young officer into the interior of the bridge, again pushing down her resurgent anger. The ensign was not the cause of her wrath, and Chowdhury reminded herself she needed to stay in control and not let any of the overflow splash onto the girl who had done such an exceptional job of recapturing the ship.

"Ensign," Chowdhury began, "you have done an exemplary job here. I need a status report."

"Lieutenant."

The forceful word brought Chowdhury up short and she turned to look at Aichele.

"Gunny?"

"She should be referred to as Lieutenant or as Captain, Major. She is currently the senior Warner Fleet officer on this vessel and was promoted by the former Commander Leung to Lieutenant and made the XO of this ship. She should receive that designation when you refer to her. Now that Captain Brighton has returned, I imagine that he will return and command the ship. If you do not want to designate her with the responsibility of commanding this ship, she should still hold her rank and be referred to as such."

Chowdhury was shocked by Aichele's outburst. He hardly ever spoke out and never corrected anyone in public. This was highly unusual. She turned to look at Samuels. The girl was red in the face and had a hand on one of the silver rank pins as if trying to hide it but she was looking at Chowdhury squarely.

"Samuels, is this true?"

"Yes, ma'am."

Chowdhury stepped over to Samuels and looked into her face. She knew her own reputation with the ensigns and intended to make the girl less at ease. She saw Aichele moving closer to give the girl support and she gave him a slight hand gesture to keep him back.

"Were you working with Leung and Teach and then decided to double-cross them for a better deal with Fleet?"

She saw the girl turn from red to white and swallow, but her face never turned away.

"No, ma'am. The captain sent me back onboard. I didn't know what he wanted me to do so I pretended to help Commander Leung while I worked against her. Finally, I found Gunny Aichele and Sergeant Burton were also working trying to stop her and they were able to take back the ship with some help from me."

Chowdhury turned to Aichele at this point.

"Can you support this statement."

"Mostly. She understates her importance. I believe she would have succeeded without our support, it just would have taken longer. We merely streamlined her plan and added personnel."

Chowdhury nodded and took a step back, giving Samuels some room.

"Very well. Again, well done, Lieutenant Samuels. I need a complete report please."

Samuels stood tall and nodded back, a small tear running down one cheek.

"Yes, ma'am. The ship is secure. We have five Forrest technicians being held in Hold Five and we had four Forrest Marines secured in the brig, but we have since released them with beacon-equipped pressure suits. We were able to take back the ship, but in the process we had several casualties, four of them fatal. We lost Ensign Omundson, Crewman Morrison, and Warrants Fields and Calvi when the Forresters tried to take the ship from us. All other former mutineers are working with the expectation of some possibility of amnesty, or at least leniency. Lieutenant Commander Leung is also helping with the rebuild, but under constant close guard. Crewman Chin has been assigned to keep her under observation at all times when either Burton or Aichele are otherwise assigned. The comm transmitter is still inoperative, but we have limited weapons and propulsion restored."

Samuels was so caught up in her own reliving of the traumatic events that she was cataloguing, she missed the slight tightening on Chowdhury's face at the mention of further deaths.

Chowdhury raised her armored right hand in a 'hold on' motion to Samuels and turned to Mdembe.

"Get back to the shuttle and contact *Yargus*. Get all our comm techs on their way over and any parts they might need to completely rebuild the communications suite."

"Yes, ma'am."

He began moving toward the hatch when Burton raised her face sheepishly.

"He will need to bring at least one external antenna … I broke all the others off the ship and the replacement we pulled from stores is non-functional."

Chowdhury's eyes widened slightly, but she only nodded to the departing lieutenant as he glanced back. When the hatch closed behind him, Chowdhury turned back to Samuels.

"I reported back to the Commodore as soon as I knew the ship was secured and I have the jump coordinates for Earth. Are there sufficient personnel to operate the ship?"

"Yes, ma'am, I believe so. If the Marines are willing to pitch in. Sergeant Burton and Gunny Aichele have been helping out in Engineering when they aren't busy guarding Leung. Our scan is still down and propulsion is marginal, so it may take some extra lead time to build up transition speed, but I believe we are ready to get under weigh if we don't have to rely on our astrogation computer. We could use some more fleet personnel who could run the bridge consoles. Marines are capable of doing that but they are not trained and we could eliminate the possibilities of mistakes with fleet people. We could get by with what we've got if we have to."

Chowdhury turned to the slender officer and nodded sharply.

"My Marines will help run whatever stations you deem necessary and we'll get what other people we can. We must be ready to move as soon as the commodore is ready to implement his plan and that may limit our options on transfers. He will cover our movement and let us jump away before following himself."

Samuels began moving to the command console with a cautious glance back at the security officer.

"Yes, ma'am. I can cover all other bridge consoles if you could assign enough people to man Engineering and Weapons for now."

Chowdhury motioned to Aichele and Burton and they both started toward the hatch.

"Very well. Aichele, rig a temporary comm line from here to the shuttle. We need to have communications back up here in the bridge."

* * * * *

WNS *Yargus*

"Ms. Samuels believes we can depart immediately, but a few hours repairs would allow *Pathfinder* to make better speed," came Chowdhury's voice from the commodore's speaker less than an hour later. "We now have temporary comm capability restored and we are ready to move when ordered."

The commodore leaned slightly back in his chair on *Yargus* as he watched Major Chowdhury make her report from *Pathfinder*.

"Very well. Keep me advised as things develop."

The Major turned slightly in her seat and her head turned to the commodore.

"Yes, sir. There is also something else."

Brighton's eyebrows rose at the unexpected tone in Chowdhury's voice. She almost sounded hesitant.

"Yes?" he prompted when she didn't immediately continue.

"I would like to put my commendations on record for Ensign Samuels, Dr. Johnson, Gunnery Sergeant Aichele, Staff Sergeant Burton, and Specialist Sullivan. They all performed above and beyond the call of duty and in the best spirit of the fleet. I would also recommend that you confirm Samuels' promotion to lieutenant. She clearly has the support and respect of the rest of the loyal crew and she would be a great asset to the fleet. They have all far exceeded expectations."

Brighton was silent for several moments, his fingers steepled in front of his face. He knew that praise from Chowdhury was usually very sparing; they must have done an extraordinary job.

"Yes, I have been studying the logs that you forwarded. Were you aware that Samuels was promoted to lieutenant by Lieutenant Commander Leung?"

"Yes, sir. It might be suspicious, but I believe her story and her loyalty completely. Her actions clearly demonstrate where those loyalties lie. But beside the fact that Leung promoted her in order to act as her XO, if she hadn't Samuels would have had to have assumed the rank in order to take command, which she had to do, by Warner regulations."

Brighton's eyebrows rose at the endorsement, but he made no comment. It was not like Chowdhury to make such a blanket statement about anyone's trustworthiness.

"Very well," he said, changing the subject. "I don't want Leung to have the run of the ship. Keep her monitored or restrained."

"Yes, sir."

"Also, you need to get the ship moving toward the gate. The jump coordinates are based on that jumppoint. Leave Samuels in charge of ship operations. Have her jump to the Gravitas research yard in Gateway as soon as you reach the gate. That's the nearest secure facility where we can protect the technology from recapture. We will cover your escape and jump to Tannar to intercept *Dagger* before she can jump into Worth. Despite my earlier bluff, I have no interest in fighting this Forrest fleet without considerably greater forces at my back."

"Yes, sir. I'll pass on that message and we'll get under weigh," Chowdhury said just before the screen went blank.

Brighton sat quietly for several moments before turning to Captain Ramirez.

"Put us into position to protect *Pathfinder*. Prepare a missile salvo aimed at the lead ship as soon as it gets into range."

"Aye, sir."

Brighton sat quietly again while the bridge became a storm of frenetic movement as Ramirez followed through on his orders. There were too many variables here to properly predict any sure result, but he needed to get his ships free of this system and report its takeover. They needed much more firepower than they had available to be able to take on the ships arrayed before them with confidence. With Forrest holding the jump gate, their best hope was to escape with the intelligence they had gathered. With the Forresters in control of the gate platform, this was only possible because both *Pathfinder* and *Yargus* were two of the three ships in the universe able to jump without a gate.

"Gate activation!" Ensign Judd called excitedly from his scan console. All eyes on the bridge turned to him, and he followed that announcement with, "IFF confirms *Dagger* has jumped into the system."

CHAPTER 7
18 October
WNS *Pathfinder*

Katherine Leung moved down the corridor toward the makeshift brig in the aft section of the boatbay. She had worked hard to feign cooperation with Samuels and the others and she had actually helped get the main engines and control systems back online. The ship could now move on her own, much better than the embarrassing, limping action that had gotten them into this orbit on the outer edges of the shipyard and construction area.

Leung had been biding her time until she saw an opportunity to take back the ship. Samuels, at least, had seemed to accept her story and let her help with ship repairs.

Now the time had finally come to make her move. It was not the move she had intended to make, however. With that trusting simpleton, Samuels, in charge, it was just a matter of time until she would have had an opening to take back control of the ship. *Her* ship! She looked at the bulkheads as she walked, full of conduits and pipes. She knew the function and purpose of every one. She knew this ship, it was hers. She hated leaving *Pathfinder*, but she had run out of options here. She would never be able to regain control now. With the arrival of Major Chowdhury and her two shuttles full of Marines, all opportunities were evaporating like a mist on a sunny day. She had barely been able to get by Chowdhury's earlier efforts by pointing her at Jhonsruud. She didn't have any similar options now. She had to get off the ship if she was going to survive. Leung had created several tentative plans in her head, for emergencies, but this one was a longshot. It also looked like it might be her only remaining chance.

But waiting on *Pathfinder*, with Chowdhury onboard, was not a survivable option.

As she exited the corridor and stepped through into the cavernous boatbay, she had her third piece of luck; the first two had been getting away from her personal guard, and also relieving him of a weapon. The boatbay was the single largest compartment on the ship, and it was placed directly between the engineering section and the living and operating section. As such, it had a near constant flow of personnel moving through to Engineering or busy with different tasks in one of the many holds that had their entry hatches at one side or the other of the area. This morning, however, there were only two other people in the boatbay when she entered. Unfortunately, they were both armed Marines assigned to guard the Forrest engineers who were being kept prisoner in Hold Five, the largest of the internal holds. The same engineers that Leung had come here to set free. She had known about the guards, however, so she had come prepared and brought a light stunner. It would be tricky to be able to get both of them, but she was desperate enough that she had very little choice.

Being an engineer, she didn't like to leave anything to chance, so she had adjusted the odds in her favor as much as possible. She strode purposefully around the large shipping containers and boxes that still haphazardly filled the bay from the crew's breakneck attempt to get the ship fully functional. Several of the containers still showed burns and other signs of the fighting which had taken place earlier that week. Once she was near the guards, they straightened and became more alert.

"I need to talk to Nishimura," she said with her hands behind her.

"No contact is allowed with the prisoners," the taller of the two guards said in a dismissive tone, without looking directly at her.

She clutched the stunner more tightly at his insulting tone, but otherwise she made no outward reaction. Internally, though, she was seething. She recognized the fact that she needed to remain in control, but she fought to keep her temper in check. She struggled so much with her emotions that, when her prearranged distraction came, in the form of a small explosion to the guard's right, she almost missed her opportunity. She quickly regained her composure and brought her stunner up while the guards were trying to assess the new situation, and stunned them each in quick succession. After they were down, she began to kick them in any unprotected areas she could find until, finally, her rage subsided and she moved forward to open the hold.

There were five Forrest engineers locked inside the compartment. They had been sent aboard from Granada, at Leung's request, to help reverse-engineer the new jump engines on *Pathfinder*. They had been rounded up by Sergeant Burton during the Warner takeover of the ship. That takeover had triggered drastic retaliation by the Forrest Marines in which several of the *Pathfinder* crewmen and one officer had been killed. The mood on the ship, currently, was just short of murderous, so the engineers had remained in detention as much for their own safety as for any other reason. The Forrest Marines, who had been captured at the same time as the engineers, had been moved out of the ship and were being housed in EVA suits outside the ship instead of the small brig in the security suite without her knowledge.

"Can anyone pilot a shuttle?" she called out as she opened the hatch. The prisoners sat dumbly, looking at her as they blinked their eyes at the sudden, blinding light.

The large overweight man in the rear of the group raised his hand tentatively.

"I've got a civilian license, but I've never flown anything as big as the military shuttles."

"Good, that should work. The way is clear to your shuttle. Give me ten minutes to get the locking clamps disabled and then head for the access. I'm also going to release your Marines from the brig, if I can manage it, so give us a few minutes to get to the shuttle and then we can launch. You will want to head directly to the ship docks in orbit rather than trying to land on the planet, unless one of the Marines is certified as a pilot and is capable of a planetary landing."

At their uncertain nods, she turned and headed toward the brig. The docking clamps were already disabled. She had lied to them about that, too. She had disabled them before releasing the prisoners. They might be too tempted with thoughts of escape and decide not to wait for her or their fellow prisoners.

Leung moved cautiously through the corridor leading past the security offices. Major Chowdhury and her cohorts were supposed to be in a meeting in the "captain's" office with Samuels, but she wasn't going to assume anything until she was off this ship and safely hidden from the Marine's justice.

Her release of the Marines was much more complicated than taking out two unarmored guards in the boatbay. She had needed to plan very specifically and very thoroughly to find a way to take out the armored Marine who was guarding the armory and cells where the Forrest Marines were being confined. She found several possible methods during her research, but none of them had a high enough probability of success to warrant risking her life on them. Finally, she chose a brute force method to accomplish her goal. She dropped her stunner into a recycler chute on her way back to her cabin. She stepped in just long enough to grab the MK97 blast rifle that she had stowed there. With Samuels' accessing of the armory for the takeover, she had inadvertently given Leung access as well. Leung had put a tracking program in place just in case Lamont, whom she still thought to be alive at the time, had been able to get the armory open and it had dutifully recorded the access codes. It had been a simple matter, from there, to gain access when no one else was around. The MK 97 was the smallest weapon in the armory that was capable of penetrating heavy armor with one shot. It was designed to be carried by unarmored troops and therefore it was designed to be as portable as possible. That did not mean it was light, just that it was possible for a strong and fit Marine to carry. She moved through the corridor as quickly as she could with her burden and arrived in front of the security suite with no issues. She hefted the weapon in front of her and hit the hatch release.

The hatch slid quickly to the side with a soft whoosh. She expected the Marine to be in the cell block, down a corridor to the back and right of the main office area, but when the hatch opened, she found him standing right at the back of the office space at a desk, with his back to her. She raised her weapon as he started to turn and she fired a burst that struck him squarely in the back. He went down without making a sound. She dropped the heavy weapon and went to release the rest of the prisoners.

There were none to release.

*　*　*　*　*

Trying to think quickly, Leung backtracked into the main room. Actually, it did not change her plans all that much. When the alarm sounded, the engineers were smart enough to leave without waiting.

Leung looked down at the crumpled form of the Warner Marine on the floor in front of her. He was quite possibly the smallest Marine she had ever seen. Most looked like they had just stepped down from a recruiting poster, but this one was only slightly larger than she was herself. She cursed her luck. She had spent the night adapting a set of stolen armor to fit her small form when she could have stolen this set and saved herself the work. With another small curse, she moved to the stairway at the end of the cross corridor. She continued down to the first landing and checked her tell-tales on the entry door to the interstitial spaces. Finding everything in order, she opened the hatch and moved through quickly. She had spoofed the electronics to be oblivious to her entry and she moved forward to the spot she had prepared to hide in. As she reached the darkened area between the decks, she lay down among the boxes and modified armor and pulled out her hand-comp. She opened her secure computer access and triggered an alarm. With luck, the Forresters would launch immediately, without waiting for her. She switched her scans to internal and lay down to enjoy the show.

* * * * *

Samuels looked up sharply at the alarm. She tapped the comm, intending to call Sergeant Burton before remembering that Major Chowdhury was now in command of the security of the ship. She paused in indecision. It had been hard enough to force herself to give orders to Aichele, Burton and Sullivan in the beginning, but Major Chowdhury was a whole order of magnitude more intimidating. While Chowdhury was a Marine and, technically, outside the chain of command for the ship, she still outranked the lieutenant; even if she acknowledged the legitimacy of that rank to begin with.

Finally, she put through the call.

She needn't have bothered.

Major Chowdhury came through the hatch onto the bridge within seconds, obviously on her way before any call could have summoned her.

"We have a breakout of the Forresters," she said without preamble. "My team is working on rounding up those we can reach."

"Why can't you reach all of them?" asked Samuels in confusion. There was nowhere on the ship that was not accessible to the Marines.

As if in answer, she felt the tremor through the deck that was the indication of a small craft releasing itself from *Pathfinder* and using maneuvering jets to propel itself away.

"Orders, Captain?" Samuels was struck speechless by shock. Chowdhury had acknowledged her authority as captain, at least for now, and she was turning to her for orders when she obviously had more knowledge and infinitely more experience in these matters. Samuels took a deep breath and thought carefully about her answer. In the end, she adopted the same approach in this as she had with Aichele during the takeover.

"I will bow to your superior knowledge in security matters," she began. "They must not be allowed to escape, however. We still have no defenses and the Forresters would make short work of us if they found out we hold this ship."

"Aye, ma'am," Chowdhury replied as she moved to the newly reconstructed comm console. She didn't ask how they were going to stop them with no fully functional weapons or targeting systems, since those had been repurposed to comms. As she moved to the console, the hatch opened again, with the characteristic whooshing sound of the airtight seal of the blast door breaking. Samuels turned in relief to see Gunnery Sergeant Aichele enter. He gave a small nod to Samuels before moving across the back of the compartment to join Chowdhury at the communications console. She took a few moments to lock the tightbeam comm laser onto the fleeing shuttle before hitting the transmit key.

"Attention Forrest shuttle," she began, "as escaping prisoners charged with accessory to murder of prisoners during a period of armed peace, you are subject to destruction under the Treaty of Dallas if you fail to surrender for trial. Heave to or you will be destroyed."

There was no response. Chowdhury looked at Samuels, who looked pale but did not turn away. The major waited quietly for a few more moments before turning to Aichele.

"Do you think you can get a lock with the laser array long enough to burn through the shuttles' shielding?"

"Yes, ma'am," Aichele said with a lopsided grin. "But there might be an easier answer."

Chowdhury said nothing. A raised eyebrow and a scowl were her only responses.

"Ahem, ah, yes," Aichele stammered, "Burton and I thought we had better have a failsafe after they almost got away from us. We weren't up to full strength and weren't sure we had gotten all of the conspirators, so…Well, ma'am, we set a bomb on board their shuttle, just in case."

"I see," she said, "can you activate it from here?"

"Yes, ma'am."

"That would have been problematic if they had discovered it and decided to take us with them, don't you think?"

"Yes, ma'am, but that never seemed very likely," he added with another grin.

Chowdhury nodded and turned her attention back to the comm.

"Forrest shuttle. Surrender, now. This is your last warning."

The hatch cycled again to admit Burton. Like Aichele, she was wearing crisp, new fatigues, but her right arm was immobilized against her torso. She glanced back and forth between Samuels and Chowdhury before finally turning her gaze to the midpoint between them, as if unsure who she was reporting to and, straightening, said, "Hutchings is awake in Hold Five, ma'am. He says it was Leung that stunned him and let the Forresters loose."

Samuels stood and looked at Burton with urgency.

"Find Chin. Did she escape from him or is he still with her? Is she with the Forresters on the shuttle?"

Burton raised her left hand and turned to face Samuels fully.

"Sorry, ma'am, I should have reported that earlier. Chin was also found. She knocked him out. He's in medbay. We haven't gotten a report yet from Dr. Johnson. As far as Leung, she is very likely with them, ma'am."

Chowdhury turned slightly from the comm console and looked squarely at Samuels.

"Have your orders changed, Captain?"

Samuels stood without moving for several heartbeats, and then turned to face Chowdhury and Aichele.

"No, Major, they have not," she said firmly. "Destroy the shuttle."

Aichele put action to her words; flipping two switches to unlock and arm the hidden device. Samuels sat down heavily in the captain's chair and faced the forward viewscreen, so she missed the approving nod and thoughtful look from Chowdhury.

With a flick of a toggle on the weapons console, Aichele sent the signal that ended the escape with a sudden finality.

CHAPTER 8
18 October
Asunción Military Base – Granada

Granada Central Combined Marine and Naval Base, a mouthful for anyone to recite, had always been called Hub-Q. This was due to its design of concentric rings, which looked like a spoked wheel from the air, and the fact that it was the headquarters for Warner's joint military forces on Grenada. Or, it had been.

Located just northeast of Granada City, Hub-Q had been turned into a glassy hole in the ground. It had once been the center of all military operations, the apex of the naval and Marine hierarchies, which made it the first target Forrest had hit with kinetic rounds from orbit in their initial attack.

During the take-over, the Forresters had brought several ships into the system on what appeared to be legitimate business. These ships had moved subtly into position, killing all the tracking satellites on their way further in, blinding those on the ground to what was happening above. The first rounds were fragile, designed to break apart and scatter reflective chaff everywhere, confusing the radar and other tracking systems on the surface. The next volley was composed of heavy tubes of lead with hardened ceramic outer shells. Even without seeing the threat clearly, Warner automated defenses had responded well, and only two of the forty-odd metal cylinders had made it through the counter-missiles and ground-to-air fire.

Two had been enough.

The kinetic energy released on impact had translated into heat and light enough to make it look like binary suns had appeared on the planet. The shockwave blew apart buildings for kilometers, and shattered windows all the way across the city. Nothing, and no one, in the vicinity of Hub-Q survived.

All of Warner's bases on Granada were in similar states. Not all had been hit from orbit, though more than ninety percent had, but none had been left in a usable condition. That had required Forrest to build their own defensible strongholds for their occupation forces, which they accomplished in short order from prefabricated pieces. Foremost among these was Asunción, designed to be the headquarters of the Forrest military troops, with operation, munition, communication and housing facilities for two complete companies of Marines.

Asunción's location would seem, at first sight, to be somewhat strange, and perhaps morbid. The base lay smack in the middle of the same field of now-scorched earth where Hub-Q had once been found. Logistically, however, it was ideally located. It was, for all realistic purposes, a part of the capital city; tied into the government's control and communications lines. Plus, from the Marines' point of view, the base was somewhat isolated, with clear fields of fire and sight lines for over three kilometers in every direction.

Admiral Juan Epstein, ranking naval officer of the fledgling Forrest Family Forces-Navy in the Worth System, happened to be dirtside on the morning of the 18th, and thus in the center of the new base. The reason he was not in his normal workplace, an office in the orbital construction area known as Caspar Yards, was that he was attending another conference intended to iron out problems and conflicts arising from the military's newfound responsibilities in this system. In addition to the areas the military was used to overseeing; security, law enforcement, crowd control, system traffic; they had just been handed an armload of new areas for which they had no training, no experience, and no desire to take care of. That morning, the admiral had sat through three hours of debate about who should be in charge of food distribution scheduling. *Three hours!* Eventually, the debate had returned back to the same question it always did: How had Epi Solomon dealt with that?

The woman had been arrogant, dismissive, and with a volcanic temper Epstein was pleased only to have seen through a comm call while safely in his office off-planet, but clearly she had also been a logistical and organizational genius. Given how much time was being wasted trying to absorb all the work she had been managing, letting her go seemed more and more short-sighted of the Board to him. Still, his superiors assured him it was both necessary and a positive move for the navy. He hoped so.

Epstein checked the chronoplate on the wall of his second office while he finished his lunch. He had twelve minutes before he would have to be back in the conference room again. He pulled the lower left drawer of his desk open and retrieved a bottle and glass kept there for just such emergencies and issued himself a healthy dose. After a second's consideration, he added another liberal amount, until the dose was significantly less healthy.

He had the bottle stowed, but the evidence had not yet been disposed of when his office door opened unexpectedly to admit Lieutenant Commander Ames. He relaxed when he saw it was only his staff officer, but when the look in her eyes registered, he jumped to his feet.

"What is it, Jacqui?"

"There's been an unscheduled gate activation, sir."

Epstein headed for the door, but turned back to down his drink before he double-timed it behind Ames to the Operations Center. That room was abuzz with activity when he entered. Forty or more officers flowed between comm, analysis, and simulation stations trying to come to grips with the new situation and to have answers ready before their superiors asked for them.

"Show me what you have," Epstein ordered as he strode to the holographic display tank in the center of the room. Captain Halliday was already studying the pieces of the puzzle, and he directed the duty tech to run everything back to the point where the jump gate opened.

"Sir, a little over thirty minutes ago, the Warner gate to Betre opened and was transited by a single ship, which we have identified as a Warner *Reina*-class destroyer," the duty officer, a florid-faced lieutenant, began as the display altered to match his words. "*Hammer* was on rotation for gate security, and issued the initial challenge. Per standing orders, the other eight destroyers immediately began reforming their dispositions to align toward the gate and began advancing on the new ship.

"Here, at time D+3 minutes," the lieutenant continued, "*Hammer* received a transmission in response to her challenge. The commanding officer identified himself as Commodore Brighton, called on our ships to stand down, and said he was commanding a task force."

"Is that what Warner's calling a task force these days? A sixty-year-old tin can?" Captain Halliday snorted.

Epstein looked at him blankly, and Halliday cleared his throat, motioning for the lieutenant to continue.

"IFF from gate control identifies the ship as WNS *Yargus*, but we have no record of a ship by that name. *Yargus* began decelerating right after entering the system, but you can see here, at time D+7, they add a lateral vector to push out toward system west. Given the positions of our ships, that course was their best chance to avoid action.

"Now here, at D+11 minutes, it's clear that our ships have more accel than they expected, so they turn again, dead away from pursuit. At this point, there is another exchange. *Hammer* calls on *Yargus* to surrender. *Yargus* responds that they have the power to destroy every ship in this system, and they will not hesitate to use it if their ROE shows a state of war exists."

"He's bluffing," Halliday stated flatly. "There is no weapon that could fit on a destroyer that could have that kind of firepower."

Epstein repeated the blank look. "Is that so, Captain?"

Halliday looked confused at the admiral's reaction. "Of course, sir. If there were such a weapon, everyone would know about it."

"I see," Epstein said calmly. "Just like everyone knows that Warner has developed a mobile jump gate platform, right?"

Epstein was fully prepared to lambaste the unfortunate captain further, but he could see the wheels turning and the lights going on behind his eyes. Instead, he added more input for Halliday to process. "And what did Warner use to build this mobile jump gate platform? A sixty-year-old tin can. Why don't we have any record of a *Yargus* on the Warner lists? Because they renamed it after they were done refitting it to whatever new model they had in mind. Just like they did with *Pathfinder*. And why does Commodore Brighton claim to be commanding a task force, when we only see one ship? Possibly because he's scouting for the rest of the group, which are waiting just on the other side of the gate.

"It's possible the man is bluffing, Captain, but I am not nearly as convinced of that as you seem to be."

"All right, then," Halliday put forth, "are there any assumptions at all that we can make about *Yargus'* capabilities? Can we, for instance, trust the information we received that *Pathfinder* is a unique prototype, and she and *Vanguard* are the only existing ships with mobile gate generators? It might make sense for Warner to be recycling ships for research, but whatever they put in *Yargus* could be completely unrelated to the Jump Drive that we wanted *Pathfinder* for."

"True, and that would match Brighton's claim that one ship could take on the whole system defense fleet, if the project involving *Yargus* were armament-related instead," Epstein added. "Brighton…where have I heard that name?"

Halliday looked blank and shrugged. The duty officer, Lieutenant Khalid, looked equally puzzled. As always, Commander Ames had the information her admiral needed. "That was the name of the replacement CO for *Pathfinder* after Captain Vanderjagt's sudden death, though we show him listed as only a captain."

"Can't be the same man, then," Halliday noted. "*Pathfinder's* captain was stranded in the Antoc system."

"What was that Brighton's first name?" Epstein fired at Ames. For once, she didn't have an answer ready. "I don't know, sir. I will find out." Ames stepped away from the display and linked her pad into the base servers to find the information.

"So, possibility one – they've got some kind of secret weapon, possibility two – they have a jump drive, and possibility three – they've got both. How do we direct our ships to go after them?" Halliday wanted to know.

Epstein was deep in thought and didn't answer directly. "How long does it take a jump drive to recharge after it is used?" He looked at Ames, but she was already fully engaged in looking up an answer to his last question. When he turned to Halliday and Khalid, neither of them had a clue.

"Get me a vocom link to *Pathfinder*. I need to speak to one of our engineers there," Epstein ordered in the general direction of the comm station.

A junior officer turned to acknowledge the order, responding with, "I'm sorry, sir, but *Pathfinder's* comms are still down. They can receive but not transmit."

"What?" The admiral didn't raise his voice, but it was clear that he was unaware of the communications breakdown. "Then how have we been getting information from them?"

"If I understand the process correctly, sir," Khalid offered, "we submit an information request to the Marine liaison officer, who passes it on to their communications office, who contacts the security force on the ship, who then provides the request to the engineers, and then the process reverses itself for the return trip."

Epstein said nothing for several tense heartbeats. "Seriously?"

"Uh—yes, sir."

"Of all the cockamamie—" The rest was bitten off behind his clenched teeth. He turned back to the comm station. "Contact General Franks and get her down here. Then start the normal process as a plan B."

He turned back to check the system display for changes, but abruptly spun back to the comm officer. "You said *Pathfinder* can hear us?"

"Yes, sir. But—"

"Transmit orders for them to reposition themselves on the other side of the planet from the intruder."

"Aye, sir. Transmitting. If I may, sir?"

"What is it, Lieutenant?"

"It's just that...well, sir...we've tried communicating this way before, but they don't actually have any communications watchstanders up there, so it hasn't ever worked. We've always been forced to go through the Marines."

Epstein's jaw clenched again. He said a few things under his breath that no one near him could make out. "Thank you, Lieutenant, for letting me know. I will add it to my growing list of things that will have to change."

The admiral moved back to the holographic chart, and Halliday was quick to get him back on his previous train of thought. "Do you have orders for the system defense force?"

Again, Epstein didn't answer directly. "Ames, what did you find out?"

"Sir, it's the same man, but listen to this. He *was* stranded in Antoc, but he somehow made it back to Earth in seven and a half weeks. The last information we had, he was given command of a task force of four ships and sent back to Antoc to try to find out what happened to his ship."

"That makes no sense," Captain Halliday complained. "How would he have known to come looking here?"

Epstein ignored Halliday, as he wasn't offering anything useful to the conversation. Instead he turned back to Ames. "You said he had four ships. What classifications are they?"

The commander referred back to her pad, still tied into the base net. "A *Hiramoto*-class corvette, a *Foundation*-class CB, *Yargus*, and Brighton's flag ship is a *Rapier*-class light cruiser."

"All right, then," Epstein clapped his hands, "we know that *Yargus* can generate a jump gate."

All eyes in the room turned to him, but only Ames asked the pervasive question. "How do we know this, exactly?"

Rather than annoyed, Epstein grinned at the opportunity to show his cleverness. "So Brighton is shipped off to Antoc with four ships to hunt for *Pathfinder*, right?" Ames nodded. "But all of his ships were not hunters, one was a Construction Battalion ship. Why?"

Ames cocked her head to the side, and Halliday furrowed his brow. Epstein only let them stew for a second. "Because Antoc had no gate generator on that side of the jump point! So the inclusion of the CB ship is one key piece of the puzzle, and the other is that Brighton is not currently on his own flagship."

"Right," Ames said, catching on, "because *Yargus* could leave the system on her own, while the others were trapped there."

"Exactly. Which further means that there are no reinforcements coming, just this one ship," the admiral concluded.

Halliday wasn't sure he had followed the links of logic chain Epstein had skipped over, but he was sure of one thing: the admiral still hadn't answered his question. "Orders for the fleet, sir?"

"Comms, order all ships to press the attack with everything they have! We need to destroy the ship or knock out her jump drive before she has the chance to escape and sound the warning!"

CHAPTER 5
18 October
WNS *Yargus* / WNS *Pathfinder*

Brighton paced along the now familiar track behind his command chair on *Yargus*. His plans were no longer viable. With the arrival of *Dagger*, they would not be able to jump out of the system without abandoning the light cruiser. She could not jump back out of the Worth system without the control of the Granada Gate Control Platform which was being held by the Forrest Family Marines. He wasn't ready to abandon her yet. With their jump from the outer system, they had bought the time they needed to make things work. He just needed to make the right choices… and hope they really had enough time.

He looked at Captain Ramirez, seated in his command chair, just in front of his own chair. The captain had put his fears behind him and looked to be in control of his emotions.

"Captain, set a course to intercept *Pathfinder*."

"Aye, sir."

"Captain, with your permission, I need to make some orders to the rest of the task force. Permission to use your bridge crew for a few moments?"

Ramirez waved a hand. "By all means, sir."

He turned to the communications console at the back of the bridge and began to give orders.

"Comm, send a message to *Dagger*; tell them to rendezvous with us at *Pathfinder*. Their primary responsibility is to protect that ship at all costs.

"Lieutenant Weaver," he called to the tactical officer, "I want you to get with Ensign Roberts and Lieutenant Amaya-Garcia to flesh out three options and turn them into operational plans. Our first option is to remove the remaining six Forrester ships with the goal to hold this system. Our second option would be for the Marines from *Dagger* and *Pathfinder* to take and hold the Gate Control Platform long enough for all three ships to jump to the Tanner system. Our third option, which is a last resort, is for all personnel to transfer to *Pathfinder* and *Yargus*, scuttle *Dagger* and jump directly to Gateway."

Brighton moved from his position behind his chair to stand behind Ramirez. He placed his hand on the young captain's shoulder. Ramirez turned to look up at the tall commodore.

"Captain Ramirez, you have done well here. I will need to transfer my flag to *Pathfinder* as soon as we close the distance. I wish to take any of my former crew that are on *Dagger* who want to return to that ship and any other crew that you feel you can spare from *Yargus*. I would appreciate it if you would make those arrangements."

"Aye-aye, sir."

Before the commodore could say more, they were interrupted by a call from Kent at the scan console.

"Sir, I'm picking up a ship moving away from the station."

Brighton turned and asked a clarifying question without waiting for the captain.

"Can you identify it? Why is it moving away from us?"

The comm operator automatically responded to the command in the commodore's voice.

"Its drive signatures nearly match those of the other Forrest destroyers, but I'm not detecting any weapons signatures, however. Its course puts it coming out of the shipyards. It might be an unfinished new construction ship."

Brighton sat very still in his command chair for several moments, his index finger running up and down his jawline, his eyes unfocussed. He turned suddenly to Ramirez.

"I will also require one or two of your senior lieutenants, possibly Lieutenant Weaver and possibly Lieutenant Amaya-Garcia."

He stood and motioned to the officer, sitting at his post at the tactical station.

"Yes," he said cryptically, "That should do it."

"Aye-aye, sir" Ramirez called as Brighton moved to the hatch and exited the bridge, a wary Lieutenant Weaver and Lieutenant Amaya-Garcia in tow.

* * * * *

"That's the last of them, sir," Captain Ramirez reported thirty-two minutes later as Ensign Lyle and Lieutenant Weaver disappeared down the access hatch, with their duffels, to board the shuttle for transfer to *Pathfinder*. In the end, all the former *Pathfinder* crew had volunteered to transfer back to their original ship and Captain Ramirez had only needed to augment that complement with a few additions.

"There should be plenty of hands to get the necessary work done to make *Pathfinder* fully functional."

"Thank you, Captain. It has been an honor to be aboard your ship. You and your crew have performed in an exemplary manner," Brighton said as he saluted the young commanding officer and moved into the accessway to the shuttle. He didn't see the way doubt and concern transformed themselves on Ramirez' face as he watched Brighton's retreating back.

As Brighton seated himself on the shuttle and fastened his restraints, he thought about his time on *Yargus* and was struck again by how alike she was to his own ship *Pathfinder*. *Yargus* and *Pathfinder* were sister ships, built almost sixty years ago. They were two of the three oldest surviving destroyers in the fleet, along with their other sister, *Hanford*. They had been built in a time when destroyers were gaining prominence in the fleet; designed to explore and protect.

He had never let Ramirez know that *Yargus* felt to him as if it were still his own *Reigna*.

Reigna, his home that once had been. He knew that it could take the pounding that the Forresters could give because it had once taken a much harder pounding from pirates in the small Humboldt system and survived time after time with most of his friends still alive. Most of his friends…but not all. And now he headed back to his other home. The ship where he had lost other friends. *Pathfinder*. The ship where he had lost the man who he had thought was his best friend.

Pathfinder had begun her existence as the destroyer *Risea*. For the Argo Project, she had been stripped down and converted into a survey vessel and had lost much of her armament. As he sat in the shuttle, his mind was racing with plans on what he needed to do now with the ship that was left.

So far, he had received very little specific data on the status of *Pathfinder*. He knew that they had completed most of the work on the main engines and those had tested out fine, as had the jump engines. Now, they had only a few hours to make it capable of going into battle. His operational planners had suggested that they send the Marines to take and hold the Gate Control Platform at the same time that they implemented Plan A, which was to attack and eliminate the remaining enemy destroyers. With a few alterations, he had decided to go with their recommendation. There were a few new wrinkles he needed to iron out, but the plan was coming together in his head.

With the addition of *Dagger*, they had the firepower to go toe-to-toe with the more numerous enemy and still have a high probability of success. This was not what worried him. *Dagger* could protect the smaller ships. What worried him was whether or not he ought to risk either of the priceless, smaller ships. Admiral Cosina had made it clear that the future success of the Warner Family depended on the prototype engines developed on *Pathfinder* and installed, now, on *Yargus* as well. Those two engines were the only full-sized examples of the engines in existence. They needed to arrive safely at Gateway or this whole exercise was in vain.

On the other hand, if *Dagger* tried to take on the enemy alone, the Warner destroyers would have time to escape, but the light cruiser and her crew likely would not be able to disengage and retreat. And she would have nowhere to retreat to without the GCP. As a logical exercise, he had no problem asking one ship to sacrifice itself for the continued existence of the entire Family, but he had an instinctive problem with being on one of the ships that would escape.

Finally, the chime sounded to alert him that the shuttle had arrived and he must disembark onto his ship. He rose and moved to the hatch as the other passengers remained seated to allow him first egress. He strode out of the shuttle and up the access corridor before emerging from the hatch into the boatbay of *Pathfinder*. He saluted Lieutenant Samuels as she stood rigidly at attention and he felt moisture welling up in his eyes as he asked, "Permission to come aboard?"

"Permission granted," she said through the emotion closing her own throat. "Welcome home, sir. You have no idea how good it is to see you."

Brighton looked at the small young lieutenant standing in front of him and wondered how she was going to react when he told her he was not only going to take her first command away from her, but also send her on an assignment somewhere else.

CHAPTER 10
18 October
Shuttle *Gerard* / FFF *Scythe*

Lieutenant Monica Samuels looked across to where Commodore Brighton stood at the edge of *Pathfinder*'s boatbay, watching as she loaded her force into the shuttle access. He stood well back, obviously not wanting to interfere with her new command.

It was still staggering to her as she thought back through the events of the last hour. Commodore Brighton had walked her to the bridge, where he was to relieve her and assume command. He had no words of blame for the wreckage that she and her troops had caused in their efforts to take back the ship.

"Lieutenant, I have endorsed your promotion," he said without preamble, once the brief ceremony was complete. "Your efforts, and your success, warrant at least that reward. There is always a possibility that the Admiralty Board will not ratify it, but I will act as if it were confirmed until I hear specifically otherwise."

"Thank you, sir," she stammered, unsure what to say. She certainly had not expected the promotion to stand. Lieutenant Commander Leung had given her the promotion when she thought Samuels was a member of her conspiracy to steal the ship. Samuels was one of the only two other officers left on the ship with Leung, and the pirate had needed a second-in-command. The computer, limited as it had become, would not accept anyone in that position who was not at least a lieutenant in rank. So the promotion had been nothing more than a convenient fiction. To hear that Brighton did not consider it so, was a shock. While she had used the promotion to coerce the enlisted troops to follow her in the efforts to reclaim the ship, she had not ever really believed it herself. She would have gone back to being an ensign once the shooting had stopped if it hadn't been for Gunny Aichele's insistence that she had to be a lieutenant to captain a ship even more than to be an XO. By regulations, she would have had to have promoted herself!

Brighton interrupted her thoughts as he continued. "We have just intercepted an interesting transmission from Granada."

"Sir?" she said, caught off guard by his abrupt change of topic.

"I had thought to keep you on *Pathfinder* as my XO, but unfortunately, circumstances will now make that impossible."

"Sir, I assure you my loyalty —"

"I have no doubts about your loyalty, Lieutenant," he interrupted. "I find that I have a more pressing assignment for you, instead."

"Yes, sir," she said, feeling her stomach begin to knot at the thought of not being in control of the ship that she had fought so hard to protect. She felt the stirrings of an irrational anger at the thought of what was being taken away from her. She hadn't realized how strong her attachment had become to a ship that she had always known to be just a convenient stepping stone to what she truly needed and wanted to get from the Warner Fleet. The anger, and the attachment that caused it, caught her off guard and forced her to reevaluate her true feelings. She had never intended to make Warner Fleet her long-term home, but the abruptness with which her condition was changing had brought all of those possessive feelings to the fore.

As she stood, now, on the boatbay deck and watched the twenty Marines, and her own executive officer, climb down the damaged access hatch to board her shuttle, she was struck by how things had come full circle again. From very near this spot, she had watched as Brighton and his loyal troops had been forced down this same access into the ship's launch, *Vanguard*. In fact, after a slight hesitation, she had joined him.

Less than half a year had passed since that event, but truly a lifetime's worth of experiences had been jammed into that time.

She watched as Ensign Roberts stood stiffly at the entrance to the access hatch, and she wondered why her friend seemed to be barely in control of her emotions. She assumed it must be that same echo of memory from her previous trip down that access into *Vanguard* that Samuels was feeling which was causing the stir in Roberts. She knew how hard it had been for her, but she wondered what her friend's experience had been during that last half year.

Samuels didn't consider those questions for very long, and her thoughts were drawn back to Brighton and the bombshell he had dropped on her on the bridge.

"It seems that the Forresters have another completed destroyer here in the system and I want you to lead a small force and take it away from them before they can use it to challenge the safety of this ship."

"Sir, I don't have the experience to command—"

Brighton had raised a hand and given her a slight smile.

"You have more experience in leading shipboard action than any officer aboard, Lieutenant, myself included," Brighton cut off her excuses before they could get started. "Talk to Major Chowdhury. She will give you as many Marines as she can spare from the gate assault. Are there any questions?"

"Um," she stammered. "Could I have Ensign Roberts as the XO of my prize crew?"

"Certainly. That is an excellent idea, and as it is not a Warner ship, we won't even have to promote her," he added with a chuckle.

And that was what had brought her to this point, ready to take on the responsibilities of an independent command. In her mind, the brief command of *Pathfinder* did not fall into that category. She had never really commanded the ship; she had only taken it away from those who had stolen it from the Warner Family. As she watched, Roberts disappeared down the accessway. Her thoughts went back to their previous track and she realized how that first step into the access hatch must have been very difficult. The last time Ensign Roberts had gone down that passage, she had begun a string of events that had nearly cost her life several times.

Lieutenant Samuels' musings were cut short as she watched Gunnery Sergeant Aichele and Sergeant Burton enter the boatbay in full armor and stride over to her with the easy glide that only experienced wearers of combat armor ever achieved.

"Permission to join the assault, ma'am?" Aichele said as they both performed parade ground salutes.

"What are you two doing out of medbay? Does Dr. Johnson know where you are?"

"Of course, ma'am, she sent us."

Samuels looked at them skeptically. Her desire to protect them from further injury warring with the comfort she felt to have her protectors near during this new experience. She was just about to send them back to medbay when they were interrupted again by Amber Sullivan striding through the hatch. Incongruously, she had the same experienced glide that the Marines had exhibited. She wore a suit of full Marine heavy armor with the helmet cradled under her left arm and a heavy blast rifle and a sniper's railgun slung over her right shoulder. Samuels was watching Aichele as Sullivan strode into the boatbay and his smile vanished as his lips tightened nearly imperceptibly. His eyes narrowed as he also noticed the glide.

"Permission to board, ma'am?" Sullivan asked as she approached. She was either oblivious to the looks of the Marines or doing a fine job of pretending that she was.

"Permission granted," Samuels responded, ignoring the looks of her two non-coms. She could tell they were not happy with her continued trust in Sullivan.

Samuels realized that with her acceptance of Sullivan into the boarding party she had lost any chance of excluding the two Marines. She ignored their continued unhappiness as she turned and silently led them down the hatch. When she looked back to nod to Commodore Brighton, he was gone.

* * * * *

"Still no reaction from the target, ma'am," the petite scan tech commented without looking up from her console.

"Very well," Samuels acknowledged from her position, standing just outside the assault shuttle's flight deck. She turned to the Marine captain at her shoulder.

"Major Tunny," she began, giving him the courtesy promotion, "take your team in first. You will proceed aft to secure the engines. Make sure the objective is secured, but do not fire on anyone who is not armed. We do not know if there are Granada citizens on board or not. If there are, you are to treat them as Warner subjects in a hostage situation. I will take my team forward to secure the bridge with the same objectives. Ensign Roberts will take her team and secure the weapons control room. Any questions?"

"No, ma'am," both Tunny and Roberts said at once, though Roberts' voice seemed a bit strained. *She must be as nervous about this command as I am*, Samuels thought.

"Very well, create the breach."

"Yes, ma'am," he said as he saluted and turned to his entry team. These three Marines were specialists in boarding actions. Samuels wondered briefly, not for the first time, how you became a specialist in something that had not been done in actual combat for over a century. She dismissed the thought and concentrated on her tasks.

She forced down the knot that had formed in her stomach. This was not the first time she had gone into combat, but she had had a clear understanding of the odds and opposition when her team had begun the fight to take back *Pathfinder*. This time she had a much better team behind her, but no foreknowledge of what they were going to face. *Well, maybe not better*, she thought, glancing at Aichele, Burton, and Sullivan, *but certainly larger.*

The entry team cycled out the forward airlock and deployed on tethers toward the ship they were pacing. She forced herself to release the breath she had been holding and waited with as little outward anxiety as she could manage. The lead member of the entry team floated across the distance with a calming grace and made contact just forward of the destroyer's amidships lock. He deployed the portable airlock around himself and locked it in place magnetically to the hull. Just as he finished locking it in place the second member of his team touched down just aft of his position. She anchored herself to the lock frame and carefully began to circle the new lock, applying sealant to the seam where the lock made contact to the hull. The third member of the team touched down just as she passed the halfway point on her circuit. The new man immediately started passing the breaching charges through the outer door to the first man who was still inside the uninflated airlock. He placed the directional charges and finished just as the second woman finished sealing the airlock to the hull.

Samuels had been so engrossed by the intricate choreography of the entry team that she had missed Major Tunny's first assault group as they left the shuttle, only realizing their position when they impeded her view of the airlock.

"Okay," she called to her team, "move to the airlock."

She entered just as the inner door showed a green light and she moved to the outer hatch until all had entered.

"All blue team members are in," Ensign Roberts called as she closed the hatch from the outside, where she stood with her team. Her tone was strained.

"Acknowledged," Samuels called back, closing her faceshield. "Comm check."

"Reading you five by five," Roberts replied.

"Venting pressure in three, two, and one. Venting pressure," Samuels called as she matched actions to her words.

The squealing whine of the high speed pumps could be heard through the helmets, gradually growing fainter as the air pressure dropped. Samuels took the opportunity to look out the viewport as she waited for the light to signal vacuum in the lock, allowing her to open the outer hatch. She could see the entry team completing their work and getting ready to blow a hole in the target ship.

"Gunny Aichele, bring up the rear and make sure we stay tight."

"Yes, ma'am."

She watched the entry group as they set off the charges to enter the destroyer and knew that time was moving quickly. The light flashed green and she wasted no time hitting the button to open the outer hatch and launch herself out into the void. Before she could move more than a few meters, she reached out carefully with her left hand and snapped her tether to the guide line the entry team had run between the ships. She had not had the opportunity to do any zero-gee work since the academy, and it was her greatest fear that she would screw something up on this mission and show herself to be a failure in front of her new crew. Luckily, her youthful working trips on ships with her father had put her in good shape and the long-unused skills came back readily enough. She pulled herself along gracefully and touched down lightly on the hull of the destroyer with the softness of a seasoned veteran. The temporary lock stood open at the outside and a Marine private stood in the hatch. He moved back as he motioned her in. When her team had all arrived and entered, Aichele called, "All present, outer hatch secured."

Samuels turned to the private and motioned to the inner hatch. He wordlessly hit the cycle switch and she heard the roar of the pumps as they forced in the air much more rapidly than a normal air lock would be able to. Within seconds, the green light came on and the hatch opened in. Samuels grabbed the hand holds on either side of the hatch and pulled herself into the hatch feet first. As she went through the hatch, she felt the pull of the artificial gravity begin to take effect. She felt a slight disorientation as it pulled her through and the far wall became the floor as she fell. She managed to turn and land on her feet, but the maneuver was far from graceful. She snatched her rifle from its mount on her back and turned to move forward down the corridor. She could hear the rest of her team hit the deck behind her and move to follow her. Major Tunney should be halfway to Engineering by now and Roberts should be right behind her from the shuttle. Samuels wished she had more Marines in her team, but there had not been enough to spare from Major Chowdhury's assault of the jump gate control station. Half of her assault force had, of necessity, been filled out from fleet crew and non-coms. Most of Samuels' Marines had gone to Engineering because that was where they expected the most resistance.

Samuels' own Blue Team consisted of six members in addition to its commander. Her only Marines were Sergeant Burton, Gunny Aichele, and Lieutenant Mdembe, an electronic warfare specialist from *Dagger*. In addition to the Marines, she had Amber Sullivan, CPO Rick Young and Ben Danis. As Samuels moved cautiously down the corridor, Burton rushed past her to take the point. Sullivan and Mdembe were right behind her.

The corridor was eerily quiet as they moved forward. A startled civilian contractor in the dark green worksuit of the Granada civilian space administration stepped out of one of the side rooms. She was quickly tackled to the deck by Mdembe. The rest of the team kept moving as Samuels heard the called, "Clear" from the Marine. They encountered no one else in their sprint. Burton was the first to arrive at the bridge hatch and she pulled a small disk from her pouch with her left hand as she crossed the last few meters. She slapped it on the bridge control and called, "Fire in the hole," as she rolled to the side, still partly cradling her right arm to her chest with her blast rifle held loosely. A puff of debris flew back, but Samuels heard very little of the noise through her light Marine armor. Aichele moved to the hatch before Burton could even rise from the deck. He jammed a large pry bar into the joint at the edge of the hatch and, with augmented muscles, heaved the hatch open. It was fortunate the blast door had not been locked down, or the process would have been much more difficult and time-consuming.

Burton flung herself though the opening as soon as the gap allowed. She hit the deck and came up with her blast rifle tracking for any targets. She was hit with a glancing shot to her left side as she came through and she returned fire as soon as she came up to a knee. Her shot was on target and the Forrester Marine had no armor to protect himself. The shot went through the railing he was sheltering behind, penetrated just above his breastbone and shattered a display screen above the engineering console. Aichele followed her in and tracked from right to left looking for other targets. He was not prepared for the three Granadan technicians that rose up as one and attacked the remaining three Forrester Marines who had, up until that moment, been their guards and captors. All three had picked up whatever tools had been handy. Blood flew as each of the erstwhile guards were caught from behind. The technicians did not stop pounding when the guards went down and they had to be physically restrained to stop the bloodshed.

Samuels stepped in after the others had restored order. She had to fight down her nausea when she saw what was left of the Forresters and she was thankful that she was spared the smell because of her armor.

As she was assessing the situation, her command circuit opened and she heard Roberts report, "Weapons room secure, no resistance."

"Acknowledged," she responded. "Keep Goodwin there and send Giannini forward to help with the bridge."

"Aye-aye."

"She was just turning to Aichele, who had stepped up to report, when her comm circuit opened again and Tunney reported the engineering spaces were secured. She held up a hand, palm outward to indicate to Aichele to stand by and responded to Tunney. "Check for any booby traps or devices. Once that is done, locate the brig and secure your prisoners.

Then I want a thorough sweep from aft to fore and make sure we didn't miss any Forresters."

"Yes, ma'am. What do you want me to do with the Granadans? I don't think they are safe to be left on their own."

"Put them in the galley. Mdembe's headed down with the three from the bridge."

"Understood."

Monica Samuels removed her helmet, despite the charnelhouse smell of the bridge and sat heavily in the captain's chair and let out a long calming breath. For the second time in as many weeks, she had captured a ship from enemy troops. She hoped it was the last time in her life she would be forced to do that.

CHAPTER 11
19 October
WNS *Pathfinder* / Worth Jump Gate Control Station

Katherine Leung, formerly Lieutenant Commander in the Warner Space Navy, strode purposefully down the corridor toward the boatbay. It felt good to be free from her self-imposed hiding since she had faked her death during the Forrest prisoner escape. From the snippets she had been able to overhear, everyone else on the ship thought she was dead. If she hadn't let them believe that fiction, there was a good chance that the fiction would have become fact.

She had heard stories about Chowdhury. But then, who hadn't? And she had seen how the Marine had been able to ferret out one of the moles on *Pathfinder*, and that had made her group of conspirators so nervous that they decided to start the takeover early. And when they had started, Morales was supposed to have taken Chowdhury out as the opening move, before anything else went down. But Morales and Brand had been the ones who ended up dead.

No, Leung didn't plan to underestimate Chowdhury again. She planned to get as far away from the Marine as she possibly could.

Leung tried to move her arm naturally and groaned as the metal joint tore at her shoulder where she had adjusted the mechanism. She found it difficult to move at all in the unfamiliar stolen armor. She had kept it hidden until this moment, now that stealth was no longer possible. Her anxiety was causing the faceshield to fog up as she walked and the enviro systems couldn't seem to keep up. She forced herself to try to walk normally, but she cursed the lack of adjustment and it was rubbing into her left shoulder and right thigh. She forced herself to continue forward with no outward indication of her discomfort.

Leung had been horrified when Major Chowdhury had re-entered the ship three hours ago. The woman terrified her in a way that no one else ever had and she knew she could not keep her intentions hidden from the security officer for long, if at all. She had avoided contact with any of the Warner Marines until she could formulate some plan that offered at least a possibility of success. She had arranged the Forrester's escape as a preparatory step that would allow her to disappear. If they got away or were destroyed, Leung would have been assumed to be on the shuttle and therefore beyond the reach of the security team. The only risk had been the slight possibility that they would be recaptured. Her cover would then have been blown beyond retrieving. However, things had worked out perfectly and she had been able to disappear into the bowels of the ship. Her searches of the ship while looking for the missing astrogator, Lieutenant Lamont, had shown her several hiding places.

Unnecessarily, as it turned out. She had detected no searches of the ship looking for her. They, apparently, had completely believed the story she planted about being on the shuttle. Now she needed to take some risks to get away before *Pathfinder* left the Worth system. While moving now was less dangerous than it would be later, it did not mean her current attempt was without risk. This morning's action was the most dangerous part of her escape plan. She had stolen the armor just in case she needed it to fight back. She didn't intend to go quietly this time. Now, however, it was going to allow her to sneak off the ship with those selfsame Marines who thought her dead. In order to do so, however, she would have to fool Chowdhury.

A cold shiver went up her spine at the thought, but she didn't stop walking.

* * * * *

Major Sheli Chowdhury stood at the front of her shuttle, getting ready for an assault for the second time in the same day. With the arrival of *Dagger*, the only Warner ship in the system without a working '*Pathfinder* Type' jump engine, they needed to take over the gate control station in order to make it possible for *Dagger* to get home. Based on the number of warships on the Forrest side of the engagement, that escape could become necessary at any time. So, once again, the Marines had a job to do.

"Okay, listen up," she called to get their attention as the shuttle came to rest near the airlock of the gate control station. "You all know your assignments. We are going in on the main level and we will have responsibility for everything from our entry point to the command center."

She looked down the rows of Marines and saw most faces looking attentively at her as well as a few closed faceshields facing her direction.

"We will be going in through the airlock for section seven on the main level. Everybody stay sharp and do your jobs. Resistance should be light, but don't get overconfident. Even with the blown airlock, it is a natural choke point and they could be waiting for us in force."

Chowdhury signaled with a nod to her breach team and they stood and began to exercise their craft. Like the previous assault, she followed them into the tube as soon as they had created an entry and her team followed her into the access. She launched herself out into the corridor as soon as the breaching charge created an opening, rolling upright and tracking her weapon across her assigned fire zone. She saw an armed guard standing at the corner of the nearest intersection and she shot him with a quick burst from her light assault blaster. He went down with a hit to his torso before he had completely turned to identify the threat. A few civilians scattered to shelter among the doorways and alcoves but didn't interfere in any way with the progress of the troops. They acted as if they had no warning of the impending attack. How was that possible? Their shuttles would have been visible on sensors for the entirety of the trip from *Pathfinder*.

Chowdhury gave a hand signal and the dragoon moved forward with her on point. The resistance was sparse, so they continued to push the pace in order to gain as much ground as possible before the Forresters could organize any meaningful resistance. In the forward rush, no one noticed the small, armored figure which separated itself from the group and slipped away down a small cross-corridor.

Chowdhury and her team were able to move forward another forty meters past the section seal before they were halted by a temporary barricade thrown up by the defenders. The Warner Marines threw themselves into any hiding spot they could find as the defenders opened up with light blasters. The weapons were really not designed to fight troops in heavy armor, but a lucky shot could still be fatal. The Marines were taking no chances.

"Burik," Chowdhury called on the command circuit, "bring up your team."

"Yes, ma'am," he called as he signaled his fire team to move up to the front from their position in a side corridor. As soon as they were clear of any friendly troops, Corporal Koissi went to the deck with a lightweight missile launcher and Private Lacey went to one knee beside him. Neither action was an easy feat in full armor, but they did it without effort or thinking.

"HE up," Koissi called, choosing his target and changing the selector on the weapon to high explosive.

"Clear," called Lacey after a quick check of the position of all his teammates and tapping Koissi on the back of his helmet.

The small projectile launched from the front of the compact shoulder-fired weapon and the thermal bloom reached two meters to each side and in front of the corporal. The missile slammed into the make-shift barricade and exploded with gratifying results. Pieces of heavy furniture disappeared in a flashing boom that could be felt even through armor, the narrow confines focusing the shockwave. The eight defenders were thrown back against the curve of the corridor and their light armor was very little protection against either the initial explosion or the secondary impact.

Chowdhury led her point group forward before the smoke had cleared and they quickly dispatched any surviving Forresters.

Having moved this far toward their objective without seeing any heavy weapons on the station, Chowdhury took the calculated risk that there would be none if they could keep pushing, so she raced the remaining sixty yards to the control center hatch. She signaled her breach team forward but the hatch slid open before they could arrive.

Chowdhury stood her ground with her pistol in her right hand at her side because she could do little else. As the hatch slid open, she saw a Forrest Ground Forces colonel standing there with a pregnant civilian employee in front of her as a shield. She wore no armor and a cursory glance showed that none of the ten soldiers in the command center had armor of any kind. The Forrest colonel held a Berlinni, Model 2303, flechette pistol to the woman's temple.

"Drop your weapons and stand down," the Forrest officer commanded.

"I am taking control of this station," Chowdhury called, ignoring the Forrest officer's commands. "If you are in command, I will give you one chance to surrender."

"I said..." the colonel began before Major Chowdhury's weapon fired. No one saw the Marine's arm move, despite the cumbersomeness of the heavy armor, but the results were obvious. The Forrest officer's head exploded from the hydrostatic shock of Chowdhury's round.

"Now who is in command?" the major asked calmly.

"We surrender!!" came the chorus, though none claimed the now vacant command.

* * * * *

One hour later, Chowdhury closed the file on the screen. Her emotions churning at the events that she had seen. She sat back in the comfortable chair in the late colonel's office and rubbed her head with a gesture that had more to do with habit than fatigue, though the exhaustion was present as well. She had removed her armor, which lay in a pile behind the chair, though the pistol still lay on the desk in front of her.

There was a tone at the door and she looked up.

"Yes, ...enter."

Lieutenant Kelly entered and saluted. Chowdhury turned her mind from the images on the viewscreen back to her job of taking the station from the Forresters.

"Lieutenant, where are we with gaining control of the station?"

"We have all critical areas under firm control. There is no evidence of any booby-traps or sabotage from the Forresters in any of the gate control operations."

"Very well. What about the prisoners?"

The tall lieutenant shook his head before answering.

"There were only 72 Forresters taken prisoner during the action and they are being kept well away from the Granadan citizens on the station. We had several deaths, both Forrester and civilian, before all the Forresters were rounded up. Apparently, the occupation of the planet was fairly brutal and the Granadans were taking revenge against their former occupiers before we could take them captive."

Chowdhury waved a hand in disgust at her viewscreen.

"Yeah, I've been looking through the visual files of the take-over. Mass executions, men, women and children; the Forresters were brutal. I don't know how we can leave here and leave them in charge down there. It makes my blood boil."

Kelly stood still and didn't interrupt his commander. He knew her and knew she needed to vent.

Finally, her head came up and she looked at him, pointing again at the viewscreen.

"I know, our main duty is to get *Pathfinder* home, but I swear that whoever is responsible for these atrocities is going to pay!"

CHAPTER 12
18 October
Asunción Military Base – Granada

"How should I know?" General Sophia Franks shouted back at Epstein, moving to within centimeters of his face. "I've had my hands full maintaining order on the surface. Spaceships are your responsibility!"

Admiral Epstein sat in his seat and tried to force down the heat that climbed up the back of his neck and tried to break through his control.

"If these were normal conditions, I might agree with you, General! But *you* had the only line of communication with *Pathfinder*! If you hadn't put so much red tape in the way of sending a message, we could have repositioned her. If we had been able to move her behind the planet when Brighton first arrived, maybe we could have kept her out of their hands! And don't think the Board is not going to hear about this!"

Franks ignored the roar that filled the ending of the admiral's last pronouncement and gave a slight laugh of her own.

"That's an empty threat, and you know it, Juan! Once Brighton leaves this system and returns to Earth with proof, the Board will have far more important worries than finding who to blame! Like how to continue breathing!"

That remark brought Admiral Epstein up short. A lump of ice settled in his gut. She was right, he realized. If Brighton were allowed to leave this system, the Forrest Family would almost certainly cease to exist within a short period of time, exactly the way the list of Families was reduced by one after the Vector Rebellion. There would be no way to hide the extent of their works. There would be trials, and Franks was right about one other thing; there would be executions. Juan Epstein and Sophia Franks were likely to be on that chopping block, along with a lot of good people caught in the backlash of a bad policy. The only way to forestall those executions was to begin hostilities with all the other Families, which would only postpone the inevitable for himself and the Family, as well as getting a lot more people dead along the way.

"You're right," the naval officer said calmly, quickly deflating. Far too calmly for Franks, who had to bite back the next salvo she had loaded and ready to fire. It took her a moment to realize she must have won the argument, though she wasn't quite sure how she had accomplished that.

"You're right," Epstein repeated, "especially about the consequences if we allow Brighton to leave Worth. And you're right that we have more important worries than finding who to blame. We have got to make sure none of the Warner crews are able to report back. We need to give the rest of the Family time to prepare our defenses."

"If the Warners have captured *Pathfinder*, and it seems clear that's the case, then they have *two* ships capable of leaving the system on their own power! How the trash are we supposed to stop that?!" Franks wanted to know.

"What sort of shape are *Pathfinder*'s engines in? We may have lost control of her, but can she even maneuver right now?"

"How should I know?" Franks played her recurring theme once more. "Engineering reports go directly to the shipyards, and that's your bailiwick!"

"But *you* had the only line of communication with *Pathfinder*!" Epstein roared in response. After a silent few moments of exchanged glares, he physically slapped his forehead with his open palm to keep from retracing the same ground any further.

"Ames!"

"Yes, sir." Jacqui had been more than willing to stay out from between the two commanding officers, considering it a less than salubrious environment on the whole. It looked like her luck had run out, however.

"Look up all the reports we have received from *Pathfinder* at the Caspar Yards and give me a status report on her engines."

"Aye, sir."

Franks leapt on the availability of a productive course of action and turned to her own flag lieutenant.

"Wickham, review the reports from our security team and see if there's any information on the ship's status."

"Yes, ma'am," the staff lieutenant acknowledged before disappearing behind her screens.

Franks turned back to Epstein. "Do you have the firepower to take these Warners out?"

Epstein directed her back to the holotank, where it was easier to spell out the situation. "Yes, I'm pretty sure we can do the job, but the problem is that Brighton suckered us out of position. We had essentially the same problem when they arrived. There was enough evidence that we suspected they had an onboard jump drive, so we had no choice but to push them as hard as we could to destroy them before they could recharge and jump out of the system.

"Clearly, they were able to hold us off long enough to recharge, and we didn't do enough damage to hold them here. What we *hadn't* anticipated was them jumping back into Worth instead of running for it. Now, all our ships have finally killed their outbound velocities and started heading back insystem, but it will still be hours before they will be in range to do anything.

"*Yargus* has already had enough time to recharge, based on the time between their two previous jumps, so they could leave now, if they wanted, and we couldn't stop them." Epstein's frustration showed clearly, but for the first time in the better part of an hour, it wasn't directed at the Marine.

"And that's all of your ships?" Franks asked.

"Yes. *Scythe* is pretty much complete, but we don't have a crew to operate her. There are a couple others that will fly and fight, though not very effectively, but they have no crews, either."

"What if we take a page from their book?" Franks offered.

"What do you mean?" Epstein asked.

"Sir?" Ames attempted to get her boss' attention.

"I mean, what if we use Marines on assault shuttles, like they did?" Franks clarified.

"Ma'am?" Lieutenant Wickham tried unsuccessfully to interrupt.

"Hmm. How large a force are we talking about, General?" Epstein asked of Franks, both ignoring their assistants.

"Enemy ships launching!" the scan officer sang out.

Epstein spun back to the main display. "Where away?"

"I could get thirty ships in the air within a half hour," Franks answered his question, though Epstein barely heard. He had to handle the immediate threat first, and that's where his focus was.

"Two point-sources separating from *Pathfinder*, one is headed outsystem, the other is turning west by southwest."

"What's west by southwest?" Franks wanted to know. Epstein wasn't sure if she was asking what destination might lay on that heading, or if she were completely unfamiliar with system directionals. He decided to assume the former.

"The shipyards are that direction. Brighton is probably going to try to destroy those ships still in process while they're defenseless."

"It might be an opportunity, sir," Captain Halliday opined.

"Sierra one is shaping course toward the Warner cruiser that just arrived," the scan officer interjected, using the standard designation for an enemy shuttle.

"What might be?" Epstein asked of Halliday.

"What sort of loadout can you put together in that time?" Ames asked the Marine leader, referring to the half hour she had stated it would take her to get shuttles launched.

"Well, it just occurred to me, sir," Halliday explained, "that the departure of those assault shuttles is very good news for us."

"Destinations locked in and on the board," the lieutenant at the scan station reported. "Hostiles designated Sierra-1 and Sierra-2."

"We'd probably modify the standard gear with several heavy armor sets per squad, maybe even heavy armor for everyone, breaching charges for sweeping room to room, that sort of configuration," Franks decided.

"Firstly," Halliday continued, "with assault parties separated from their mother ships, Brighton can't leave the system without abandoning his own people. Those shuttles aren't built to handle a jump."

"Ma'am, I do have news that you need to hear," Wickham insisted.

Epstein was listening to Halliday, who was thankfully thinking ahead and analyzing the situation. The admiral was glad now that he hadn't chewed the man out earlier, which might have left him resentful rather than thoughtful.

The scan officer's report had triggered a new priority for the Marine officer.

"Comm," General Franks directed at the Marine lieutenant who manned the communications board, "raise *Scythe* and tell her that a shuttle full of Warner Marines is headed their way. Have them make necessary preparations to receive them."

"Admiral, I would recommend we follow the general's recommendation to gather an assault force of Marines from the planet," Ames slid in before Epstein could turn back to Halliday.

Halliday didn't wait to have an audience. "And secondly, from the timing of events and the fact that one of those shuttles is headed toward Gate Control, it may mean they have decided that they won't be able to get the jump engines on *Pathfinder* running before our destroyers are back in range of them."

"Comm, message to Gate Control to set condition zero, by my authority. Then get me a shielded vocom line to Colonel Hazen in flight operations," Franks ordered.

"Which would give us more time to get at them and stop them from escaping," Epstein concluded. "General, I concur with Commander Ames. We may have a brief window where Brighton is compelled to remain in this system. Let's get your birds in the air and make him regret coming back!"

"*Scythe* acknowledges orders," the comm duty officer reported.

"Ma'am?" Wickham tried again, but it was only half-hearted.

"Was that Lieutenant Rizzoli you spoke to, Lieutenant?" Franks asked of the communications officer.

"That was a first rate analysis, Captain," Epstein remarked to Halliday, then turned to Ames. "Did you have something to report, Jacqui?"

"Uh, yes, sir."

"No, ma'am," Lieutenant Ramakumar at the comm station replied to Franks. "One of the shipyard engineers had the communications watch. He's notifying the Marines now."

"Sir, I pulled all the data on the *Pathfinder* engines from the Caspar servers, as you requested," Ames began, before being interrupted.

"Ma'am, there haven't been any reports from the *Pathfinder* Marines for two days," Wickham finally got out in a rush.

"There is no data, sir," Ames concluded.

CHAPTER 13
18 October
Forrest Main Complex – Earth

"Yes, I'm afraid that *is* how I see things," Gerald Warner said calmly. "I know you want to see my evidence before you call a Board meeting, as would I in your place, but such is not required in the bylaws. That being the case, I will hold onto it until the meeting convenes. Good day, Mr. Chairman."

Amanda Forrest ended the playback with a subtle motion of her hand, then let out a sigh and leaned back into her comfortable chair. She couldn't say that the content of the conversation was unexpected, but it was worrisome. *No, don't try to minimize it, even to yourself. This was potentially catastrophic.*

The CEO thought carefully, reviewing everything that had been said. Warner was obviously being cagy about what proof he might have been able to uncover. She had been hoping he would have been more open with Rial and give them some hint of what preparations to make. Now, it would be very difficult to know what strategy to employ against them. If she tried to counter something the Warners didn't already know, it might supply a clue that would be all too revealing.

What action could she take that would improve the Family's position regardless of what Warner knows? She only had a few days before the Board would meet, which didn't give her very much time to act or prepare.

Time! That was the biggest problem. Everything was coming into the light much too soon. Another eight or ten weeks, and she would have given them very good odds of their eventual success. Even one more month would have shifted the balance of power in their favor. Well, one more month if her people had kept to their original projected schedules, she admitted to herself.

Was there anything she could do to buy more time? She considered that idea for many minutes, but none of the possibilities that occurred to her seemed likely to produce results. Now that Warner had gone to Rial, there was nothing she could do to stop the meeting, or even delay it.

If there was no chance of stalling, what about maneuvering to get other votes? She had two possibilities there; spin the media to favor her view, and using political influence to pressure the other Families into supporting her. The latter had worked in dealing with Rial, and there were a few others that she had enough evidence of shady deals on to push them where she needed them. That wouldn't work in every case, though, and not in enough cases to change the outcome.

Amanda moved to her desk as she decided that she was going to have to use every dirty trick she could think of to get enough support, to at least delay an adverse response from the Council. She would probably need all the clean tricks she could think of too. She signaled her assistant as soon as she arrived at her desk and sat down.

"James, get word to Kristiana that I need to speak to her urgently. Then have the comm office contact Paola DaGama for me," Amanda said to the empty room.

She hadn't finished thinking the thought when there was a tap on the door and James entered, carrying a communications set. "Miss Van der Waal for you, ma'am."

"Kristiana, how are you this evening?"

"Well enough, ma'am. Your man said that you had some important business? If it is really urgent, I can probably get it inserted into the midnight feeds, but I'll have to move quickly."

"I appreciate that, and yes, it is that pressing. I need you to begin Operation Sideshow right away, but accelerate the pacing of the messages. The first five stages need to be circulating by 8:00 am the day after tomorrow."

Kristiana, Director of Media Relations, said nothing for a few stunned seconds, then regained her normal unflappability. "Whatever you say, ma'am. Is everything else to remain the same, though? No changes to the financial or physical damages?"

It was a good question, Amanda thought. It showed the younger woman was thinking ahead.

"I think we have already crafted the right tone, so no other changes. I wish we didn't need to change anything, because the operations plan was a thing of genius." No sense letting the woman think she wasn't trusted, especially when the praise was truly deserved. "Unfortunately, we have a very short window, and I need the maximum effect we can produce in that time."

"In that case, ma'am, might I suggest including stage nine on the final morning? The original timing relied on a slow percolation of public outrage, but if we speed up the rate that atrocities are being reported, it would make sense for things to come to a boil much more rapidly."

Good girl! "Can you make it happen that soon?"

"I think so, ma'am," Kristiana said after a moment's reflection. "In fact, I am certain of it."

"Do so, then. I'll expect a report after each stage as to the effectiveness of the messages, and how the overall operation is proceeding."

"Of course, ma'am," Kristiana acknowledged with a smile. "Was there anything else?"

"No, there's nothing else. Not that you'd have any time to spare if there were."

"Good night then, ma'am. I'll have the first report by 3:00, and the second by 6:00 or 7:00."

"Very well," Amanda said, then disconnected.

James poked his head in while Amanda's finger was still pressing the button. He raised two fingers, and then slipped back out of sight. Amanda reconnected on channel two and was met by Paola DaGama's well-tanned, scowling face.

"What is it?" the other woman demanded.

"We have a mutual problem, Paola."

"That's it? No apology? No greetings? No 'How are you today, Paola. Sorry I so completely screwed you that your Family will probably disincorporate this year'?"

Amanda stared back at the woman, refusing to show any remorse outwardly. Internally, she did regret the course of action the Family's executive board had mandated. It had made logical sense for the bottom line, but it was very short-sighted, something of a recurring problem for them. Rather than building a solid ally, they, and she, she admitted, had created yet another enemy.

"Do you want an apology, or do you want help avoiding the 'disincorporation' scenario?"

DaGama didn't ponder long. She flicked her dark hair negligently out of her eyes. "Why would I even consider getting back in bed with you lot of vipers? What could possibly convince me to believe a word you say?"

"Well, first, of course, there's the whole idea of avoiding the collapse of the DaGama Family," Amanda said lightly. Paola failed to see any humor in the statement. "And second, as I said before, the problem you have is a mutual one; one we both share. It makes good business sense for us to work together to achieve our aims."

"Oh, you're just full of barbs today, aren't you," Paola spat back. Amanda looked puzzled, clearly not understanding, so the DaGama head spelled it out for her. "Those are very nearly the exact words I said to you two years ago when we brought you in on our plan to take Warner's jump engine designs. Do you remember now?!"

Amanda did remember, the events of the past replaying in her mind, zipping by like a maglev train. It had been DaGama that had ferreted out the secret project Warner had put together to design a new breed of ships. They had all the knowledge, and the spy inside the program, but they did not have the manufacturing capability to take advantage of their captured data anytime soon. DaGama's board had decided, therefore, to ally with someone who both had the ability to produce their own ships and the desire to get out from under the dominance of the four spacefaring Families. Forrest had been the obvious choice.

After being approached, and given access to all the information already gathered, however, Forrest's spymaster had been able to make his own contact on the top-secret project. At that point, the Forrest board had decided that DaGama had nothing more to offer in the partnership and began taking steps to sever the relationship.

Amanda did remember, and was aghast at her unbelievable gaff.

"I'm sorry, Paola." she said, and meant it.

In all honesty, she was sorrier for the misstep in trying to win the other Family's support than for the cause of the rift, but she was genuinely sorry, nonetheless.

"There now, that wasn't so hard, was it?" Paola asked mockingly.

"I'll live," Amanda replied. After a moment, she continued, "All right, you don't trust me. That's fine. I wouldn't trust me, either. But that still leaves the first reason. If you do nothing, Warner will take what it knows of your actions to the Ruling Council and demand reparations. And their demands are likely to be so steep you'll never recover.

"I'm offering you a way out. It's still a slim hope, but it's the only straw around to grasp at."

Paola leaned forward and sighed, then she looked back up and again flipped her dark hair out of her face. "All right. I do *not* trust you. I do *not* like you. But I will listen to what you have to say for the next sixty seconds."

"Then I won't waste any time. There are two things that are currently threatening our two Families: The first is the evidence that Warner has compiled which implicates us in acts of piracy and war, and the second is Warner's military power which would allow them to take matters into their own hands if they so choose.

"There is one solution to both problems, and that is to have a solid majority of votes on the Ruling Council backing us and our version of events. In order to arrange that, I need not only your vote, but your help in calling in as many favors as you can to procure the other votes we need."

DaGama did not move for several moments. "What specific evidence does Warner have?"

"I don't know for sure. My people estimate that it can't be much, but...but I don't know. What I *do* know is that Warner has enough that he feels justified in calling an emergency Council meeting for later this week."

Paola sat bolt upright and slammed her hands on the table before her. "When did you hear this?!"

"Felix Rial is one of the favors I've already called in. He's been keeping me apprised of Warner's communications. I expect he will be informing each of the Families very shortly."

Paola pushed away from the table and leaned back. Her eyes became unfocused as she processed the relevant information and fit it into what she already knew.

"All right. I can see how buying, cajoling, or strongarming a majority of votes can keep us from facing a formal reprimand...or anything stronger that might be legislated, and it *would* make sense to coordinate that effort so that a consistent version of the counterargument comes out, but that only covers the first problem. Warner still fields the largest navy, and Gerald certainly possesses the will to use it, given the provocation we've provided him. Having the vote go against him will only make him that much more likely to come after us himself."

"You're wrong, Paola."

"In what regard? You don't think Warner would go to war over what we've already done?" Paola made a rude noise. "Got a herd of magical space-unicorns that will go out and protect us? We've been working to put a navy of our own together for two years now, and we would be lucky to put a dozen ships into space, all small compared to Warner designs. If it comes to shooting, we wouldn't last a day!"

"No, you're not wrong about any of that, and we've been doing much the same thing — though on a larger scale than you. Still, we're not in a position to take on Warner in an all-out fight. The point I disagree with is your assertion that Warner has the largest navy.

"The largest navy is the Combined Fleet, and Combined Fleet is under the direct orders of the Ruling Council, not any individual Family."

Paola sat with her mouth open for several seconds, then the hint of a smile began to appear. "I'm in."

CHAPTER 14
18 October
Warner Shuttle / WNS *Pathfinder*

"Hey, it could be worse." Ensign Jordan Hayes said to his friend, working hard to keep his expression clear of any humor. "They could have assigned Reed to help with the repairs."

Ensign Josiah Mitchell rolled his eyes but maintained his somber silence. He had been dour and resigned since his confrontation with the chief engineer on *Dagger*, and it hadn't helped that Captain Johnson had supported his position in front of the senior officers.

Lieutenant Reed had received an official reprimand, which made it certain he would spend a minimum of three extra years before the promotion board would consider him for a lieutenant commander slot. Ensign Mitchell hadn't gotten away without punishment either, however, even though he had been correct in his assessment that the information was critical, he had been deemed insubordinate and had been assigned extra duties and had also been stripped of three months' seniority. No reprimand, thankfully, but three months represented most of the seniority he had! To add insult to injury, most of the engineering crew, who he had to work with every day, had begun to ignore him whenever they thought they could get away with it. Normally, Jordan's kidding around would brighten his outlook, but today it seemed to be having the opposite effect on his mood.

"No, seriously," Hayes tried again, "they could have sent Reed and Durrant. You know the Captain wanted to get them off the ship and she could have used this as an excuse, but instead, she grants you an escape. Face it, for you, it's Christmas come early. We get to go on vacation with the rest of the *Vanguard* crew," he motioned to the other members of the crew seated with them on the shuttle. "It's like a reunion cruise."

"Hmm, I don't think it will work out that way," Mitchell said darkly.

Whatever Hayes had intended to say next was cut off by the docking alarm, and immediately thereafter by the thump of the shuttle moving onto the docking mechanism under *Pathfinder*. Most of the crew fell silent as they considered the cycle of events that left them about to board the ship they had been ejected from four months earlier. The shuttle was quickly attached to the airlock and the hatch opened.

The two ensigns followed Lieutenant Amaya-Garcia as he led the enlisted crew out through the lock and down the accessway. Each in turn climbed the ladder that led them into the very boatbay from which they had been expelled a lifetime ago.

The scene was quite different, now. Commodore Brighton stood rigidly at attention with Lieutenant Weaver, from *Yargus*, standing at his side, both saluting. The rest of the crew was arrayed behind them. Hayes and Mitchell instinctively moved out of the path of those flowing in from below and snapped to attention to return the commodore's salute.

When the shuttle was emptied and the passengers arrayed behind the two ensigns and Lieutenant Amaya-Garcia, Commodore Brighton dropped his salute and cleared his throat.

"At ease," he said and waited while the crew relaxed their posture. "Several months ago, I made several promises to most of you. One of those was redeemed on the third planet of Antoc-A. Now, I am able to deliver on the most important of those promises. Today, we are reunited aboard our ship and we are prepared to return with it to our home. We have worked hard and endured much to arrive at this time and place and I want to acknowledge your efforts and sacrifices to get us here. I also want to acknowledge the sacrifices of those who weren't able to return to this ship, who made the ultimate sacrifice for the crimes of the pirates. I especially want you to be aware of the sacrifices of those who remained behind. Not all remained by their own choice and we owe them a debt. They risked their lives every day to allow us to be able to stand here. If you get the opportunity to see Lieutenant Samuels, Gunnery Sergeant Aichele, Staff Sergeant Burton, Doctor Johnson, or Specialist Sullivan," Mitchell and Hayes both opened their eyes wider at the new rank of their former schoolmate, "be sure to convey your appreciation."

The commodore took one step closer to the newcomers and continued.

"Having said that, we still have a lot of work to do on this ship to enable us to survive the coming days. You will all be expected to work hard to make that happen." He motioned to his right and said, "This is Lieutenant Weaver, for those of you who do not know him, he will assume the duties of Executive Officer here on *Pathfinder*. Ensign Hayes, you will assist Lieutenant Amaya at Tactical and Weapons. Senior Chief Quèneau, please take over the Scan department."

Brighton then took a slight step forward and straightened.

"Ensign Mitchell, you will assume the duties of Chief Engineer with Warrant Long as your assistant. As I have come to find out, Warner Navy has a few rules that I cannot break. As Lieutenant Samuels discovered, you cannot command a ship as an ensign, neither can you be the Chief Engineer. Therefore, Ensign Mitchell, I am promoting you to lieutenant junior grade to fill this position. This promotion will have to be verified and accepted by the Board upon our return to Earth, and with everything that has gone on, I would expect that to be an interesting Board review, but congratulations.

"All others, please return to your former assignments. Section heads, supply a list of repairs to the chief engineer by 1300 today. We need to be spaceworthy and able to fight by 2300 today, so prioritize the repairs based on those needs.

Mitchell felt as if he were going to fall over. Lieutenant? A few minutes ago, he thought his career was in the slime hole and now he gets a promotion? Before he could get his bearings, Brighton continued.

"Lieutenant Mitchell, requisition any parts you need from *Dagger* or *Yargus*. Are there any questions?" Brighton's blue eyes cut into every person there as he waited for an answer and Mitchell felt them very strongly cutting into him. Did he have any questions? Of course he had questions. What was he supposed to do as Chief Engineer? He hadn't even been able to get Durrant and Long to work together on *Dagger*. His thoughts were cut off as Brighton was satisfied with everyone's acceptance of his orders.

"Very well, dismissed," the commodore's voice cut through everything and the crew began to move off to their duties.

Mitchell turned to Hayes, expecting to cut off one of his friend's jokes, only to see Hayes' face blank and he appeared to be struck speechless for the first time in anyone's memory. Before he could begin to try to figure out his new situation, Long stepped over to them, came to attention and saluted.

"What are your orders, sir?" he asked with no trace of mockery.

Mitchell returned the salute and shook his head slightly.

"I have no idea, yet, Mr. Long. I guess we'd better go to Engineering and get a report."

Much as he'd thought Reed was going about his job the wrong way, Mitchell had never expected to have the same job thrust upon him. Especially not so unexpectedly. And certainly not with a promotion after all of the problems on *Dagger*.

* * * * *

"Commodore, the in-system engines check out fully, and the jump engines pass all preliminary tests."

Commodore Brighton looked at Lieutenant Mitchell on the comm screen as he reported at 2250. Mitchell rubbed a dirty hand across his forehead, leaving a dark, dirty stripe he didn't seem to notice. His eyes were red and looked heavy and Brighton wondered if the young officer had taken a break at all since he returned to the ship. If he hadn't, then Brighton was probably right in his choice of a Chief Engineer. He ignored that thought and asked instead about the other things he needed to know.

"What about the weapons systems?"

Mitchell nodded his head and sat up a little straighter in his chair.

"We've gotten all the weapons under manual control, now that the software upload is complete. When we get the weapons console rewiring done, the weapons system should be fully functional from the bridge."

"Very well, Lieutenant. Rotate your first watch off duty. We will need everyone rested and ready for action soon."

"Aye-aye, sir."

Brighton switched off the comm and turned to his new XO. "Lieutenant Weaver, how close are we to buttoning up all those consoles?" he asked with a wave at the chaos behind him at the back of the bridge.

"Sir, Weapons and Scan should be done in the next quarter hour, but we still have several hours of troubleshooting on Astrogation. Warrant Long said that he can't get consistent results and I would hate to count on it if we needed to use it."

"Very well. If we need to jump, we can double check the calculations with *Yargus*."

"Humph," came a muffled noise from under the astrogation console, where Long's legs protruded.

"What was that, Mr. Long?"

"Nothing, sir. I was just amazed that *Pathfinder* arrived here at all with this set up," came the muffled reply.

"Of course," Brighton replied under his breath.

* * * * *

"Hey, did you hear?" Ensign Hayes, coming in through the center hatch to Engineering, whispered loudly enough to be heard from twenty meters away.

"Hear what?" Mitchell replied absently from his position on the deck, where he was in the process of securing the cover on the back of the engine monitor station.

"About Durrant."

"What?! Is he here?" Mitchell jumped up from the floor and looked wildly around.

"No, no," Hayes said, laughing. "Man, you looked like you bumped into an open circuit there. Are you that scared of him?"

Mitchell settled back to work on the cover with a dubious look at his friend.

"I'm not scared of him. Just...rationally cautious."

Hayes leaned against the monitor station and bit into the apple he had carried in with him.

"Sure, that's why your pants are wet. You just spilled, right?"

Mitchell glared at Hayes.

"My pants are not wet. And you couldn't tell if they were wet or not. They're black, you idiot. Quit joking around and tell me what you know."

Hayes pointed at his friend with his apple. His face a portrait of concern.

"Are you sure you don't need to go change first?"

Mitchell aimed his wrench at Hayes. "Come on, spill it."

Hayes looked shocked. "Didn't you already do that?"

Mitchell raised his wrench. "Your life is hanging by a thread, here."

Hayes took another bite of his apple. "Okay, okay, if you're done jawing, I have news."

Mitchell stood, his wrench swinging. "Just remember, I'm not responsible."

"Okay, I just got off the comm with Ensign Leslie on *Dagger*. I had to reload the weapons software, so I needed a clean copy." He took another bite of his apple. "Have you noticed how cute she is?"

Mitchell put his wrench down on the monitor console and shook his head, his eyes wide with wonder. "Durrant? You think Durrant is cute?"

Hayes gasped on his next apple bite. "No, Loren Leslie."

"I thought we were talking about Durrant."

Finally, Hayes gave up his game as a draw. Waving his half-eaten apple, he began, "Okay, here it is. Durrant was going around crowing about being the new bosun on *Dagger* now that Quèneau and Mackey are gone, and within two hours he was transferred to *Yargus*."

"What? Jurnigan is bosun on *Yargus*."

"That's right. *Master* Chief Jurnigan was already there when *Senior* Chief Durrant arrived."

"Oh, that's classic," Mitchell chuckled.

"It gets better. Who does that leave on *Dagger*?"

Mitchell cocked his head to the side momentarily as he ran through the enlisted roster. "No... Giovanni?"

"I think Chief Giovanni will be exemplary as bosun, don't you?" Warrant Long said from centimeters behind Hayes' head. Hayes jumped and lost his apple to the deck as Long continued to walk past them to return his tool bag to his locker.

Mitchell laughed quietly.

"Do you need to go change *your* pants, Hayes?"

Before Hayes could respond, the general quarters klaxon started to sound.

CHAPTER 15
19 October
WNS *Peru*

Lieutenant Monica Samuels pulled herself away from reviewing the latest updates which appeared on her screen and checked the time on the aft bulkhead. It read 1102, which meant she was two minutes late beginning the meeting, and that her XO was two minutes late in arriving. She was about to get started anyway, when something about the clock caught her attention and she looked at it more closely.

She'd known there'd be a chrono in that spot without thinking. Had it been one of the freighters operated by her own family, the timepiece would have been either above the hatch to the corridor, or else affixed to the forward bulkhead. This chrono, though, was exactly the same, and in the same position, as she would have found aboard *Pathfinder*. She wondered what else might be the exact same as other Warner ships.

Monica turned to the man two seats to her left. "Mr. Fuentes?"

"Bernardo please, Lieutenant," the Granadan smiled and said. His accent seemed normal; that is, the way he pronounced the words was the same as Samuels was used to, but his cadence was a little off, giving his words a slightly foreign feel to them.

"Captain," Major Tunney corrected.

"My apologies. Captain."

"No problem. When did construction begin on this ship, and who provided the schematics, Forrest or us?"

"We laid the keel back in April of '85. It was originally going to be WNS *Peru*, one of the *Brazil*-class destroyers, until they renamed it FFF *Scythe*. The Forresters, they made some modifications to the design, expanded the power plant for one thing, but I don't think there were too many others. The hull was already complete, and they had begun working on the interior, so there weren't that many modifications they could make. As far as I know, anyway; I wasn't given access to the full design, and I wasn't involved with this ship at all until almost a year after The Fall."

"And when exactly was 'The Fall'?"

"November fourth, 2785," he responded darkly, clearly not relishing the memory.

Samuels' eyebrows climbed up her forehead. "That's almost two years ago! How could this system be overrun without anyone on Earth being aware of it? And how could they have kept anyone from finding out for so long?"

"Both of these are excellent questions, which I have pondered myself on many occasions, but I do not have answers to them. Part of how this happened I understand. Once they had eliminated all military forces in the system, they did not keep everyone out as you would think, but regular transport shipping continued. Deliveries were made to orbital warehouses, where everything appeared to be normal. They were very careful not to let anyone go to the planet if they could avoid it, and if they insisted, they were not allowed to leave. Entire ships, also, if they insisted on delivering to the planet, were then not allowed clearance to pass through the gate."

"Wouldn't the ships be missed by the transport company when they didn't arrive at their next port?"

"Of course, Captain, but false messages are sent to explain their delay; mechanical issues, medical issues, some story is fabricated.

"What I do not understand, though," he continued, "is how Forrest was able to bring warships here without alerting the Warner Navy. There is a common rumor that the Family was paid off to allow this invasion. Another which claims that Gateway knew, but did not care."

The Marines sat up and were about to respond, but Samuels raised a hand and they let her take the lead. She leaned forward and folded her hands together.

"I assure you, Bernardo, that was not the case. No one outside this system knew of what had happened, or we would have responded immediately. This system is part of Warner territory, and every Granadan is a full Warner citizen. We would never allow its people to suffer," Samuels replied levelly.

Abruptly, her focus shifted and she separated her hands to initiate the connection to the central data system. Then her fingers tapped on the table surface. "There was something in what you said that has me wondering. How *did* Forrest manage to get warships into the system past Gate Control? For that matter, how did they get warships? X—"

Samuels stopped short, realizing that her executive officer was still missing. She glanced at the chrono, 1110, and was reminded that there was another thread she needed to follow up on, and no XO to make a note to do so. Although, that particular thread was one that she couldn't share with her exec anyway.

Samuels brought up the comm screen at her seat and keyed in a two-digit code. The response was almost immediate.

"Communications Room, Sergeant Brassey."

"Sergeant, this is Lieutenant Samuels."

"Yes, Captain?" Brassey's voice was suddenly much more attentive.

"Please have the comm steward on watch, report to Conference Room One to record a report to the commodore, and please have the XO paged to the same room."

"Yes, ma'am."

"Do you see something the commodore needs to know?" Burton asked.

Samuels was about to respond when Ensign Roberts walked in and took a seat. "Sorry," was all Roberts said by way of apology.

"Ensign Roberts to Conference Room One. Ensign Roberts, please report to Conference Room One," sounded over the ship-wide, and Roberts blushed.

"All right, let's make this as brief as possible so we can get back to work," Samuels said instead of responding verbally to the Marine or pursuing Roberts' tardiness. She did make the Marine hand signal for 'hold in place,' though.

She scanned around the room to make sure she had everyone's attention. Aside from Samuels and Roberts, the only two naval officers, there were four Marines — Aichele, Burton, Major Tunney, and Lieutenant Mdembe; two engineering techs — Giannini and Sullivan; and two Granadans, the older Fuentes and a slender youth named Hastings.

"I wouldn't have called you away at all except I think we need to change our priorities, and our assignments with them. First, though, let's have a quick report on where each of you are. Major Tunney, what's the status on your end?"

"Secure," he said. He followed that up by folding his hands in front of him on the table and saying nothing else. A few seconds passed before Samuels realized that was the extent of the report. *Sheesh, he's as bad as Chowdhury,* the young captain thought. *I wonder if it's required for Marine officers to use fewer words than glowers each day.*

"Prisoners?" Samuels prompted.

"Also secure," Tunney replied.

So far, Samuels thought her theory was still watertight.

"What about external sensors?"

"Nominal." She thought he was going for the hat trick, but he continued after only a brief pause. "We have a solid view of everything within twelve light-seconds."

The comm steward, a lanky Marine private with a brownish buzzcut, entered as his superior spoke. Samuels transferred the short message she'd prepared while others were speaking to the private's pad, then thumbprinted it.

"Private Pettinato, please send this to the commodore with priority two encoding."

"Yes, ma'am," he said, and saluted before he turned sharply to leave at a normal pace. Priority two meant important, but not urgent. Priority one would have sent him racing at top speed.

Samuels turned back to the table and picked up where she had left off. Silently, she blessed her father for teaching her to keep mental track of multiple issues at once. It was an essential talent in the business world, where everyone had assumed she would end up, but she knew of no one else in any of her Academy classes who could do it.

"And is that view coming from gear that we brought with us, or from this ship's systems? I'm asking because a) I think it's almost certain the Forresters are going to hit us to get this ship back, and b) it was evident when we arrived that the Forresters already here never saw us coming."

"Oh, that was because of Cipi," Fuentes said.

"Sippy?"

"I'm sorry, Cipriano Felix; he goes by Cipi. He's the one who arranged for the PMs to have no clue of your coming."

Samuels looked around the room, but didn't see anyone who appeared to know what he was saying any more than she did.

"Okay. First, what is a 'PM?' Second, how did this Cipi make that happen?"

Fuentes blushed.

"Well, Lieutenant...it is...well...our name for the invaders. It is a shortening of a Spanish phrase which I would prefer not to repeat here."

"Captain," Tunney insisted. Fuentes blushed, and nodded.

Samuels had picked up enough Spanish, as spoken by sailors and dock workers, to have a number of guesses as to the phrase in question, but she let that drop in favor of the important topic.

"And Cipriano?"

"Oh, yes," Fuentes continued, blushing a third time, "that. So, Cipi, he works on this ship in the vocom room. I don't know for sure that he works also with GU, though I think it is so, but he has a cousin, Pablo, who definitely does work with GU, and Pablo works on the tactical equipment of this ship, and the two of them have worked out this code where, if there is ever something going on outside of the ship which the PMs should not know, one of them will send up the code, and between the two of them, they will keep them in the dark. It happened, then, last night, that when you and your people set off to come here, this was seen by the PMs on the ground, and they sent word to this ship that such is happening. But the PMs, they are lazy, and a communications watch is boring, so they tell us Granadans to handle it. So we do, but not like they want. The PM in charge, he doesn't want to be bothered to verify receipt of orders and messages, so he gives to Cipi his codes, and so when word of your coming arrives, it is to Cipi, and not to the PMs. Then Cipi gives word to Pablo, and the situation in the tactical department is only a little different, and Pablo is able to fool the others with a replay of the data from the day before, and so no one except the two Felixes knew you would be here to liberate us!"

Major Tunney surprised the group by speaking without being spoken to.

"I had been wondering about that."

Samuels was getting a little more clarity on what had gone on before her arrival, and the story alleviated one of her fears; that they would be blind to any possible counter-attack by the Forresters; but the story also generated a new set of questions.

"Where are these two Felixes now, and what is a GU?"

"You have not heard of GU, the great underground movement working to free our people?"

"You have a group working against the Forresters, and they named themselves Great Underground?"

Fuentes looked confused for several seconds, then his face cleared. "No, Captain, you misunderstand. The name of the group is Granada Unfettered. They mark their victories by leaving this sign at the place of their attacks." Fuentes drew an interlocked G and U at his screen and sent it to the main board for all to see. "So they are mostly known as GU."

Looking back at the screen took her gaze past the chrono, and she realized that she was wasting time she did not have in abundance.

"I see. And these two men—Nevermind. XO, would you have both of them meet with me in this room at 1300?"

"Yes, Captain." Something in Roberts' stressing of the last word caused a few heads to turn her direction, but Samuels gave no indication she had noticed anything amiss and moved on.

"Very well. Giannini, how is Engineering shaping up?"

"Ma'am, it's not as bad as my first report indicated. That report was based on the state we found things in when we arrived, and after Security cleared the Granadan engineers and technicians and got them to help us, we found that all of the systems which were tagged down had very simple solutions, all of which someone knew exactly how to correct. Everything appears to be in working order now, but we're still many hours away from finishing requalification tests."

"Is this more of GU?" Samuels asked of Fuentes.

It was Hastings who answered. While younger than Fuentes, the man appeared at least two decades older than Samuels. Appearances might be deceiving, though, depending on how available anti-aging therapies were this far away from the central systems. Samuels was all too aware of her own very youthful looks.

"Nothing nearly that coordinated, ma'am. It was just a bunch of people looking for ways to slow down the enemy without getting caught. There was no organization behind it."

"Makes sense. When can I have full maneuvering, Giannini?"

"In an emergency, you could have it now. All the faults have been corrected, but some of them are bailing wire engineering because we just don't have the right parts available, and we can't exactly whistle them up. If you want to be sure of everything, we need at least twenty hours. And that's if quals go smoothly."

"Expedite as best you can. I can't guarantee you twenty hours."

Roberts made a soft snorting sound, causing eyes to turn her direction again. Samuels moved on to the next item without any noticeable pause.

"Sullivan." Three sets of eyes sharpened at the name; Sullivan herself, and the two Marines that had worked with her and Samuels on *Pathfinder*. In Sullivan's case, it was simply because she knew it was her turn to report. For Burton and Aichele, it was the wariness of a predator, looking for any misstep that they could pounce on. Samuels knew she was going to have to do something about that before more problems arose, but her promise not to break Sullivan's cover made it all but impossible to satisfy the sergeants' distrust. Although, maybe there was a way...

"What does Tactical look like?" Samuels asked, filing yet another thread away for future consideration.

"The two main issues we initially discovered are still not resolved. Our tactical feeds are currently coming from *Yargus* via one of the data channels and fed into the net through the comm system. Major Tunney is correct that we have visibility out to a few light-seconds, but the interface delay causes a five-second lag in what we are seeing, in addition to the normal lightspeed lag for detection and communications. That's what we can do right now, but it's too long for real security. Top priority is running the new data lines to our own external sensors, which are fortunately already installed. Three more hours to complete that, and then we'll test."

"How long to test?"

"Until it works," Sullivan said.

Samuels grinned. "Fair enough. What about the second issue you raised?"

"Well, when I told you the tactical software the Forresters had installed was a piece of garbage, I may have been exaggerating somewhat."

"It's salvageable, then?"

"No, it's worse than I had thought. After twelve simulated attacks, ten times the system chose the wrong responses, and seven times a human operator would have responded more quickly. With permission, I'd like to ask *Yargus* for a copy of their tactical set, and then modify it to interface with the hardware on this ship."

"That sounds like a major undertaking. I don't think we're going to have time to get it done, and we don't have the trained manpower to run weapons and tactical manually. Does anyone else have a suggestion?"

"Captain," Sullivan said, "you're right that it is a major undertaking, but if we do get hit with the current system, we won't stand a chance. Let me at least replace the automatic response algorithms. There are four technicians here that really know their stuff. Between the five of us, I can guarantee a functional, and improved, system in three hours."

Roberts snorted again, this time louder than before. Samuels heard it, but shrugged it off. She didn't blame Jherri for doubting Amber's claim, but Roberts didn't know the breadth of Sullivan's capabilities. For that matter, Monica doubted *she* could claim to know them either.

"All right, Sullivan. I trust your assessment. But if you are not going to make that timeline, I want to know about it immediately." Aichele looked like he wanted to object, but after a few seconds he settled back into his former demeanor.

The comm steward walked back in during the lull in conversation and handed Samuels a message pad. Everyone waited quietly as she read it and handed it back to the private. "Acknowledge receipt when you get back to the comm room, and pass on a request for a full operational system copy, with priority on tactical and weapons control."

"Yes, Captain."

"Okay, back to business. Ensign Roberts, let's have your report."

"The assignment you gave me, to assess the Granadan civilians on this ship for possible disloyalty, is complete. The people themselves made it very easy. All of them were willing to give evidence while sitting in the chair, and there were no signs of deception, though several of serious emotional distress. Most of them have lost people close to them, and all of them are only here working for Forrest because their families are being held as insurance for their good behavior."

"Do you have any reservations about any of them?"

"No, ma'am. None."

"I am very glad to hear that, because we need every hand we can get. Here's what I'm thinking, and, please, if any of you see something I'm overlooking, I want you to let me hear about it.

"First, the Forresters are very much aware of the current condition of this ship, and they have accurate specs and diagrams to help plan an assault. They have their own Marines and their own assault craft available to them in great numbers. I think the chances that someone in their command structure fails to come up with the thought that turnabout is fair play are exactly zero.

"Second, that squadron of destroyers that Commodore Brighton led on a merry chase are going to be returning for a rematch in about five hours. *Yargus*, *Pathfinder*, and *Dagger* are going to have to position themselves to best intercept them, which means they can't stay behind to help us.

"Third, the Forresters can do the same math I can, and so five hours from now would be an ideal time for them to try retaking this ship, when they know we'll have no support. So that is our deadline.

"Major Tunney, I need you and your Marines to create a defensive plan to repel boarders, no matter what axis they choose to come at us from. Giannini, I need functioning engines ASAP. Sullivan, we're going to be a big target. We need to be able to knock down incoming fire, as well as serve up some of our own. We can't assume that they're willing to try boarding and taking the ship back. While that would be a big plus in their eyes, they have to keep us from leaving the system with proof of what they're doing, and I'm sure they'd be willing to sacrifice a whole ship to see that happen.

"Is there anything I'm overlooking?"

"Captain?" Hastings actually raised his hand to be recognized. At Samuels' nod, he continued. "We don't actually have any ship-to-ship weapons on board, and the only hand-to-hand weapons are what you brought and what the Forresters carried around with them. They didn't want us getting ideas about raiding the armory."

"So much for plan A, *Captain*," Roberts whispered into the silence which followed.

CHAPTER 16
19 October
Asunción Military Base – Granada

Colonel Rochelle Kadison, Forrest Family Forces-Marines, had a headache. Undoubtedly, the predominant causes were stress and lack of sleep, but listening to four generals and five admirals shouting at each other for more than six hours over the question of which branch of service should have primacy in the proposed joint action certainly had not helped.

Kadison could have settled it very quickly if the final decision were hers. It was clearly a Marine op, pure and simple. In the Warner and most other militaries, that's exactly what the case would have been. An assault on another ship was under the purview of the Marines, and the Navy provided the ships and pilots for the Marines to do their assigned duties. The Marines took orders from Navy officers, but Navy officers were trained for combat of the ship-to-ship kind, not the hand-to-hand variety, and they didn't accompany assault forces, as a rule.

That was one reason Kadison wanted to move now, instead of waiting for agreement from all parties. There had been no second wave of shuttles to dock with the *Scythe*, so the only troops on board right now were the single group of Warner Marines, which she knew how to handle. If they waited until a prize crew of Navy personnel got aboard, chances were that Kadison would have to wade through a good deal of that ship-to-ship combat before she could get her troops to their own battle.

That was her first reason, and it was the most important one. She also hated how a simple question of tactics had turned into a political discussion. There had never in the history of the Forrest Family, been a joint operation with the Marines and the Navy, since there hadn't been any Forrest Navy five years ago. The only military the Family had ever had before had been the Marines, which were known as the FFF, Forrest Family Forces. Now the military had to hang a "-Marines" or "-Navy" on the end.

Nor had there ever been an incursion operation to board a ship in enemy hands. This was not a scenario any of her Marines had ever trained for, which meant the planning had to deal with a lot of new variables.

But instead of looking at what needed to happen to make this one operation successful, the questions being raised were all about what sort of precedent was being set for future operations. Which branch should have overall command? Who got to call the shots? Who got to earn political capital when this op was successful? *Gah! Who cared?* Just get the win, and then worry about the future!

And then, not content to argue over who was taking orders from whom, they had to start arguing over which ship to go after. There, at least, there had been a modicum of reason. *Pathfinder* was forming up in formation to take on the destroyers headed inbound, so it made sense to leave that ship to be retaken by the numerically superior Forrest fleet. And that meant that Kadison and her troops were now headed for *Scythe*, instead. As far as she could tell, that was the one sane decision in a sea of madness.

It didn't appear that universal rationality was due to break out anytime soon, either. If they couldn't agree to put the Marines in charge, she would have been willing to accept the first compromise that Admiral Epstein had suggested. He said that the operation had two distinct stages and each branch should call the shots during the stage in their element. The Navy ran the show from deployment to delivery at the target, Marines took charge once the target was breached. That was at least a reasonable and *workable* idea. The arguing was settling down now and it looked like the final solution was going to be anything but reasonable or workable.

The new division of responsibility looked like an unholy mess. Navy crews commanded their ships at all times. Marine officers were to be in command of their troops at all times. Reasonable so far. But the Marines didn't want to be mere passengers on the shuttles, so they insisted that they be consulted on all decisions, and variance from the flight plan had to be approved by the Marine commander on the scene before implementation. If the naval and Marine officers disagreed, then they would have to appeal to the ground base to settle it. And once that was argued and approved, the Navy fought just as hard to have input on the Marine's movements once inside the target. Madness!

And unworkable. *If* this was the SOP that she wound up with, she was planning to ignore them once she was off the transport ship. How could those rules be enforced? There were no Navy officers who were going in with her, so who would know if she improvised?

As usual, the rear echelon tried to make policy without asking those at the sharp end what would actually work. The one thing they were doing correctly, though, was to assign enough troops to do the job; probably three times what would actually be needed. An overwhelming force would cover a lot of other problems with a bad plan of attack. And if that was the hand she was dealt, she could make it work.

Her plan was simple. There was no way a single Warner was ever leaving the *Scythe* alive.

CHAPTER 17
19 October
Pathfinder

Commodore William Brighton sat back in the command chair of *Pathfinder*.

His command chair.

He looked over the bridge of his recaptured command as they moved to intercept the incoming Forrester Fleet.

He had anticipated a greater feeling of accomplishment to be seated here again, but the feeling was somehow empty without the capture of Teach, Leung or Lamont, who had all died before Brighton could take them. The first was dead during the piracy, killed by his own supporters, Leung had died during an attempted escape, and the last became a victim of his own sabotage. With none of the officers left to take into custody for the crimes, he felt incomplete. And now he was dealing with something he had not expected or planned for. He was looking at a complete takeover of the Worth system by a foreign Family. Something that had taken him by surprise. He had hypothesized to Admiral Cosina that the Forresters must be building a fleet, but he had not supposed they would be doing it inside a Warner system.

He looked back at his small console to check the repeat of the scan monitor.

The Forresters were now maneuvering back toward them from the outer edges of the system, where they had been left by *Yargus'* sudden jump.

This had given the Warners the time they needed to transfer people to *Pathfinder* and to takeover the newly completed destroyer *Peru*.

After all the ordeals he and his *Vanguard* crew had gone through to get to this point, it felt right that they should all be entering this battle together on *Pathfinder*. When given the opportunity, all had come from *Yargus*, thus lightening the burden on that ship's environmental systems, but a few had come from *Dagger* to rejoin their original ship. Warrant Officer Long sat at the engineering console monitoring the patched together engines. He had worked like a dervish since returning to the smaller ship, helping the young Lieutenant Mitchell with the innumerable engineering duties. He was working tirelessly to put the ship back together with no sign of the resentment or anger that had seemed to dominate his personality since their ejection from this ship nearly four months previous. Lieutenant Mitchell and Ensign Hayes had joined Lieutenant Amaya at the weapons controls. They seemed as unruly as ever, harrying the poor lieutenant with questions about tactics and preferences. Amaya had an expression on his face indicating he might be regretting his decision to volunteer to transfer from *Dagger* to *Pathfinder*. Mitchell kept glancing at Brighton as if he expected to be banished to the engine room at any moment, but he still managed to ask more questions than the irrepressible Hayes.

Quèneau sat at the scan console, monitoring the enemy fleet as it approached. CWO Lear was at the helm, having come over from *Yargus* to take the place of the absent Elle Williams and Fyonna Johnson, *Pathfinder's* former helmswomen. He was about to move on in his perusal, when he noticed the helm seat had not been replaced, and it still bore the gouges of fletchettes which Teach had fired at Williams on that day. Williams had been stalwart in her loyalty, but the mental strain of their ordeal had taken a heavy toll on her. The last report he'd had of her told of a slow but steady recovery, however.

Brighton turned his mind next to the situation with Samuels. The task he had assigned to her and Roberts might turn out to be harder than the one she had miraculously performed with Aichele and Burton. He would like to have seen Major Chowdhury's face when she stepped off the shuttle and found the three of them standing there. Chowdhury has made a career of keeping her face straight and scaring junior officers nearly to death, but he would place a bet anywhere that she had a hard time keeping an impassive mien at that unexpected sight.

"Commodore, the Forrest fleet is turning over and braking. Their speed is coming down." Quèneau reported from scan, interrupting his thoughts.

Brighton pulled his attention back to the present and concentrated on the problem at hand. He smiled at the way this was developing, also.

Lieutenant Amaya had noticed the same issues. "Rookie mistake."

"What do you mean?" Hayes asked almost immediately.

Before Amaya could respond, Commodore Brighton answered for him.

"A rookie mistake, Ensign, is an error made by someone because they haven't the experience to know any better."

Brighton had to turn his head away as he couldn't quite keep a smile from his face. Warrant Long, at the engineering console, suddenly developed a coughing fit. Brighton realized that he shouldn't really taunt the youngsters, but they seemed so eager, without the ability to sit still and listen in order to learn. They had to jump in with both feet without thinking beforehand if they could swim or not; or even if there was any water. He thought about some of the comments that Captain Cosina had made to him on *Courser* so many years ago and they now had clearer meaning. He supposed that he had been just as much an 'Ensign' as these two young men.

Lieutenant Amaya finally took pity on them and explained.

"There are several factors involved, Ensign. Most important is the velocity of the missiles. If you can keep your speed higher, that is imparted to your missiles as an initial velocity. They will therefore reach their target more rapidly and have a higher terminal velocity, making them a much harder target to defend against. It will also increase the range at which you can engage the target. The only reason to give up these advantages is if you feel that you have such overwhelming superiority, that you want to prolong the engagement window to allow yourself to do more damage. With *Dagger's* power on our side offsetting the enemy's numbers, they should have tried to keep their speed advantage."

"Passing point for turnover, if you'd like a zero-zero, sir," Quèneau interrupted.

"Maintain course and acceleration."

"Aye, sir," responded Lear from the helm.

"Approaching maximum range for missiles," Amaya called from his weapons console.

"Signal to the fleet: Prepare to engage with all forward tubes. Take targeting from *Pathfinder*."

"Signal sent, sir," called Ensign Lee from the communications console. With personnel at a premium on *Pathfinder*, the ensign had also been 'invited' to join the company as they departed *Yargus*. "Receipt confirmed from *Dagger* and *Yargus*, sir," he added a few moments later.

Brighton studied the enemy formation as it raced toward them.

The six ships were still trying to spread across his route of advance, trying to optimize their area of coverage. This also was something of a 'rookie mistake.' The enemy commander was diluting his defensive firepower and minimizing his ability for mutual support. Brighton did some quick mental calculations and determined that, because of the velocity advantage, they would have two volleys from their forward launchers before the Forrest ships would be able to respond. If he spread his first volley out among the entire enemy formation, he would be able to judge their defensive capabilities.

"Lieutenant Amaya, on the first volley, please target Tango-1 and Tango-2, assign -2, -3, -4, and -5 to *Dagger* and -5 and -6 to *Yargus*. For the second volley, I want all ships to concentrate on Tangos 2, 3, and 4."

"Targets designated, sir."

"Fire when ready."

Commodore Brighton felt the slight tremor as missiles were catapulted from *Pathfinder's* two forward launch tubes. His monitor showed sixteen more launching from *Dagger* and, after a slight delay, four more from *Yargus*. His eyebrows went up slightly as he realized that Captain Johnson must have maneuvered her ship to launch her broadside against the enemy as *Dagger* only held ten missiles in her forward batteries. That would give them a slightly higher punch with this first salvo than he hed been expecting.

"All missiles away, sir," called Amaya, not noting the expenditure from *Dagger*.

Brighton nodded, but did not respond. Instead, he watched the twenty-two missiles spread out to attack their targets.

"Volley two is away, sir. Volley one in final acquisition," Amaya said just as Brighton felt the launch.

Brighton watched in fascination as the first missiles engaged the enemy. He was one of the unfortunate few within the WSN who had experienced combat before. He knew the costs of any battle, and he was not looking forward to the death or the destruction that was about to be visited on his enemies; but that would not keep him from doing his duty.

The missiles spread out and began their final approach. The six enemy destroyers launched their defensive missiles. Just as he suspected, their effectiveness was minimized by their distance from each other. Still, he was surprised by how well his command demonstrated their accuracy. Brighton had expected about twenty percent of his missiles to get through the opponent's defenses. In the end, he achieved five hits. Three of them on his primary target.

The three M-17 missiles impacted nearly together on the starboard flank of Tango-3. There was a single hit on -5 and another on -2. Tangos 2 and 5 continued on with no discernable damage, but T-3 staggered and her acceleration dropped to almost half of its previous output.

"Tell the fleet to concentrate the next volley on targets three and five only," Brighton told his comm officer. "Let's try to even the odds just a bit."

"Aye-aye, sir,"

"Incoming. Brace for impact," called Quèneau from her scan station.

Two missiles impacted on *Pathfinder* seconds later. Brighton was thrown against his shock straps and the bindings cut into his left shoulder as the lighting went out, to be replaced almost immediately by dim green emergency lighting. Lear scrambled forward to put out a small fire on his console.

Warrant Long seemed unconcerned by the shaking as he directed damage control parties from his station. There was no evidence that he had ever been thrown out of his chair but Brighton could see him putting on the lap belting that he had apparently forgotten to strap on earlier.

"Damage to port, Frame 113 through 116. Missile five is out of action, sir" Long reported to Brighton as the commodore adjusted his left shoulder strap. "Hold Seven is open to space. No other damage. Unknown casualties from Missile 5."

Brighton simply nodded in the direction of the engineering console. He knew from post battle walk-throughs after his actions in Humboldt what those areas looked like; what his people were feeling and suffering through. He forced those thoughts from his mind and did not let any of them show on his face. He had an aura to project to the crew. He sat a little straighter in his chair and pulled all his shock straps just a little tighter.

"Comm, new targeting instructions for *Dagger* and *Yargus*."

Cheney

CHAPTER 18
19 October
WNS Peru

Monica sat back down and rubbed her chin while she thought. It reminded Roberts of the way Commodore Brighton looked when he was thinking. Finally, she turned to focus on the other people sitting at the conference table.

"Okay, as far as I can see, there are only two places we can get weapons from, either borrowing them from *Pathfinder* or *Yargus*, or stealing them from the stores the Forresters have accumulated. Both of these have problems. The first thing on the list would have to be, will the missiles on *Yargus* match the tubes on *Peru*? Anyone?"

"Why is everything a list with her?" Roberts whispered to Mdembe.

Hastings raised his hand and looked across the table in both directions from his place in the middle.

"I know the gun ports were set before Forrest arrived, so the tubes are the same size as the Warner Mark-20s. Is that what *Yargus* or *Pathfinder* carries?"

"No," Giannini chimed in. "*Yargus* and *Pathfinder* both carry the older Mark-17s."

"What about *Dagger*?" Samuels asked.

"Nope," Roberts supplied, "cruiser missiles are a completely different class. She carries Mark C-07s, I believe."

Samuels sat back in her chair and looked at the far wall.

"That rules out the easy answer. What about our second option? Bernardo, do you know where Forrest stores its weapons?"

"Yes, but you will not like what I will tell you. The storehouse is located on the planet surface, in Nueva Torreon."

Samuels turned to her Marine Commander.

"Major?"

"I'm sorry, Captain, but I don't see how we can make a successful grab for them. I don't know what strength they'll have there, but I'm sure it won't be nothing, and they'll have a ready response force there within a few minutes. Even if we had all of Major Chowdhury's Marines with us, we couldn't hold the facility long enough to steal a collier ship and load it up with missiles."

The Captain picked up her stylus and tapped it a few times on the table while she thought through her list before turning to Giannini.

"Could the Mark-20 tubes be altered to fire the Mark-17s?"

The dark-haired tech shook her head and grimaced.

"I'm sorry, Captain, but not in five hours. And not without more materials than what we have."

Samuels lifted her hands and waved them slightly in the air.

"Okay, I'm open to any suggestions."

"I've got one," Roberts said.

"Let's hear it."

"We might not be able to hit the planet surface, but the Caspar Shipyard facilities are a quick sprint to starboard. Maybe they don't have live ordnance on hand, though that's not certain, since the destroyers that went up against Commodore Brighton couldn't have been armed on the surface, but even if missiles aren't available there, a lot of the other materials that Engineering is lacking are. I think it's worth at least looking at what's there."

"That's a good idea, Jherri. Bernardo, do you know what's on hand at the shipyards?"

"I cannot say. The PMs did not allow any of us to leave this ship. I know only that the missiles are constructed and stockpiled in Nueva Torreon. This much I know only because it was one of the few sites which successfully held off a GU attack."

Samuels turned back to her Marine commander.

"Major, is what Ensign Roberts described within our capabilities?"

"I believe so, yes. If we move quickly, the forces on the ground wouldn't be able to respond before we were gone. I'll take one shuttle and put Lieutenant Mdembe in charge of the other."

"I'm not going to order otherwise, but I think you should turn this operation over to Lieutenant Mdembe to command. I still need you here to plan our defenses. If we don't get any ordnance at Caspar, then we are definitely going to be boarded, and in large numbers."

"I do see your point, but I hate to send my people into battle without me. I'll think seriously on it before I decide."

Samuels nodded at the older Marine.

"Very well, but I'm not going to give you too long to consider. I want the assault launched in an hour, and back here in three. Ensign Roberts, I'm giving you overall command of the operation. Coordinate with the Marines and put the plan together, then meet with me in half an hour to go over it. Make sure you've got a shopping list from Giannini, Sullivan, Mr. Hastings, and Mr. Fuentes."

"Half an hour? To plan an operation?"

"Far from ideal, I know, Jherri. But it's what we have to work with."

Roberts looked shocked at the idea, but she nodded after a few moments.

"All right. Your decision, Captain."

"I know," Samuels said with a sigh. "Anyone else have ideas? Suggestions? Comments? Okay, let's get to it, then."

As people began rising, Samuels called to Roberts.

"XO, could you change the meeting with the Felixes to 1130? I'd like to see them before you and I go over your plans."

When Monica saw Aichele and Burton trailing the crowd to the hatch, she motioned to them.

"Gunny Aichele, Sergeant Burton, would you two stay behind for just a moment, please?"

The two Marines exchanged a look and reclaimed their seats.

CHAPTER 19
19 October
WNS *Peru*

Mdembe was waiting in the corridor for Roberts to exit the meeting. He fell into step with her as she walked, but he waited until they were out of earshot of the others before speaking.

"What was that all about?"

"What was what about?"

"I thought you and Samuels were old friends."

Jherri said nothing for several moments, trying to define in her own mind how she felt. Were they still friends? Could they still be friends when she had to take orders from Samuels? Samuels had taken orders from her when she was cadet wing commander, and yet they had maintained their friendship. So, what was so different now?

There shouldn't be anything different, Roberts knew, and yet there was. She felt betrayed by Samuels because Samuels had been promoted, and Roberts had not. It was not a rational thing, she knew, and it made her feel guilty because of the way she felt. She knew that her own guilt was surfacing as anger, and it was affecting her behavior, yet she couldn't just set it aside.

"I thought so too," she finally responded, before her rational mind had any input.

Mdembe kept walking, saying nothing all the way down the main corridor until they turned to port on the cross corridor leading to the aft ladderway.

"This is a problem, Ensign. Or rather, you have made this a problem."

She turned to look up into Lieutenant Mdembe's dark brown face as she walked beside him.

"What do you mean?"

There was another long pause as their banging feet on the steps would have made communication difficult anyway.

"I mean," he finally said, "that whatever personal feelings you had would not have been a problem if you had been professional enough to keep them to yourself. Now that you have publicly displayed your dissatisfaction with your commanding officer, this is a problem."

"What? I didn't do that."

"Yes, you did. Do you think anyone in that room had any doubts about who *you* thought should have been giving the orders?"

"Uh —" She played back the meeting in her head, and she had to admit there may have been some hint of how she felt, but nothing that overt. Certainly nothing to warrant this lecture from another of her friends.

"I think you are overreacting," she said defensively.

"Am I? Tell me, have you ever seen a subordinate question orders before?"

She remembered Warrant Officer Long on one of the planets they had visited in their exodus from the Antoc system questioning Captain Brighton's orders. She nodded her head at Mdembe. "Yes."

"Did the officer just let it go, or did he or she come down hard on the offense?"

"It was Captain Brighton, and he came down harder than I have ever seen before or since."

"Okay. So what would Captain Brighton have done if you'd received his orders the way you received Lieutenant Samuels'? Better yet, answer me this: If you had given that tone to Major Chowdhury, would your head still be attached to the rest of you?"

"Uh—" she said again, turning pale at the mention of Chowdhury's probable response. "I didn't think—"

"No, you didn't," Mdembe interrupted before she could finish the excuse. "You have got to apologize to Captain Samuels, and you've got to do it soon, and in public."

"Why should I?"

She knew the words made her seem like a petulant child as soon as they left her mouth, but she really didn't see that her offense had been grave enough for all this fuss.

The muscles in Mdembe's jaw tightened. He turned to face her, stopping their progress and opened his mouth, then just as abruptly shut it again. His center of mass dropped suddenly, his leg shooting out and sweeping ankle high. Jherri's legs flew forward and she hit hard on her back, air exploding out of her lungs. Before she could inhale, Mdembe's boot pressed onto her chest and she stared up at his sidearm, not quite aimed at her head.

"If I have your attention now..."

Roberts nodded vigorously, not having breath enough to speak. Mdembe removed his foot and crouched down next to her, folding his arms, but not putting the fletchette gun back in its holster.

"This ship is preparing for battle. Again. This is no time for whiney little girls to moan about how life isn't fair, or how they deserve more than they have. Commodore Brighton has placed you under the orders of Lieutenant Samuels. She *asked* for you to be her executive officer. Your oath as a Warner naval officer *demands* that you support the decisions she makes, no matter what your feelings are.

"Now, you may think that the commodore put you in a tough spot, having to take orders from someone you feel is your inferior." Roberts drew in a gulp of air and made as if to protest, but Mdembe's glare made her subside. "But look at the position Samuels is in. She's got to command a bunch of Marines with ten times her experience, with every reason to feel that maybe they know better than her what should happen. She's got to get this ship ready to fight, a ship she'd never seen before last night, full of technicians and engineers who know the workings of the ship far better than her, with every reason to feel that maybe they know better than her what should happen. I'm sure she walked into that meeting expecting that she was going to have to demonstrate her ability to lead, or she would never gain the confidence of those under her command, confidence they need to have to do their jobs without hesitation when it really matters. I'm sure she thought that at least she wouldn't have to worry about you or the men and women of *Pathfinder* who know her.

"Instead, by your words you've let everyone who was there, who had any doubts about *your friend's* ability, know that there's room for even more doubt. *Captain* Samuels cannot allow that doubt to exist. And in order to dispel it, she has to come down hard on you. She *has* to. There is no other way for her to regain the trust you just did your level best to destroy.

"And if you think that I'm making a bigger deal out of this than I ought to, just let these words sink in a little: insubordination, dereliction of duty, conduct unbecoming an officer. Now consider what your chances for promotion would amount to if you had to face those charges at a court martial. *That* is how hard she could come down on you for your actions in that meeting.

"Major Chowdhury has told me that you once blamed yourself for a crewman's death, which was not your fault. *That* may not have been your fault, but I am telling you now, if anyone dies on this ship because they hesitated when they received orders, tried to analyze them to see if they made sense instead of just doing them, those deaths will be yours to carry until the day you die. There is absolutely no room for your petty arrogance in the chain of command. I'm telling you as a friend, if you don't go take care of it yourself at the first opportunity, then you will deserve whatever overly harsh punishment the captain of this ship is forced to give you in order to make an example of you."

With that, Mdembe stood and walked away, leaving Roberts on the deck, gasping for air.

CHAPTER 20
19 October
WNS *Dagger*

WNS *Dagger* shot through the void of the Worth system like a shark through Terran oceans. From the core outward she had been designed for one function, to kill enemy ships. For the first time in her existence, she was doing the job for which she had been built.

Though the Warner ships were outnumbered and slightly outgunned, *Dagger* had easily double the mass and displacement of any other ship in the engagement. As such, the Forresters were concentrating their fire on her. This was another tactical mistake on the part of the inexperienced Forrest commanders. *Dagger* was a *Rapier*-class light cruiser; designed as a fast, heavily-armed combatant to be able to stand toe to toe with larger ships in a missile engagement. At 80,000 tons, *Dagger* could absorb an incredible amount of damage. The better strategy would have been to eliminate the smaller, more vulnerable weapons platforms, thus reducing the offensive and defensive capabilities of your opponent for the least investment of time and munitions. The problem the Forresters were facing was that both *Pathfinder* and *Yargus* had engine systems that they wanted to steal. They didn't want to destroy either ship. They wanted to capture one or both of them after the battle. So far, *Yargus* had taken several hits during the earlier engagement in the outer system, but currently had all systems functional and was able to fight effectively. She was also largely being ignored by the Forrest ships. *Pathfinder* had been hit by a few missiles, but that looked to have been accidental.

Commodore Brighton, aboard *Pathfinder*, was not making the same mistake. He knew the more missile launchers he could take out of action, the better his chances of winning this engagement. For that reason, he had ordered all his ship's launchers to concentrate on one ship at a time and pound her to scrap.

Nothing larger than a light cruiser, such as *Dagger*, had been built by any of the Families for over fifty years. The remaining heavy cruisers still in existence were left over from the first interstellar struggle. As a consequence of that first experience with space warfare, one Family had been destroyed and the allied Combined Fleet had been created, where missile platforms were king.

The Forresters had six remaining destroyers to the Warner task force's three ships. All of Forrest's destroyers were slightly larger than either of the antiquated destroyers under Brighton's command. To compound the commodore's problem, *Pathfinder* was no longer a warship. As part of Project Argo, *Pathfinder* had been converted from a destroyer to an exploration ship, and her fighting ability had been gutted to provide space for the larger engines and enhanced sensors. There had also been damage to *Pathfinder* that had been self-inflicted; starting with the damage from Brighton invoking his modified piracy protocols, then the sabotage to keep the pirates from escaping with their prize, and finally, the damage incurred in the battle to retake the ship.

Johnson ignored the damage to her old ship and focused on the battle ahead of her.

"Amanda, put us in a position slightly ahead of *Yargus* and *Pathfinder* with one on either flank. Keep them inside our defensive envelope," she told the helmswoman from her command seat on the bridge of *Dagger*.

"Aye-aye, ma'am."

Captain Johnson eyed the helm controls for a moment as if longing to sit and control the power that was harnessed there;

but only for an instant. Ensign Tory was a talented and capable officer and there would be very little that Johnson could do to improve on her shiphandling, no matter how much she longed for the simpler days when all she had to concern herself with was the proper maneuvering of the ship. Now she had to worry about every aspect of the cruiser and her untested crew.

"Ma'am, orders from the flag. We are to concentrate our fire on tango three," her comm tech, T. K. Hiramoto, relayed.

"Confirm to the flag. Haskins…"

"Shifting now, ma'am," the tactical officer responded from her console before the captain could complete the order. "Locked onto the assigned target."

"Fire double broadside at the target."

The slight shudder of the departing missiles crept up Captain Johnson's back, followed a few moments later as the ship rolled on its axis and launched from the opposite broadside to add to the total missile count flying toward the lone ship which was moving ahead of the other five as it couldn't keep up with the braking of its fellows as they had turned for a zero-zero intercept with Brighton's task force.

Their sixteen missiles were joined on their outbound journey by six from the two small destroyers.

The incoming missiles from the Forresters interpenetrated with the outbound missiles, but neither set was disrupted by the confluence. Unlike two duelists standing in a field, both ships were aiming for where the other was going to be when it arrived, and so each followed different tracks to their respective targets. The projectiles placidly ignored each other on their way to their impending immolations.

The Forrester ships began to maneuver to evade the wave of missiles, but their efforts were in vain. In another example of a 'rookie mistake,' the squadron commander had not matched the lower acceleration of her sister ship, allowing it to creep farther and farther in advance of the others. Tango-3 had moved outside the envelope where it could gain supporting defensive fire from her cohorts. Task Force Ten's missiles were nearly unopposed, and bore in on the sixth ship at the fore of the enemy fleet.

Twenty-two missiles began to make their final runs on the target. The Forresters did manage to eliminate five missiles as they passed through the defense of a single ship. Six more lost their lock on the target as it went into desperate gyrations, but it was far too little to make any meaningful difference. The other eleven homed in and detonated against the shields of the target.

A destroyer is designed to be strong, and the Forresters had made their new ships even larger and tougher than any that had been previously produced, but that was not enough to help FFF *Hammer* as she was hit by eleven nearly concurrent blasts of nuclear energy in the ten-kiloton range. *Hammer* vaporized as the shields failed and the energy was transferred directly to the hull in a giant wave of heat and plasma.

Captain Johnson watched from her screens as Tango-3 blinked out. *Such a passive response to represent such violent destruction and death,* she thought.

The inexperience of the opposing officers and crews was beginning to tell. It was certainly improving the odds of her ship coming off as the conquerors, for which she had not the slightest qualm about mercilessly taking advantage of every mistake the other side cared to commit. The Forrester crews were getting better, however, with each successive wave of warheads they defended. The quicker they could bring this engagement to an end, the better it would work out for the smaller Warner fleet.

"Shift target to next designated ship," Johnson said as she glanced at the incoming missiles on her screen. "Free all inner perimeter weaponry and brace for impact."

She felt the missiles leave their silos and the smaller rail guns and lasers begin to engage the targets that were speeding to destroy her ship. A small corner of her mind noticed *Pathfinder* and *Yargus* doing the same. The forty-eight incoming missiles were still targeted on all three Warner ships, even though it looked like only two were going after *Pathfinder*. All three ships erupted with lasers and projectiles in defense, with overlapping fields of fire. While *Yargus* and *Pathfinder* were able to put out a slightly smaller amount than each of their Forrest counterparts, *Dagger* was able to easily blanket the space around all three ships with destruction. By expanding her fire in order to defend the two destroyers, she was able to ensure that none of the missiles targeted on those smaller ships was able to complete their journey. Of the forty-eight missiles launched by the six Forrest ships, only three impacted on *Dagger*, and none at all on either of her smaller sisters.

Johnson watched while damage reports scrolled across her screens. The ship shuddered with another double launch, before she had absorbed all the information. It could have been much worse, she knew. They had taken all the incoming missiles on the port side. They were losing atmosphere from a rupture on G deck, aft. They had also lost three antimissile rail guns from the same blast.

Captain Johnson glanced over her shoulder to the weapons console to see Lieutenant Haskins rapidly rewriting the tasking algorithm to cover for the missing guns even as the next salvo raced in. The tactical officer was sitting calmly in her chair as if at afternoon tea, but her hands were flying over the keys. She had overall responsibility for the engagement and was directing the combined defense of the flotilla, but you could never tell from her body language that she was anything but calm and in control.

By contrast, her number two at the weapons station was not covering his stress nearly so well. Next to her at the weapons console, Lieutenant Andy Gordon looked harried in trying to orchestrate the roll of the ship to clear the way for each successive broadside salvo as he managed the offensive weaponry of *Dagger*. Sweat soaked his hair and uniform, but his dark eyes never wavered from his displays and his hands flew nearly as quickly as his boss'. This was a new assignment for the young tactical officer, since he had been bumped up to the first team after the loss of Lieutenant Amaya-Garcia to *Pathfinder*. Under normal circumstances, the backup tactical officer would have been with the XO on the auxiliary bridge in the stern to avoid a single shot taking out all the ranking officers. Instead, Lieutenant Pol Strachowitz, normally the communications officer, was manning Tactical in the auxiliary bridge with Lieutenant j. g. Heidi Szoke as his weapons officer. Both of those officers had tactical experience, though no prior taste of actual combat. In the case of Strachowitz, more experience even than Gordon.

Gordon ignored all the turmoil around him and fired another double broadside at the designated target. Just after the launch, the impact of the incoming missiles rocked the bridge. The inertial dampeners kept much of the impact from being felt through the ship, but lights dimmed momentarily and the noise was nearly overwhelming on already overtaxed senses.

Haskins swore quietly under her breath, though no one could have heard a shout over the cacophony, and redoubled her efforts to kill the incoming missiles.

As the two fleets closed with each other, the time between launch and impact decreased, until there was no way for human reflexes to affect the hammering they were receiving from the Forresters, and more and more defensive systems were operating solely on automatic. Each salvo was getting smaller, however, as Commodore Brighton's targeting plan took its toll on the enemy fleet. Each ship targeted was being eliminated. The second ship, FFF *Conqueror*, had not been destroyed outright, as its companion had been, but it continued on its previous trajectory as a battered, lifeless, atmosphere-streaming hulk.

The bridge of *Dagger* again was shaken by the impacts of several missiles. Captain Johnson looked quickly at her damage control screen and saw that they had received a missile directly over the starboard #3 missile silo. The silo was completely destroyed and the communication to the rest of the area was disrupted. Fortunately, the tube was empty at the time; the missile having left a handful of seconds before, and the automated reload not having finished yet.

"Captain, *Yargus* is reporting damage to their forward port laser array. They are requesting that we allow them to pull in closer to help cover their blind spot."

"Signal affirmative."

FFF *Defender* joined her two sisters in destruction six minutes later, when the Warner's next salvo arrived at her position.

Just as *Defender* was destroyed, *Dagger* was again shaken by the impact of six missiles that got through the diminishing defenses.

One of these detonated directly in front of the bridge, unleashing hellish heat and concussive force through the fore of the ship. Captain Johnson's world turned black as her seat was torn from the deck and thrown to the back of the bridge, as if it were no more than a capricious child's toy.

CHAPTER 21
19 October
WNS *Peru*

When the last of those excused had left and the hatch sealed itself shut, Samuels turned to Burton and Aichele in their seats and paused before she said anything. She knew this discussion needed to happen, but finding the way to broach the subject delicately was beyond her. She trusted both of them, and she felt that they trusted her, but that trust still did not extend to Sullivan, and that was going to cause problems if she let it slide.

"That's going to be a problem if you let it slide," Burton said.

Samuels stared at her, wondering how Burton could identify herself as the problem without solving it herself. Aichele clarified, giving Burton a warning look.

"It may be out of place for us to point out, ma'am, but you are going to have to deal with Roberts before long. I would recommend today, if you're expecting action before tomorrow."

Roberts? Samuels' mind lurched. *What was wrong with Jherri that needed dealing with?*

"Gunny, it's not out of place, because I have no idea what you're talking about."

Aichele looked at Burton, who returned the flat gaze before speaking, "Ensign Roberts is jealous of your promotion, L-T," Jill clarified.

"Captain," Aichele corrected.

"Sorry, Captain."

"What? Why would she be jealous? I'd get rid of these headaches in a minute, if I could!"

Both Marines looked at each other as if trying to decide which would be the one to pursue the issue. After a few seconds, Aichele nodded and continued.

"I've seen this before, many times. Tell me, Captain, what sort of person is Roberts? How would you sum up her character?"

Samuels tipped her head to the side, as if thinking through the question.

"Well, she's smart, and witty, and bubbly, and dependable, and a good friend."

Aichele nodded.

"What about competitive?"

Samuels smiled at the question.

"Oh, yeah, she is that. I was glad, though, because I did better at the Academy knowing she was working just as hard to stay ahead of me."

"How did you rank at the end?"

"Roberts was first. We were tied going into the last day of trials. I beat her by three points on the Naval Systems final, but she got a 99.2 to my 94.5 on the Military History exam, so I took second. Then it was Omundson, Mitchell, and then Hayes."

Aichele nodded again, his face turning serious.

"So, is it possible that, in her mind, she was expecting to be promoted to lieutenant before you, considering that she came out of the Academy ahead of you?"

Samuels sighed. "I don't know. Maybe. As long as she's following orders, though, what does it matter how she feels about it?"

Burton and Aichele shared the same look again, but this time Burton answered. "Because, unless you and your XO are on the same page, the troops are going to get mixed signals. And going into a combat situation, mixed signals can get people killed."

Monica pressed her palms into her temples and stared at the table while she slowly exhaled. She had seen people die in combat, and the images were now fresh in her mind, because Burton's comment brought them all flooding back. She would do everything in her power to avoid adding more images to her collection. "Okay," she finally said, "I'll talk with her. I'm sure you guys are exaggerating the problem, but I'll talk to her."

"Was that everything?" Aichele asked, beginning to rise.

"No. Sit down." The tone of command was unmistakable, and Aichele dropped back into his chair. "I have two other matters to discuss with you, which, you will be happy to know, involves getting the two of you on the same page as me."

"Captain?" Aichele asked. The single word coming from someone old enough to be her grandfather had made her very uncomfortable a few days before, but she barely noticed it anymore.

"First, I want the two of you to check out the security office on this ship and see if there is an Omega Room somewhere."

"What made you think of that?" Aichele asked.

"Believe it or not, it was the clock on the wall while we were waiting for Roberts. It's mounted exactly where it would be on a Warner ship. Then Fuentes confirmed that construction of this ship began before the Forresters arrived, so any modifications they made had to fit in with what was already built. The question is, whether or not the Omega Room was completed first."

"Chances are good that it's there, but that won't help us get in. We don't have any codes for this ship," Burton said.

"Just find out and report back. If it's there, I'll see if I can find a way in. If I have time."

"Yes, ma'am. Then what was the second item?" Aichele asked.

"Sullivan." Both Marines stiffened. "You don't trust her. I do. I need you to be on the same page with me on this. Just like the Roberts issue, we can't show any conflict. We're not on the same page."

"Yes, ma'am," Aichele agreed, while making it clear he wasn't actually retreating a millimeter.

"And I think it is putting this assignment in jeopardy for that distrust to continue."

"Ma'am, you know the reason I don't trust her. Her story is full of holes. She has lied to all of us several times. You know this. I don't understand why you trust her."

"Gunny, I would tell you my reasons if I —" She cut herself off before she revealed too much, then sudden inspiration caused her to change her approach. "Gunny, I told you once that Sullivan had explained herself to my satisfaction, correct?"

Both Marines nodded. "I have given my word that I would not *tell* you anything about that explanation. The reasons for not sharing what was revealed to me, I also found satisfactory."

"I understand that, ma'am," Aichele acknowledged.

"Right. Both of you understand what I have told you. But neither of you has explored what that information implies."

Jill turned to look at Aichele, who continued looking at Samuels with narrowed eyes.

"You trust Sullivan's loyalty," Eric stated. Monica nodded.

"As much as you trust mine, or Burton's?" She nodded again.

"And this trust comes from the story she told you?"

Nod. "Plus, that her actions are consistent with her story," Samuels added.

"That story accounts for her pre-knowledge of Omega Rooms?" Nod.

"Her sharpshooting?" Nod.

"The fact that she had a suit of heavy armor, custom-fitted to her body, sitting in our armory? And no one in Security was aware of the fact?" Pause.

"I hadn't thought of that. Have you discussed that with Major Chowdhury since her return, to find out if she was aware of that?"

"Well, no. There hasn't been time."

"Regardless, her story also accounts for that, though it shows a level of paranoia and preparation I didn't expect."

Burton broke in for the first time. "Did you say 'paranoia'?" Nod.

Burton and Aichele shared another of their looks, and Burton mouthed the words, "We see you." Aichele's eyebrows shot up for an instant and then he squinted and stared at nothing, considering the new possibility. The involvement of WICIU, the Warner Internal Counter-Intelligence Unit, would actually make sense. After several seconds he leaned back in his chair and shook his head slowly.

"Wow," he finally said. "A counter-intelligence officer would cover all the known facts. Does she outrank you? Should we be taking orders from her? Never mind, she couldn't issue orders without breaking cover, which, I assume, she is still not willing to do. Wow.

"Wait, are *you* taking orders from her?"

"I cannot confirm or deny the accuracy of your suppositions, of course. But I will confirm that I am the ranking naval officer on this ship, and Commodore Brighton is the only person to whom I am accountable. Now, may I ask if we still have the same trust issue to deal with?"

"No, ma'am," they both said in unison.

"Very well, dismissed."

The two Marines rose, saluted, and walked out into the corridor.

Aichele turned and looked at Burton.

"You know, with those spooks' reputations, we've got an entirely different set of trust issues now," he said acidly.

CHAPTER 22
19 October
WNS *Peru*

"Pablo Felix," the man said as he stepped into the conference room, extending his hand as Samuels rose.

"Lieutenant Samuels," she countered, accepting the hand and offering hers to the next man as well. "Cipriano."

For cousins, the two men did not look very similar. Pablo was of medium height, perhaps a few centimeters taller than Samuels, and slender, with dusky skin and a thin black mustache. Cipi was twenty centimeters shorter and carrying more mass. His skin was fairer, but he had an identical mustache.

"Thank you, gentlemen for agreeing to see me."

"Of course," Pablo smiled. Samuels decided he was also the more handsome of the two.

The three of them sat, Samuels at one end of the table, and Pablo and Cipi in the two nearest seats to her left.

"I wish I had time to chit-chat with you, but I simply don't." Both men nodded. "Are both of you a part of GU?"

The two men exchanged a look, then Pablo nodded.

"Who on this ship holds the most authority in your group?"

Again the exchange, and again Pablo responded. "Cipriano does."

"Very well, Mr. Felix, I'd like to offer you a position on my crew."

"As gopher?"

"Excuse me?"

"Someone to go-for this and go-for that. A lackey. A minion. A lickspittle. A peon."

Samuels was shocked at the malice in his words, especially as the first words he'd said to her, but they confirmed her sense of the Granadans' feelings she'd picked up so far. It also confirmed that she was making the right move. She owed another thank you to her father, for teaching her how to manage a new crew.

"No, nothing like that," she smiled. "I'd like you to take the position of bosun of the ship."

"What's a bosun?" Pablo asked.

"The bosun is the highest ranking noncommissioned officer. He makes sure personnel issues are handled fairly, and that the necessary work gets done. Effectively, he's a buffer between the crew and the officers."

"Why do want me to be this...bosun?" Cipi asked, carefully pronouncing the unfamiliar word.

"Because the Granadans are not my people, they are yours, and you are already their leader. And like I said, I am pressed for time. So rather than trying to convince all 95 of you to trust me, I am going to convince you, and let you represent me to the crew. We don't have the time for the whole crew to get to know me."

"What makes you think I will ever trust you, or any Warner?"

"That's a fair question," she said, leaning back in her seat and deliberately not paying any attention to the tone in which the rhetorical question was thrown at her. "Let me start by saying that I don't know you, and I don't know what you've been through. I do know that you have reason to want the Forresters gone. I know that you feel Warner has broken faith with you, by allowing Forrest to take over this system. Mr. Fuentes said that some people believe Warner sold your people out. I will tell you what I told him, that is not the case. If we had known the situation, the Warner Navy would have been here at once.

"But, there's no reason for you to accept my word, if you already don't trust me. So instead, let's look at this logically. You hate the Forresters and you want them gone. The only thing you know about me is that I brought people onto your ship and took it away from the Forresters. Surely, that is enough to buy me a little trust in your eyes."

"Not really."

Samuels hadn't expected that response, and she looked at Pablo, who remained blank-faced. "Why is that?"

"I have talked with some of your people. You did not come here to help Granada. You came here looking for something you lost. No one asked you to come here, and we'll take care of the problem ourselves without you. What right do you have to claim this is a Warner vessel? Warner didn't build it. This is a Granadan ship. You took command by force, and you forcing us to work for you is no better than what Forrest was doing."

Samuels gaped. "Seriously? You think we're the same as the Forresters? *You're a Warner citizen!*"

"Not anymore. I was abandoned by Warner when Forrest claimed this system as theirs."

Samuels clamped down on her anger and forced herself to look at the facts. She consciously leaned back in her chair and considered his point of view. Legally, he probably could not support his position, but there was enough gray area that it might actually make it to the courts before it was settled.

That wouldn't help her, though. Whatever the legality, or lack thereof, of the current situation, she had orders to fulfill. Commodore Brighton had ordered her to take *and keep* this ship as evidence of what Forrest had been up to. Those orders were nondiscretionary. Besides, what did Felix expect, that she would leave and let him take over? That wouldn't stop Forrest from hitting the ship in a few more hours.

She ought to just insist, pointedly, that she was the one with the guns and Marines and if he didn't like it, he could get out and walk. But if she did, she'd just be proving his point for him. Time to try the unexpected instead.

"Tell me what you think should happen."

"I think you should turn this ship over to GU. I think it should be renamed *Redentor*, and it should be the first ship in the Worth System Defense Force. I think you should be taking orders from us."

"All right."

The agreement hit him just as he was preparing to angrily defend his assertions, and he almost couldn't believe his ears. "Really?"

"Well, I can't take orders from you without orders from my commanding officer to do so, but I'll agree to the rest. My people and I will just load up on our shuttles and be on our way."

Samuels rose from her seat, smiled at both men and walked toward the door.

"Cipi?" Pablo said.

"Wait," Cipi said. "You cannot do this thing."

"Why not? You won't take orders from me, I can't take orders from you. Let's just part amicably. Good luck!"

"But you have all the weapons."

"That's true, but it doesn't change the nature of our relationship. I'm not going to use my weapons to force you to do anything you don't want to."

"But we can't hold this ship without you," Pablo cut in. Cipi glared at him as if he'd been betrayed.

"Not my ship, not my problem. We'll be off *your* ship in the next twenty minutes or so." She resumed walking toward the hatch, but had only made it one step before there was another call.

"Captain—"

"Lieutenant," she corrected. "I can't be a captain without a ship."

Pablo followed her out into the corridor. "Captain, please, come back and sit down. I'm sure we can come to some arrangement."

"Like what?" she said, not slowing down.

"Please, Captain. Without you, not only will all of us die, but so will our families on the surface."

The thought of all those deaths wrenched her heart, but she gave no sign. "Not my problem anymore."

"Wait, Capitán," Cipi spoke for the first time since she'd left her seat. She obligingly stopped walking and turned to face him.

"I told you, I'm not a captain if I don't have a ship."

"I know, Capitán," he said with a sigh. "I will accept your authority to issue orders on *your* ship."

"Thank you, Cipriano. I'm not trying to bully you into accepting me—"

"No?"

"No. But like I said, I am very pressed for time. And this was the quickest way to get you to face the realities of the situation we are in. Neither of us is going to make it without the other. Of the two of us, you're better suited to lead your people, and I'm better suited to fight the ship."

Cipriano looked at her in amazement, and newfound respect.

"Okay, let's go back and work out the details."

"Yes, ma'am."

CHAPTER 23
19 October
WNS *Pathfinder*

Commodore Brighton leaned forward to better examine the unfolding battle from his station on *Pathfinder's* bridge. The command seat felt right to him. It was probably the only thing on the bridge that did. The remainder of the command deck looked as if a tornado had swept through on its way to Oz.

There was evidence of the destruction he himself had initiated with his additions to the piracy protocols, but the damage was much more extensive than his contributions could account for. Lieutenant Samuels had done an extensive job of sabotage in her efforts to keep *Pathfinder* in the Antoc system, and the charred consoles and half-repaired wiring runs as a result of her work were nearly everywhere his glance fell. He could not blame her, however. That was what he had assigned her to do. He had not really believed she could accomplish her task. In fact, she had not accomplished what he had wished, since the ship escaped to Worth eventually, despite her efforts, and those of the two Marines.

He had wanted the ship kept in Antoc, where he himself could recapture her. He had wanted to redeem his ship and exact vengeance from his old friend Edward Teach. As it turned out, he had been able to do neither. The ship was retaken before he could return for her, and Teach had been killed by one of his co-conspirators before he could answer to Brighton's justice.

None of this diminished the accomplishments of Samuels, however. Truth be told, she had exceeded her assignment greatly. He had not really believed that she would be able to accomplish the limited task he had left to her. In fact, he was not even sure she would be able to derive his meaning when he told her to stay on board *Pathfinder*. Perhaps, he reflected, that was why she had gone beyond what duty could have asked of her; she had misunderstood what he wanted of her. She had always seemed to be too straightforward and literal in her dealings. She simply hadn't seemed to be capable of the subterfuge necessary to understand the implicit order, or to execute it if she did comprehend. It seemed, however, she had been capable of both. Once again, he had proved to himself that he was a poor hand at understanding people.

"Lieutenant Amaya," he called over his shoulder as he continued to scan the display mounted on his right armrest and designated the proper blip with his cursor. "Next target, please."

"Aye-aye, sir," the weapons officer responded. "Orders relayed to the fleet."

"Very well," Brighton responded. He turned his thoughts back to Samuels. Brighton was unsure if Leung had had any other desires in the promotion, but Samuels had more than earned the new rank with her efforts to retake *Pathfinder*. He had confirmed her field promotion in his earliest dispatches to Earth. Those dispatches would not be able to leave the system until Chowdhury could secure the jump gate, but he was acting as if they were already confirmed.

Leung, it seemed, had bestowed that rank on the only officers available. Samuels had become her XO and Omundson had become her chief engineer. Odd that she had given Samuels the promotion, but had officially left Omundson as assistant chief engineer while retaining the higher position for herself. Nevertheless, she had promoted Samuels. Now, he had confirmed that promotion and sent her out to take over her own independent command. In the process, he may have gotten her, and all those with her, killed. It looked as if the Forresters had sent several shuttles to try to take that ship back from her. He had seen the ship separated from the rest of its cohorts and had felt it would make great evidence of the havoc and disruption the Forresters had created here in Worth. If they could hold on to it, it would still do so. With that thought in his mind, he turned all of his attention to the battle. Samuels future was a problem that he could tackle later, if they all survived.

He refocused on the screen by his chair and studied the ships arranged against his small fleet. The engagement had unfolded in much the way he had hoped that it would to this point, but the battle had moved much farther toward the outer reaches of the system than he had expected. As a result, Samuels and her destroyer would soon have no clear path back to the small Warner fleet. If Brighton failed to defeat the Forresters, Samuels and the destroyer she had named *Peru* would be cut off from both the gate and his fleet. They would most likely die or be retaken at that point, since *Peru* had no armaments installed for their protection. Brighton studied the display but could see no choice in the matter. Tactically, he must maintain a path to the jump gate for himself and his fleet; both to protect his retreat and to be able to assist Chowdhury and her team on the control station, if such a move became necessary. It didn't look as if he could maintain that pathway and a pathway for Samuels' at the same time. Unfortunately, she must look out for herself; something at which she had proven herself to be quite adept.

"Bogey nine destroyed," Lieutenant Amaya said, interrupting Brighton's reverie. "*Dagger* took a big hit forward."

Brighton turned to look at Quèneau at scan.

"Damage report."

The report came from Ensign Lee at communications instead.

"Contact from Lieutenant Grant. Damage to bridge and missile silos three and five."

Brighton was caught short by the report; not because of its content, he had expected that, but by its source. The only reason Grant would respond for *Dagger* was if the bridge was out of action and he was directing the ship from Auxiliary Control. He would only do this if Captain Johnson were dead or out of communication. The thought hit Brighton as a physical blow. Fyonna Johnson was a part of his family in a way that few others were, or ever could be. She had been with him on *Pathfinder* before the piracy and accompanied him into exile on *Vanguard*. She had supported him and stood by him throughout all the ordeals of their escape from Antoc and the recovery on Earth. She had volunteered to accompany him back to recover his ship. He was stunned by her sudden loss.

He straightened and pulled down his tunic.

He wouldn't get ahead of himself.

They could have just lost communication to the bridge.

He turned back to the helm.

"Helm, turn us over and begin braking. Let's stay within the inner system."

"Yes, sir."

Brighton then turned to Ensign Lyle at communications.

"Open communications to the Forresters."

"Live mic, Commodore."

"Forrest fleet, surrender now and avoid the destruction of your ships and the loss of your lives. There is no point in dying for no gain. Your destroyers stand no chance against a light cruiser. Stand down now."

"Sent, sir." After a lengthy pause, the ensign said, "No response."

Brighton shook his head at the stubborn refusal. The cruiser did make this a one-sided affair even if they didn't want to believe it. Their refusal to fire missiles at *Pathfinder* and *Yargus* had doomed them. They didn't have enough missiles to take down a cruiser with two supporting destroyers. He didn't let any of his emotions show on his face as he gave the next orders.

"Very well," Brighton replied and then turned to the Weapons console. "Next target, Lieutenant."

"Aye, sir," Amaya acknowledged.

Brighton felt the ship shudder under him as another volley was sent on its way toward the enemy fleet. This shudder was followed almost immediately by another and another as the two fleets hurled toward each other at increasing closing velocities.

The closer the two fleets got to each other, the harder it was to defend against the incoming missiles. There simply wasn't time for the complex detection and course predictions necessary to isolate targeting vectors that would guarantee the destruction of the hostile warheads. *Yargus* took a hit from two missiles in quick succession and rolled over to present her undamaged port side as she struggled to repair missile batteries on the starboard. *Pathfinder* rang from the impact of a single missile near the bow that took out a thankfully unmanned laser emplacement, but Brighton hardly noticed as he watched four more impacts on *Dagger*. The missile output from the massive light cruiser never slackened. The density of the volleys diminished slightly as they had lost two silos, but they stayed on task and their rate of fire never faltered.

The Forrester ships took an equal beating and only a single destroyer emerged from the other side of the melee after the two fleets passed through each other. She was damaged and alone.

"Forrest destroyer," Brighton called again over the comm, "surrender and prepare to be boarded."

"No response, Commodore."

Before Brighton could repeat his request for surrender, Ensign Hayes called out from his tactical board next to Lieutenant Amaya-Garcia.

"They are firing missiles, sir."

"Return fire, Weapons," Brighton called as he sat back in his command chair. "Comm, send to the fleet: Reverse course and head for the gate. Destroy any ship that engages you." He felt the missiles launch from his own ship and knew the small, damaged target had no possibility of defending itself from the missile storm that was about to descend upon it from the spatial equivalent of point blank range.

"Aye, sir." Lyle responded.

"Four hits on the target, sir. There is nothing left. Only one of their missiles got through to *Dagger*. No hits on either of the other ships.

"Tactical, what is the status of the damaged ships as well as those in the outer system?"

"Sir, final bogie in this fleet is destroyed, two ships limping in from the outer system. One, designated Tango-2, is making about two-thirds former speed and should arrive in the inner system in 4.2 hours. The other, designated Tango-6, will not arrive for nearly three hours after that. None of the nearer ships are moving or appear to be under power. If there are life pods deployed, they are not using a standard emergency beacon frequency."

He shook his head at the tragic loss of life, even if it had been an enemy of his Family.

"Thank you," Brighton said sadly. He forced his thoughts to the other frying pans he had in the metaphorical fire. "Comm, contact Major Chowdhury. Tell her I need a report, then get me *Dagger*."

"Aye, sir."

"Commodore, this is Lieutenant Grant," came the response after a slight delay.

"What is your status, Lieutenant?"

"Sir, we were hit pretty hard amidships and forward. We still have 94% capacity on the engines and we lost three missile launchers. Both forward lasers are out of action, but we are still capable of defending ourselves."

"How about casualties."

Grant seemed to hesitate slightly, as if he were moving to areas where he didn't want to go, then straightened and began, "Captain Johnson is severely injured and we lost several officers and crew from the main bridge. There are nearly sixty known casualties, including twenty-four dead in the forward spaces. Fifteen still missing. The medical team is working on the captain. I'll let you know as soon as I have an update from them, sir."

"Thank you, Lieutenant. Your ship fought well and was a credit to the Warner Space Navy. Please relay that to your crew."

"Thank you, sir."

"Brighton out." He called *Yargus* and relayed the same message and was happy to hear there had been no fatalities on that ship despite heavy damage.

Brighton sat back in his chair and tried to relax while his first message traveled the distance from their present position to the gate control station and Major Chowdhury could respond. He considered his next steps, trying to forget the friend who was still fighting for her life in *Dagger*.

He could see only two paths to pursue going forward. The open presence of foreign warships in a Warner-owned system was not only an act of war, but did not speak favorably about the conditions of the Warner citizens on the system's only inhabited planet, Granada. Brighton already knew the orbital shipbuilding platform was in Forrest hands. Undoubtedly, the planetary surface was as well. All Chowdhury's Marines had either been tasked to take back Gate Control or else had accompanied Samuels to take the destroyer that was completing its builder trials. Brighton did not have nearly enough personnel to begin a ground campaign on the surface of Granada until he could receive reinforcements from Warner Fleet.

The second major consideration was that neither Cosina nor the Admiralty Board had any idea about the scope of the disaster that was brewing out here in the fringes. The suppositions and clues that Brighton had been able to forward did not rise to the degree of proof that would be needed to confront DaGama and Forrest at the highest levels. For that, he or his representative, would need to carry evidence of this incursion back to Earth.

"Sir, message from Major Chowdhury."

"Shunt it to my console, Ensign."

"Aye, sir."

He looked to his screen and saw Chowdhury's image filling it. She began to make her report without waiting for any response. With the time lag to the station, he had expected that.

"Sir," she began, "the Forresters are contained in sections seven through nine. We hold Gate Control, Engineering, and the External Weapons Control Center. They have approximately twenty-three civilian hostages in their section with them, but the majority of the Warner citizens have been liberated. To this point, we have sixteen casualties among our Marines with three fatalities. There are estimates of over one hundred civilian casualties, but the reports are not clear at this time. Many of those casualties might have occurred before we landed. Our current plan is to contain the Forresters at the perimeter of section nine and try to work our way in through section seven. We estimate we should have control of the station within the next two to three hours. What are your orders, sir?"

He looked at all of his screens.

Brighton sat back in his seat, closed his eyes and began to rub his forehead slowly. After a few moments, he sat back up, straightened and motioned to Lyle at the comm.

"Prepare to record a message to Major Chowdhury."

"Aye, sir. Ready."

Brighton took a deep breath and pushed the switch on his chair arm to start the recording.

"Major, you are to proceed as you see fit in any remaining combat situations. Consider the Forresters to be in a state of war with the Warner Family and take whatever actions you feel are necessary to protect Warner lives. We are en route to the station and should arrive 116 minutes from now," he glanced at his chrono, "at approximately 1855.

We will use the Gate Control Station as our base for now. All wounded from the three ships will be transferred to the station as well as available medical personnel. Please have all available Marines ready to embark onto *Dagger*. We will be headed back to the planet as soon as possible.

"Message sent, sir."

"Comm, also send movement orders to *Dagger* and *Yargus* to rendezvous with Major Chowdhury at Gate Control."

"Aye-aye, Commodore."

"Very well. Helm, make our best speed to the Gate Control."

"Aye, sir."

CHAPTER 24
19 October
WNS *Peru*

Ensign Roberts made way for the Felix cousins to go past her through the doorway, then poked her head in. "Are you ready for me, Captain?"

"Yes, Jherri. Come in. Grab a seat."

Rather than allowing the meeting to become that casual, Roberts stopped behind the indicated seat and came to attention. "Captain Samuels, I need to apologize for my earlier insubordination, and I present myself for disciplinary action."

Samuels pressed the heels of her hands into her temples and let out a long breath. "Oh, will you sit down," she said exasperatedly.

Roberts hesitated, then sunk into the chair.

"Look, Jherri, I've been advised that I need to come down hard on you, in order to bolster my position as the leader."

"Yes, ma'am. I've heard the same."

"Not my philosophy."

"Pardon?"

"Look, there are a lot of different management styles, right?"

Roberts looked at Samuels as if she hadn't quite understood the question.

"Yes, ma'am."

"Well, the Navy and the Marines have decided that everyone should use the one they know best. But that one doesn't fit my way of doing things, so I'll do things my way instead."

Roberts looked at Samuels as if she was still on the outside of an aquarium trying to understand the fish floating inside.

"So, what is your way of doing things?"

"According to 'The Way Things Are to Be Done,' I have to make an example of you because you've disparaged my competency."

"Yes, ma'am, I heard that from one of the Marines."

Samuels nodded to her friend.

"I heard it from two of the other Marines. But that is not the *only* way to resolve this problem. From what I can tell, the best way to deal with you is not to deal with you."

Roberts shook her head.

"How's that?"

Samuels leaned across the table and tapped on it.

"Okay, general policy is that if someone criticizes the one in charge, then it could lead to distrust or lack of confidence in the leader, low morale, that sort of thing."

Roberts leaned in slightly, nodding her head.

"Okay, following you so far."

Samuels leaned back in her seat and let it swing slightly under her.

"But coming down hard on critics can have the opposite effect. It can make the leader look like they're trying to shore up their own confidence. I think the best way to appear to be a strong leader is to lead. Have a plan. Have a vision. Share the vision with everyone you talk to. Get them to support you because you know what you're doing, and they want to be going the same way you're going. Then it doesn't matter whether you're criticized or not, because others already trust your leadership. When someone criticizes a strong leader that the people trust, it's the critic that looks bad."

"So...you're not going to relieve me of duty, or bring me up on charges?"

"No. Nothing like that."

"Then what are you going to do?"

"Nothing."

"Nothing?"

"Are you seriously jealous of me?"

The sudden shift caught her off guard. "No."

Samuels raised an eyebrow.

"Not exactly," Roberts amended.

"All right, then, can you follow orders if they come from me without complaining in front of the crew?"

"Yes. Absolutely."

"Good. Then the other issue doesn't really matter."

"It doesn't matter that you beat me to lieutenant?"

Samuels smiled. "In the Academy, when you had your career all mapped out, when did you expect to make lieutenant?"

This second abrupt change in topic caught her by surprise all over again.

"Uh, three years."

Samuels' eyebrows lifted slightly.

"Pretty ambitious."

Roberts smiled but didn't drop her gaze. Samuels nodded and her lips straightened into a thin line.

"Right. That's a good summary of you. Pretty and ambitious."

Roberts sat up straighter and her eyes narrowed.

"Hopefully, that's not all there is to me."

Samuels waved a hand and laughed slightly.

"No. Sorry. I just had your ambition pointed out to me less than an hour ago by those Marines and I was just thinking about what they said. Anyway, the reason I am saying it doesn't matter, is that I can almost guarantee you'll beat your planned schedule by at least a couple of years."

Roberts let the anger slide from her face as she tried to piece together where Samuels was going with this.

"What do you mean?"

Samuels tapped lightly on the table in front of her.

"Well, let's make a quick review of your current resume." Another tap on the table. "Top of her class at the Academy." Tap. "Junior officer on a high-security prototype." Tap. "Staff

168

officer to a commodore, which is traditionally a billet for a lieutenant." Tap. "Executive officer on a ship in combat, another lieutenant's slot." A double tap. "And, to top it all off, Warner is almost certainly going to war over this whole situation, and as the Navy gears up to a war footing, promotions happen more frequently."

Roberts was thoughtful for a moment. Then she shook her head.

"Yeah, but you still beat me to lieutenant."

Samuels leaned back and smiled.

"Well, first, it wasn't exactly my choice." She held up a hand as Roberts started to lean forward to make a comment. "I'm not complaining, mind you, but my promotion was not a personal assault on you. Second, I can't undo it. Even if I wanted to, I couldn't.

"And third," she smiled to take the sting out of her words, "life is tough. Learn to deal with it."

Roberts let out a slight grimace and looked up with a small grin.

"Yeah. I've heard that advice before. And why *is* everything a list with you."

Samuels looked over at her friend, and let her in on the secret.

"It's a mental trick to keep from forgetting anything. Now, enough chit-chatting. Let's go over your plans to raid the shipyards."

* * * * *

"Well hello, handsome! What brings you down to the hind end of the ship?"

Eric Aichele and Jill Burton had just passed through the hatch into the Power Control Room in search of the speaker, but it was clear she had eyes only for the short-haired gunnery sergeant.

"Rounding up strays, unfortunately for you, Giannini. Burton and I need to get all the Marines you've got working on the engines back up to the boatbay and ready to deploy for the raid."

"Not a problem, Gunny. Most of them think they're on guard duty anyway. They're just lounging around, 'keeping an eye on things.' As if a Marine could do engineering work, right?"

Aichele pulled back in mock offense.

"I have it on very good authority that Warner Marines are capable of completing any task, real or imagined. All of us are three meters tall, forged of mystical alloys, strong as an elephant, and imbued with the stamina of ten men."

"Now there is a claim I'd like to put to the test."

Aichele grinned, and Burton cleared her throat.

"Not to put too much of a damper on things, but we've got a time limit here."

"Right," Aichele said, the grin disappearing. "Ensign Roberts says she assigned fourteen troops to you. Where can I find them?"

"Fourteen? Are you sure?" Giannini got a distant look and began ticking her fingers. "Preston and Fleer are moving cables to interstitial 1. Gomez, in the power room, has five of them with him. There are three with the team isolating a localized fault in the CNC lines up on A deck. That's all of them I know about. If there's four more, I don't know where to find them."

"Burton, why don't you gather the ones in the power room and on deck A. I'll head to interstitial 1 and send them to the briefing, then look for the others. Don't have them wait for us to start."

"Okay, Gunny."

"How about if I go with you to find your missing Marines?" Giannini said, after Burton had left.

"Do you have time for that?"

"I've got fifty top priorities right now, so probably not. One of those priorities is to get updates from all the teams and see when we can start testing, though."

Aichele grinned again. "Lead on, McDuff." he said, gesturing with the arm on his less injured side at the hatch.

"Who's McDuff?"

"No idea. It's just something my dad always says."

Conversation halted while they maneuvered their way out of the crowded and active engineering section. Once forward of the bulkhead that separated Engineering from the rest of the ship, they took the starboard ladderway up toward the interstitial space between A and B decks, at a slower pace than Giannini was used to.

"Are you all right, Eric? I can deliver your message for you, if the stairs are too much."

"I'll be fine," Aichele winced.

"I'd heard you were wounded in the fighting. How bad was it?"

"I've had worse." Giannini could tell it was taking an effort for him to ascend, and that speaking was making it harder, so she waited until they had stopped at the landing before continuing.

"Have you actually had worse injuries, or is that just what you tell people to get them to stop bothering you?"

Aichele's boyish grin reappeared. "You know me well, Crystal. While it is true that I've had worse injuries than this, this is the first time I've been this banged up without spending weeks on the sick roll."

"No evasions, how bad is it?"

"Three cracked ribs, two broken, punctured lung, lacerated kidney, burns, contusions, and a few torn muscles. Doctor Johnson said everything is glued back together, but not completely healed. She did as much as she could without an immobile patient."

"So why aren't you immobile?"

It was a simple question, and it had a simple answer, but Aichele paused before responding. He knew Giannini didn't see life the way he did, and he didn't want to come off sounding condescending. For Crystal, the Navy was her job; for Eric, the

Marines was more than that. The Corps defined who he was as a person.

"Because I can't do anything else but this. I can't lie down and sit this out while others are taking risks and there's anything I can contribute. It's just not in me."

Giannini said, "I know," before leaning in and kissing him. It wasn't a short kiss, and when they broke contact, Eric was speechless. "That's in case you manage to kill yourself before I have a chance later.

"Now, you may not take orders from Dr. Johnson, but I'm running Engineering now, until they decide to lock me up, and you are going to take mine. I am not having you climbing and ducking and weaving through the guts of the ship in your condition. You are going to stand right here on this landing until I come back out with the Marines you're looking for. Clear?"

"Yes, ma'am. And...thank you."

"For running your errands for you, or teaching you how to kiss?" she asked, but disappeared into the hatch before he could pick either response.

CHAPTER 25
19 October
WNS *Peru*

Aichele walked into the briefing with the last four Marines, whom he found in an unused room on D deck playing cards, and tried to stand unobtrusively at the back. The four others with him had the same desire to be as unnoticed as possible, but for different reasons. The others wanted their goldbricking to be overlooked; Aichele wanted no one to forbid him expressly from going on the raid.

Ensign Roberts stood at the front, leading the briefing. Already past the approach and insertion portions of the plan, she was handing out assignments to individuals and groups.

"Corporal Braithwaite will take two squads and search the three lowest levels. Given what information we have from when the yards were under Warner control, that is the most likely storage area for missiles. In addition to munitions, look for anything on the list in Appendix A of your briefing folio. The list is prioritized, so you know what to grab first if you have to choose. Two engineers will be accompanying you, Silva and Maldonado. They are authorized to change the priorities on the list or add something new if they see something worth grabbing, but they are *not* authorized to issue orders of any kind. If either of them do anything to compromise safety or security, you have my permission to render them unconscious. Clear?"

"Yes, ma'am." Braithwaite acknowledged with a grin.

Silva and Maldonado looked pale.

"Sergeant Myer will lead two squads through the main level and the level just above. The same parameters apply for your team, and you'll have Reyes and Smith with you."

"Understood, ma'am."

"Mdembe will take one squad to the top level. You'll have the same priority list if you find supplies up there, but we're expecting that level to be mostly administrative offices. If you find anything which might implicate the Forresters, you are to take it or copy it. We don't have time to search records and determine what is useful during this mission, so just grab it and go. Cipriano Felix will be accompanying you. Mr. Felix *is* authorized to issue orders; as the ship's bosun, he is technically in the chain of command. That being said, Cipi, I would advise you not to try to tell these Marines how to fight. They know their jobs."

Mdembe and Cipriano both nodded acknowledgement.

"Two more squads are being held in reserve at the breach point, led by Corporal Vo. I will be there also, along with twenty from the engineering department whose job will be to move equipment and ordnance once we've located what we need. Vocom circuits for each squad are assigned and listed in Appendix C. Command authority is on circuit 4. Call in if you encounter resistance or if you spot items on our shopping list.

"Any questions?"

Cipi spoke up almost before the words were out of Roberts' mouth. "Will we Granadans be armed?"

Roberts turned and looked at the man.

"Those accompanying the advance Marines will be issued light protective gear and sidearms. That is for personal protection only. Their job is not to fight, but to advise on the scene. Those Granadans held in reserve will be unarmed, but are not expected to enter any area not already secured."

"Are we short of weapons?"

Roberts paused a moment before speaking. "That's not an easy question to answer. Thanks to Captain Samuels, we have access to the ship's armory, which was almost empty, as we had been told to expect. That means we basically have what we brought with us, and what we've taken from the Forresters killed or captured. The problem is that we don't know how much firepower we will need to hold this ship, and we don't know if we can replace the ammunition we expend on this mission from what we are able to locate at the yards. So yes, we are short of weapons and ammunition as far as what would be ideal. If we can't find both long-range weapons and close-quarters ammunition, we're going to be in a very difficult position.

"That's not the reason we're not arming everyone, though. Everyone who is expected to come within shooting distance of the enemy will be armed. The rest are going to keep their heads down until the shooting is over."

"What if we could have a better idea of where to find what we need? What would that be worth to you?"

Roberts' eyes narrowed, and her voice became harsh. "Mr. Felix, I am not about to bargain with you to get information which could potentially save the lives of my people. If you know something that will help us, I want it added to this briefing. Now."

"Do not threaten me, chica," he said in a low tone that had every Marine in the room shifting positions. They had all been in enough bar fights to recognize that feeling that things might be about to happen.

Cipi sensed it too, apparently, and, not liking the odds, modified his tone. Most of the Marines visibly relaxed at his next words. "Perhaps the way I phrased the question gave you the wrong impression, Ensign. I do not know anything about what is to be found at Caspar, or where we could find any of the items for which we seek. But I do have a GU contact in the communications room there. I was thinking that it might be possible to get them to do the scouting for us, before we arrive. However, that's asking her group to take a big risk, especially with so little notice. These people have survived by not taking risks which might be avoided if there is no equivalent reward."

"And Warner Marines clearing out all the Forresters on their station is not sufficient reward?"

"Ay caray, girl! Do you think this is going to be a pleasure cruise?" Felix looked from face to face, and while the tension was back, it was clear that none of them grasped his meaning.

"'Clearing out all the Forresters,' you said. What sort of security force are you expecting to have to deal with?"

"Well," Roberts began tentatively, "our records of Caspar from three years ago show a security detail of forty Marines, with twelve on duty at all times. We used that as our basis, and estimated double that, to be conservative."

Cipi's mouth opened and stayed that way for several seconds. "So, two dozens on duty, and eighty total? You *are* expecting a pleasure cruise.

Felix held up a hand at Robert's angry expression.

Cipi shook his head.

"Look, how many Granadans are on this ship?"

"Ninety-five."

"Right. And how many Forresters were here to provide 'security forces?'"

"Uh, 51. But this is a different situation. This is a military ship, and you would expect more military presence here."

"You're still looking at this in the wrong way. You people *still* do not understand what we Granadans have been suffering through the past two years! This ship was not commissioned yet. There were no navy people here. This was simply another place of work until you arrived. And the Forresters have discovered that it takes about half as many guards as slaves to maintain order.

"You and your team are planning to take seven squads, which is what, 50 or 60 soldiers? Like I said, I don't know any specifics about the situation at Caspar, but I would be estimating the same ratio there as here. There are probably

5,000 Granadans working there, so there's roughly 2,500 Forrest Marines with whom you will have to deal."

Now it was Roberts' turn to let her jaw drop.

CHAPTER 26
19 October
Forrest Assault Shuttle

"We're all buttoned up, Colonel."

Finally, Kadison thought.

"Thank you, Sergeant. Please inform Lieutenant Oliver that we are ready to lift off, and that we approve the current flight plan."

"Yes, ma'am."

The added weight of takeoff pushed her into her acceleration couch, but it was an easy two gees. She wasn't worried about the extra weight as she knew they could enjoy their anti-gravity plates as soon as they got out of the atmosphere. Besides, her Marines were trained to take much more, and usually did, but Oliver knew the brass were all watching, and he opted not to push his ships at anything approaching their limits. She hoped he wasn't planning to pussyfoot along all the way to target. She hadn't looked closely at the acceleration numbers when the flight plan was sent to her for approval. By that point, her attention to detail had already been shredded by the incredible number of decisions that she had been forced to make.

As it was, the course they were going to take was far too circuitous for Kadison's liking. They were planning to come at their target the long way around, so that their approach would be from sunward. Kadison's protestations that speed and force were the two essential elements in the operation's success fell on deaf ears, and eventually she'd accepted this trajectory just to keep from wasting more time arguing.

They should have been en route within a half hour of Warner's move to take *Scythe*. Delays only made the enemy's position stronger. You would think that, at some point in their careers, someone might have explained that to at least one of the generals or admirals who compromised and bickered this plan into existence. If someone had, there was no evidence of the fact.

Kadison watched the gradual darkening of the viewport as they left Granada's atmosphere behind. The pressure shifted to the antigravity plates but she could still feel some of the extra push from the engines that were driving them to their target. The compensation plates on these assault shuttles weren't perfect yet. There was no change in the pressure, and there wouldn't be until it increased for the attack run. At least, if she was remembering the final version of the plan correctly.

"Colonel Kadison?" Lieutenant Oliver's voice sounded in her helmet's earpiece. "Could you come up to the flight deck?"

"On my way."

The slight changes in gravity from the plates were not burdensome while in her seat, but standing and walking forward under those conditions took more effort and focus than she had expected it would. Just another reason to curse the Warners and their firm, gripping control of the antigrav systems and engines. Warner and Sterling, the two leading Space-faring Families, jointly owned Gravitas, Inc., the only source of high-grade grav plates. And just like everything else they owned, Warner milked the market for all it would give. Price was a few less important consideration than operational security, but as a result, both the propulsion and compensation systems on these shuttles was far from flawless.

Fortunately, her assigned seat was next to the forward bulkhead separating the Marines from the flight deck, for just this reason; so she could be consulted if there happened to be any change in the plan.

When the hatch opened, Oliver didn't wait for any pleasantries. "There's activity at the target. Looks like their assault shuttles that have been standing guard are moving back toward the ship."

"Any other information that might explain why?"

"No, Colonel. What you see is what we know."

"Well, until we know more, I don't think there's any reason to alter our plans."

"I concur. Just wanted you to be aware of the change."

"Thank you, Lieutenant. I'll return to my seat, but let me know if anything else changes."

She turned and thumped heavily back to her seat and was just about to secure the restraints when Lieutenant Oliver's voice sounded in her helmet's earpiece once again. "Both shuttles are entering the launch bay simultaneously."

"Both at once? Are you thinking emergency evac?"

"Not sure yet. For all I know, maybe that's standard practice for Warners."

"If they are abandoning the ship, does that alter our plan?"

Oliver chuckled. "That's what I was going to ask you, Colonel."

Kadison smiled, though Oliver couldn't see it. If she had to put up with cumbersome operational requirements, at least they'd given her a pilot that didn't seem difficult to work with.

A thought occurred to her, and she voiced it.

"Any chance they're clearing the ship because they saw us launch and know we're headed their way?"

"Possible. Central Command cut them off from access to the navigation network, but who knows what gear they brought with them? My guess would be no, that we'd still be lost in the clutter of activity around the planet. We're not headed right for them at the moment, so even if they suspect we're targeting them, there's no evidence to support it yet. Certainly not enough to cause a panicked exit."

Kadison had presumed the same, but wasn't familiar enough with this kind of operation to feel confident in her gut feelings. That Oliver came to the same conclusion was comforting.

"All right, Lieutenant. I think for now we stick with the plan and await developments."

"Seems reasonable to me, Colonel. Oliver out."

As it turned out, further developments were only ten minutes in coming.

"Colonel Kadison? This is Lieutenant Oliver on the flight deck."

"Go ahead."

"I've got both of those Warner shuttles separating from *Scythe* now."

"Heading back to that destroyer out-system?"

"Well, that's the odd thing. It looks like they're headed toward system west."

"West? What's that direction?" Kadison was trying to pull a system map up on her helmet's display even as she asked, and she found the obvious answer the same time Oliver answered.

"If I had to guess, I'd say they were making for the shipyards."

CHAPTER 27
19 October
WNS *Peru*

"Captain to the bridge!" sounded for the third time over the all-hands net.

Samuels came through the door at a run. "Status," she yelled as soon as her first foot hit the bridge deck. Lieutenant Tucker, one of the Marines, stood from the command chair. "Captain on the bridge!

"Confirmation that we have an inbound force with hostile intentions, Captain."

Samuels checked the main board and absorbed the salient points almost instantly. Fifteen *Kilo*-class assault shuttles, or whatever the equivalent class was called by the new Forrest Navy, were directly to sunward of their position. It might have been a good tactic to mask their approach if *Peru* hadn't been getting her tactical feeds from *Yargus*. From that angle, their approach was not disguised in the least.

"How long at current closing velocity?" she asked, turning to the scan station and only then realizing that it was Amber Sullivan who sat there.

"One hour, thirty-eight minutes with current relative speeds and acceleration. Two hours, forty-two, if they turn over for zero-zero intercept."

Monica was about to ask more questions, but realized a part of her mind had already done the math, and the results were there when she needed them. There wasn't anything they could do, except delay the inevitable. The approaching force already had too great a velocity advantage for them to be able to overcome it. If they ran directly away, the force would keep building on their accumulated speed and eventually catch them. If they ran a different direction, it only meant they would be caught sooner as the ships cut across the arc between them. They had no weapons to hold them off, so there was no way to keep them from boarding. And fifteen shuttles of that size would carry a *lot* of Marines.

Unless they could do something to alter the situation in the next two hours, they had no options at all.

"Captain," Sullivan interrupted Samuels' thoughts. "Roberts in CR1 needs a word, if you're not too busy."

"'If I'm not too busy,' she says," Monica mumbled. "Tell her I'm on my way. Ensign Roberts' assignment has just become our only chance. Hopefully, she just needs final approval and everything will proceed on schedule."

"Of course, Captain," Amber said, and Samuels wasn't sure if she were being mocked or not.

"Your bridge, Mr. Tucker," Monica said, and headed back out the security hatch she had entered only a minute before.

* * * * *

"Sorry to pull you into this, Captain, but there's going to need to be major revisions to the plan I went over with you earlier." Ensign Roberts rose and shifted over one seat as she spoke, allowing Samuels to slip into the spot at the end of the conference table. The newly-minted captain let out a long breath as she sat.

"Of course, there will," Samuels mumbled. "All right, let's have it," she directed loudly enough to be heard.

"Capitán," Cipi began, inclining his head in deference, "I think the original planning has underestimated the number of Forrester combatants likely to be at Caspar Shipyards. By a lot."

"How many are you expecting there?"

"Two to three thousand."

Samuels' eyes swung immediately to Major Tunney, but he did not comment. He didn't look happy, though. Samuels' mind tried to process the latest information, looking at what part of the current plan might be kept and modified to account for this change.

After thirty seconds, she leaned forward and pressed her palms into her temples. There was *no* part of the plan that could be kept, except that they would still use the assault shuttles to get there. Moreover, there was *no* chance of success.

Hit and run tactics, which would normally be called for against a significantly more numerous foe, could not be employed, because they would need to hold that position for a considerable time to move the materiel and ordnance they needed. With no chance of grabbing stand-off weapons, there was no chance of preventing boarders, and thus, no chance of keeping 900 or so Marines from taking this ship away from her and her people.

Or, put another way, no chance, period.

"Options?" she asked of the room, hoping someone had an idea that was at least possible.

Cipi replied hesitantly. "I may have a way to get a better idea of the current situation at the shipyards."

"How so?"

"I have a contact in GU that works in the Caspar communications department. She and her contacts may be able to tell us how the soldiers are deployed, and where to find the missiles we need to fight the Forresters here on *Redentor*."

"*Peru*," Samuels corrected automatically.

Cipi smiled. "As you say, Capitán. But, to get that information, and get it to us quickly, they will need to take considerable risks. They will not wish to do this if there is not some benefit to them."

Samuels' eyes narrowed, just as Roberts' had a few minutes earlier, but the captain remained silent for several seconds while she considered. "That seems reasonable to me," she finally said, and meant it. Quid pro quo was so ingrained into her way of thinking from her business world upbringing, that such a position on the part of GU was not at all surprising. "What do you think we might offer to enlist their aid?"

"Hope and weapons," Cipi answered at once. "But mostly weapons."

Samuels smiled despite herself. She was growing to like the brash Granadan since they'd come to an understanding.

"I've already explained that we're short of supplies ourselves," Roberts interjected. "We just don't have anything to spare."

"I know, XO, but I've just come from the bridge. We're expecting company in less than two hours, maybe as little as one. And if they off-load all those shuttles into *Peru*, we're done."

The pronouncement left the meeting room silent, but Samuels moved on as if she hadn't noticed. Entering a routing code into her display, she waited for a response.

"Bridge, Tucker."

"Lieutenant, this is Samuels. Has the incoming force begun decelerating, and if so, at what time?"

"Yes, Captain. They initiated braking four and a half minutes ago."

"I just had a thought, but I need Tactical to tell me if it might work. Ask Sullivan to see if it is possible for us to accelerate toward them far enough that they won't be able to slow down enough to engage with us, and if that's possible, what's our window to get moving?"

"On it, Captain," she heard Sullivan's voice in the background.

"Thanks. Samuels clear." She closed the link without waiting for Tucker to respond. "Well, if we wait, that gives us almost two hours to work with."

The rest of the people in the room didn't seem very happy about the news that they probably had an extra forty minutes to live.

"Mr. Felix, this contact of yours, can we set up two-way communications, or is it more of a communications dead-drop arrangement?"

Cipi checked the chronometer on the bulkhead. "I can probably set up a standard vocom connection right now. She'll be on duty in the comm center."

"Okay, I have another plan, but no time to explain it. Major, I need at least twenty Marines who can think on their feet and can look menacing. Jherri, I need all the undamaged Forrest uniforms rounded up. I need someone who can rekey an ident pod, maybe Burton or Sullivan. Try Burton first; Sullivan is checking on Plan A. Take Pablo Felix with you and talk to the Granadans. See if you can find thirty volunteers for a very dangerous assignment. Make sure they're also the kind that can keep their cool under pressure. Mr. Felix, let's go talk to your contact.

Samuels stood and motioned to the rest of the team.

"Let's move people. We do not have enough time as it is."

CHAPTER 28
19 October
WNS *Peru*

Fernandez, a girl who looked too young to Aichele to be allowed out unchaperoned, killed the torch, pushed up her face shield and looked up at the Gunnery Sergeant.

"How's that?"

Aichele inspected the weld on the ad hoc barricade by eye, then dropped his own face shield back down and selected microscopic view, then subsonic imaging. The seam wasn't completely cool yet, but he could tell it was quality work, without any bubbles or other imperfections.

"Fine as frog's hair."

Fernandez squinted, trying to decide if that was a good or a bad thing.

Aichele smiled at her uncertainty.

"It's perfect. If we have time, I'd like to add braces at the center and each side to strengthen against high-energy rounds. Shooting ports would be nice, too, but I doubt we'll have that kind of time."

Fernandez motioned with her gloved hand across the corridor space.

"If you know how big and where, I can cut a hole for you in half a minute. Braces wouldn't take all that long either, if they're already cut. Three beams, two ends, a line at top and bottom, that's twelve welds...maybe twenty minutes?"

Aichele was surprised at the speed she claimed she could achieve, but remembered how quickly and surely the current weld had been made. He considered a moment. "Where are you assigned next, and when do you have to be there?"

She shook her head and pointed at him.

"I'm assigned wherever you say, Gunny, but the welder has to be in corridor B12 in five minutes for that barricade."

"Okay, put holes here, here and here. High enough for an upward angle from a prone position. Then one at either end about yea high." Aichele indicated a point just as far down as he could reach without causing his ribs to complain. "Make the holes about five centimeters across. Then get the torch down to the next corridor, and meet me in Engineering."

She nodded and made a half-hearted salute with her gloved hand.

"All right, Jefe. Consider it done."

Aichele left her to the task, satisfied that she knew her business. The same could not be said of all those he had checked on, and he needed to follow up with them before heading to Engineering and asking for braces to be cut. If there were people available to cut them. If there was time for them to be cut. If they lived long enough to put them in place.

Aichele was aware there was way too much "if" for his personal comfort.

* * * * *

Brassey was still in the comm room when Samuels and Cipi arrived, and it seemed like he might put up a fuss about being kicked out, but something in the captain's demeanor told him it was not the time to quote regs. He cleared everyone out and sealed the door himself.

Once isolated, Cipi wasted no time in configuring the familiar equipment to his liking, and keying the mic.

"Caspar Control, Lima-one-niner requesting position check."

"Lima-one-niner, Caspar, wait one."

It was more than one minute, but eventually a new voice responded.

"Lima-one-niner, Caspar. We're showing a clean scan for quadrant three."

"Try quad five."

"Cipi, it's good to hear your voice. We've been worried since we heard your ship was being deployed. So, what has you making emergency contact?"

"The Warners hit the ship and took it over. I've got their captain here with me. She wants to talk with you. We're in a tight spot over here, Elena, and we need some help."

"Do you trust her?"

"Yes, I think she genuinely wants to do right by us. I trust her."

"*You* trust her? A Warner?" Elena let out a low whistle. "That must be some captain. Wait a second. Is she good-looking?"

"Yes, she is, but that's not what this is about. And I don't have time to banter. I vouch for her, and here she is."

"Elena. My name is Lieutenant Monica Samuels, and I need to know what the situation is at Caspar."

"Heightened alert. The PMs know there's a Warner warship in the system, but not much more than that. We're out of the communications loop for operations, and we don't have system-level scanners, just the local space navigation type."

There was something familiar about Elena's voice that tickled the back of Samuels' brain, but she pushed it aside for a more appropriate time. "How much oversight do you get from the Forresters, and how much access do you have into their systems?"

Elena hesitated. "I'll need to review that with Travis before I can answer definitively," she finally said.

Cipi cut in, "Elena, I recognize the code word, and I assure you, I am not being coerced. Jelly bean. Now, please answer the captain's question. We really need to move fast."

Elena was still not ready to reveal anything meaningful. "You sound like Cipi, and you know the all-clear phrase, but I don't know if I can trust you. We can't use the bandwidth for visual comms without being noticed, and even if you look like Cipi, and are Cipi, you still might be coerced into what you're saying. We've been led into traps before. Unless you have some way to convince me otherwise, I think we're done."

The last phrase tickled Samuels' memory again, this time bringing a name and image to her mind. "Elena, can you hold the line for a minute?"

She sounded doubtful, but Elena agreed. Samuels reached over and muted the audio pickup, then turned to Cipi. "Is Elena a native Granadan?"

Cipi looked at Samuels for a long while, puzzling out what she was getting at. "Why do you ask this question?"

Samuels was also a while in answering; for her part, trying to find a way to be honest without giving too much away. "It may be that I have met Elena before, but if she was born on Granada, she would not be the person I am thinking of. If she is who I'm thinking of, I may be able to convince her to trust me."

Again, Cipi did not answer at once, analyzing her words for as much information as he could. Finally, he decided that he didn't know enough about the captain to decide if it was important or not, but he was certain that Samuels was holding something back.

"She was not born on Granada. I do not know where she was born, but I know that she was an officer on a freighter that was trapped here more than a year ago. The Forresters put her to work in communications because she had some experience there."

"A Warner freighter?"

This question also seemed odd to Cipi, and he spent many seconds trying to understand why this point would matter to the young woman, or why it would even occur to her. Most Warners assumed everything came from Warner. Something seemed different about this girl, but he didn't have enough pieces to put the puzzle together.

"I don't know for sure, but I doubt it. The Forresters would not have trusted her if she were a full Warner citizen instead of one of the affiliated trading families."

It was still a remote possibility that this was the Elena Monica knew, but at least nothing Cipi had said removed all chance. "Would you step out while I talk to Elena?" she asked, turning back to activate the mic.

"No." The flat word stopped Samuels and she turned back to face him.

"Why?"

"You're hiding something, something important. I think the reason you want me to leave is that you have intelligence that is not good for Granadans, and you can't share it with Elena unless she isn't Granadan. If that is the case, I want to know what this information is."

Samuels' thin face started to turn red as her frustration started to kindle her anger.

"That's not it."

Cipi's anger also seemed to be kicking in as his lips got thinner and his moustache narrowed out across his upper lip as he spat the next sentence at Samuels.

"No? Then what is it?"

"It's—" She was about to say it was none of his business, but stopped herself in time. She fought down her anger and got herself under control. Their trust was just building and that would have crushed it in its infancy. She took a deep breath and started again.

"It's not that. I have no such information."

He was not quite ready to give in yet. He still didn't trust her or anything else that wasn't explained.

"Then what are you hiding?"

"You told Elena that you trust me, that you felt I intend to do right by you. You were right to trust me, and I do mean to help you and all Granadans in any way I can. Please believe that. And you're right that I am hiding something, something I intend to keep hidden. I may have to share it with Elena to prove my trustworthiness, though I won't if I can avoid it. It has nothing whatsoever to do with Granada. But it is personal information that may be harmful to me, individually, if it were to be known.

"Please, Cipi, can you simply trust me?"

"No," he finally said, after a long delay. "I *feel* I can trust you, Capitán, but that is not enough. I know only what I have seen of you and what you have told me. Before, I believed that was enough. Now I know that there is more to you than what I already know, and that you fear to share that part of you because of how I might react. In this case, I must assume that your fear is that I will withdraw my support of you if I know whatever you still hide. With that information, I must then conclude that you are right, and I must not support you any longer."

Samuels rubbed at her temples with her palms. *Why did nothing ever come easy?* There really was no viable option outside of sharing her secret. She had to have weapons to defend the ship and she had to have everyone working together. Had to. Otherwise, people were going to die, and Forrest was going to carry the day. Neither of those outcomes were worth her secret, even if they sent her to prison for it.

Samuels reached over and opened the vocom connection again.

"Are you still there, Elena?"

"Yes."

"Please hold on a little longer while I secure comms at my end."

Samuels left the line open while she logged into the communications control system as the ship's commanding officer. Setting up that account had been the very first thing she had done once the ship was secure. Thirty seconds later, all logging was disabled. Cipi could see and understand what she was doing, since this was his department, and Samuels made no effort to shield his view.

"Elena, Cipi tells me that you used to be an officer on a trading ship before your current position, is that right?"

"Yes," Elena answered hesitantly.

"Was that ship named *Freudian Ship,* by any chance?"

"I suppose Cipi told you that, too."

"I didn't ask that information of Cipi. I am familiar in my own right with many of the ships of Bybee family registry. Your voice sounded familiar when I first heard it, and I knew an Elena Chavez that served on that ship. In fact, I knew her before she was married, back when she was still Elena Patel. Is that you?"

"Quoting stats that the Forresters could look up is not going to convince me to trust you, if that's what you're thinking, Warner."

Samuels took a deep breath, then plunged in. "I am not a Warner. I am a Bybee. Your voice is familiar to me because I was on the *Freudian Ship* with you for four months; me and my father, Victor Bybee. In fact, you spent most of the first two months teaching me communication systems and cyphers. By the end, I was covering watches for you so you could take off with Ricky. When you and Ricky decided to get married, Dad offered our estate for the venue."

Samuels watched Cipi for some reaction, but there was none, until Elena responded and confirmed that she was the one Samuels remembered. There wasn't much of a reaction, even then, but he leaned in to better hear the exchange.

"Mica? Mica Bybee? No. There's no way. First, Mica would be...maybe 20 or 21 now. Certainly not old enough to be in command of a Warner strike force. And second, you can't join the Warner Navy without full Warner citizenship. The Bybees have almost always been affiliated with Warner, since their areas of business intersect, but full citizens they are not.

"Sorry, not buying it."

Samuels nodded slightly to herself as Elena spoke and then began as soon as she stopped.

"Okay, let's assume, for the sake of argument, that I'm telling you the truth. At one point, I confided in you and shared my middle name, which I have never liked. Do you remember it?"

"Samantha, I think."

"Cipi, what's my last name?"

"Samuels."

"And how old do I look?"

"You look about twelve."

"Very funny. How old do you believe I am?"

"I'm still not sure. You look very young, but you are deceptively wise. Perhaps eighteen, nineteen at most?"

"It's the freckles, isn't it? They always make me look like a little girl."

"Yes...I suppose so. That and the ponytail."

"I can't really do anything about either one of those. Navy regs; no loose hairstyles. If I braid it into a queue, I look even younger. I'm 23, just for the record. "

Elena cut in. "Did you say freckles? Cipi, what does she look like?"

"About 45, 50 kilos, 165 centimeters or so. Maybe a bit more. Brunette, with a little bit of red in it. Not many curves yet, but maybe after puberty — "

Elena heard a smacking sound. "She is also quite sensitive about her appearance, and fairly strong." Cipi added more faintly, as if he were farther away from the audio pickup.

"Cipi, we don't have time for your humor, if that's what you call it. Can we please stick to business?"

"Yes, Capitán," he said, though without any hint of remorse.

"Elena, do you believe me now? Will you accept I am who I say I am, and that I am not working with the Forresters?"

"Well, let's say I am partially convinced. But you still haven't given me any reasonable explanation of how you could have wound up in the Warner Navy."

Samuels ran her finger along her jawline and looked sidelong at Cipi, but decided there was no point in holding anything back from him at this point. *In for a penny...*

"All right, this is the half minute version, and I'll fill you in with the details if there's more time later." *If we live that long.*

"Do you remember, five or six years ago, when Bybee ships were being outbid on a lot of our contracts?"

"Yeah. I spent a very dull six months in Idyll while we tried to fill our holds."

"What no one outside of the head office knew was that was more than just the normal ups and downs of business. Hightower Interglobal managed to break into our secure corporate systems and found information on all of our sealed bids, plus the formula we used to calculate what we would bid on any new contract. Then they used that information to target our business, contracts we had won consistently for years, and bid just a little less than we did.

"Well, you can see the strategic advantage that gave them; more work and profit in the short-term, and less competition in the long-term if they could drive us out of business. Obviously, we had to do something about it, both on the business side, and also to secure our systems.

"On the business side, we got word out through normal channels with updated bids, and put misinformation into our files. Slowly, we started getting things moving again, but we took a big hit from typical income for all of the next year.

"Securing our servers again was a lot less straightforward. We contacted the Data Guild to contract them to plug all our leaks, and they were happy to help us, for a price. About halfway through the process, the DG wanted to know if we were interested in renegotiating the contract and adding a retaliation clause. They said they could force their way into Hightower and get us access to all their secrets, for an additional fee."

"You're not serious," Elena accused.

"I am very serious. It looks like DG has started a protection racket, where they're playing both sides off against each other, for a bigger profit.

"Well, it was clear how Hightower had gotten into our systems, and equally clear that we couldn't trust the DG to provide us with any long-term security. Unfortunately, they're also the only place we had to go to. They don't actually have a monopoly on system security, since almost all of the major Families have their own resources to draw on, but for us minor families, there aren't any other options."

"Unless you get what you need from one of the major Families," Elena guessed.

"Right. A Warner citizen could, say, enroll at the Naval Academy, and specialize in Data Security. Such a citizen could spend four years at the Academy, finish their initial cruise, ask for an extended leave, put together a top-of-the-line firewall, and then quietly finish off her eight-year minimum requirement."

"But why you?" Cipi asked. Samuels was pleased the questions sounded curious, without the overtones of suspicion which were evident earlier.

"Primarily, because it was illegal. And the consequences of discovery were so high. And not just for me personally. If I am found out, the backlash against Bybee Freight will be severe enough to close our doors forever. With the stakes that high, we couldn't trust anyone outside of the core family. And of the three cousins that were the right age range to be headed for university...well...let's just say the other two did not have the right traits for the job."

There was a laugh over the comm.

"Are you referring to Sebastian?" Elena asked.

"Yes. Him and Margarethe, though Maggie might also have been disqualified for a long-standing dispute between her mother and Aunt Carlotta."

"But how did you convince the Warners that you were a citizen?" Cipi asked now.

Samuels glanced at the chrono on the bulkhead. "Can we save details for later?"

"Yes, certainly." Cipi said, and Samuels felt the tension leave her shoulders.

"All right, Mica, I am convinced. What can I do to help?"

"First, you have to stop calling me Mica. That's a nickname that belongs to a different person."

"What do I call you instead?"

"Samuels, or even Monica, should be fine."

"She is Capitán Samuels, Elena. There can be no hint that you have a friendship with her. If you keep things formal, that should help."

"All right, let's get down to business, then, here's what we're going to need." Samuels began.

CHAPTER 29
19 October
WNS *Peru*

Samuels and Cipi were just turning the Vocom Room back over to Brassey and heading aft when Sullivan found them.

"Captain?"

"Amber. Have you met Mr. Felix?"

Sullivan nodded slightly at the young man.

"Briefly, yes."

"Ms. Sullivan," Cipi said, giving her a moderate bow.

Samuels looked at Sullivan and her serious expression.

"What did you bring me?"

"Bad news, I'm afraid. My analysis is complete, and there isn't any way to make your plan work. The inbound shuttles are not maxing out their drives; I'd estimate they're using no more than 80% of full thrust. With accel in reserve, they can match any move we make in the ranges that matter. We could probably pull away from them if we ran for it, since our top end is probably much higher, but even then, we'd be in their weapons envelope for at least three hours."

Samuels nodded and matched Sullivan's expression.

"And the odds of us keeping our engines running at max for three hours under fire are not high."

Sullivan did not nod but the indication of agreement was there. "Yes, ma'am. Microscopic."

"What about rekeying an IFF squawker? Did Roberts talk to you about that?"

Sullivan lifted her head slightly and looked curiously at Samuels. "No. Was she supposed to?"

"Well, you or Burton. I'll check with Roberts to make sure we can cover that angle. Anything else to report?"

"No, ma'am."

Samuels looked at Sullivan thoughtfully for a moment.

"Does it seem odd to you at all for you to call me ma'am, when we've been on first-name standing since the day we met?"

"Not at all, ma'am," Sullivan responded seriously. "You've always outranked me."

I'm still not sure I outrank you, Samuels thought, but let the matter drop. There was no time to pursue it, and Cipi had proven astute enough that she didn't want to expose him to the thought that there might be another secret out there for him to puzzle out.

"Cipi, have you had a chance to gauge the feelings of the crew?"

"Not really, Capitán. I have not had the time to sit back and discuss recent events with my colleagues over a drink." The line was delivered deadpan, but the hint of a smile made it clear that this was more of his droll wit at work.

Samuels turned back to Sullivan so he wouldn't see her eyes rolling.

"All right. So, we can't run for it," Samuels said, bringing the conversation back to the former subject. "I hate not having a backup plan, but sometimes you just have to play the cards you were dealt." Samuels turned back to Cipi. "Unless you have some ideas you're holding out on me? An ace up your sleeve, to continue the metaphor?"

"I cannot say if I have an alternative to offer, when I have no idea what it is that you plan."

Samuels stopped walking and stared at Cipi, then turned to Amber, who simply stared back blankly. "Garbage," Samuels cursed, then turned and jogged back forward. Felix and Sullivan glanced at each other, then moved to keep pace.

Samuels used the frame of the Vocom Room hatch to aid in her deceleration, poking her head in without fully entering. "Sergeant Brassey."

The named man jumped to his feet, startled. "Captain?"

"Please send a general page to all volunteers to gather in the boatbay for final briefing and departure."

"Yes, ma'am."

Samuels didn't wait to hear his acknowledgement, but was already moving aft again, Cipi and Amber in her wake. When they caught up, she said, "Sorry I haven't provided more details, but at this point, we don't have time for me to explain things twice. Since I haven't already shared, please point out any weaknesses you see in the plan as I describe it."

"As you say, Capitán," Cipi said noncommittally. Sullivan made no comment, nor indicated she had heard.

Samuels stopped. "I am serious, both of you. I don't care if you think it will make me look ineffective if you poke holes in my plan. What I am worried about is anticipating and dealing with any problem now, before it's too late to fix. I want everyone to come back alive. Anything that helps meet that goal is worth any embarrassment to me."

"As you say, Capitán," Cipi repeated, and Samuels wasn't sure if her words had had any effect at all. Regardless, she didn't have time to do any more convincing.

The ship-wide address system activated, and Sergeant Brassey's voice could be heard giving clear instructions that were much more detailed than those he had received. Cipi and Amber had nothing more to add before the three of them entered the expansive boatbay.

* * * * *

The bay was a study in cacophonous Brownian motion. Samuels made her way toward the aft end, where she could see Roberts talking with one of the Marines. Major Tunney arrived at the same time, and Samuels asked both of them for a report.

Finding things were prepared enough, including Burton's efforts to jury-rig two IFF transponders, she turned toward the gathered Warners and Granadans.

"Okay, listen up." The volume level dropped immediately, but it took a few additional seconds for the conversations to die down enough for the captain to be heard.

"All right. This is the part of an operation where the commanding officer comes in and delivers a rousing speech to motivate the troops." A few chuckles sounded here and there in the crowd. "Well, I haven't had time to learn any of those, and if the incoming Forrest assault shuttles are not motivation enough, I doubt anything I say will have any positive effect."

There were no chuckles this time, but the reminder of the likelihood that people would be dying soon cast a pall on the gathering. Samuels recognized the false step after it was made, and realized that it was the kind of flub an experienced officer wouldn't have made. For a moment, she wanted to just run and let someone else take over; Jherri would be happy to move into the slot. It was a fleeting urge, though. The job was hers and she would give her utmost to see it done. The task was Herculean in scope, but really no more impossible than the task of retaking *Pathfinder* had seemed a few months ago.

It came to her, then, how everyone else in the room must be viewing the mission they were undertaking. Except for the four people in the bay who had been through the struggle on her previous ship, and Jherri, with her own nearly insurmountable task, none of these people had faced odds this long before. Scanning the faces in front of her, she could see that there was little or no belief that they were going to survive this.

A second look showed her that all of them were going to move forward anyway, regardless of the odds against them.

But they needed a little faith if they were going to succeed, and, unfortunately, she was the only one who could give it to them.

She really didn't want to deliver a speech; hadn't remotely had the time to prepare one; but she could see that one was needed. And there was no time for her to build up their confidence in her abilities by demonstrating them. It was time, once again, to take the non-traditional approach. Instead of showing her competence, she was going to have to tell about it. Besides being contrary to her nature, it wasn't all that effective a means of engendering confidence. It was all she had time for now.

Maybe that wasn't exactly the right tack, either. They needed faith in her, but they also needed to believe in themselves.

"I'm glad to see that all of you are taking our situation seriously, because we are definitely in a tight spot. Fortunately, this is not a new experience for me, any more than it is for you. All of you have been in a tight spot for almost two years now. For most of you, fighting the Forresters directly has been more of a wish than a reality up to now. Instead, you've all had to keep your heads down and feet shuffling in order to avoid notice, just to survive. I know that all of you can do difficult things. The fact that you are still here proves that. Today, though, may be the most difficult thing anyone has ever asked of you, because before the day is over, you are going to be up against enemy Marines.

"This is not the first time I've taken on Forrest Marines. Most of you are fully aware of the odds against us. This is not the first time I've faced heavy odds. Many of you have realized that there is a good chance that you may not live through what is to come. As I said, this is not the first time I've gone up against Forrest Marines. But I'm still breathing, and they are not. This is not the first time I've risked my life to do what needed doing.

"So, here's what I think needs doing now. Forrest had no right to attack this system. They had no right to destroy your homes. They had no right to kill your friends and families. And they had no right to enslave an entire planet. For all of these things, they need to be brought to a reckoning."

She paused to let that sink in, and she could see the anger building in the faces turned her way. Now, instead of thinking about what might happen to them, they were thinking about what had already happened to them, and that this could be a way to get some retribution. That was almost as dangerous an attitude as the possibility of them freezing up, or giving up, but it was a necessary step in getting them in the right frame of mind. Now, she just needed to get them to harness that anger and focus it, and most of all, be patient.

"I have never been in the position you are in, so I won't pretend to know what you all are feeling. I can imagine, though, that all of you volunteered for this mission because you want to make the Forresters pay for what they have done. I guarantee you that before the day is over, we will have a chance to *start* exacting that payment.

"But a final reckoning cannot, absolutely cannot, happen with this phase of the plan. This operation depends on making the Forresters believe what we want them to believe. To see weakness where we are strong. To see surrender where there is defiance. To see the usual where there is something out of the ordinary. If you show them the truth in your faces, we will not be able to prepare ourselves to fight back, and the Forrest Family's final reckoning will be delayed.

"All of you have had to work in close contact with the enemy for months now, and I'm sure you've already learned how to put on a mask, so no one can see the real you. *That* is exactly what we need for this part of the plan. We need you to lock that anger and outrage and thirst for justice away inside you where no one can see it. I'm only asking for a short time. Once we are back on this ship, and we have the tools we need, you can let it all out. And *that* will be the time to make the Forresters pay.

"Can you all do that for the next few hours?"

Few spoke their agreement, but everyone else was nodding quietly. The anger that was there before was still there, but now it had been tempered and controlled behind a look of determination. It was exactly the attitude Samuels had been aiming for.

"All right, then. I apologize that we have not had time to brief you on this operation sooner, but there were too many details to arrange. If we had weeks of planning, though, I don't think we could have some up with anything more sure of success than what we are about to do to the Forresters. If everyone does their part, they will never see us coming.

"Here is what we're going to do..."

CHAPTER 30
19 October
WNS *Peru*

"I'm afraid, if there are more questions, we'll have to answer them on the way. We have to board now and get moving, or we'll miss our window. Mr. Mdembe, would you see to it?"

People began moving right away, and Samuels noted that the new bosun was helping Lieutenant Mdembe to organize the embarkation. Roberts had reported the IFF rigged up, and Tunney was planning to accompany his troops on the raid. That left a couple of things for her to do before she boarded as well. Which included letting her crew know that she was boarding as well.

The Marines had gathered on one side of the bay and were changing out of their black and gray fatigues and into the olive and tan uniforms of the Forresters. Samuels' worries that the injuries inflicted during the fighting would not leave them a large enough supply proved to be unfounded. Major Tunney had sent a squad down to the laundry bay and they had returned with more than enough clean and pressed uniforms.

Roberts was there with the Marines, and she acted as if this were where she belonged. When Samuels was able to identify the two she was looking for, made easier by the slow and careful movement they were exhibiting, she moved over to speak to them quietly.

"Gunny, could I have a word with you and Sergeant Burton?"

Aichele stood up straight when he was addressed, rising and turning to face the ship's captain. His state of undress put many of his recent injuries on display, and Samuels stopped short at the sight. It wrenched her heart to see what it had cost him to follow her orders during the battle to take back *Pathfinder*. He had already been critically injured before the 'Battle of the Boatbay,' as many were calling it, and to see him now, she couldn't imagine how much effort it must be taking for him just to stay on his feet.

Burton also rose, and she was trying to mask the fact that she was having difficulty moving her right arm enough to do up her blouse. Samuels had to fight back tears that would betray her feelings. She wished more than anything that these two could have been spared the suffering they were continuing to endure. She didn't have the option of ordering them to medbay, though; she needed them too much.

She looked behind her until she was sure she had her expression and voice under control before turning back to them.

"I have an assignment for the two of you."

"Ma'am?"

"Gunny, I'm appointing you as head of ship's security, with Burton as your second. In keeping with your new position, I have received permission to issue you a field promotion to the rank of lieutenant, effective immediately. With Major Tunney accompanying us on the raid, you two are the most knowledgeable about what we can do to prepare a fitting welcome for uninvited guests. So, I need the two of you to stay behind and oversee the work on our defenses."

"Ma'am," Aichele began, and then paused, apparently reconsidering what he had been about to say. "That is a very dirty trick," he finally finished.

"Lieutenant, it was not meant to be. If you think I want you two out of harm's way, you would be right. But I know what it means to the two of you to stand up and do your duty as you see it. I would never order you to avoid a fight unless it was necessary. In this case, I believe that's what it is.

"You know that there is no one else I would trust more to have my back in a fight. But the situation we are heading into is not supposed to be a fight. If it becomes a fight at all, we will have already lost. But with the condition the two of you are in, well, you look like you've been in a fight. With the roles you're supposed to play, there is no reason why you should have been in a fight, and you might get one of those Forresters to use her brain and start asking questions.

"We simply can't have that. It's too much risk. And you and Burton have the experience I need to prepare the ship."

"I suppose Sullivan will be going on the raid," Burton put in.

"Can you think of someone better suited to pretending to be someone she's not?"

Aichele chuckled. "You can't argue with that, Jill."

"No, I suppose not. But I will point out that she was also seriously injured in the fighting on *Pathfinder*."

"I know she was, but her injuries are not visible, and she doesn't move like she's injured."

"You're right, Captain," Aichele said thoughtfully. "That seems odd, when you think about it. With her burns, she's got to be in a lot of pain, but she doesn't move like it bothers her at all."

"How do you know how badly she's injured?" Burton asked.

"Dr. Johnson reported what happened in the brig with the Forresters. She had been called in to treat the injured prisoners, by you I think, Jill, and she made a comment that I didn't pay much attention to at the time. She said she couldn't believe Sullivan was capable of moving, let alone inflicting that kind of damage on multiple people."

"Great. One more thing to add to the pile of what doesn't add up about that woman."

"No. It's more like one more piece of the puzzle that will explain her story. I'm beginning to think that her assignment and organization are only part of the answer."

"You're as bad as Cipi, Lieutenant. He can't leave a mystery alone, either. But right now, I need you focused on getting the ship ready for company."

"Very well, Captain, I accept the promotion and the new position. Now, as head of your security force, however, I cannot allow you to leave the ship during a state of high alert."

"Wait, you think *you're* going on this raid and leaving us behind? That really is a dirty trick, L-T."

Aichele gave Burton a sour grin.

"She's the captain. I'm the L-T."

Burton tossed her Forrest uniform top into the pile in front of her.

"Right. And here I had just gotten used to her being a lieutenant instead of an ensign."

Samuels sighed.

"I know it is a dirty trick, Burton, but I don't have any choice. There wasn't time to cover every detail of the new plan in the briefing, so I've got to go to keep handing out instructions on the way. It was also one of the conditions I agreed to in order to get the Granadans at the shipyards to help us."

"Granados," Burton corrected.

"What?"

"They prefer the term 'Granados' to Granadans."

"When did you learn this?"

"A few minutes ago while I was waiting for the briefing to start. I was talking with a couple of Granados to pass the time."

"Huh. All right, Granados it is, then. Funny that Cipi hasn't corrected me. He's been prickly about everything else."

"Back to the issue at hand," Aichele prompted, "will Roberts also be going on the raid?"

"Yes. I assigned her to run this operation; I can't very well take that away from her now. It would send the wrong message."

"And the bosun?"

"Also going. It's his people taking the biggest risk, and he needs to be there."

"So, you are taking away both naval officers, the bosun, half the Granadans—"

"Granados."

"—and all the Marines except the two of us, and you want us to accomplish anything at all? What are you expecting, Captain? Who's supposed to take charge of all this?"

"You are, *Lieutenant*. At least the ship's security portion. Giannini is the highest in the Navy chain of command, so that puts her in charge of the ship. Not that I want the ship moving anywhere, so she won't need to take the conn, she just needs to keep Engineering going. Although, that means I probably need to promote her too, now that she's running a department, but the top priority is preparing defenses. So I'm leaving you in charge of personnel assignments."

Aichele's jaw clenched several times before he said anything. "I wish to point out, again, that what you are doing is a very dirty trick. Captain."

"Sometimes desperate captains use desperate measures. But the smart ones know who they can rely on to do what they have to do. Seriously, I know I'm handing you a basket full of snakes, and you have every right to hate me. But I also know you'll roll up your sleeves, tighten your bandages, and get the job done."

"'A basket full of snakes?' I never heard that one before."

"It's a phrase my dad used all the time."

"Then your father has a gift for metaphor. A basket full of snakes is precisely what this is. But, like you said, I'll take it and do what needs doing."

"I know you will, Gu— Lieutenant. And I'll go fly to the shipyards and come back with some weapons, because that's what needs doing. And if I live through today, I think I shall sit down and have a good cry. No time for it now."

Aichele shined his boyish grin again.

"If I live through today, I'm going to check myself back into medianninibay."

"If I make it, I'll probably do both." Burton looked near tears already.

Samuels stood up straighter and nodded to her two friends. The difference in rank didn't let her reach out and hug them like she wanted to and she felt a wetness in her eyes as she looked at them.

"I need to go, but there's something I need to say to both of you first. Thank you. Genuinely. I was in so far over my head when I was working on my own, and I wouldn't have survived, let alone succeeded, without both of you."

Aichele and Burton both stood a little straighter also and looked her straight in the eye, but it was Aichele who said what they were both feeling.

"Captain, Sergeant Burton and I not only owe you our thanks, but a debt of honor as well. Do you know the last time a successful mutiny occurred while Warner Marines were in charge of security?"

"No, I can't say that I do."

"Never. It had never happened before. Not once. And now, since it was the crew of *Pathfinder* which regained control, instead of being recovered by outside forces, the honor of the Corps is still unblemished. It's just a very lengthy internal struggle for ownership. Not a successful mutiny."

Samuels sighed. She spoke very softly, "It's what needed to be done. And it came at a very high cost."

Aichele came to attention and saluted. "Agreed. And thank *you*, Captain."

Samuels returned the salute crisply. "Make me proud again, Marines.

"And help me find a uniform that will fit me before my ride decides to leave without me."

CHAPTER 32
19 October
WNS *Peru*

Samuels was unable to find a uniform that would fit her thin frame. She was about to settle 'reluctantly' for a comfortable worker's shipsuit to fit in with the Granadans, until Aichele dashed her hopes.

"It won't work, ma'am. People are still going to be looking to you to direct them, even subconsciously. If having wounded Marines might give away the ruse, Marines checking with a Granadan—"

"Granado," Jill corrected.

"—will give it away just as surely. And wouldn't she technically be a Granada?"

"Technically, yes, but wouldn't that get confused with the name of the planet?"

"Then what am I supposed to do?" the Captain cut in before the conversation devolved any further. "If I wear a uniform that fits me like a tent, I will still be suspect."

"Burton, grab me a med kit from the alcove over there. Captain, if you'll grab a uniform pants that fit at the waist and a blouse that fits at the shoulders, we can fix the rest."

True to his word, Aichele used sure stitches with suture thread to take in the waist of the blouse, and wound sealant to hem the sleeves and legs to the correct length. When he was done, Samuels looked like the uniform had been tailor-made for her. Still, it took an extra fifteen minutes, and there wasn't enough time in the schedule as it was.

Samuels sprinted onto the second shuttle; the first had already launched; and the conveyor was sliding it through the lock and into the launch bay before she was completely up the ramp. Aichele and Burton stood and watched until the lock had cycled and the shuttle was away.

"Okay, Sergeant, time to earn our pay," Aichele said.

"Yes, and with all that extra officer's salary, you're going to have to do more to earn it."

"Probably true, but there's no shortage of work to be done today."

From the boatbay, the two Marines headed aft into Engineering country. The ship seemed almost deserted compared to the frenetic activity of an hour earlier. The hum of machinery and power lines was still evident, but the sound of working and shouting had diminished to nearly nothing. Due to the near silence, Giannini was not hard to locate by following the sounds of banging and cursing.

"Crystal," Aichele called when he arrived, "I need some information."

She put down a large hammer and stood up, leaving two techs working on securing the newly installed engine monitor. She wiped at a dark spot on her left arm as she moved to them.

"Like what?"

Aichele nodded back at the two workers.

"First, what shape are the engines in? Then, how many people can you spare me to prepare defenses? And third, how tough are the corridor walls?"

She leaned back against the rail that separated them from the engine and gave him a narrow gaze. She held up her hand and counted off fingers as she answered.

"The engines should be good to go, but the testing is not complete. I have nine people left in my department, and you can have seven of them. And I'm not answering that last one until you tell me why you need to know."

She lowered her fingers and stared at him, waiting for an answer.

"Oh, just an idea I had that may or may not work."

"An idea that involves potentially tearing the ship apart?"

Aichele shrugged his shoulders and shook his head. He grinned a bit sheepishly.

"Well, obviously, I'd like to avoid that outcome. That's why I want to know how much force the corridor walls and hull can take *before* they buckle."

"Let me tell you a secret, Eric. The answer to every engineering question is always the same. 'It depends.' Where is the force being applied? What directionality? What duration? What frequency? All of those will change the answer."

He held up a hand to stop her outpouring.

"Okay, let me simplify. I'm considering planting mines on the ceilings or upper corners of the corridors most likely to see fighting, with shrapnel packages attached. Say two kilos of material. How much explosive force can I apply before I risk rupturing the seams of the corners or the ceiling?"

"Why not just use what you think you'll need and worry about fixing what you break if and when we survive?"

"I'm not worried about damaging the ship. But if I put a hole in the corridor, then I'm letting energy escape to somewhere that it doesn't do me any good. And if I have any explosives at all, I'm not going to have much. I need to make it count."

"You know, Gunny, for a Marine, you think an awful lot like an engineer."

"I'll take that as a compliment."

"It was meant that way."

"So how much?"

"What type of explosive?"

"I don't know yet."

"Haven't you already inventoried the armory?"

"Yes. No mines or charges there."

"Then where are these explosives coming from?"

"It just occurred to me while I was trying to think of any potential threat that the Forresters must have scuttling charges set, and that they are likely able to be activated remotely. I was planning on making that my first task, to find and disarm those. But then I was thinking it would be a shame to let all that ordnance go to waste..."

"I take it back. You do still think like a paranoid security guard, but in this case, I'm very glad you do."

"So how much can I use?"

"If this were *Pathfinder*, I could probably give you a close guess. As it is...tell you what. You go get the explosives and tell me what type they are, and I'll pull up the virtual model and run some numbers for you."

"Deal. Burton will grab six of the seven and put them to work. If you have a skilled electrotech you'd recommend, I'll take him."

"Why don't you take Fernandez? She's one of the best we've got left, though power systems are not her forte."

"Fernandez is still here? I would have expected her to have gone on the raid."

"She had too many welding assignments to finish, and missed the briefing. She's not happy about staying here, though."

Aichele nodded.

"I can certainly understand that. Fernandez it is, then." He turned to his second and continued, "Burton, you know what sort of defenses we need to prepare. If I were them, I would come in exactly the same way we did, and split to take Bridge and Engineering first. That will give us likely lines of advance. Plan on setting up at least four fallback positions per line. Also, spend some time thinking about where they might breach if they're feeling particularly sneaky, and see what we can do about those."

"Not asking much, are you, L-T? We've got what, 80 or 90 minutes before they hit us? What do you want done first?"

Giannini looked at Burton and then over to Aichele.

"Lieutenant?"

"Long story," Aichele said, taking the last question first. "Actually, it's a short story. Captain didn't want me along, and gave me a promotion and the Security Chief job to mollify me."

Giannini made a rude sound. "That is not fair to Captain Samuels, who is doing a remarkable job of getting the most out of her people, and it downplays the level of trust she has in your considerable abilities. Now, let me be the first to congratulate you on a well-deserved recognition of your value."

Burton tried to look away in embarrassment, but the kiss lasted so long she eventually had to look back, and then to wonder if either of them were still getting any oxygen.

"Thank you," he said, once there was an opportunity. Then it was back to business.

"To answer your questions, Burton, most of the fallbacks have already been created. I just need you to check them all for any problems that we can fix in the next hour. Do the checking yourself, but if you find problems, have the techs do the fixing. Once that's done, worry about the unexpected. I don't know how long I will be with my pet project, so don't come looking for me every time a decision needs to be made. Just make the best call you can, with my blessing. Consider this another RIO opportunity."

"Great. The last time I was released for independent operations, it worked out so well for me."

"We recovered the ship, didn't we?"

"Yes, but I went six weeks without a shower, and spent more time inside a space suit than out of it. Do you know what I smelled like? My sinuses may never recover!"

"Well, I wasn't going to mention it..."

Burton smacked him playfully on his good arm, then fell back a step and saluted with her left hand. "Orders understood, sir."

Aichele straightened and returned the gesture. "Carry on, Sergeant."

Burton hurried off at a double-time march, but while the left arm swung in cadence with her steps, her right was held rigidly in place against her torso.

"Where can I find Fernandez?"

"Deck C, just forward of the boatbay in corridor four. Tell her I said she was authorized for overtime."

Aichele had started away, but turned back with a questioning look at the last line.

"Inside joke. She'll get it, and know that you cleared her new assignment with me."

"Good enough. And Crystal, if I survive this, we should sit down and talk."

"If I survive this, we should do more than that."

Aichele grinned and hurried away.

CHAPTER 33
19 October
Forrest Assault Shuttle

"If I had to guess, I'd say they were making for the shipyards," the pilot said.

Kadison swore as possible explanations crowded into her mind, fighting for supremacy. The idea which won was that they had never intended to stay on the ship, and they were now moving on to their next target.

The more she thought about it, the less sense that made, though. If they had intended to disable the ship so that it could not be used against them, then why not attack and destroy it from a safe distance? *Scythe* couldn't retaliate in kind. Of course, they wouldn't have known that. There were also native civilians on the ship, but they wouldn't have known that either. So why would they board the ship, and then just leave again? Something must have happened to change their goals.

What if the new decision was related to what they didn't know before they arrived on the ship?

"Any change in our current plan, Colonel?" Oliver asked politely over vocom.

"Not yet. I need to figure out why they're doing what they're doing before I know what to do about it. Do you mind if I come up to the flight deck to talk it over with you?"

"Not at all, but I don't know how much clairvoyance I can offer."

"Maybe not clairvoyance, but you have more experience with how a naval officer might think than I do. On my way."

Kadison thumped her way the few meters she needed to reach the pilot's compartment, and took the open seat just aft of the co-pilot's chair, which was currently occupied by a rating named Karen Van Duyk. With internal gravity to compensate for the external thrust, she shouldn't have had to deal with the extra weight. Unfortunately, the engineers had to trade off some compensator efficiency to get the acceleration numbers the contract had demanded, or so Kadison had been told. She cursed them in her mind, anyway.

"First thing we should do is get a warning to the shipyards that company is coming," Kadison said.

"I already thought of that, but that would mean breaking our comm silence order. And it might be for no reason. Other eyes are going to be watching what's happening, and they can get word to Caspar as well as we could."

"I suppose that's true, but there may not be a need for comm silence either, if we're going to abort, or if the plan changes to the point that we lose our approach from the sun line."

"Granted, Colonel. But let's not take that step until we know that it won't matter. And, may I suggest we slow our approach?"

She looked at the young pilot, whose eyes were fixed on the controls in front of him while he continued to maneuver the ship. "Why would we want to do that?"

He finally turned to glance at her as he started his next sentence. "Well, it occurs to me, that if they were able to take the ship, and are now abandoning it, they would want to scuttle it so that it could not be used against them. That they haven't, may mean that they've booby-trapped it instead, or that they've rigged it to detonate by remote signal when they see us try to board it."

He held up his hands in a shrugging gesture. She nodded and cringed at the thought.

"I'll grant that may be a possibility, but how does slowing down help?"

"For one thing, it lets them get farther away. There may be a range limit on their trigger. For another, if we stop accelerating, we have fewer gravitic emissions, which makes it harder for them to see us coming. And finally, it gives us more time to figure out what we should do next."

She gave him another nod, though he was not looking at her. "All right, do it then."

There was a pause in the conversation while Van Duyk communicated with the rest of the shuttles, and at a signal they all dropped power to the Gravitas field that had been pushing them along. They were maintaining the same velocity, just not adding much to it anymore.

When the pilot finished that task, Kadison continued, "It looks like the next step is deciding what we're going to do."

"I thought you said figuring out what those Warners are up to was the first step."

She gave him a slight chuckle. "Well, I guess I was including that in the first step. But you're right; that's where we need to start. Any ideas what they're after?"

"Spreading FUD, maybe?"

"What?"

He turned to her with a small grin. "You know, fear, uncertainty, and doubt. Being unpredictable, seeking targets of opportunity, terrorizing the citizenry, doing as much damage as they can without being pinned down anywhere."

She sat up a little straighter. "They're certainly being unpredictable. And a hit and run operation was the first thing I thought of, too. But if they want to hit a target of opportunity without being pinned down, why did they board *Scythe*? Wouldn't it have made more sense to pound the ship to scrap from a distance?"

He held up a hand and waved it up and down slightly. "Well, look at it from their point of view. They must have deduced that the ship wasn't ready to field yet, since it wasn't out on patrol with the other destroyers. But maybe they thought the ship was at least armed, so they wanted to close as quickly as possible to avoid unnecessary time trading shots in an open field."

She shrugged. "I suppose that would make sense, once they decided to hit the ship. My question is, why did they decide that? You would think that Warner destroyer would have its hands full with eight other ships after it. And it looked like it was a near thing that they got that new drive system powered up again to let them jump, and even then, they didn't have enough power to go very far. So why, after they barely escape, would they send a boarding party to another ship that wasn't threatening them at all?"

"Maybe that's the reason," Oliver opined.

"What is?"

"The power, or the hurried exit. Maybe they didn't get very far because they're damaged, or their experimental jump drive system isn't working right. Maybe they're trapped here until they can find replacement parts, and the boarding party was looking for what they need, but couldn't find it on the ship. And if that's the case, their next stop would be the shipyards, which will almost certainly have what they need."

Colonel Kadison sat considering for a moment. "I could see how that's possible, and it would account for them trying to take *Scythe*, but I'm still having trouble accepting the leap to them heading to the shipyards now. They have to know that it's suicide. With conditions on the planet being what they are, Marine Command has been rotating units off-planet at regular intervals. I'd wager that there are 8,000 troops on the station right now. Like I said, suicide."

He turned and looked at her. "Do they? Have to know, I mean. Have you heard how many Warner Marines were at the yards when we took over?"

She shook her head, trying to think if she had ever heard that information. "No, I don't think I have."

He gave a knowing nod. "There were only a couple dozen on the main station, and another dozen or so spread out over all the outlying docks."

Her eyes opened in shock. "You're kidding me."

He held up a hand as if being sworn in to testify in court. "I am not. So maybe that was what they were expecting to have to deal with when they arrive."

Kadison's face showed a predatory smile as she considered that thought. "If you're right, those poor saps are walking straight into a meat grinder."

CHAPTER 34
19 October
Warner Assault Shuttle

The shuttle lurched sideways before Samuels made it all the way inside the hatch. A conveyor moved the shuttle from the boatbay to the launch bay and the enormous lock sealed to allow pumps to remove the air before the outer doors would open. Samuels hurried to try to get strapped into her seat before they were away, but the boat's inertial compensators made it impossible to tell if she made it or not.

She had been headed forward to the flight deck; traditional Navy territory on a Marine assault shuttle, but stopped short when she saw an open spot next to Cipi. She abruptly altered course to that aisle and slid herself into the seat, letting out a lungful of air in a rush. She suddenly felt enormously tired and wished she could just slip into a week-long nap.

"Capitán," Cipi said in his drawn out accent.

"Bosun," she replied easily. "Might I ask you a question?"

The man turned to face her and scrutinized her up and down. He paused so long that Samuels expected he was going to deny the request, when he finally said, "Of course, Capitán."

"Why didn't you tell me that your people prefer the term Granados to Granadans?"

If anything, the question made his dour scrutiny increase in intensity. Then, much to her surprise, he started laughing.

"At first, I thought you were trying to play a joke on me, but I can see you are in earnest. Who told you this thing?"

"One of the Marines heard it from one of the Gran—your people," she said. "Now are you going to tell me why it's so funny?"

He stopped laughing eventually, and wiped at one eye. "Tell me, how much do you know of Granadan history?"

"A little, I suppose. The Worth System was discovered in the third expansion push, somewhere around the mid-2600s, and settled later that century, which makes Granada about a hundred years old. It spent a longer than average period as a protectorate, but has been fully represented on the Family Board for at least fifty years."

"Hmph. Well, that is more than most Warners know of us."

"My dad traveled a lot."

"So, as you said, Granada has been inhabited for more than a century. The first city, Toledo, was established in 2662. The first settlers, though, were not altogether of one mind on many things. The greatest of these disputes was on heritage."

"What do you mean, 'heritage?' Didn't you have a new world to start over in?"

"Yes and no. It was a time and place to start anew and create fresh traditions, but the people themselves were not new. They brought with them heritages from their individual upbringings."

"I thought all Granadans had come from the Spain province of Earth."

"No, not all. In fact, only about a fourth. Other groups had come from Argentina, Chile, Ecuador, and France. And part of what people brought with them that they felt was part of their identity was their traditional language. For the majority, that was Spanish, and they called themselves Granados. The minority who remembered French wanted to be known as Grenadiers. And they were serious about it. It was a source of great discord for many years, and people would take offense if the wrong name were to be applied to them."

Samuels looked at him askance. "Are *you* trying to play a joke on me, now?"

He chuckled. "No, but I am getting to the funny part. So, to sum up, there was great discord, and it was turning to animosity and, in some cases, to open hostility. The Governor at that time, a man named Hector de la Planche, made one of the finest political moves in human history. In his first Address to the People speech, he declared that, while it was a good thing to remember where one's people had come from, it was not a good thing to allow a people's history to mar a whole planet's future. Since the official language of the Warner Family was neither Spanish nor French, but English, all official documents would from that time forward speak only of Granadans."

"Sounds like an excellent compromise, but I don't see what's funny about it."

"I'm still getting to the funny part. Be patient, please."

"Sorry."

"Okay, so this one move essentially ends the dispute. A few hotheads still tried to hold onto their victimhood, but before long, even they bow to the inevitable, and everyone is equally a Granadan.

"Many years go by, and Granada grows and flourishes. We begin producing goods for export and importing other goods. One thing we cannot export is the natural beauty to be found here, and so there are numerous tourists to visit our planet, especially in the equatorial islands.

"I do not know how this next part got started, but tour guides began telling visitors to forget about what they have read in guide books, and that they must call the locals 'Granados' or risk offending them. The locals play along with this, and they know that if someone enters their shop looking for 'Granado wares,' they must be from off-planet, and they may safely charge them twice the normal price, because they will be unfamiliar with local conditions.

"So, it seems that one of us 'locals' is playing a long-standing joke on what he considers a 'tourist.' That is what I think is so funny."

Samuels smiled, then chuckled softly. "That is a good one. I'm half tempted to start calling you all Grenadiers the next time I have to say anything."

"I'm pretty sure I know who is the one responsible, and believe me, he does not need that kind of encouragement."

"All right then, what can I do to help coach the Granadans on what they need to do?"

"For us, I do not think there is a need. You have cast us in the role we have been playing for the last two years. I am more worried about the Marines acting in the right way."

"What do you mean?"

"I mean that they think of us as people, and the Forresters do not. I fear that this will show when the Forresters on the station observe us."

Samuels considered what he was getting at, and briefly thought about pointing out that he was undermining his original argument that in his mind there was no difference between Warner and Forrest. Clearly, it had been an exaggeration meant to justify his defiance. Either that, or he had greatly changed his opinion in the course of a couple hours. "Can you give me some examples? If we had some specific actions to tell people, that would be easier than portraying a mindset."

"Hm. I am having difficulty in thinking of instances. They must act more callous, more self-satisfied. They must gloat more; knowing that those they are guarding are powerless to do anything against them. They must be ready to hit us and kick us and treat us like unruly dogs, knowing that for us to strike back would be suicide."

"I see. If we do behave that way, though, will that drive a wedge between the Granadans and the Marines?"

"I do not think so, but I will warn everyone beforehand what must happen, and that should minimize any misunderstandings."

"All right. Why don't you do that, and I'll spend my time coaching the Marines instead."

"As you say, Capitán," he said, rising to gather people together in the next aisle.

Samuels rose also, and checked her chrono on her way to the rear section, where the Marines had congregated. Still more than thirty minutes of flight time before they docked at Caspar. With as pressed for time as they were, the forced inactivity was hard for her to bear. Hopefully, talking and practicing with the Marines would make that feeling go away.

She doubted it would. That countdown to when the Foresters would hit *Peru* was still ticking away in the back of her brain, pushing her to do *something*.

"Major," she said, once she had arrived at the ranking Marine's seat, "could I have a word with you and the other officers for a few minutes?"

"Of course, Captain." He popped to his feet and with a few hand gestures had all four of the other Marine officers moving their way.

When they were gathered in close, she wasted no time in sharing her thoughts. "The new bosun is the closest thing we have to an expert on what the Forresters are going to expect when we arrive, and he is concerned that you Marines are not going to be able to put on a believable performance."

Casting aspersion on their abilities, definitely got their attention. "Is that so," Lieutenant Tucker said with a drawl.

Samuels pushed just a little more. She didn't want to make them so mad they went overboard and hurt someone, but at the same time, she wanted them a little worked up. "Yes. He's afraid that all of you are too nice to make realistic Forresters."

"Too nice?!" Mdembe snorted. "Perhaps you would like to ask Ensign Roberts her opinion on that topic. She has the bruises to prove otherwise."

"Look, all kidding aside, he's got a point. You're going to have to act and talk like Forrester Marines, and the people you have to fool are Forrester Marines. It's going to be really easy to say or do the wrong thing and make people start wondering about us. And that absolutely must not happen. If we break character, even for a moment, it could be the end of the mission for us."

"What do you want for us to do, ma'am?" Major Tunney asked quietly. "We're Marines. We can improvise, we can adapt. Just tell us what you want."

Samuels smiled, despite her desire to stress to the Marines the need to take this problem seriously. "What I really want is for every one of us to walk back out of the shipyards in one piece. Here's how you all need to behave to make that happen. I'll walk you through it once or twice, then I need you to take those lessons and practice them with all your people. You're probably only going to have a few minutes with them, so let's be quick about it.

"Let's start with..."

CHAPTER 35
19 October
Caspar Shipyards

The shuttle slid effortlessly into its assigned berth and there was a loud clicking sound as the dock clamps took their hold. The extensible tube sealed around the starboard lock, and began filling with breathable air. Captain Samuels was at the front of the line to transit from the shuttle into the station, and swam the twenty meters like a pro. Major Tunney was impressed with the natural grace she displayed, half-fearing he'd have to help her get back to an artificial gravity field, but then, he didn't know she'd made such transitions hundreds of times before.

A Marine sergeant, a medium-height man with blond hair and a confident posture, met them as they crossed into the gravity field that indicated they were in the station proper. Samuels had a moment of panic when she realized that she had no idea what the correct protocol was for entering a station among the Forresters. She didn't think there was anyone who could help her, either, since the Forresters had never owned a space station before.

She fell back on general military procedure and blatant honesty. After the sergeant had saluted, Samuels stood straight and returned it, then asked, "My first time on a Family-owned station, Sergeant. Do I need permission to enter or some such?"

"No, Lieutenant. If you'll follow me, the colonel would like to see you. Apparently, there's some questions about the orders we only just now received."

"Certainly, Sergeant...Hammond," Samuels said, reading the name tag on the big man's chest. "Top," she called, turning to Major Tunney, currently in an NCO's rank tabs. The lieutenant's uniform Samuels currently had on was the only one close enough to her size that a hasty job of tailoring could make work. Since they didn't want anyone to outrank her, everyone else was a non-com or a private.

"Ma'am," Tunney replied, trotting over.

"I'm going to see the colonel to...clarify...our orders. Keep the herd together, and don't let them stray. They've got work to do, so minimize injuries, if you can."

Samuels could see in the tightening of the major's jaw that he considered coming with her, role-playing or not. Samuels looked at him sternly, and he finally nodded. "Yes, ma'am."

The sergeant appeared not to give any special attention to the silent exchange. He strode purposefully across the bay, and Samuels had to exert herself to keep up. Samuels wasn't sure what was really going on, but she tried to convince herself that if their story hadn't convinced the Forresters, they never would have let them get off the shuttles. It wasn't a very effective argument to allay her fears, and she instead tried distracting herself by making sure the return route was being burned into her memory. You never knew when it might be needed.

After many turns and level changes, the sergeant showed her into a tube seat for a four-minute ride from Tenth Ring to First Ring. The sergeant said no more than one-syllable responses to her attempts at conversation. Three more levels up and nine turns were added to her internal map until he paused before a hatch labeled "Station Commanding Officer – Colonel Marsha Kern" on a plate that did not match the rest of the wall, and had clearly been recently added, and motioned her inside. The door led into an outer office, and three non-coms were busy at various tasks within. The blond sergeant snaked around her to knock on the door in the center of the back wall. Samuels was still musing over the inefficiency of the sergeant's waiting for her to enter first, then hurrying around her to announce her presence when the sergeant again opened the door and motioned for her to enter.

"Lieutenant Bixby, as you requested, ma'am," the sergeant said, giving the name Samuels had provided as an alias. He held his salute until the Marine colonel returned it brusquely. The sergeant left, closing the hatch behind him.

Once the seal hissed, Samuels gave her best imitation of the salute the sergeant had given, which was subtly different from what a Warner would have delivered. When it was returned, Samuels said, "You asked to see me, ma'am?"

"Yes, Lieutenant. I'm hoping you can shed some light on these orders I've received."

Samuels had worked up three different potential strategies as to how to handle this interview. Thanks to her father's training, she could gather clues from minor things to get a quick read on someone's personality. Since entering the outer office, she'd collected quite a bit of information. The aides just outside were all busy, and there was no communication going on between them. That indicated that the colonel was more interested in results than in building camaraderie among her troops. This observation was bolstered by the five awards on one wall for unit efficiency, awards she had clearly worked hard for and was proud of.

Also on the wall were two diplomas, both with honors attached. So, intelligent and educated. Notably missing from the wall or desk were any personal images; friends or family. So, either unattached to anyone, or else of the opinion that personal items did not belong at work. Either might be the case, but they both led to roughly the same conclusion.

Normally, such a personality would be best approached from a position of greater knowledge or authority. Unfortunately, Samuels didn't believe she could pull off either act. She was already outranked, so no greater authority, and she didn't really have enough information on the Forrester's organization or normal procedures to give a convincing performance. Someone this intelligent was more than likely to trip up her story at some point.

Nor did she think playing the opposite position would work out. If she pretended to have no knowledge to share, she couldn't build any trust, and without trust, this seemed the sort of person to hold stubbornly to her last known orders until she had confirmation from some other source; a source that would be far outside Samuels' control.

Her best chance, she decided within only a few seconds, was going to be to take the middle road; she didn't have all the answers, but she knew enough to do her job.

"I'll certainly help answer anything I can, ma'am, but I don't know what specific orders you received."

"Please, Lieutenant, have a seat," the colonel said, indicating one of the two chairs set to face her desk. Samuels took one, and the station commander continued. "The orders I've been given are to turn over a shuttle-full of Mark 20s to you as well as emptying any extra anti-personnel weapons and ammunition from my armory. Can you explain the rationale behind those orders? I've tried to ask my superior, but he hasn't even acknowledged my message yet."

"Well, I can give you a partial answer. I know the rationale for the missiles, because my orders include both where to pick them up and where to drop them off. Those are supposed to be delivered to the destroyer fleet that is currently in pursuit of the intruder. The rationale being that, since the Warner ship can't rearm, all we have to do is keep them fighting long enough until they run dry and then they'll have to surrender. Someone above my pay grade thinks there is something of value on the ship, and they want to capture it intact instead of simply destroying it.

"As for the small arms I'm supposed to pick up, I really don't know. My orders don't include where to take them, just that I'm supposed to remove them from the station."

The colonel rubbed her chin in thought and Samuels tried to remain calm. The first hurdle, that the station commander had received orders to cover what they were doing, had been passed, and for that she owed the Granadans a vast debt. While that was an enormous relief, it was far from the last thing that could go wrong. She really didn't understand how the Forresters were lax enough to allow the communications watchstanders to be all Granadans, but she wasn't about to look a gift horse in the mouth. Still, if the colonel wasn't convinced and decided to look into things personally, or wait for confirmation from the planet, or even just delay things too long, then the mission was going to be a failure.

If things went badly enough, she could get caught up here at the station center while the nearest support was all the way at the outer edge. Samuels' nerves were starting to get to her, and she really wanted to be on her way. She wasn't sure what she could do to move things along, though. What would be in character for her right now...?

"Ma'am, begging your pardon, but if there's nothing else, I do have a rendezvous schedule to keep."

"Hmm? Oh, yes. Thank you for the explanation on the missiles. That does help. Unfortunately, I think I know what's going on with the small arms transfer, and I'm going to hold them here instead of sending them with you."

"As you say, ma'am. Might I respectfully ask for your rationale? I am sure that I will be asked to provide it at some point in the near future."

"Of course, Lieutenant. This has nothing to do with the defense of this system. This is all about political maneuvering. In the last report to the home office, there were several excuses offered as to why certain Marine units were not able to remove Granada Unfettered, and the delays they represent, once and for all. In the home office's reply, those excuses were not accepted, and the security record of Caspar was held up as a counter-example of an effective force. Which predictably painted a giant target on our backs labeled "Stick Knife Here."

My guess is that some genius dirtside thinks they can demonstrate an imagined security problem by showing we had to transfer our small arms off station because we weren't certain we could keep them out of the hands of the natives. Well, that's not the case, and I'm not about to give anyone at headquarters any such ammunition against us.

"Thank you, ma'am. That's very clear. Permission to carry out the remainder of my orders?"

"Granted."

A quick exchange of salutes, and Samuels was on her way, with one more huge problem to solve.

How was she going to deliver on her promise to the Granadans? And if she couldn't, was GU still going to keep theirs?

CHAPTER 36
19 October
WNS Peru

Aichele moved with purpose to Deck C, his mind shifting from evaluating where to begin the search to how to best employ the devious tactic that had been developing in his mind over the past several hours. True to the description from Crystal, he found Fernandez just forward of the boat bay in corridor four.

He was still off balance by how such a diminutive individual could contain such a fierce presence, and yet he liked working with her even more because of it. He liked surprising things that could be brought to his advantage.

"Fernandez, can I interrupt you?" he called to her as she lowered her gear to stare appraisingly at him.

"That depends Gunny," she began.

Aichele cut her off before he could get caught in the all too common "that depends" lecture from another engineering type. "Look, I need your help, and Giannini has already authorized the overtime, whatever that is supposed to mean."

"Why didn't you lead with that?" she asked as she began to gather up her things. "Tell me what you need Gunny."

Aichele let the incorrect rank slide as well. That was how he's been introduced to her, and it wasn't worth the lost time to explain his change in status. "I have been thinking that it is most likely that the Forresters would have planted scuttling charges aboard. I want to locate them, disable them and then repurpose them to make a nasty welcome for our would-be assailants who are inbound," Aichele said without any preamble, "as quickly as we possibly can."

Fernandez scrutinized the Marine for a few moments, and then grinned at him. "Well, Gunny, this might be your lucky day. You see, it occurred to us quite a while back to look for those scuttling charges and disable them. They're all already disabled, and better, I know where they all are," she said while flashing her teeth in an ear to ear smile.

"Can you take me to one of them so that we can get an exact ID on the type of ordinance and what type of detonators we have to work with?" he asked her while reaching to take one of her bags of gear.

"I really like this line of thinking. Can do, Gunny, let's go," she replied grabbing the rest of her gear and setting out to the nearest charge.

"Fernandez, if you like the plain old boring line of thinking I started with, I think you are going to love how cunningly devious we are going to be on the other end of it," he answered with a small smile as he stepped into pace behind her.

While Fernandez led him to the closest set of charges, he began telling her a story about how much he had hated the ancient history lessons he had been forced to suffer through in military history classes. Since she assumed he was taking the long way around to his point, she held back any criticism about how hearing about these classes didn't sound like a great load of fun either. It would certainly pass the time while they went further below deck.

After a bit more context, Aichele delivered the point.

"You see Fernandez, as military strongholds went, castles, fortresses and the like were pretty powerful in their day. They did get assaulted though, and the people who built them planned for a lot of options for defensive warfare inside of them. As we have been structuring our defensive plan for this ship, these fortress concepts have rattled in and out of my thoughts. Using the defensive junctions, position control, and armor and barricades where possible to be a screen for us. I keep coming back to something we are missing though," he said smiling as they were at the hatch she had indicated that they were headed towards.

"Oh, what's that," she said, genuinely interested now.

"Murder holes," he said smiling.

"Gunny, that name sounds great. What's a murder hole?" she asked, not sure she wanted to know this answer.

"I'll tell you once we get this ordinance ID solved so that we can run the numbers on how to not blow a hole in the ship," Aichele responded, still not caring to correct Fernandez' repeatedly incorrect usage of his old rank. He liked being Gunny, and had no desire to correct people into using L-T.

The two of them descended the hatch to get a look at the charges placed in the interstitial space beneath the decking, against the innermost side of the outer hull. They both lit their lights and began reviewing the ordinance.

"Well Gunny, it looks to be all XABX, and looks like it has a linear shape charge arrangement, with these acting independently," she said indicating the panel charges laid out in front of them. "We've obviously pulled all the detonators, but the team of us Granadans doing the work weren't really comfortable moving any of it."

"This should all be stable enough, but from what I understand, scuttling charges aren't usually too concerned about being precise in their blast damage," Aichele said, eyeing the layout formation and beginning to think through his options.

"Space bound vessels are somewhat easier to scuttle from the inside, Gunny. While from a pressure perspective, the strength of the hull is positioned to keep a significantly higher pressure inside than outside, warships are armored extensively on the outer hull to protect against all kinds of damage, but especially against explosions," Fernandez explained, "which is why internal scuttling charges don't require tight precision in their explosive force map."

"So, I think we both agree that this ordinance may need some minor modifications, or some leeway, in its use if we don't want collateral damage," he concluded.

Aichele hit the comms to reach out to Giannini again.

"Crystal, you copy?" he asked.

A few seconds later, her voice came over the comm. "Copy L-T, did you find it already? That was faster than I thought by far. What did you find?"

"L-T?" Fernandez said in a confused tone while shooting him a look that equaled her voice.

"Looks like XABX, with linear shape charged panels, and yeah Fernandez and her fellows already had these located and disabled, so we caught a break there." He replied, ignoring the question Fernandez had thrown him.

"L-T?" Fernandez asked again.

"Well, it could be worse Eric," Giannini began, "since they are panel shaped charges, we'll get cleaner blast pressure waves. They are likely also a little indiscriminate with their shrapnel and back pressure blast since they are meant to destroy everything around them. Read me a model number off one of those panels and I'll start running some models."

Aichele did so and then turned back to Fernandez with a weary glance.

"Yes, L-T Fernandez, long story and not a big deal," Aichele said to the confused Granadan.

"Okay Crystal, MN reads X-ray, Foxtrot, Mike, Six, Bravo, Three, Three, X-ray, Alpha, Alpha, Five," he said after running his light over the model number stamped on the panel.

"Strong copy Eric. I'll get to work and let you know as soon as I have the right model worked out for these," she replied and cut from the comm.

"Well, Lieutenant," Fernandez said dramatically, over-emphasizing the rank, "how should we proceed?"

"Let's take one of these panels back to Engineering so that Giannini can validate any alterations or specific instructions for placement we need to follow," he paused, "and along the way,

I can tell you all about murder holes, and how they were used to rain death on the enemy from hiding spots above."

* * * * *

Sergeant Jill Burton was moving busily from location to location to validate the preparations in progress and to keep those working focused.

As she rounded a corner out of sight of everyone else, she allowed herself to wince. Everything still felt like it hurt, but her shoulder and arm were radiating serious amounts of pain.

She didn't want to mask the pain with medication that would leave her thoughts sluggish. In the role of overseer that she currently had, the ship needed her mind at its best far more than an able body.

She also didn't want to show her pain in front of the team, because they might assume she wasn't enthused about their options or their chances in the upcoming fight.

She wasn't even remotely enthused about either if she were being honest with herself. They didn't have good odds, and they didn't have enough time nor resources to make their planning cost the enemy enough based on what she could see.

While the reality was grim, it didn't mean she could lose hope, and more importantly, couldn't be seen to have lost hope. Her husband was waiting for her back home. With everything she had been through up to this point, there was nothing that would make her back down. Either she'd get back home to see her loved ones, or she'd die in the attempt.

She entered another work area and began reviewing the additional defensive screening the team had assembled, along with the now welded obstacles in the corridor that would prohibit large groups from making an easy passage.

"Can one of you please check that weld. It's flimsy looking," she indicated where a screen had been attached to the bulkhead, and began moving on.

She was moving back towards the boatbay, and began thinking about the work that Lieutenant Aichele was undertaking. She smiled to herself as she thought about his very recent promotion. She wasn't jealous, she realized, because she didn't care about promotions any more. She had already made up her mind that if she got out of this scrape, she was out. She planned to retire after this mission, and take up full time, stay at home, planet *wifelihood*. She didn't really know what that statement really meant, even to herself, but she planned to find out.

Her walk-through had seen a few things to correct, and a few more that would need a second check, but she paused to think strategically about the upcoming engagement rather than just tactically. She thought about where she would hit the ship if she were the enemy. What weak spot would she exploit with multiple attacking vessels? As she ran through the weak points for breaches, she also realized that they might decide to breach multiple locations simultaneously in the hopes that some groups would not be facing direct resistance.

"Well, that won't do," she muttered to herself, realizing that she'd need to make some additional alterations to accommodate multiple potential entry points from multiple ships, possibly all simultaneous.

What they needed was some way to have warning if that was they enemy's plan.

She hurried back to where several of the Granados were standing. "Do any of you have EVA experience?"

* * * * *

"So, Fernandez, if we have murder holes in our interstitial spaces, with nasty surprises to be dropped on the unsuspecting infiltrating hordes, it might augment our successes enough to make it too expensive of a butcher's bill to uproot us," he said as they reached Engineering.

"Nice timing, Lieutenant Gunny," Fernandez said passing through the hatch in search of Giannini, "but that is a great idea. We'll need some folks to assign to it."

Crystal was at her station, already started on simulations modeled on the explosive in the passageways.

"Here's what we are dealing with Crystal," Aichele said as he set down the explosive panel.

"Thanks Eric," Giannini said, turning to face the two. "I'll need to validate that we can make the modifications we need to this, but the model shows that as long we keep them focused with the cone inward facing, and we locate them in strong points I have on the schematic, we can keep from blowing any holes to vacuum, and we'll keep much of the explosive force directed into the space likely to be occupied by our enemies."

"Okay, Fernandez and I will grab the rest of these charges, and then I'll head to the areas I want to use them in. We'll comm when we are there and you can help us make whatever modifications we need to, and confirm where we can locate them," Aichele said, turning now to Fernandez with a wry smile, "and you can get started on the murder holes. Let's keep them out of the areas I might be blowing up though. Just as a precaution in case we still have less precise ordinance than we'd prefer when I get done."

"Grab who you need to, and make sure Burton is aware of what you are up to. Once we have things in order, there's a lot of the team that could use a bit of a rest before the action hits," Crystal said to both of their backs as they were already on their way out.

A raised arm in a wave and a backward glance from Eric, still with that wry smile on his face, told her that he wasn't sure there would be any time to stand down before the action started.

CHAPTER 37
19 October
Caspar Shipyards

Samuels looked to either side as she stepped out of the commander's office. She was glad to see that her escort was no longer waiting for her. She needed some time to try to come up with another plan, not carry on a meaningless conversation with a Forrester. Although, come to think of it, he hadn't said a lot on the way in. Maybe it was more of an officer-enlisted thing. 'Thou shalt not speak unless spoken to.' No, couldn't be that either, since she had attempted speaking to him here and there.

Whatever the case, she didn't need any distractions, because try as she might, she couldn't think of any way to get the small arms she had promised the Granadans.

Passing the busy workers, she left the outer office and began retracing her route back toward the docks. She made it as far as the tube station before her surroundings registered. Even then, it was only because there was no car on the line to keep her moving forward that disturbed her desperate attempts to think of some idea. She had to look around to find the reader board which let her know that it would be seven more minutes until the next car heading outward arrived. Samuels moved forward and joined the throng of would-be passengers and let her problems again take full control of her thoughts.

A disturbance to her right barely penetrated her mental labors, until it started getting closer. The motion and grumbling were not only getting closer, but headed right for her.

Abruptly, there was a break in the wall of people and a small woman appeared in front of her. Her skin was dark, and it immediately made Samuels think of Chief Mackey, though the new individual was not quite so dark as him.

"Lieutenant,' the woman said once she was in sight, "I'm so glad I caught you before you left. There's a message for you in the comm room. Could you come back and sign for it, please?"

Samuels was so shocked at being recognized, she nearly panicked and ran for it. It took her a moment to realize that 'Lieutenant' also applied to her current role. Still, how could anyone be looking for her here? There must be a mistake, but how to deal with it without attracting attention? And how to do so quickly? She had no time for anything but what she was already dealing with.

She stood a little straighter and tried to project that she didn't have time for any extra duties.

"A message for me? Who is it from?"

"I don't know, ma'am. Just that it's flagged private for Lieutenant Bixby. Could you come with me, please?" The words were subservient, but the tone was not at all. Something smelled off about this, and Samuels' anxiety increased. Had her cover been blown? Had something happened at the docks that tipped their hand? Was this an attempt to remove her from the crowd so she could be arrested quietly with no chance to evade?

Apparently, some trace of Samuels' thoughts must have reached her face, despite the normal control of her features. The other woman leaned in closer and said, sotto voce, "Elena sent me. She needs to talk."

Relief flooded Monica, and she followed the other woman back toward the corridor she had just exited.

Samuels fell into step behind the woman and within a few dozen meters they were out of the press and beyond the range where others might overhear.

"Is there a problem?" Samuels asked, while thinking that there were already more problems than she knew how to handle.

"Yes," the woman said. Then followed with, "Not here."

Samuels remained silent thereafter while they wended their way down two levels and then farther outstation. Eventually, they turned into an alley between businesses in the food district. They went up a flight of stairs and entered a building above a Korean restaurant, down a short hallway, and stopped at the third door. The woman knocked with a peculiar pattern, then stood back and waited while she was scanned from within.

After a few moments, the door opened and the woman gestured for Samuels to precede her. Once inside, she took a quick look around to gauge her surroundings and found little of note. It looked like a run of the mill apartment, with only a few modifications. The front wall and door had been reinforced with metal plating. There were no standard furnishings in the front room, only an electronics workbench that ran the full length of one wall, and three weapons racks along the two others.

Elena came walking out from somewhere in the back, and Ricky, her husband, was at her heels. Another woman, even shorter than Samuels' guide, appeared from behind her after resealing the door. As stressful as her last few days had been, seeing two friends from her previous life did her heart good. The woman who had been her guide and the other were unknowns, though, so she kept to her incognito status. Her old incognito persona, not her new one. *When did I sign up for this complicated a life?* She silently asked herself.

"You must be Elena," she said, before Elena could say anything that might betray their history.

"That's right," Elena said, picking up on the hint. "And you are Captain Samuels?"

"Yes, good to meet you."

"Auger," the doorkeeper said, though there was no French accent to accompany the odd pronunciation. "My name is Srini," the guide introduced herself, extending her hand to shake.

"Ricardo." He stepped around his wife to make the same gesture.

"Good to meet you all, and I'd love to chit-chat, but I'm on a very tight schedule. Srini says there's a problem. What is it?"

Elena smiled. "You sound just like...a boss I used to have." She caught herself before letting any felines out of flexible containers in front of Srini or Auger. "The problem is that we heard the PMs are not going to let you take any arms from the station, which puts us in a tough spot, since we had already started making plans based on having those in our possession."

"That's right, but how did you hear about it so quickly? I had just come from the colonel's office when Srini came to find me."

"We have sources that are...close...to the colonel," Auger supplied.

Samuels accepted that at face value, and didn't attempt to pry further. "Anyway, I've been racking my brain since I left the colonel, trying to figure out what I can do, but I just can't see anything else I can do to get those weapons for you. And I don't really have time to put together another plan, since if I don't get the missiles that the colonel will let me take back to my ship in the next eighty minutes, everyone there will be sitting ducks."

"You made us a promise, Warner," Srini said coldly. "I suppose I shouldn't be surprised. Warner guaranteed to defend our system, and look how well they've kept their word on that. We have been suffering and dying here for years, and Warner only now noticed us at all."

"I know," Samuels responded quietly, "but what else can I do? We gambled on the best plan we could put together, but all our bets didn't pay off as we expected. That's not reneging, that's the way taking chances works. Not every throw of the dice comes up sixes. And trust me, it could have gone a lot worse than it did."

"Not for you and yours, Warner. You're getting what you came for, and leaving us to fend for ourselves. Again. It's like I told you, Auger. We can't trust Warners to help us. We have to move on our own."

Samuels turned to face the small, dark woman, frustration and anger starting to build within her.

"Srini, all Warner naval officers have taken an oath to defend Warner citizens, and that includes you and every Granadan. But I cannot work miracles. In the short term, I am not doing anything to help you out of your plight, but in the long term, I am.

"By protecting that captured ship and taking it and our Forrester prisoners back to Earth, we can prove what's been done to your people. Once that happens, it won't be just Warner that comes back here, it will be all of Combined Fleet. Forrest won't last an entire day after that happens. I just need you to understand that that's all I can do right now. I don't have any more dice to throw."

Srini made a derisive sound and turned her back on Samuels. "I think we still have to go now. The Warners aren't helping us directly, or even knowingly, but they are creating a lot of confusion. I say we take advantage of it and make a run for the armory ourselves."

"Srini, sometimes you have the patience of a lightning bolt. You always want to go, and go now," Elena added.

Srini spun and faced Elena. "It's better than sitting on my hands and waiting for *Warners* to do anything."

"Ladies," Ricky interposed, sticking his hand in between the two would-be combatants. "You are not each other's enemies, and neither are the Warners. Let's just let Cozette decide what we'll do."

All eyes turned to Auger, who mumbled something.

"I'm sorry, what was that?" Samuels asked.

"I'm thinking," Auger responded.

"I think you think too much," Srini muttered to herself, but Samuels heard it all too clearly.

Auger must have caught it too, for she glared at Srini. "We're going to have to wait for another opportunity," the woman decided. "You're right that there is greater confusion in the Forrest ranks right now, but that also means that everyone is on heightened alert. And just like the captain here, I can't think of a plan to get to those weapons with any chance of success. If we had any such plan, we would have tried for them sooner than this."

Srini clenched her fists and tensed every muscle in her body. Samuels was afraid she was going to start a fight with everyone in the room, but finally she let out a loud snarl and stomped over to a stool by the electronics bench. Plopping herself down, she said, "I just get so tired of doing nothing! I know why we wait for the right moment, but sometimes I think the 'right moment' is never going to arrive and we should just do...*something*...even if it's not the perfect situation!"

"Srini, they have the weapons, and the power. We have to move only when we clearly will gain an advantage. This is chess, not Battleship," Auger answered, referencing two ancient games. "We can't simply attack at random times and places and hope we cause damage. They'll eat us alive if we try that."

The small woman threw up her hands and turned away. "I know, I know! You remind me of that every time."

"To be successful in freeing ourselves, we have to have focused, directed attacks. We need a specific objective which leads us toward our eventual goal, and plans for every likely contingency. If someone could show me that, and if there were a reasonable chance of success, I'd be willing to discuss it. But no one has shown me anything which does yet."

Samuels moved closer to the main group. "Um, Auger? I just thought of something that might work. Might. Still very long odds, and high risk."

"Well, trot it out and let's discuss it."

"Okay, the main reason our current plan fell apart was that the colonel won't let any weapons be transferred off the station, because she thinks it's a political maneuver by someone to make her look bad, right?"

"Right."

"And most likely, she's contacted the armory to inform them that they are not to turn over anything to me, no matter what orders I present."

"Most likely," Auger agreed.

"But the majority of what we had to convince them to give us those weapons were official orders, which you provided, official uniforms, which we provided, and the ability to display the right attitude so no one got suspicious. That last part, you could perform as easily as we Warners could, if you picked the right sort of people."

Auger shook her head. "Yeah, but they're not going to give us weapons because they've already been warned not to by their commanding officer."

Samuels held up a hand, holding back the protest. "Except that what they've been warned against is letting them be transferred off-station. If you can produce official orders as easily as it appears you can, they can say anything, including moving them somewhere other than off the station and delivering them to someone other than Lieutenant Bixby."

"Hm. I don't know. We were able to generate those orders because they 'officially' came from groundside, so it was a matter of inserting them into the communications logs. That wouldn't work for what you're suggesting, because the weapons aren't going off the station, so orders to move them wouldn't have originated on Granada. And having been warned, the armory is likely to check with higher authority before they do anything."

"What about the person close to the colonel you mentioned. Could they forge official orders? Could they intercept a confirmation call?" Samuels offered.

"Hm," Auger said again, and for a time said nothing else while she considered. "Possibly, but it would be a considerable risk."

"Risky yes, Auger," Srini pounced on the opportunity, "but it meets your requirements. It's a specific objective, it gets us closer to our eventual goal, and it has a reasonable chance of success. I say we go."

"Easy. I said those were my requirements to discuss the plan, not to endorse it. With the previous plan, we could take the weapons and stash them away for later use. No one would have been looking for them, because they would assume the arms were gone from the station. With this plan, as soon as the weapons don't arrive at where they're supposed to be going, someone will notice. If we take them this way, we have to use them immediately. And that will involve a lot more planning."

"Are you certain of that?" Elena asked. "That someone will notice, I mean. Is it common practice for the armory officer to check in with the destination to make sure they arrived? Or is it more likely that once the soldiers who pick them up have signed for them, the attitude would be that it's no longer their responsibility?"

"That seems more likely to me," Srini opined. "Plus, we could put the op together quickly enough to still take advantage of the confusion having Warner warships in the system provides. Unusual circumstances often lead to unusual orders, and people won't bat an eye at seeing something new come their way."

"Hm," Auger considered. "All right, it's worth pursuing a little further, at least. Let's put our heads together, and start looking at contingencies."

"Auger?" Samuels interrupted. "I'm sorry, but I really can't stay to help any more than offering an idea. I've already used up ten of my remaining eighty minutes. I've got to be going."

"Right," Auger said, crossing to Samuels. "Best of luck to you. Elena will guide you back to the docks, and collect the uniforms we'll need. Srini, Ricky and I will keep working on a plan."

"Nothing but success to you, Auger."

"Please, call me Cozette."

"Monica." They clasped hands firmly but briefly, and then Samuels and Elena were out the door and gone.

Samuels found it difficult to keep from breaking into a sprint, but she did not want to draw any attention to herself. For her part, Elena had a hard time not peppering Samuels with questions, but slaves did not talk over old times with Forrest officers.

They continued in silence until they had reached their destination. Major Tunney was noticeably relieved to see her when Samuels arrived. They were nearly finished loading the missiles, and he was facing the question of what to do about not having his ship's captain on hand when it was time to go.

"It's good to see you, ma'am. How did the other part of our orders go?"

"They didn't, Top. Would you join me inside the shuttle to discuss some changes?"

His eyebrows rose, and he looked suspiciously at Elena, but he said only, "Certainly, ma'am."

Others had also noticed her arrival, and Roberts and Cipi were right behind Tunney coming up the loading ramp and into the shuttle. Cipi and Elena embraced briefly, then he made introductions all around.

"What's going on, Captain," Roberts asked.

"The plan to deliver weapons to the GU fell apart. Instead, we're going to give them our uniforms and let them work out their own plan to get the weapons they need." Samuels turned to Elena. "Is there somewhere near here where we can get some shipsuits?"

"Uh, not really. Most freighters would have some in their slop chests, but this is the wrong part of the station to find them."

"Garbage. Guess it's going to be a cold ride back to *Peru*."

"Ma'am?" Tunney again had his eyebrows up in his hairline.

"Well, I am not going to let modesty get in the way of keeping my promise, especially not after I failed to deliver the weapons I said I could. All you Marines, Roberts, and I are going to ride home in our undies. Do you have a problem with that?"

"No, ma'am. Marines have their modesty surgically removed in Basic. But I think I will use the term 'skivvies' instead of 'undies' when I brief the troops."

Samuels grinned at the big soldier, despite herself. "Good man. You round up all the duffel, and get it into a bag for Elena here to take back with her. Elena, you go with him. Roberts, you get the pilot started on the departure request, then peel. Cipi, you supervise getting the last of the missiles loaded, and make sure all our people are accounted for. Let's move it."

Tunney and Roberts jumped to obey, but Cipi and Elena held back.

"You cannot do this thing, Capitán. For a leader to go unclothed is...indecorous. The people will lose respect for you."

"Cipi, a good leader does not ask her people to do anything which she is not willing to do herself. And I do not have the time to argue with you. Now go, Bosun."

"Yes, Capitán," he said unhappily, but moved to obey.

Once he left, Elena looked around to be sure they were alone. "It was good to see you, Mica. I wish it were better circumstances."

"You and me both, Elena. I am in so far over my head, I can't even see the surface anymore."

"I don't think so. From what I've observed, you've got people around you who aren't afraid to disagree with you, but still follow your direction. I think you've got the same knack for leading that your father has. He never made the mistake of thinking a leader was the person who everyone had to obey. He led by making connections with people, and building relationships based on trust. You'll do fine, kid."

With that, Elena hugged the younger woman and made her way down the ramp to catch up with Major Tunney.

Within five minutes, the hatch was sealed and they were pulling away from the docks. Within five more minutes, nine men had approached and politely offered her their shirt. She politely declined each with increasing exasperation, then finally accepted the tenth with, "Oh, for heaven's sake. Fine."

CHAPTER 38
19 October
WSMC Assault Shuttle

Samuels leaned back in her seat, closed her eyes, and let out a long, slow breath. It would be at least a thirty-minute transit back to *Peru*, and the thought of napping during that time was very tempting. Unfortunately, tired as she was physically, her brain was looking ahead at what had to happen next. It, at lea st, was too amped up to let her rest.

If she stopped for a break at times like this, where she knew fighting was coming soon, she invariably saw the panic-stricken face of Morrison when she ordered him to go with her into the boatbay. Twenty minutes later, he had been dead, so his panic had turned out to be well warranted. She had grown somewhat accustomed to the image, and used it as a reminder that if there was anything, anything at all, she could do to avoid more deaths, she needed to do it. She could always sleep after the battle, and if she died fighting, well, that would just be a longer rest.

She arose from her seat and made her way forward. The walking was awkward, since every available space, aisles included, had been packed with munitions or engineering spares. Traditional shuttles had commodious holds and minimal berthing, since they were usually meant for short-term duty, getting things from point A to point B. Assault shuttles, by contrast, sometimes had lengthy deployments, with the goal of delivering an effective fighting force to point B, which consisted of equal parts personnel and gear. Part of keeping up appearances had been the transfer of loads suitable for normal transport vehicles, so the sheer volume of cargo aboard far exceeded what would fit in the lower compartments.

At the forward bulkhead, she had to climb over a crate to get to the flight deck, scraping her bare legs as she slid off the opposite side. She ignored the pain; if there was no time to sleep, she wasn't about to let minor injuries get in her way.

Auberjonois, a lanky Granadan woman, was co-piloting next to Staff Sergeant McMurray, who had what she considered the "helm," though in Marine lingo, he had the "stick."

"Can either of you tell me where those inbound Forrest shuttles are? Are we going to beat them back? I know we were behind our planned exit from Caspar," Samuels asked while dropping carefully into the astrogator's seat.

"Tracking them now, ma'am," McMurray said, making a quick adjustment that allowed her to see his heads-up display.

Samuels leaned across so she could see the HUD display. "Hm. Looks like they're behind schedule, too. Why would they have slowed their approach?"

The pilot shook his head. "No idea, ma'am, but I can't say it breaks my heart."

"Nor mine, Sergeant. I make it 72 minutes from our arrival at *Peru* to theirs. Any way we can add to that?"

Auberjonois chimed in, "Caspar will be monitoring local traffic, so we thought it best to leave that envelope before increasing speed, so we will not look suspicious."

Samuels nodded, though she wasn't sure either of the pilots could see her, as she sat behind them. "How far out are we now?"

"Not quite 600 kilometers."

Samuels considered a moment before responding. "That's far enough. Let's go for maximum thrust now. There's not much they can do to us at this point. At least not that they aren't already planning on."

"But what about GU? Aren't we leaving them exposed if we do something ... wonky?"

"Wonky, huh? No, it shouldn't. As far as the Forresters know, there is no connection between us and Granada Unfettered. And they know we have orders to deliver these munitions to their system fleet, which could easily include orders to hurry. I think we're okay to expedite."

"Expedite the captain asks for, expedite the captain gets." McMurray leaned forward and adjusted a few controls. Samuels watched as another digit was added to the number of newtons on the 'Net Thrust' line of the HUD.

That was the only change she could detect. There was no sense of acceleration, no objects near enough see any change in position, nothing. Only numbers on a screen to indicate they were pushing the small craft to near its limits.

"Thank you, Sergeant. Now, have either of you been in contact with *Peru*? So they know we've left the station, and so they know when to expect those hostiles? Unless I miss my guess, Lieutenant Aichele is going to have every able body working on defenses, and that will include any sort of Bridge or Comm watch."

Auberjonois answered, "No, ma'am. I'll do that now."

"Yes, please do that. If you can get Aichele on the vocom, call me back up here. It'll be a pleasure to tell him we've got more time in hand than we thought we would. In the meantime, I'm going to go finalize our plans with the Marines."

"Yes, ma'am," McMurray said to her retreating back.

When Auberjonois could see she had shimmied back over the crate blocking the short passage up to the flight deck, she said, "What do you think of Captain Samuels?"

"Well, she's pretty enough, but a little young for me."

The non-com received a smack on the arm for his efforts. "That's not what I meant."

"Then what exactly did you mean?"

"She looks like a skinny little girl who belongs in secondary. And we're supposed to trust her to save us from a light regiment of Forrest Marines that are about to hit *Redentor*."

"You mean *Peru*."

"We'll see."

"Well, I suppose we will, and there's still the possibility the ship will wind up being called *Scythe* again, too."

"Right. But you didn't tell me what you really think of the captain."

"I take it you haven't heard any of the stories about her, then?"

"What stories?"

"I was one of the Marines that was sent in to recapture *Pathfinder*. I have to admit, I was a little nervous going in, because while I had trained and drilled on what to do, and what to expect, I hadn't ever had to actually fight my way into a ship and take it away from anybody. So, I'm amped up and scared, and mad, and ready to kick some Forrest butt when we breached the hull and came storming into the boatbay." He stopped speaking and chuckled.

"And then what?"

"And then Captain Samuels throws us a salute and gives us permission to come aboard. She and two Marines had taken out a full platoon of Forresters, including heavy armor, before we even arrived.

"That's better than five to one odds, and all three of them came through it banged up, but alive. So, that's what I think of our captain. She may look like my baby sister, but any commander that can bring her people out from under those kind of odds is the kind of commander I want planning my ops."

McMurray turned and looked squarely at his co-pilot. "Do you know who Chowdhury is?"

"Chowdhury? Wasn't she the one in the center of that Humboldt uprising a bunch of years ago?"

"That's the one. Anyway, she's my CO. And she has a well-earned reputation as a *very* tough Marine. Well, I overheard her telling Commodore Brighton that she couldn't have executed a better plan herself."

Auberjonois was silent for a handful of seconds after the sergeant finished. "Wow," she finally said. "Sounds like we're in pretty good hands, then."

"The best," McMurray confirmed. "Now you better follow her orders and contact *Peru*."

"You mean *Redentor*."

* * * * *

Samuels pushed off with her hands and used her legs to swing herself away from the crate, avoiding a repeat of the scrapes she had already collected. Landing gracefully, she headed aft until she spotted Cipi, and she waved for him and Pablo to join her. She continued aft and the two Felixes trotted up behind her just as she reached her goal, a collection of Marine officers having a low-pitched discussion. Roberts, also wearing a borrowed shirt, was speaking with Mdembe a little to one side, but they moved in when they saw Samuels approaching.

"Major, do you mind if I intrude?"

"Of course not, Captain. May I be the first to congratulate you on a completely successful raid?"

"Thank you, but the credit belongs to your Marines and Cipi's people. They're the ones who made it all work."

Cipi said, "It is true that the people were able to carry out the plan very well, but do not minimize your own part. The plan itself was entirely of your devising, and it was far more audacious than any of us would have dared to propose."

"The bosun is correct, ma'am. This was your victory more than anyone else's."

"Fine," she said, blushing, and then even more embarrassed about blushing. "Thank you again. Now, let's assume the boss has been sufficiently buttered up and move on to our next steps. After all, this victory is not permanent, and we have a long way to go before we are out of the woods."

The major's face became serious. "No victory is permanent, ma'am."

"You're right, Major, and I know we need to celebrate just a little. Make sure your people know that I'm proud of them. Same for you, Cipi."

"Yes, ma'am," Tunney said, right on top of Cipi's, "I will do this thing."

"Now, the next thing we need to firmly establish is the chain of command." Everyone looked at her strangely at that, but she could see she had their full attention. "We have to be clear up front. Everyone has to know who's calling the shots, and who takes over if the captain is incapacitated.

"So, at the top, defense of *Peru* is my responsibility, and I am the ultimate authority unless Commodore Brighton specifically orders otherwise. Ensign Roberts is my second, and she may issue orders in my name until further notice. She and I will have to be covering different areas during the fighting, and I don't want her to try running every decision past me first. Clear so far?"

A chorus of "Yes, ma'am"s and nods were her answer.

"Good, because this is where we depart from tradition."

That same strange look came over the faces of all the Marines. Cipi's face did not change, but his eyes sharpened noticeably.

"Cipi, I don't know how much of Warner's military structure you're familiar with, but normally, the Marines and Navy are completely separate, except at the very top. So, I can tell Major Tunney what I what done, but I can't order any individual Marine to do it.

"By the same token, the bosun and the crew are under naval command, so if a Marine wants a crewman to do something, she has to send it up the Marine chain to the commander, who talks to the captain, who sends the commands down her chain until it gets to the crewman affected."

"It sounds very... inefficient," Cipi noted.

"It is, but it keeps things organized, and keeps one branch from stepping on the other's toes. But right now, inefficiency is the last thing we need. So, again, until further notice, the Marines are in charge of ship defense, so they get to tell you what to do, as if it came from the captain. Is that clear?"

"Yes, Capitán."

"And now for the more difficult change," Samuels said, turning to Major Tunney. His eyebrows rose, but he said nothing.

"Lieutenant Aichele is the head of security for *Peru*, so I am temporarily placing you under his command and that of his deputy, Staff Sergeant Burton."

Samuels paused and waited for the eruption, marshalling her arguments to defend her decision.

"You do realize just how many of those 'Marine's toes' you're stepping on here, don't you? I don't think even a ship's captain has the authority to make that order stick. And *Lieutenant* Aichele?"

"Believe me, Major, I do recognize all that. And I am not acting out of caprice or favoritism. If you'll recall, I recommended that you stay with the ship and organize defenses instead of going on this raid. I understand your reasons for coming with us, and I agree the reasons were good ones, but by doing so, I had to ask someone else to make a defensive plan and prepare the ship. At this point, we don't have time to switch leaders, and the one with the plan should be the one to see it executed. And a ship's chief security officer has to be an officer, so I petitioned Major Chowdhury, who is still listed as his current CO, to give him a field promotion. Which she did."

Tunney was silent for a few moments, absorbing the statements. Finally, he said, "As you say, Captain, this isn't the time, either for confusion in the chain of command, or for power struggles. I will still command my own troops, but will place myself under the orders of the man on the scene. And may I add, Captain, that Aichele amply deserves his promotion."

"Thank you, Major. I am certainly glad that we can spend what time we have getting ready, rather than — "

"Captain to the Flight Deck," sounded everywhere at once.

"Okay, got to run. All of you here put your heads together and organize everyone into teams of one or two Marines with two or three Granadans. Then introduce them so they know who they're going to be working with. First priority when we dock will be getting those missiles loaded into tubes. After that, if everyone already has a team, Aichele can just assign them a location to defend, and he can divide them up as he sees fit. Except for Sullivan. Don't assign her to a team, because I have a special assignment for her.

"Jherri, you come with me."

Samuels turned and jogged back the way she had come, weaving around spare parts and missiles. Roberts fell in behind her, and Samuels could hear the beginnings of animated conversation in her wake.

Samuels went up and over the obstructing crate much more quickly this time, and without any additional damage, diving feet-first through the opening and reaching over her head to grab the hatch sill as she went by, landing softly on her feet. More and more, the skills she had developed during her time working on crowded transports was resurfacing when she needed it. Plus, there were times when her skinniness was an asset.

Auberjonois stared at her with her mouth open, and McMurray gave the co-pilot a knowing grin. Samuels ignored the byplay and said aloud, "You there, Aichele?"

There was no audible response, but the sergeant handed her a headset. "Can you put it on the overhead? I want Ensign Roberts to participate."

"Overhead the captain asks for, overhead the captain gets."

"Can you hear me, Lieutenant?"

"Yes, Captain. I'm in the comm room with Sergeant Burton, and Ms. Auberjonois has already given us an update on the expected arrival of the Forresters, though it looks like they've seen you coming back and have increased acceleration again."

"How are the defenses looking?"

"Not perfect, but not bad. As you know, the basic plan is for a layered defense, with the expectation to fall back if needed, but still have some protection set up. I've added a few wrinkles to that which should be unexpected for the enemy troops."

"Knowing you, that does not surprise me. I think I've come up with a wrinkle or two myself, one of which I need to discuss with Sergeant McMurray, and the other we can discuss when we arrive, which will be in..."

"Five minutes, eighteen seconds," McMurray supplied.

"What? What's your thrust output?"

"Emergency maximum, ma'am." Samuels' eyebrows rose sharply. "The captain did say, 'expedite,'" he said unapologetically.

She grinned at him. "Well, it's no wonder those Forrester shuttles noticed us. Aichele, I'm planning to fight with the group defending the bridge, and I'm sending Ensign Roberts to Engineering. We can cover details when we dock, but you should be aware that I've suspended the normal chain of command for the duration of the fighting. All Warner and Granadan crew will be under the command of the Marines, and Major Tunney will be taking orders from you and Sergeant Burton."

"You did what?" she heard Burton's strangled voice from somewhere away from the pickup.

"Ma'am, I don't believe you can actually do that. Legally, I mean."

"Oh, I know that, and so does Major Tunney. If I survive, I'll probably face charges and you'll be working with Captain Roberts. Until then, I think it will save people's lives for you to be coordinating all the wrinkles in our ship's defense, and that's all I care about."

There was another long pause before Aichele spoke. "All right. I'll certainly do my best."

"You always do, Lieutenant."

"Yes. Well, I have one more wrinkle I'm still working on, so I'd best get to it, if there's nothing else, Captain?"

"I have another wrinkle myself, which I am about to explain to Sergeant McMurray when we're done. But there is one more thing. Could you have someone meet the shuttles with a fresh uniform for myself, Ensign Roberts, and all the Marines? We seem to have … misplaced ours."

"You did what?" Burton repeated.

CHAPTER 39
19 October
WNS *Peru*

The newly-minted Lieutenant Aichele stood next to the massive airlock doors that separated the expansive boatbay from the starboard hangar, waiting for the pressure to equalize so that it might open. Next to him were all the remaining crew, except for Fernandez and two other specialists who were still working on his latest "wrinkle." Between each pair of them was an anti-grav pallet with specialized cradles designed to fit the Mark-20 ship-to-ship missiles.

The indicator switched to green and the door unsealed at the deck, rising upward and allowing a blast of frigid air to flow into the bay. The rear hatch of the shuttle was dropping at the same time, and Captain Samuels jumped off the end before it was three-fourths open. She jogged over to him wearing a large blue-gray shirt, with sleeves cuffed up and hanging below her knees.

Aichele came to attention and saluted, followed by all the others, the Granadans doing their best to imitate their neighbors. "Welcome aboard, Captain," he intoned.

Samuels returned the honor quickly. "Save that for when I'm not out of uniform, and when I've got spare time for such things. Speaking of which…"

"Collecting them was no problem, since everyone left theirs in a pile in the boatbay when you left, and no one's had time to clean them up yet," he said, handing over her uniform.

"Thank you," she responded, pulling the pants on under the oversized shirt, but continuing as she dressed. "Aichele, would you get everyone working on unloading, then meet me on the bridge in ten minutes to go over your defensive plan. Ask the Marine officers to join us. Jherri, I'll want you there as well. When you see Sullivan, invite her, too. Giannini, give me a quick status on Engineering, and then you oversee the transfer of missiles into the magazines."

Everyone except the chief engineer moved off after acknowledging their orders, and Samuels and Giannini moved inboard through the boatbay as they talked.

"Aye, ma'am. Propulsion systems are online and show green for all tests we were able to run—"

Samuels held up a hand and looked at her chief engineer. "What does that mean, exactly?"

Giannini smiled slightly at not being able to sneak the line by without being noticed. "Well, we followed Phase 1 of the checkout procedure to the letter, and the power plant runs perfectly, all the way up to 125% for five minutes, as prescribed. Phase 2 passed with no downchecks as well, with a stable Gravitas field created at minimal power. The problem was in Phase 3 of the checkout. We couldn't push full power into the field without actually moving the ship, which seemed like a bad idea, without checking with you, in case you had other plans..."

"I see," Samuels smiled. "You thought I had some devious plan in mind, and didn't want to spoil it?"

Giannini smiled back, "Don't you?"

Samuels raised a hand and let it waver back and forth. "Well, a plan, at any rate. You did right, but be ready to move the ship at maximum in about twenty minutes. Probably in the middle of you overseeing the arms transfer. Who do you have second to you in Engineering?"

"Greg Pineda. He was the electronics crew chief during construction. Good engineer."

"Where's Greg now?"

"Coming off the shuttle behind you."

"Okay, make sure he's briefed, but quickly. We need the capability to shoot within the next fifteen minutes."

"Fifteen minutes aye, ma'am."

Samuels put her palms to her temples as she felt the weight of the timing hit her again. "All right, skip the blow-by-blow, and just tell me what isn't working yet."

"Top of the list is an intermittent fault in the air scrubbers. That's the most critical problem, but also the one that's going to take the longest to isolate and correct. Planning to save that until after we kick the Forresters out an airlock. Acceleration compensators had a major problem until one of the Granadans remembered he had rewritten the firmware. Should be good now, but there hasn't been time for a full checkout. Primaries are good, fuel system is good, environmental is good except for the air problem I just mentioned, weapons are green, tactical is green, even the new features that I haven't ever seen in a ship before. If we can keep from being blown up by the bad guys, we should survive."

"Well, you'll have to talk to ... Lieutenant Aichele about that," Samuels said, amending at the last moment. "How are things with you two?" She asked instead.

"I didn't know the captain was aware that there was an 'us two'."

Samuels turned to look at the older woman with a smile. "I was aware way back on *Pathfinder* that there was an attraction between you, being neither blind nor stupid. And now?"

"That, my dear Captain, is yet another system that I have not had time to give a full checkout yet. I will let you know, if and when we figure it out ourselves."

"Fair enough. And good luck with that. He is a very good man, but about as stubborn as they come."

"I know. Endearing, isn't it?"

Samuels just grinned and shook her head. "Whatever you say, Chief Engineer. All right, I'm headed to the bridge. Let me know the instant we've got our first missile locked in the tube."

"Will do, ma'am. And Captain?"

"Yes?"

"I sure hope your plan is devious enough."

"Well, we're about to find out."

* * * * *

"Captain on the bridge!" Major Tunney announced.

Samuels walked onto the bridge to see everyone else already there. "As you were. I suppose you're wondering why I've called you all together here."

Aichele stifled a laugh, but the others merely looked confused. "Never mind. I suppose a joke only works to lighten the mood if everyone gets the reference."

Samuels took a moment to collect her thoughts moving from face to face of the team, wondering how many of them would still be there on the other side of the coming battle. She cleared her throat, mostly to clear her mind of such unhelpful thoughts, and began.

"Most of you should be aware, but for those who are not, Lieutenant Aichele has assumed the position of head of ship's security. As such, until this crisis is past, all of you, except Ensign Roberts and myself, are under his authority. Is everyone clear on that?"

All replied with nods or 'Yes, ma'am's. "Good. Now I'll turn this briefing over to him to review his plans, and I'll add a few things after that. I expect everyone to be looking for the weak points, and offering ways to improve. No plan is perfect, and whatever we can do now to prevent our own losses or inflict more damage on the intruders, I want to hear about. Lieutenant."

"Thank you, Captain. If you'll watch the main screen, I've overlaid the defensive positions we've constructed on *Peru*'s deckplan. We've assumed that the Forresters will try to breach as close to midships, C Deck, as they can manage."

"Why?" Pablo Felix asked, though not belligerently.

The question, unexpected, caught Aichele off guard. Surprisingly, it was Sullivan who answered. "A number of reasons contribute to that being the accepted approach for a hostile boarding. First is that the boarding team has three primary objectives, to secure Bridge, AuxBridge, and Engineering. The second is that the act of breaching the hull is the time of greatest vulnerability, so splitting your force into two units before breaching will lead to much heavier losses just getting into the ship. A midships, middecks entry gives them equal access to all three objectives with only one breach.

"Third is that there are a lot of sensitive systems concentrated around the bridge and Engineering, so if you're planning to use the ship later, which is why you board rather than destroy from a distance, then it makes sense not to create big holes in the fore or aft sections."

"I see. But don't they have enough troops coming in to be able to split them up? And if they have multiple ships attacking, how can they use the same opening?" Pablo persisted.

"That is a possibility, of course, and one that we've considered," Aichele picked up the discussion. "Normally, a shuttle that attaches itself to the hull is inside our scanners' pickup envelope. In this case, Sergeant Burton led a team EVA to connect a temporary network of security sensors to the outside of the ship, so we should be able to pinpoint where they're coming in with as little as 90 seconds, and as much as four minutes' warning. The plan takes that into account by having multiple layers of defenses. If they come in where we expect, we can bloody their noses repeatedly as we fall back. If they do something unexpected, we have a little time to reposition so we're not caught exposed. It still won't be ideal, but it won't be catastrophic, either.

"For the other point, a smart commander will concentrate his forces at the point of attack, making the defenders spread out to cover all the possible approaches so they're weaker at any given position until they're reinforced. So the attacker gains a foothold and secures it with the initial thrust from one shuttle, and has the other shuttles link airlocks to continue pouring troops in at the established bridgehead."

"Thank you, sir, for the explanation. I apologize if I am unduly slowing us down."

"Not at all. I may have been doing this job a long time, but there's no guarantee I've thought of everything. Please don't stay quiet if something doesn't make sense, or if you think there may be a better way. In addition, I'm counting on you all to spread this information around, which you can't do very well if I haven't explained it well enough to you."

"Thank you," Pablo repeated.

"So, back to the deck plan. The gray lines in the corridors show where we have erected makeshift barriers out of excess decking, with the intention of holding only so long as they provide a tactical advantage, then falling back to the next redoubt. They aren't fancy, but will offer some additional protection during the fighting."

"Enough protection for us who do not have battle armor?" Cipi asked.

"Probably not, though it depends on what the invaders are planning to use against us. They are certainly proof against fletchettes, and offer good protection for the first couple of energy hits. But they are makeshift, and the metal was not purpose-built to deflect those kinds of energies. Since I hear that the raiding party was not able to come back with additional small arms, I'm not planning to put Granadans out in these areas, where they are unprotected, if they don't have anything to fight with."

"Are you intending that we cower somewhere out of sight while others are fighting for our freedom? Do you think so little of us, that you ignore us completely in your battle plans?"

"Nothing of the sort, Mr. Felix. We are likely to be so outnumbered, that if we had a way to arm all of you, I would put you all at the front lines and let you take your chances. But we don't have the weapons to do that. So instead, we have to improvise some way for you to fight back, and hopefully, to protect you from counter fire as much as possible."

"And what is that way?"

"I'm glad you asked me." Abruptly, the display changed, showing seven decks instead of the four that had been there before.

"What are those marks on the interstitial decks?" Samuels asked.

"The first thing I did when I started planning our defense, was to pull a set of the ship's plans to work from. When I made the request of the database, what I got was the first set you were looking at before. I had occasion to go to one of the interstitial decks to retrieve some Marines a short time later, and it occurred to me that when the Forresters started planning, they pulled the same set of plans I did.

"All most Marines see of a ship are the living and operational decks, unless they've spent some time working ship security, which Forrester Marines almost certainly have not. So, to answer your question, Captain, those marks are where we've set up some nasty surprises for our guests that Granadans can man without being exposed to direct return fire."

"And what is the nature of this surprise," Pablo asked.

"I doubt any of you would have heard of them, but what we have set up at each of those markers is what was known in medieval times as a murder-hole."

Samuels made a startled sound. "What? What are you using, boiling oil?"

"No, ma'am. We don't have enough, and powered armor wouldn't even notice it. Heavy armor will shrug off most anything small enough that any of the Granadans could carry. That was the wall I kept hitting when I was looking for a way that the non-Marines could contribute. Powered armor distributes the kinetic or plasmic energy of any strike over the entire framework of the suit, and small arms just don't provide enough punch to overwhelm the energy redistribution."

"But you have found something which will do this overwhelming," Cipi surmised.

"It was Fernandez, actually, who gave me the idea. Well, her thought combined with more medieval weaponry. I was complaining about needing more mass to add to the force of a blow, and she pointed out that most of one hold contained raw hull-grade steel in standardized 58-kilo bars. It takes the machine shop about two minutes to lengthen it out and sharpen one end to make a weighty lance."

"But how do our people with only muscle power apply enough force to breach armor?" Major Tunney asked.

"The machine shop also turned out some hastily designed mortar tubes, and some of the ship's scuttling charges have been repurposed to provide the propellant. Targeting is set up with a security bug on the corridor ceiling tied into a handheld monitor. Chrysler is writing some simple code to put crosshairs on the display."

"That is...devious, Lieutenant. And exactly what we need. You have my compliments," Samuels said, somewhat in awe.

"It's what Marines do, ma'am. Improvise, adapt, and overcome. These are going to be single-use weapons, of course, and there was a limit to how much explosive material Forrest left here, so there are not as many as I would like. Once a Granadan fires, he or she should fall back to the next line of defense immediately."

"Missile 4, Bridge," sounded from a speaker at the Comm station. Sullivan took a couple steps over and toggled the line active. "Bridge, aye."

"Please inform the captain that tube 8 is loaded and active, all systems check out green. We'll load more tubes as the missiles are stocked in the magazine."

Samuels, who had crossed the command deck herself by this time, responded, "Good work, Crystal. Are all the status boards at Tactical tied in?"

"Yes, ma'am."

"Very well, we'll monitor from here. Give your people a well-earned pat on the back when the magazine is loaded, then start organizing damage control parties. It won't be long now before we'll need them."

Samuels toggled the circuit off, not waiting for an acknowledgement, then turned to her assembled staff. "Mr. Aichele, I'm going to need one of your Marines to take the Comm board. Sullivan, can you run Tactical?"

The blonde woman seemed to hesitate a few moments, as if trying to recall, then answered, "Yes, ma'am." Her voice seemed slightly altered when she said it, but Samuels was too focused on other things to notice.

"Good. Roberts, you take Helm during the ship to ship engagement, then I want you down at Engineering. Be prepared to take over command if you lose comm link to the bridge."

"Aye, ma'am."

"Lieutenant, I'm sorry we didn't finish your briefing, but it's time to move now. You and Chief Felix get your people where they need to be and tell them what they need to know. Tell them to expect company in..." She turned to Sullivan, who supplied, "Twenty-five minutes."

"...Twenty-five minutes. I'll address the troops via shipwide in five. Dismissed."

Aichele snapped to attention, and Cipi, seeing the action, did his best to imitate him. She returned the honor, then both men went quickly out, with the rest who had assignments off the bridge hurrying after.

Lieutenant Tucker had been among those in the staff meeting, and Samuels had noticed the non-verbal commands Aichele had sent her way, so she wasn't surprised to see the woman take station at Comms. Samuels took her own station, and then said, "Record for transmission."

"Ready."

"Attention, Forrest vessels. You are approaching WNS *Peru*, a warship of the Warner Space Navy, during a time of heightened alert. You are hereby directed to state your intentions, or be considered hostile combatants. Captain Samuels clear."

"Message in memory, Captain."

"Send it. Put a copy in the ship's log along with the comm log copy."

"Transmitted."

"Tactical, what's the time to message receipt?"

"Just over fifteen seconds, ma'am."

"Helm, you've got double duty, so while we're waiting, astrogate a course away from the approaching shuttles, and wait for orders to move."

"Plot new course, aye, ma'am."

Samuels toggled a switch on her command station and said, "Engineering, Bridge."

For a handful of seconds, there was no response, then, "Bridge, Engineering." It was a deep male voice, and not the familiar soprano of Crystal Giannini. Samuels assumed that meant Pineda was still covering while Crystal saw to the missile transfer.

"Engineering, prepare engines for full thrust. Validate Helm has control."

"Uh, yes, ma'am, I mean, Captain. Um, the engines are ready and Main Bridge Helm has directional and output control."

"Very good, Mr. Pineda. Bridge clear."

With nothing left for her to see was prepared, Samuels sat back and waited. After another minute, she ordered, "Comm, record new message."

Tucker jumped at the unexpected sound, but said quickly, "Ready, Captain."

"Approaching vessels. If you do not reverse course within one minute of your receipt of this message, we will assume your intentions to be hostile and we will respond accordingly. As there are forces representing a foreign Family in illegal possession of Warner territory, we are authorized to respond with deadly force. *Peru* clear."

"In memory, Captain." The tension of the moment was making Tucker very formal, but again, Samuels was too focused on the situation to pay any attention to it.

"Send it and log it, Lieutenant."

"Yes, ma'am. On its way."

"Tactical, start a 75 second countdown. How many active tubes?"

"Five, ma'am. One through three, seven and eight."

"Get them locked onto targets. Helm, get us moving."

"Aye, Captain. Engines engaged on planned course. Uh, Monica?" This last was said as quietly as she could, hoping that only her friend would hear.

Samuels rose from her seat and took the two steps that brought her behind Roberts' chair. She leaned in close and whispered, "What is it, Jherri?"

"You're not going to fire first, are you? Rules of Engagement say we can't open fire unless we have clear evidence of hostile intent. We know what they're up to, but we don't have any evidence yet."

"Doesn't apply here."

"What do you mean ROE doesn't apply? It always applies. That's what Captain Merrick said in Advanced Strategy."

"Hostilities have already opened. They fired first when they invaded, so now we are free to engage."

"But we weren't here to witness that, so we don't have a sensor log to prove they fired first."

Samuels stood up and turned. "Sullivan, do we have sensor logs on this ship of Commodore Brighton's second battle?"

"No, ma'am. We didn't have a Bridge watch at the time because of our raid."

"I see. If I order you to fire on those ships, would you consider it a legal order?"

"Yes, ma'am. No question."

"Lieutenant Tucker, in your opinion, am I justified in firing on the approaching assault shuttles?"

"Um. I hadn't given it any thought, Captain, but yes, I believe that we have given them ample opportunity to respond if their intention was anything other than hostile."

"I'm sorry. I shouldn't have asked either of you that question, because ultimately, it's my decision. And just so we're clear, I believe the squadron headed our way intends to board us and take the ship back by force. And my determination is to remove as many potential combatants as I can before they reach this ship.

"Every one of those ship we destroy will mean fewer deaths here. And I will not wait one second longer than I have to, to engage the enemy."

"Time," Sullivan announced.

"Fire all active tubes."

CHAPTER 40
19 October
Forrest Assault Shuttle

"Kadison to the flight deck."

The announcement interrupted a friendly argument between Kadison and her second-in-command, Lieutenant O'Reilly. She hopped up promptly and headed forward, signaling that she was not retreating from a challenge as she went.

She bounded up the four steps in two strides and asked, "What's changed?"

"Our comrades in arms failed to grind any meat," Oliver responded.

"What do you mean?"

"You know how you said those poor Warner saps were walking into a meat grinder?"

She didn't actually remember using those words. "Yes, of course."

"Well, those two shuttles we saw heading toward Caspar have docked, spent the better part of an hour socializing, and now they're headed away from the station."

"What the infinite hell?"

"Precisely my thought."

"Which way are they headed?"

"Back the way they came."

"Back to *Scythe*? Why would they do that? And what happened on the station? Did no one else notice them heading there and warn the station?"

"I don't know. I'm as confused as you are."

Kadison pondered a moment, then said, "Open a vocom line to Caspar."

The co-pilot, Van Duyk, responded, "That will break our comm silence. Are you sure?"

"Yes, I'm sure. There are questions we can't get answered anywhere else."

"Yes, ma'am." The young woman put a headset on and started fiddling with the communications board. "Comm attendant of the watch on the line for you, ma'am."

"This is Colonel Kadison, First Brigade, Ninth Regiment, Forrest Marines. Who is this?"

"My name is Gimelda. How can I be of service, Colonel?"

"I need to speak to the officer of the watch."

"I'm afraid the officer of this watch was called away. Would you care to leave a message?"

"Called away? What do you mean, called away? She's on watch! What's your officer's name?"

"I'm afraid I'm not allowed to divulge that information over an open vocom line. Is there something else I can help you with?"

"Yes, get me your officer's superior, so I can talk to her."

"I'm afraid that officer is also not available just now. Would you care to leave him a message?"

"No, I would not care to leave him a message! I want you to get me a Forrest officer on the line to speak to."

"If you know the name of the officer you're looking for, I can connect your vocom line. Did you have a specific officer for me to connect you to?"

"Yes, connect me with the Comm officer of the watch."

"Do you know the name of that officer, ma'am?"

Kadison was growing angrier by the second. She had to take a long breath in order to keep from shouting. "No, I don't know the name of the officer who is supposed to be standing in the same room as you. But you do, so just connect me to wherever she is."

"I'm afraid I can't do that, ma'am. If I connect you to that officer, then you would know that officer's name, and I have standing orders not to divulge that information over an open line."

"Standing orders from who?"

"I'm afraid I'm not at liberty to divulge that information over an open vocom line."

"Gimelda." Kadison was balling and flexing her hands.

"Yes, Colonel?"

"Regardless of what you have been told, this is an emergency situation, and your standing orders do not apply. I need to speak to a Forrester officer, and I need that to happen right now. So you send someone out to wherever you can find the closest officer and you inform them that there is an emergency vocom call for them, and get them in front of your audio pickup! Am I clear?"

"Yes, Colonel, quite clear. But, I'm afraid I can't do that."

"Why can't you do that?!"

"Only the station commander has the authority to declare a state of emergency."

"Then let me speak to the station commander!"

"Of course, Colonel. Do you have the name of that officer?"

Kadison put one hand over the pickup. The other was stuck in the balled up position. "Van Duyk, can you look up the name of the Caspar contingent's commanding officer?"

"Comm silence protocol disconnected us from the network. It'll take a few minutes to reestablish a link. I'll let you know when I have it." She had begun tapping keys before the first words were out of her mouth.

"Right." She pulled her hand away from the mic. "Gimelda. We are looking that up now. Stand by."

"Of course, Colonel."

"What was that sound?"

"What sound is that?"

"It sounded like a weapon firing. There. There it is again. What's going on over there?"

"Nothing, Colonel. We're all fine here. How are you?" The line went dead.

"Get them back!" Kadison ordered.

"I'm trying, but there's no response."

"What is going on?" Oliver asked.

Kadison stood up and paced the two or three steps the confined deck allowed her. "I don't know. It sounds like we may have a general uprising being attempted at Caspar. Likely triggered by whoever's on those shuttles heading back to *Scythe*."

A few more times back and forth, then she continued, "Whatever is going on, we're not in a position to help them, but we can certainly get those vermin in the shuttles and take back our property. Give me full speed on an intercept course."

"The shuttles have increased speed. They'll reach *Scythe* long before we can catch them, if that's where they're planning to stop."

"What do you mean, 'if'?"

"Well, with the vector between us now, we didn't have the sun behind us, so they've almost certainly seen us coming. We outnumber them heavily, and they have no weapons. Maybe they're planning to get back only to blow the ship and then make a run for it."

Kadison considered this, resuming her pacing.

"If they do run, can we catch them?"

Oliver looked at his console for a few moments, calculating. "Depends on how long they stop for, but it's most likely we can. If they spend more than twenty minutes on the ship, it's a certainty."

"All right, best speed, then. Things have taken a strange turn, and we should never have slowed down to begin with, but now let's go do what we were sent to do."

"Ma'am?"

"Yes?"

"Not to put too fine a point on it, but is this how you want us to come at them? Your question about catching them if they run got me thinking..."

"What do you recommend?"

"Well, look here." Oliver showed the current positions of the ships on the main screen, then they abruptly jumped to where they would be when the Warners got to *Scythe*. "We know those Warner shuttles have better acceleration compensators than we do, so in the short term they can outrun us. If we stay on this vector, they could head perpendicular to our advance, and slip beyond us before we can catch them, and our velocity will carry us past if we divert thrust to add a cross vector." The icons on the screen moved to show the scenario being described. "But if we open our line and spread out, then they can't slip past us."

"All right, that makes sense. Go ahead and order the other shuttles to deploy that way. Is there anything else we can do to prepare?"

"Nothing else I can think of. Now we just have to wait and see if they're going to run away or stay and get smashed."

Kadison chuckled, but there wasn't much mirth in it. "With our track record of predicting what they're going to do, it wouldn't surprise me if they *did* decide to stay and get smashed. In the meantime, I think I'm going to stay here and watch until we know, if that's all right with you."

Oliver shrugged. "Fine with me."

The next minutes passed slowly, and Kadison was inconsistent in her method of dealing with the wait; now sitting, then pacing, and occasionally exercising. Finally, the Warners reached the ship, which had Van Duyk commenting on the skill of the pilots as she watched the Gravitas field strength number stay higher than safety would allow all the way into the launch bay boundary.

That was a short-lived conversation, since it was clear Kadison was not in the mood to hear anything positive about the Warners. The waiting resumed, this time in near silence, until Van Duyk announced, "Incoming transmission, Colonel."

The naval rating did not wait for instructions, but rolled the log back to the beginning of the message and replayed it on the flight deck speakers. "Attention, Forrest vessels. You are approaching WNS *Peru*, a warship of the Warner Space Navy, during a time of heightened alert. You are hereby directed to state your intentions, or be considered hostile combatants. Captain Samuels clear."

Kadison said nothing, nor did anyone else, until Van Duyk couldn't take the silence any longer. "Any response, ma'am?"

"No, I don't think so. Just that short message they sent gave us more information than we had before. There's no reason to return the favor. Plus, it's a pretty weak bluff. If we don't respond, they're threatening to consider us 'hostile combatants.' I wonder what they consider us now, migratory birds?"

There was no time for either of the two pilots to comment on the rhetorical question before the next transmission arrived.

"Approaching vessels. If you do not reverse course within one minute of your receipt of this message, we will assume your intentions to be hostile and we will respond accordingly. As there are forces representing a foreign Family in illegal possession of Warner territory, we are authorized to respond with deadly force. *Peru* clear."

"You see? You never call when you're bluffing, you have to raise the stakes. So now it's 'deadly force.' They're sitting ducks, and they know it."

"Yes, ma'am. And they've already stayed sitting too long. Even if they run now, they can't avoid engaging with us," Oliver put in.

"All right, things are set up here, so I'm going to go get the Marines ready to board."

Kadison had just called O'Reilly over to start the process, when the shuttle lurched to the side suddenly, enough that Kadison had to catch her balance again. She sprinted back up to the flight deck, again cursing the engineers who couldn't design decent compensators. "What the infinite hell?"

"Missile launch!" Van Duyk supplied, while Oliver was busy jinking the shuttle around randomly.

"From *Scythe*? But they're unarmed! They —" And then it all fell into place in her mind. Those shuttles had gone to Caspar to start a rebellion, supplying weapons to the GU on the station. GU must have taken over the communications room first, to keep them from calling for help. That's why she couldn't get a Forrester on the line. And then the Warners took advantage of the confusion to grab a load of missiles.

For a moment, the abrupt change in the situation left her at a loss, but just as quickly, she could see what they needed to do. "Van Duyk, we need to close as fast as possible. Order everyone to emergency speed. Evasive maneuvers only when actively targeted. They're not going to have many missiles, but the faster we reach them the fewer we have to face."

"Aye, ma'am."

"How many missiles?"

"Three in the first wave, then they rolled ship and fired two more twenty seconds later. None since," Oliver reported.

"Anti-missile systems are up?"

"Yes, but..."

"But what?"

"Missiles are harder to hit coming straight at you, and we're too spread out for mutual support. I've already ordered us to close ranks —"

"Cancel it. We need to head straight at them. No delays."

"No, Colonel. Ship-to-ship engagements are up to the Navy. My call, not yours."

Colonels do not often get told no, and Kadison was shocked at the rebuff. She was already off-balance by the sudden turn of events, and she had become accustomed to Oliver checking with her for permission before making any move. Suddenly, all the stress and anger came boiling out. "This is *my* command, *Lieutenant*. You will do what I say —"

"Shut up, Colonel. I'm busy."

"You dare! I'll have you up on charges for insubordination, you little..." Kadison stopped, aware now that Oliver was not even listening to her. She knew he was right, but she felt like she had to do something, and being told no was...well, it was a roadblock. And roadblocks needed to be smashed.

But not this time, she realized. He was right, and she needed to stop jostling his elbow.

"Sorry, Lieutenant. Carry on." With that, she left the flight deck entirely to avoid a recurrence, and went back to the main deck. She quickly outlined the situation to O'Reilly and had him start getting the troops ready. Then she found herself headed back up to the flight deck. She couldn't hold herself away when that was the only place to be able to see what was going on.

Three of the five missiles had lived to hit their targets, despite the best the close-in lasers and EM countermeasures could do. Those three hits had entirely vaporized three shuttles, and the 58 people aboard each. That didn't seem right to her, and she wanted to ask, but at the same time didn't want to interrupt Oliver.

"These shuttles can't even stand up to a single hit? I thought they were built to be tough," she directed to Van Duyk instead.

It was Oliver who answered, anyway. "They're not firing engagement missiles. Those are Mark-20 shipkillers. Way more firepower than they need, but being as big as they are, they're nearly impossible to stop with what we're armed with."

Looking at the pilot's HUD, she could see that four more missiles were inbound, clearly launched one at a time, rather than as salvos. None of the four was targeting her shuttle.

She could also see that the enemy ship had begun moving away to open up the range between them, but had not built up much velocity yet. They were only delaying the inevitable. At the rate they were firing at the approaching force, even if each one scored a hit, they wouldn't have time to get them all before Kadison was inside *Scythe*'s firing envelope.

The slow pace of a naval engagement was very different from Kadison's Marine training and experience. On a battlefield, there was no time between firing and seeing the results. Here, minutes dragged on before knowing if you had scored a hit. Unfortunately, the first two of the four incoming did just that, wiping two more of her shuttles from existence, and one more missile had been launched.

"Can we get a visual on *Scythe* yet?" Kadison asked Van Duyk.

The woman did not respond, but an extra keystroke or two put an image of their target up in one corner of the HUD. The Marine appreciated it. She liked to have an image of what she was after.

Two of the three missiles in space impacted, further reducing Kadison's force, but there were no additional launches from *Scythe* until well after the last of those had detonated. Apparently, some internal problem was slowing down their rate of fire. Kadison wasn't about to complain. It allowed the Forresters to close up inside of what was considered the missile envelope. Too near a launch platform, and a missile would not have built up enough speed, making them easier to dodge or target in return. To illustrate the point, the last shipkiller was destroyed as she watched.

Scythe opened up with her close-in lasers after that, but the increased hull strength of the purpose-built shuttles was up to that task, and it looked like all nine of the remaining craft would survive to breach their target.

Just as Kadison had that thought, the Warners sprung one more surprise on her. Those two Warner shuttles that she had seen taking them back and forth to Caspar, and yet had never considered in her planning, came out from behind *Scythe*, where they had been hiding in her shadow. The parasites suddenly appeared, weapons firing at maximum rate, and the surprise was complete.

Two more of her ships were destroyed before the rest even returned fire, but then the greater weight of numbers quickly overwhelmed the attackers. One was destroyed outright, though it managed to kill another of her birds in the exchange. The second took a direct hit to the engines, which sent it spinning out of control and unpowered away from the immediate battle space.

That was the last thing Kadison saw or heard before running back to the main deck and sealing up her suit. She joined with her Marines just as the six remaining ships picked six entry points off the established priorities list and breached simultaneously.

CHAPTER 41
19 October
WNS *Peru*

Eric Aichele was caught in a boatbay, shooting at Forrest Marines.

Again.

How does this keep happening?

At least this time he had time to prepare some defenses. He ducked as fire started coming from his right once again.

"Burton, they're trying to flank us again!"

"I'm on it!"

He watched as one of the few other set of full Marine armor shifted from its position at the far right end of the line and moved forward out from behind the protective defenses. Shots fired out from both sides as she made her way to a small prepared firing location. Just as she reached her spot, one of the Granadans, a teenager barely old enough to shave, went down behind her. He had been hit in the junction of the shoulder and neck when he rose up to fire and the blast had nearly taken his head from his body. Aichele turned to fire at the Forrester who had taken the shot, but before he could move, Burton had fired and her heavy blaster had killed the Forrest Marine. He cursed again at the lack of any armor on this unfinished ship. The kid would have survived the hit if they had been able to put even light armor onto these troops.

A few sets or pieces of armor had been turned up in a search of the ship, but most of the Granadans were fighting without anything at all to protect themselves. As a result, Aichele had been forced to pull back in the face of these Forrest Marines much sooner than planned or else he would lose troops to random fire like that shot. He was trying to protect them with the Marines he did have in armor, and so far he had been doing a fair job, but the only way to protect them completely would be to lock them away from the danger; and none of them would submit to that.

"Fire in the hole!"

Everyone hit the deck as Burton's voice came across the headsets. The explosion from the ship-grenade blew a hole in the front of the advancing Forresters and Burton dove back across into their defenses as the smoke cleared, before anyone could recover.

Blazes, she was quick, Aichele thought. She'd be worth marrying if she weren't already taken. After their injuries on *Pathfinder*, and the work preparing for this battle, she had to still be feeling as much pain as he was. He couldn't have made that jump. *Blazes, it hurt just thinking about making that jump.* He thought about what she had done on *Pathfinder* after she pulled herself out of the medbay and he decided that she must either have a high threshold of pain, or she could tell herself to ignore what her body was feeling. *He wished he could do that. Maybe he was getting too old for this garbage.*

Aichele refocused on the battle as the Forrest line started moving again on both sides of his defenses. His line curled up at the ends to keep them from being able to get around either flank, but there was just too much room to maneuver here in the boatbay.

"Jenkins, go."

From up above the boatbay deck, small charges dropped down from above the Forresters. This was the opposite of the murder holes that he had used in the corridors. Small cuts had been made into the catwalks above the entryways and three volunteers had waited until now to fire the charges at the rear of the Forrester unit. The charges fired prepared metal projectiles into the backs of three of the Marines who were kneeling on the ground behind the barricades that Aichele and his teams had given up in their retreat. The weaker backplates of their armor were not enough to shield them, and the metallic pieces in the homemade devices cut through the armor to ravage the soldiers within.

The reaction of the Forrest Marines was immediate. They turned and started firing up into the catwalks at the poorly sheltered Granadans.

"Jenkins, Williams. Move out now."

"Yes, sir." The warning was not necessary, as plasma bolts provided all the motivation the two needed. Their shadowy forms moved straight up from the ladder on the back wall and into the upper interstitial space above the catwalk, the Forrester blaster fire lining traces around them as they moved. There was more protection up there for them, since they were out of sight. The Forresters had no access from where they were, so it was the best shot he had to get them away to safety.

He looked back at the oncoming Forresters. The bombs hadn't taken out enough of them. *Blast*, he thought. He had hoped to slow them down more. Green-suited Forrest Marines started moving out at both edges and trying to collapse the flanks once again.

Blazes, he was tired. They had fought this group of Forresters all the way from their entry point, just in front of the midpoint on Deck A. The six surviving shuttles had put out over three hundred Forrester Marines, and the six entry points had quickly converged into two forces moving fore and aft to their main objectives. Half fighting toward the bridge and the other half pushing his units toward the engineering areas. They had fought them in the lower level and then up the ladderway and down the corridor to the hatchway that lead into the boatbay.

He had run into the unit Major Tunney had been leading here on Deck B as they held the approach to the boatbay from another group at the opposite end of the corridor. Both groups had collapsed inside the large bay when they could no longer hold their ends of the corridor.

He had used nearly all of his pre-planned assaults, just to keep the Forresters from getting this far. But the truth was that he was running out of tricks and he didn't have enough people to hold the enemies in front of him.

"Burton, Tunney, start moving the Granadans back to point Omega. Have Sullivan and Pulliver hold the left flank until everyone gets pulled back. You two and Short hold that weak right side and I'll keep Hanover and Gilliam and the other Marines here in the middle. We have to hold until all of the Granadans have gotten back to the Omega defenses.

He could hear the hesitation before Burton responded. He knew she didn't want to back up into another hole. "Yes sir." He could hear her orders going out as soon as he turned his head forward. Tunney didn't hesitate. He sent orders on to his people and started firing.

As soon as the Granadans started moving, he could see the Forresters start to push out of their positions. They had seen this move before, so they knew when the Warners were about to retreat. The eleven remaining Warner Marines in armor began to put out covering fire to try to keep them down, but there were nearly five times their number pushing ahead, with more continuing to enter the boatbay. Aichele fired slowly to conserve power and watched as the Forresters moved toward a small white dot painted on the floor. He shot another one as he switched to a new covering position. It was a clean shot and the man went down, a burn hole directly through his helmet. Aichele focused again on the white dot, to check the enemy's progress. Five more steps. One more row of cover to hide behind.

He let the first row of Forresters slide past the spot on the deck and into the positions there and resume their fire against him. When he was sure each one was in position, he pulled the trigger from his belt and hit the button. The barricades in front of each Forrester erupted with a shower of ten millimeter balls, tearing five of the leading Marines to shreds through their armor.

As the remaining Forresters went down, either from the force of the blast or a sense of self-preservation, the Warners retreated back to the center access point into the engineering spaces. There were three doors leading from the boatbay into Engineering. The one on each end had been spot welded shut, leaving only this center hatch open. It would make it easier to defend, but also harder to fight out of if they got trapped in there.

Aichele assessed the situation as he pulled himself behind the barricades that they had erected here at Omega, their final holding point before Engineering. His remaining defensive force was down to eleven Marines and nineteen Granadans.

"Burton, keep a watch for them trying to get up into the catwalks."

"Roger."

"Sullivan, don't let them pull up too quickly, I think they'll be slow after that last blast but keep an eye out for anyone trying to sneak in."

"Got it."

"Tunney, you've got temporary charge while I check in with the captain."

Aichele looked up and saw the older Marine nod his head. It was a menacing sight, since something had hit the man's armor on the left arm below the shoulder, and had burned the whole left side of his suit the darkest black. His faceshield was blackened and it looked to Aichele like he felt, burned out and tired beyond belief.

With those three keeping an eye on things, he felt he had a second to check on the other half of the battle. He switched his helmet comm to the command circuit and called Samuels.

"Captain Samuels, sit-rep, please."

"Aichele, we've just had to pull back to the last defense in front of the bridge hatch. We're being pushed hard."

Aichele tried to keep his deep concern from entering his voice.

"Can you hold there?"

"We won't let them have this ship back!"

Aichele could hear an anger in the young lieutenant's voice that he hadn't heard before. Was she associating this ship with *Pathfinder* somehow?

"If you seal yourself into the bridge, they can't get through the blast armor to get in quickly."

"I know, but then we're trapped. We'll hold here as long as possible."

"Yes, ma'am. But, don't leave it too late. Don't worry, we won't give up the ship. We'll think of something."

Aichele looked up as Major Tunney tapped him on the shoulder.

"Looks like they are working their way back up the center."

Aichele nodded. He was down to his last trick and then he didn't know how he was going to hold them out of Engineering.

The one positive sign he could see was that it looked like they had quit getting any more reinforcements into the boatbay at some point in the last few minutes, but the Warners were still outnumbered by at least three to one.

He thought about his last statement to Samuels. *We'll think of something.* He would have to work on thinking of something soon… or they would all be dead.

CHAPTER 42
19 October
WNS *Peru*

Aichele grimaced and took three more shots at the Forresters advancing on his position in their dark green armor. For every one his people killed, it seemed there were seven more to take his place, like some mythical hydra. They just didn't seem to have the weapons or defenses to be able to fight the numbers that were coming at them. He had promised the Captain that he would think of something to save the ship, but he was out of ideas. He watched as the Forresters slid into the row of barricades they had just been forced to abandon. He gritted his teeth and pressed the trigger on the monitor in his hand. Five of the barricades erupted with hardened armor balls that blasted through an equal number of the Forrester Marines who had rested behind them. The other Forresters hit the deck, just as they had the last time. Aichele and his fellows came up firing at anyone they could get a shot at. Except for Sullivan. She leapt over the cover of the last set of barricades and attacked the incoming enemy.

"Holy flaming mercy!"

Aichele could understand Burton's thought as he watched Sullivan go. As much as he had admired Burton's acrobatic assault earlier, it was a childhood cartwheel compared to what Sullivan was doing now. She had her high-powered railgun in her right hand and her sidearm in her left and was firing each independently. She didn't seem to take time for aiming either, and she never missed. As quick as thought, Sullivan took out the remaining four in the front row of the Forrester attack while they were still on the ground from the explosion and jumped over them into the next set of defenses as that group was still rising to recover.

During his defense and retreat into the boatbay, Aichele had seen that the Warner armor was easier to move in than the Forrester model, though theirs was stronger in most places. He had taken advantage of that quickness to be able to survive so far by moving out of danger. Sullivan seemed to be using that quickness to an extreme he had never dreamed possible. And she was not using it in defense. She was anticipating their shots and turning in place so the shots went wide. Her shots never failed to find a target and theirs never scratched her armor. Suddenly, her amplifiers came on with high-pitched, screaming music. The heavy beat of the bass pounding as she moved and danced towards them, striking down her enemies as she went.

Aichele shook himself free from the mesmerized state he had fallen into watching her move and looked at the Marines with him.

"You four, follow me!"

"Yes sir." they chanted in chorus, tearing their eyes free from Sullivan's death dance.

He started to follow in the wake of destruction, then called back to Tunney.

"Major, take command of this group and defend Engineering at all costs. Disable the engines before you give up the room. We'll stay with her until this burns out and we'll take as many Forresters as we can."

"Understood."

With that, he motioned three of the Marines to the right and took one with him to the left.

"Cover her flanks. Don't let them get around behind her."

None of the Marines answered, but all went to work as he had directed. There had to have been nearly sixty Forester Marines in full battle gear inside the boatbay when Sullivan went over the barricade, but they were giving up ground to her in their surprise and shock. She must have killed the officers in charge first, or else they were some of the ones killed by the blast, because no one was trying to take charge and push back against her.

One of the Forresters behind her was getting up to fire. Aichele couldn't get a shot off from his position.

"Sullivan, behind you!"

Sullivan went down at the sound of Aichele's voice and the Forrester's shot went above her. She dropped behind a row of improvised barricades and a shot came from through a firing hole and out through the chest of the green suit that had just missed her. Sullivan rolled up on the other side of the barricade and fired two more shots forward into the next row of Forrester Marines and kept moving. Aichele took aim at a couple of Forresters who had crawled forward to his row. He was able to shoot both of them because they were looking forward to see where Sullivan was with her blasting music.

Aichele looked at the carefully prepared rows of barricades that they had made in preparation to defend the boatbay and Engineering and now the Forresters were using them to protect themselves from Sullivan. And he couldn't keep up with her. He looked down the row. It was clear. He motioned the other Marines up to catch Sullivan. He jumped forward two rows, ignoring the risk of going over the barricades into the open lines of fire.

A Forrest Marine saw him moving and caught him with a blast just below his right hip. He dropped flat when he hit, farther to the left than he had intended, and rolled to his back to do a quick assessment. Years of training guided his motions much more than any conscious thought. The armor had protected him, but the plasma had significantly damaged the armor itself.

He looked around the corner from his new position. *Blast.* There were three of the Forresters crawling down the row toward where he could hear her music. He was behind them so they were crawling away, but he couldn't take on three by himself, especially with his mobility hampered. With them crawling away, he didn't have much of a shot at anything but their legs, and if he sat up or stood, he would be a target for anyone who saw him. *Blast, he'd give anything for a grenade. He really was getting too old for this garbage.*

He took a deep breath and put on his old 'weapon firing instructor' hat and shot up on his knees, pulled his weapon to his shoulder, took his aim on the lead man's head and pulled the trigger. He immediately went down to a prone position and waited for the reaction. Both of the Forresters did what he expected. They spun up to a sitting position with their weapons up to fire back at whoever was behind them. He took the target to the right and then the one to the left, just as quickly as he could pull the trigger and move the barrel. He was able to get both targets in the weak part of the armor, just above the chest plate, in the neck and killed each of them. Unfortunately, the one on the left got his shot off at the same time. He wasn't quite on target but the blast hit Aichele in the right shoulder near the deck and while the deck took some of the damage, his shoulder took a lot of it too. The armor didn't open, but still his right arm went numb inside the armor. Aichele let his faceplate fall down to rest on the deck as he reached over with his left arm to pull his weapon to that side.

Definitely, getting too old for this freaking garbage.

He slid his way to the center of the row and looked forward to try to find Sullivan. He could hear her music and it sounded like she was a couple of rows ahead of him. How was it possible she was still moving? He figured they'd all be dead by now. He could hear the shots of several of the other Warner Marines behind her, so they were keeping her back clear, at least so far.

There is no way this should be working. How could she be scaring the Forresters into retreating? Any Marine with any experience could see that a large assault would kill her attack. And all of them too.

He jumped to the next row, his left leg providing most of the lift, and found it empty so he moved anther row, dragging his right leg, his right arm dangling at his side. He saw a Forrester moving away from him, so he aimed his weapon and shot him quickly from the hip. He was able to do most things equally as well with his left hand as his right, but his blaster was hard to carry and shoot one-handed. You needed another hand out at the end to support it if you were going to try to shoot it properly, so he put it on his back and drew his sidearm. It was still heavy enough to penetrate the Forrester armor if he hit them in the right spots. A couple times. He was starting to feel pins and needles in his right hand, so maybe the feeling would come back soon in his right arm. He turned his sidearm on its side and adjusted the power to the max. It would run the power out after a few shots, but it would let him cut through a helmet faceplate or the necking with a single shot.

He kept moving forward, slowly, shooting anything in his way. Sullivan was moving down the center, and he pushed a little outward to clear the edges. He saw Hanover as he moved past the edge of his row and on to the next. Aichele tried to move more quickly to follow along at his back. When they reached the next row, Aichele realized that it was the last row. Sullivan had pushed the Forresters out of the boatbay!

He saw two dark green suits coming in the end hatch, trying to reenter the bay. He lifted his pistol and fired a round that pierced the neck. Handover fired a shot that took out the Marine on his side. Aichele had never thought they could push them back out of the boatbay. It had just seemed too big a task given the size of the area and the lack of personnel.

"Tunney, pull everybody and let's secure the hatches to the boatbay. I want to push these guys out into Broadway."

"We saw what was happening. We're pushing out any remaining pieces as we come. We're almost there."

Aichele turned to see Tunny's black armor behind him, followed by the rest of the Marines and followed by the unarmored Granadans. The cavernous boatbay was awash in the outpouring of their noise as they tried to outblast Sullivan's speakers. The final Forresters were pushed out of the three hatches and into the corridor outside the bay. Aichele pushed his way through the Warner group to the main corridor that led up the center of the ship, what the crew called Broadway. From here it ran down the main line of the ship until it met at the bridge hatch where he could see flashes of fighting going on in the distance. As he gained a new secure barricade to fight from, he locked the hatch behind him. No enemy was getting back into the boatbay now. He looked at Amber Sullivan as he holstered his sidearm. His right arm hurt, but it was mobile again, and he pulled his accustomed blast rifle from its scabbard on his back.

"What the blazes was that?"

Her shoulder kicked up a tiny bit. She crouched behind a one-meter barricade and shot through the gun port at the remaining Forresters, who were down the corridor firing back.

"Just trying something new," she responded calmly, as if she had tried a new flavor of ice cream.

He let his head fall back to the hatch and he let out his breath.

"Just trying something new, huh. Well, next time... give a warning so I can try to give you some back-up."

She chuckled slightly without turning to look at him.

"Yeah, right. If I'd have told you what I was going to do, you wouldn't have let me do it. Then where would we be?"

Aichele looked at the two Granadans who had slipped out with him before the door closed They were now sitting on the outside of the boatbay shooting at the Forresters, who were also outside the boatbay, their numbers cut nearly in half. He leaned his head back on the bulkhead behind him and closed his eyes.

"My guess would be about eighty meters farther aft, getting chewed up by a determined enemy, Sullivan."

CHAPTER 43
19 October
WNS *Peru*

Samuels looked down the corridors at the Forresters who were still pushing them. She and her Marines had no further to retreat without giving up the corridors to the invaders. They already had their backs to the bridge hatch and were defending against all three corridors, holding the intersection where they met.

In one way, that was a good thing. That allowed her to combine the units commanded by Mdembe and Tucker with her own group. The bad news was that now they had three times the amount of enemy fire coming in, from three different directions.

"Mdembe, keep your group defending your corridor, but get as many of those Granandans back behind someone with armor!"

She needn't have said anything. The Marines were already forming up into three solid walls of armor that closed off the three corridors from incoming fire. One row of Marines in each wall was prone, one was on one knee, just able to fire over the improvised barricade, and a third stood behind the other two. They had pulled all the Granadans back and they were behind the Marines, trying to find holes in the Marine firing line to fire through. Almost all of these Granadans had been unarmed at the beginning of the fighting, but the first wave of murder holes had provided a few weapons, and their own fallen had provided more.

While they had been able to collect some weapons, the one thing they hadn't been able to provide the Granadans was sufficient cover. There hadn't been time to build as many of the protective barriers as Aichele had hoped to and he had decided to protect Engineering and the auxiliary control that was down in the aft end of the ship first. There were only two layers of defense at the forward end of the ship, one just aft of where each of the three corridors met the cross-corridor that passed in front of the bridge, and this semi-circular one just outside the bridge hatch. There hadn't been time to build more of the barriers here. It was always considered that if things got too bad, they could withdraw inside the armored bridge itself.

Samuels didn't want to trap herself inside the bridge yet. They still had some time.

"Captain Samuels, sit-rep, please."

Samuels was caught off guard by the voice of Aichele in her ear. She had been so concentrated on the battle in front of her that she had forgotten about the others fighting in the engineering spaces of the ship.

"Aichele, we've just had to pull back to the last defense in front of the bridge hatch. We're being pushed hard."

She could tell that Lieutenant Aichele was trying to sound flat and unconcerned, knowing he could not come to help.

"Can you hold there?"

She tried to put as much fire into her voice as she could, to let him know they were okay here, or as okay as the situation allowed.

"We won't let them have this ship back!"

She could hear the concern in his voice this time when he spoke.

"If you seal yourself into the bridge, they can't get through the blast armor to get in quickly."

She could tell that was what he wanted her to do, but he was going to let her make the decision.

Cheney

"I know, but then we're trapped. We'll hold here as long as possible."

"Yes, ma'am. But, don't leave it too late. Don't worry, we won't give up the ship. We'll think of something."

With that he clicked off and despite the chaos of the battle around her, the world felt silent. *We'll think of something*, he'd said. Like they were on the edge of a cliff with a horde of Vikings pushing them. It couldn't be that bad. They had taken back *Pathfinder*, and there were only three of them then. They had a whole troop now.

A round from the Forresters got through the Warner Marine's armor and hit the young Granadan next to her. The girl was only about Samuel's age, and now she was dead. One of the others grabbed the girl's shoulder and dragged her back to a pile near the bridge door.

She had a troop now, all right, but she was watching them all die. One after another. Just like before. Holding their ground, ground that she had ordered them to hold.

"Granadans, move inside the bridge."

She called out the order without even thinking.

That would cost them more than half their firepower. Could she even hold the corridor without them?

She still had a few of Aichele's surprises, and a couple of her own once they did end up falling back to the bridge.

She pulled the trigger from her belt and set off the remote. She looked at the corner and was shocked when nothing happened.

She looked around. She wanted to push them back with that bomb. Had they seen the remote bomb and disabled it? *What do I do now?*

Mdembe and Tucker were pushing their lines out and closing off the corridors again. *Maybe we can win this, anyway.* She turned back and watched as the Granadans made a slow withdrawal into the bridge. Keeping up firing as long as they could until their turn came to move. Soon she was down to her 23 Marines. Could they hold? No. They had to pull back. They

298

couldn't hold without the Granadans and they were getting wiped out in the open corridor with nowhere to hide.

"Mdembe, Tucker, pull your men back into the bridge."

She pushed forward into a gap to fire, so some of the Marines could pull back. She saw a Forrester poke his head out around a corner and she took a shot. The blast hit the corner near his head and he jerked back, but she doubted that he took any injury.

The Forresters jumped from their cover and ran forward from all three corridors, and Samuels and her Marines found themselves in a sudden crossfire. All her Marines returned fire and green suits went down here and there in the enemy ranks. The Forresters knew it would be a killing ground, but it was a short distance, and they had the numbers on their side. She should have pulled back sooner.

"Fall back. Get everyone inside the bridge."

She fired at the mass of Forresters as they sprinted the thirty meters down the corridor to her end of the defense. She took down four of the oncoming mass with steady aimed rounds while their wild fire flew over her head, but it didn't seem to make any difference. Then she noticed that none of the Marines around her were pulling back.

"You've got to get to the bridge!"

One of them looked up at her, she wasn't even sure if she knew his name.

"No, ma'am. We're not moving without you."

He was right and wrong. At that point, the Forresters crashed into their line and they all moved. The firing was all close range and blasters blew through armor and weapons were used as clubs as often as blasters.

Samuels started working her way back to the bridge access. Knowing that the Marines wouldn't abandon the spot if she were still there, *what a ridiculous idea*, then she needed to move to where she wanted them to be.

"Marines, work your way to the bridge."

She watched as Tucker got to the bridge access and with her height, began shooting over heads at any target she could clearly identify. She had the bridge hatch open and soon two other Marines joined her to protect it from any Forrester who broke free from the disorganized fighting to attempt to attack it.

Soon the Warners had absorbed the mass of the initial charge and were pushing the Forresters back. Grey and green suits littered the corridor and the Warners started to pull back to the hatch. Most were inside the bridge when the Forresters attacked again.

Mdembe and Tucker physically pushed Samuels and the other two remaining Marines back inside the bridge and then turned to fight off the incoming wave.

Once inside, Samuels headed straight for the command console, knowing that was the only place she could continue to make a difference once the hatch was sealed. She didn't notice that the two Marines hadn't come through the hatch with her.

CHAPTER 44
19 October
WNS *Peru*

Samuels stumbled as she was pushed inside the closing blast doors. She regained her balance and moved quickly further inside to clear sight lines for the Marines covering the entrance to the bridge. She continued the movement all the way to her command console and keyed a connection before she was seated.

"Engineering, Bridge." There was no response for several seconds, and Samuels was about to call again when Giannini's voice came on the line.

"Bridge, Engineering." She was out of breath and her voice was rushed.

"Crystal, what's the status of the fighting down there?"

The answer to the question was difficult to make out. The Marines at the door were shouting at someone, which drowned out the comm line. She had to trust the Marines to handle whatever was going on and concentrated on getting a clear picture of what was going on everywhere else on the ship. Much as she wanted to just deal with her little slice of the battle, she had a responsibility at least to keep abreast of the big picture.

"... so definitely better than it was twenty minutes ago. The push wouldn't have been possible without Sullivan, and where she learned to fight like that as a warrant officer on a technical track, I will never understand."

"Don't try. It leads to migraines," Samuels advised. "But I missed what you said to start with. Could you repeat it?"

"Yeah. We'd been pushed back and bottled up behind the Engineering firewall, defending the one choke point. Eric blasted his last bomb and took out a group of Forresters, trying to hold them back a little longer. When he did Sullivan took off with some kind of wild attack run. The Forresters were so shocked they started to back off so Eric followed with four other Marines to try to back up Sullivan. After a bit, Tunney followed with a larger group and we ended up pushing them back out of the boatbay for now. I don't know how long it will last but we're definitely better off than we were twenty minutes ago, but we're back to a stand-off, just at the forward end of the boatbay."

"Casualties?"

"I...I don't know, exactly, but it's not good. I've got three people resealing the doors to Engineering, and everyone else that's left, which is about two dozen, are still fighting."

"Thanks, Crystal. Keep your head down."

"Same to you, Captain. Clear."

A Marine stepped up to Samuels as soon as she had keyed the comm off and saluted. She couldn't tell who it was because his name plate had been burned away by an energy hit, and he still had the light-diffracting face shield closed.

"The hatch is secure, ma'am. Two wounded, and Thomason is seeing to them. Workman is collecting stats on our remaining ammo and power. We probably have thirty minutes before they can force their way in, and, of course, we have no further fallback position."

"I know, Sergeant..."

"Ramamurthy, ma'am."

"What happened to Lieutenant Mdembe? I didn't see him get hit."

"He...remained outside to see that the Forresters didn't have time to catch the door before it sealed."

Samuels bowed her head and tried not to cry. The effort was easier than it should have been. She hadn't known him well, but she did know that Roberts had been close to him. Surely she should be feeling *something*. It was as if the last few days had wrung her completely dry, as if there was nothing left of *her* anymore, just the captain, the one everyone was looking to for salvation.

She looked up finally. "I'm very sorry, Sergeant Ramamurthy." Even to herself, the voice sounded flat and emotionless.

"Yes, ma'am." His voice, too, was flat and sounded resigned.

"Make sure Thomason has whatever she needs. There are emergency supplies in a locker behind Comm. Make sure everyone eats. To the side of Tactical you'll find three universal ports where you can recharge both power packs for your weapons and armor from ship's power. Have Workman prioritize, but make sure everyone gets enough to keep going before our time runs out. I'll see what I can do to delay that as much as possible."

"Pardon me for asking, Captain, but how are you going to do that? The Forresters are on the other side of fifteen centimeters of hardened steel."

"True, but you forget that this was always part of the plan. And knowing that we were going to wind up in this exact situation, I prepared a few surprises for the big, bad wolves while they're huffing and puffing."

"Yes, ma'am. Not sure what difference it will make in the end, but right now, I'll take every extra minute I can get."

"So will I, Sergeant."

Ramamurthy turned to see to his tasks, and Samuels dropped back into the command station. First, she activated the video pickup outside the hatch and routed it to her station, just in time to see one of the Forresters fire at it. The screen flashed and went dark. A few more taps on the pre-loaded menu and a new stream appeared, this one originating from one of the security bugs she'd had installed on the opposite wall facing the bridge hatch.

The Forresters were having a debate as to the best way to proceed, so she took a moment to connect her station into the direct link to Aichele's suit. Again, she had prepared the sequence in advance, so it was available to run with one tap.

"Aichele, Bridge."

There was no response. She checked the connections from her end and could find no problem. She repeated the call with the same result, and only then realized that it might mean he was injured...or dead. The same lack of reaction to the thought she'd experienced before concerned her subconscious as being...wrong, but she didn't have time to think about it further.

She quickly tied into the Marines' command channel with another single selection. "Bridge, Burton."

"Burton."

"I tried contacting Aichele. Has he been injured?"

"I wish I knew, ma'am. Wait one."

The line was still open, and Samuels overheard her giving orders to two Marines, then directing Tunney to take over for her for a minute."

"I've tried calling both Aichele and Sullivan, but I get no response. When I tried polling his telltales, though, I get a 'unit not in network' rather than 'suit damaged' or 'occupant in distress' or any other kind of response. Best guess is that the suit's comm system was damaged somehow. So there's no telling how Aichele is doing."

"He's not there with you?"

"No. Sullivan got to the center boatbay hatch and just kept going. Aichele and a couple of Granados were close enough to follow, but by the time I got there the Forresters had recovered enough to set up a solid defense at the hatch. The rest of us are doing the same on our side, keeping them from advancing, but we don't have the numbers to overcome their defenses."

"Understood. Our team has fallen back to the bridge. We're safe for now, but eventually the Forresters are going to find a way in. When they do, I don't think we can stop them."

Burton didn't say anything for a while. "When that happens, are you going to destroy the ship?"

Samuels laughed. The back of her mind was again disturbed that she found the idea genuinely funny. Maybe she needed more sleep. "Not an option, Sergeant. We've been using all the self-destruct charges for weapons."

"Right. Forgot about that. Do you need anything else, ma'am?"

"No, Jill. Just...good luck."

"Thank you, ma'am. You too. Burton clear."

Samuels disconnected the circuit and brought her attention back to the Forresters, who she saw were finally getting organized. Time for her to get to work.

CHAPTER 45
19 October
WNS *Peru*

Aichele led the small band he was with into the starboard ladderway, trying to move as quietly as possible. That endeavor was severely hampered by the fact that damage to the right leg of his armor had left that portion unpowered, while the rest moved normally. Trying to move smoothly and quietly under those conditions was all but impossible. He was shambling like the undead, while Sullivan, bringing up the rear, seemed to float effortlessly a centimeter above the deck, for all the sound she was making.

Improvise, adapt, overcome, he reminded himself. Truth to tell, he wasn't doing that badly at remaining quiet, but he had to move very carefully to do so, and that was slowing down their advance.

And they had to advance, since the bulk of the Forresters on this level lay between them and Engineering, making retreat an impossibility. Or, if not exactly impossible, based on recent experience watching Sullivan in action, still not advisable.

Aichele reached the platform midway between decks and stopped. Above them, voices could be heard coming from the upper deck, and getting nearer. Aichele hobbled over to the door leading into the interstitial spaces and motioned the two Granadans, Varela and Bertrand, to cover the upward ladder with the heavy weapons they'd picked up along the way.

The door was locked, which was normal during a boarding action, but it was seriously inconvenient at the moment. Locking down the ship was SOP, and to gain access, someone would need both a key chip and the proper code. The code he knew, but he hadn't anticipated needing to get in, so he had no chip. He could turn his variable blast cannon on the door and be inside in a moment. Or he could use the augmented strength of his armor and tear the door out of its frame. Either of which would be heard halfway across the ship, and the enemy would swarm all over them in seconds.

Sullivan levitated up to the platform to join them. He shook his head. *How could she do that in heavy armor?* She made the Marine hand sign for "area secure" with a tilt of her head that turned it into a question. Aichele nodded, and Sullivan handed him both her massive weapons. That gave him three to handle, so he wound up cradling them in his arms like a bunch of kindling.

Sullivan walked up to the lock panel and spread her fingers out around the outer edge. Slowly, she increased pressure until a soft pop was heard and the panel came free. Without any thought or hesitation, she selected five wires and pulled them free. Two she twisted together and the other three she inserted into different locations on the connector grid. As the final connection was made, the hatch slid silently open.

Aichele motioned the Granadans inside, then followed them. Sullivan reversed the process, sticking her foot out into the door frame to keep the way open until she had popped the panel back into place.

When she had entered and the hatch was sealed again, she did a quick scan of the area to be sure it was safe, though she knew Aichele would have done the same already. When they hadn't started moving, she signaled "orders" and waited for a response.

Aichele unsealed his face plate and rotated it out of the way. "We should be able to talk in here. Machinery noise will cover our conversation."

"Okay. What next, Lieutenant?"

"Clearly, I am not as familiar with the workings of this ship as you are," he said sardonically. "Do you know where the nearest universal port would be?"

She ignored his tone and said, "Column Hotel-24, about 30 meters aft at the boatbay frame."

"And what if I asked for the nearest heading forward?"

"Golf-22."

Aichele's eyes narrowed. "What *don't* you know?"

Sullivan unsealed her face plate and flipped it up so Aichele could see her face, which wore an angry expression. "Plenty. I don't know how Forrest took over a system and built a navy with no one in the intelligence community even suspecting. I don't know if we're going to live to see tomorrow. And I really don't know what I was thinking when I accepted this assignment.

"What I do know is that you're smart enough to have figured out who and what I really am. I know you don't trust me, even more so now that you've figured it out than when you weren't sure. I know my cover is basically irrelevant at this point, so there's no need for me to hold anything back. Anything I can do, anything I know, anything you need me to be, is yours for the asking. That's what I know."

Aichele was taken aback at the sudden change in her. Varela looked at Bertrand, who simply shrugged, since she didn't understand the byplay any better than he did.

Aichele's look of shock abruptly changed into a grin. "Now, that's more like it. Let's get to G-22 and we'll make a plan while I recharge. How's your power level?"

"87%."

Aichele caught himself before he stumbled and shot a startled look at the young woman.

She bounced a fist off her nearly-pristine breastplate. "It's not the standard issue model."

"Clearly."

The team started moving forward, though awkwardly. The bulk of the massive PUMA units was difficult to maneuver through the cramped and uneven environment. Finally, Aichele hobbled up to the G-22 column and found the predicted universal port, marked with large red letters. He uncovered and unspooled his matching port and made the needed connection.

Inside the suit, indicators began changing from red to green at a snail's pace. Once his power level had dropped below 20%, the suit had shifted to power conservation mode automatically, but now that it detected the direct power feed, it was back in normal operational mode. And it was putting the power to good use, activating the self-repairing circuitry to reroute and rebuild everything within its capabilities. There were some things that would still require depot-level maintenance, but even if the armor was not in top condition, it was becoming far better than it had been.

When Aichele's leg light stopped flashing red, he experimentally raised and flexed it a few times. It squeaked twice, but by the third time that too had been detected and corrected. The sound had another consequence, however.

"Sh," Sullivan whispered. "I hear someone out there."

Aichele hadn't heard anything, and wasn't sure how anyone could over the incessant hum and whirr of the conduits and machinery all around them. There was nothing wrong with his suit's auditory pickups, either. Although, it was true that his suit *was* the standard issue model.

Instead of answering, he pulled his weapon from its holster and aimed it in the general direction Sullivan was looking. He quietly pulled his face plate into place and activated the enhanced visuals. No sooner had he done so than three men and two women came racing around a bend yelling and waving improvised weapons.

"Check fire! Check fire!" Aichele ordered, recognizing them immediately as friendlies. "Stand down, Mr. Felix. It's just us."

The group slowed and stopped, keeping their distance now. "Sargento Aichele? Is that you?"

"Teniente now, but yes, it's me." He raised the face shield so the Granadan could get a good look.

"Ah, that is very good." The group came forward now, much relieved. The two Granadans with Aichele also came out of the cover they had taken at Sullivan's warning.

"So, the battle is over now, and you have finally thought to come let us out of our prison?" Pablo said, sitting down next to Eric.

"What prison?"

"We have been locked in here for an hour now, with no way to get out."

"How did you get locked in here? Each team had a key so they could fire their lances and then fall back."

"Yes, but our teniente is not thinking ahead and asking, 'What if the person carrying the key chip is killed and the chip is destroyed?'"

"You're right, that question did not occur to me."

"Well, since you have remembered us and did not leave us here all night, all is forgiven. Now, let us go and celebrate our great victory with the others."

"The battle isn't over yet," Sullivan said flatly.

"Even better! Now there are still PMs we can make pay for their crimes."

"The lieutenant isn't ready yet, and he hasn't explained our next step to us," Bertrand added.

Aichele announced, "I've restored my comms. Stand by while I check in."

He pulled the face shield back into place, to keep the conversation private. "Aichele, Mdembe." When a repeat of the phrase still got no response, he checked Mdembe's suit telltales and discovered the fate of the young officer. Adding him to the list of those to properly mourn at a better time, he switched circuits and tried seeing if the captain had fallen back to her last redoubt yet.

"Aichele, Bridge."

"Bridge, this is Samuels. It is good to hear your voice, Lieutenant. What's your status?"

"Sullivan and I have found a place to hole up and make some repairs. We currently have seven Granadans with us. We should be back in the fight in five or ten more minutes."

"Is there any chance you can support the bridge? It's only a matter of time until they can break in, and we don't have any way to fight back in the meantime."

"How many are you facing?"

"Thirty-five."

Aichele was silent for several seconds. "We can get there without being seen. The Forresters are essentially ignoring the interstitial decks. But I don't know how much good we can do when we get there. Thirty-five armored Marines is a significant force, and surprise will only get you so far."

"I know. And I suppose I don't have any realistic expectation of living through this. I was just hoping you had one more wrinkle to throw at them."

"I don't yet, ma'am, but we're Marines. We specialize in creating wrinkles. Let me surveil the area and get back to you."

Aichele flipped his shield up again. Sullivan stepped up immediately, "Do you have a plan?"

"No, but we've got a destination. Still working on a plan."

Aichele rose and disconnected his suit. It wasn't fully charged, but he could top Sullivan's 87%, at least for now. "Pablo, did your team use all your lances?"

"No, sir. There were two which never got a PM in its crosshairs."

"Bertrand, you and Varela both helped assemble those units. Do you think you can safely take them apart and bring the explosives to me?"

Bertrand looked at Varela, who nodded. "Yes, sir," she said.

"All right. You take all the unarmored troops with you. Give someone else the weapons to stand guard. Collect the charges, and meet us at column H-12. You guys can move faster than we can in this armor. If we're not there yet, it's because we went to scout out an approach to the bridge. Just wait there for us. Got it?"

"Yes, sir. You have something else devious planned for the PMs, yes?"

"That's right. It's so devious it hasn't even been thought of yet. Now get moving. And for heaven's sake, be careful with those explosives. Have someone else carry the triggers."

"Yes, sir," Bertrand replied, and the whole troop of them took off at a jog.

Sullivan and Aichele started forward as well, but at significantly less than a jog. While Aichele was no longer shambling, the constrictive pathway required a slow pace to pick a way around and over myriad obstacles.

When they arrived at H-12, there was no one in sight or hearing. The hatch out to the forward ladderway was only a few steps away, and Sullivan repeated her performance on the locking panel, not bothering to reattach it to the wall, since it was out of sight.

Aichele found it considerably easier to move quietly on these steps than the last ladderway.

There were no Forresters between them and the hatch leading to the forward cross-corridor. The hatch had been dogged open, but Aichele and Sullivan could stay far enough back that no one would notice them unless they were looking straight at them. No one was; the Forresters had all their attention on the massive bridge hatch. No one posted to watch the approaches, no one patrolling, nothing.

Unfortunately, all thirty-something of them were standing inside the defenses that Aichele had helped to build, a semicircle of deck plating chest high that covered the entire three-way intersection in front of the bridge. The only entrances were two narrow openings against the forward bulkhead.

"Nice of us to provide such sturdy defenses for them," Aichele whispered on local vocom. "If only we had a way to turn their strength into a —" And then he had it.

"Let's get back upstairs," he whispered with a grin.

CHAPTER 47
19-20 October
WNS *Peru*

As it turned out, the lack of popcorn wasn't a problem, because there wasn't much to see.

Samuels had the feed from the spybug showing on the main screen of the bridge, along with a countdown timer which had dropped steadily from ten minutes since she put it up. It still had almost a minute left when the screen flashed bright and went dark. The whole bridge shook, catching everyone unaware and launching them out of seats or off the floor for a second or two.

Samuels attempted to restore the feed in order to see what was going on, but nothing in range of the bridge hatch was transmitting.

She wanted to unseal the hatch and take a look, but remembered Aichele's warning not to do so until she got an all clear from him. When two more minutes had gone by with no communications from him, she activated his channel herself. "Bridge, Aichele." There was no response, and Samuels immediately assumed the worst. Her second thought was that he had been without vocom capability not long ago, and perhaps the shock had simply knocked loose whatever patch job he had done to get them back. No one else had a comm set out there...except Sullivan. Did she tie her suit into the shipwide network? Maybe local comm would reach her.

Before Samuels had a chance to try, there was another message for her. "Bridge, Burton."

"Bridge, this is Samuels. Go."

"What was that shaking?"

"That was Aichele."

"Aichele? What did he do?"

"I still don't know, but my guess would be improvising, adapting—"

"—and overcoming," Burton finished.

"Right. He set off some sort of explosion outside the bridge hatch, but I've lost visuals. I tried calling Aichele, but his comms are out again. I was about to try Sullivan when you called. Does she have her suit tied into the network?"

"Yes. She's on the Squad 12 circuit. Individual line is 12-Echo," Burton said, pulling the data up on her HUD to be sure she remembered correctly.

"How are things on your end?"

"Mostly unchanged. Our side doesn't have enough people to make a push past the boatbay choke point. Their side has enough people, but they just got pushed backward pretty hard. It's going to take a while for the non-coms to be ready to push back. We're still trading shots back and forth without much effect.

"When the push does come, though, we'll be hard pressed to stop it. Our ammo and power are running very low. I'm cycling a few back to Engineering every ten minutes to try to recharge their suits, but we're not really gaining much ground. Any chance we can expect support from forward?"

"I still don't know what the situation is up here, Burton, but I'll do everything I can."

"I know you will, Captain. Burton clear."

There was such resignation in Burton's voice it nearly brought tears to Samuels' eyes. She fought them back as best she could and set her unit to 12-Echo. "Bridge, Sullivan."

"Sullivan here, ma'am. I was just about to report. If you'll give us another couple minutes to clear debris, you should be able to open the blast door."

"What happened out there?"

"Aichele didn't fill you in on the plan?"

"He said there was no time. What happened?"

"All the Forresters were collected together inside the defenses we built. Aichele managed to drop a suitable application of high explosives in the middle of them, and they ceased to be a problem."

"Where's Aichele?"

"His suit says unconscious and concussed, but in no immediate danger. Do you have a corpsman in there with you?"

"Yes. Once the door's open, I'll have her give Aichele a look. What shape are your troops in?"

"No other injuries to report. There are seven Granadans with me, all armed with heavy weapons. Five of them are upset that they didn't have a chance to get in the fight. The other two have some spark of intelligence."

"Tell them there's more fighting still in Engineering, and we're going there next."

"Yes, ma'am. Even though I don't like to encourage them. Try the door now, ma'am."

Samuels did so, entering the key code she hadn't needed to resequence even once. The door responded with a soft pop, followed by high-pitched squealing, but the giant actuators pushed the door open slowly.

Thomason, having heard the conversation, headed out to check on Aichele as soon as she could fit through the opening. Samuels heard her exclamation of "Holy hell!" when she got out, and when the door opened fully, Samuels had to agree.

The corridor was filled with the evil smell of burnt offerings and chemical compounds. Shrapnel had torn long gouges into the walls, radiating away from the central junction, some of the metal shards still protruding from the walls. The temporary barricade was simply gone, as was a four square meter section of the ceiling. The floor was still there, but deformed and bowed downward. A greasy black paint coated everything, and Samuels' stomach attempted to turn itself inside out when she realized that the 'paint' was what was left after you put thirty-odd Marines in a blender and then threw it into a furnace.

"It's hell, all right, but there's nothing holy about it," Samuels said quietly to herself.

Sullivan had come up behind her to report. "War is hell, ma'am. Always was, always will be. The goal is to send the other gal there ahead of you."

"I know, at least up here," Samuels said, pointing to her head. "But this is a sight and smell that I will never be able to get rid of."

"And every time you think of it, just remember that they had the same or worse planned for you. These troops died quick and easy, never seeing the end coming."

"Thoughts for another time. Right now, we've got people dying in Engineering, and we need to support them. So, let's gather everyone up and anything we can fight with and get down there."

"You ever hunt turkeys, ma'am?"

"What? No. What has that got to do with anything?"

"Well, I knew you were a fan of classics, so I thought you'd get the reference. Anyway, sending everyone in, guns blazing, to storm the castle is seldom the best tactic. Turkeys run single file, and if you just fire at random, they all notice and scatter. But if you start at the back and work your way forward, you can often get all of them before they notice.

"When we get down to the boatbay, chances are those Forresters are going to be just like these, focused on the threat ahead instead of watching their flanks. If we sneak up on them and use the bulwarks to mask our approach, we can probably get the ones in the rear, likely officers, before they're aware we have them pincered."

"All right. I can see that. Can you do the sniping?" Samuels had first-hand knowledge of Sullivan's level of marksmanship.

"That was my plan."

"Sergeant Ramamurthy, get everyone together and ready to move. We're heading out ASAP."

"And by 'we' you mean us, and not you, Captain." It was a statement, rather than a question.

"No, I mean 'we' as in 'we.' You do understand English, right? Now gather up the troops."

"The captain needs to remain with the bridge. The executive officer is already involved in the fighting in Engineering, and both of you should not be risked in the same location."

"But there are no other officers to take command."

"Precisely why you should stay here while the XO is there."

"No, I mean there are no other officers to command this group."

"You can give Sullivan command, or give it to me, but you should not go with us, ma'am, by your own plan."

"Not me," Sullivan interjected. "I don't know the first thing about being an officer."

"I don't give orders I'm not willing to follow, Sergeant," Samuels fired back, ignoring the absurdity of Sullivan's comment.

"Ma'am, I apologize if anything I have said or done indicated that I thought otherwise. You have more than amply demonstrated your willingness to take the same risks as the rest of us. There are a lot of men and women here who can fight, but there are only two people who can command this ship. One of them needs to be on the bridge."

He was right, and she knew he was right. She was tempted to override him and go anyway, but finally decided not to.

"All right, Ramamurthy," she sighed. "You're in command until you join up with higher authority. Sullivan has a good idea, and I think you should follow her advice for the initial approach and engagement. I'll stay here, along with the wounded."

Ramamurthy saluted, and very diplomatically did not smile. She returned it, and very diplomatically did not kick him.

The sergeant then sent two corporals around to gather everyone together. Samuels went back to her command console and pulled up security feeds from the boatbay.

* * * * *

Sullivan raised her hypervelocity rail gun up and over the half wall in front of her, resting its weight on the immobile metal. As quick as thought, she moved Nancy into the driver's seat. Cynthia had been better at the running battle tactics she had used getting out of the boatbay, but Nancy had the patience to do this right, which was not running straight into the thick of the action without thinking. Also, Nancy had no fondness for neo-acid grunge music. There was no way Cynthia could do this quietly.

Once the weapon came to rest, she sighted down Broadway on her selected target and squeezed the trigger. The steel-jacketed round had significant mass, so Sullivan used part of the expected recoil to pull the gun back and out of sight.

She dropped down behind the cover, and used one of the gun ports to spot the results. The magnetic field that gave her armor-piercing rounds their deadly speed was absolutely silent. The report when the round struck its target was anything but. The Forresters knew they were being hunted, as the multiple shouts of "Sniper!" attested, but they were still looking aft into the boatbay trying to spot the source.

Nancy/Sullivan hoped she could get off two more shots before the enemy figured it out and Ramamurthy turned everyone loose.

Wanting to make the most of her opportunity, she spent a little extra time scanning the Forresters through the firing hole and identifying anyone who might be an officer. Once she had their positions in mind, she stood, squeezed off three rounds in the same second at three targets and dropped back under cover. The augmented muscles of her suit handled the recoil easily, so there was no wasted time or motion in recentering the sights of the weapon.

Smack-smack-smack, and the Forrester array became a hornet's nest of movement, everyone diving down to keep from exposing any part of their armor above the barricade that separated them from the boatbay. Nancy/Sullivan still had a clear line of fire, but with all her targets' backs against the barricade, she was sure to be spotted as soon as she moved again.

"Sullivan, Ramamurthy."

"Ram, go."

"Be ready to move. I'm about to make myself a big target. Clear."

"Copy. Ready to move. Out."

She took another look out her peephole and couldn't see any officers left. So it wouldn't matter who she shot at, and this would be her last clean shot opportunity. She took a few extra seconds to eject her magazine and replace the four rounds she'd expended before locking it back into place. She took a deep breath, let it half out, and then rose and started firing as quickly as she could pull the trigger starting at her right and walking her fire to her left.

The hornet's nest buzzed into action, but she had made eight shots before the first return fire glanced off her left arm and she dropped back behind her cover. As expected, she was a big target now, and blast after blast of high-energy plasma hit the improvised barrier, and spots of orange heat appeared here and there.

With all their attention focused on her, the Forresters did not notice the Marines and Granadans taking up firing positions at either end of the cross-corridor, until they opened up. Shots quit hitting her position as they shifted fire to handle the new threat, and she rose and fired off four more quick rounds.

She was about to pop back up and send more fire downrange when Ramamurthy broke in on the all-call circuit. "Check fire, check fire. White flag."

She took a quick look and saw that it was true. With no leadership to organize a response, the Forresters had surrendered. As she watched, the enemy was throwing down their weapons and putting their hands on top of their helmets.

* * * * *

"Welcome back to the world of the conscious," Samuels told Aichele with a grin when she saw his eyes open. She might have spoken too soon. The Marine lieutenant had a distant look in his eyes, and didn't appear to have understood her words. Gradually, his eyes focused, but he still looked confused.

"Where am I? What's the ship's status?" he said, trying to rise. He moaned in pain and laid down again.

"Don't move until I've set the bones, L-T," Thomason advised.

"Which ones?" Aichele wanted to know.

"Those same ribs that weren't healed yet. You're also concussed, and exhausted. I think you should stay down for a few weeks."

"Not likely," Samuels opined. "He's allergic to medbay."

"Am I on the bridge?" he asked, not willing to move his head to investigate.

"Yes," the captain answered. "Though, technically, it is also medbay at the moment, until we have control of the rest of the ship."

"What's our status, then?"

"I don't think we should tell you before you promise not to try to get back to the fighting," Thomason stated.

"Don't worry about him going anywhere. Even if he were able to move without armor to support him, the blast door is sealed again, and only Roberts or I can open it at the moment." The captain talked across his prone form at Thomason, as if he weren't there. "Can you prop him up with something so he can see the forward screen?"

"I can sit up," he protested.

"Don't," Thomason advised shortly.

"Just as well, I suppose. The fighting is over, so there's not much to see." The captain was about to continue, but the vocom line activated first.

"Bridge, Burton."

"This is Samuels. Go ahead, Sergeant."

"Captain, we've accepted the surrender of all the Forresters attacking the aft section. Major Tunney is organizing a means of securing them all. Corpsman Derat is setting up an infirmary in what will someday be this ship's medbay, and we're transporting our wounded there. Forrester wounded are being seen to in the boatbay. Do you have any further orders, ma'am?"

"Yes, Sergeant. I've been in contact with the remaining crews of the assault shuttles and explained the situation to them. They have surrendered as well, which seemed logical of them, since they think we still have missiles in the tubes. I told each of them to disarm and meet security forces at the breach point in...five minutes from now," she explained, checking the time on the chronometer. "Please organize a squad to take them into custody. There should be only two or three per shuttle."

"Understood. Anything else, Captain?"

"Do you have a rated shuttle pilot among your Marines?"

"I'll ask the major, but I don't think so."

"Nevermind. Grab Roberts or Sullivan. Once we've got the Forresters off those shuttles, we need to take one and recover the crew from one of our birds that took damage holding off boarders. Tell whoever you send to contact the bridge. We've got a track running on them, but we can't raise them on vocom."

"Yes, Captain. Was that it?"

"Have Corpsman Derat send someone to the bridge to get the wounded here, once he's got things organized in medbay."

"I'll do that. Is Aichele awake yet?"

Samuels paused to check over her shoulder. "He was, but it looks like he's drifted off again. He'll be okay."

"Yes, ma'am. I hate to ask, but, is there anything else?"

Samuels chuckled, and felt the tension finally drain out of her. "No, Sergeant. I think that's everything."

Once again, the ship was entirely under Warner control.

CHAPTER 48
20 October
Pathfinder

"So, we should have all the civilians removed from the Gate Control Platform in another hour. Several Granadan technicians have agreed to man the platform and keep the systems running, but all others are being evacuated." Brighton listened to the report and forced himself not to comment on the bedraggled state of his former flag captain. Johnson wore a white bandage wrapped around her head and it looked like most of her already shortened hair was gone. In addition, her left arm was in a sling and she had two black eyes. Brighton wondered how much other damage was not visible.

Captain Johnson broke his train of thought as she continued, "Major Chowdhury is en route to *Pathfinder* with two shuttles full of Marines. "

"Very well, Captain. Please expedite the evacuation of the GCP. Once that is completed, stand *Dagger* off a safe distance to guard against any unauthorized transits. You are to consider us to be at war with the Forrest Family and adjust your rules of engagement accordingly. We have our injured transferred so We will be headed back to Granada as soon as Major Chowdhury is aboard. I'll contact you with further orders, depending on what we find at the planet, for now your most important role is to protect the gate."

"Aye-aye, sir."

As the connection closed, he pulled his thoughts away from her physical condition. Dr. Tyson, on *Dagger*, would not have let her out of Medbay, regardless of her rank or position, if he thought she were still in any danger. She would have been transferred to the medical facilities on the station with all of the other wounded. With the details of the GCP taken care of, his mind moved ahead to the potential problems that would exist on the planet.

The initial reports from the civilians and prisoners on the gate platform had estimated somewhere in the neighborhood of 500,000 Forrest ground troops on the planet, not including whatever fleet personnel were manning the ships and shipyards. He had managed to take away their newest destroyer as it was conducting its builder's trials, but *Peru's* scans, that Samuels had brought, showed another twelve ships in various states of completion. All but one seemed to be destroyers, but there was also one heavy cruiser about midway through its construction. Those ships were being constructed in Warner shipyards by Warner personnel, so those ships belonged to the Warner Family. He needed to find a way to take that construction intact if possible, but at a minimum, he needed to deny it to the enemy. He would also prefer to take the shipyards intact, which would enable them to repair their own damage to *Dagger* and *Yargus*. Pathfinder *might do with a little repair, too*, he thought sardonically.

The comm chime broke his thoughts.

"The shuttles are docked."

"Very well, have Major Chowdhury rest her marines and order the helm to get us under weigh to the planet."

Ensign Lee nodded on the screen.

"Yes, sir."

In his mind, he ran through the schedule again. It would be two more hours before they arrived in orbit so he might as well try to rest. As he put his head to the pillow, he immediately went still and began to snore quietly.

* * * * *

"As I see it," Major Chowdhury said, a few hours later, "we have several options. I think we need to take the orbital shipyards first, however. We need to wait for reinforcements before we can tackle the surface. I'm not sure we can take the shipyards, either, with our current personnel. The station is too vast and the Forrest troops will be too spread out to be able to take in one surprise engagement, as we were able to do at the GCP. It would take a sustained assault, with the casualties that would entail. Having said that, we stand ready to take whatever action you deem necessary."

She sat back down as the room took on a hushed expectancy. All eyes turned to the Commodore. *Dagger* remained near the gate platform and the able members of her crew were doing repairs on the cruiser, but many of the repairs were too extensive to be completed, or even begun, given their limited capacity to carry spares, and would require the resources of a shipyard. *Yargus* had also sustained damage and *Pathfinder* was suffering not only from the damage incurred during the battle, but also from the pre-existing damage the loyalists had used to try to prevent the movement of the ship to this system after the theft. All of these things were points in favor of assaulting the shipyards sooner rather than later, if they planned on being able to hold this system.

"Let's not forget we still have Forrest ships still in this system," Lieutenant Amaya-Garcia said into the silence. "Those first two destroyers may be limping back into the system, but they would arrive before we could deal with the shipyards or any of the other orbital facilities."

Brighton nodded slowly. "That is certainly a factor in any decision," he began. "Also, we need to notify the Board about the extent of the current developments. That will factor into any plan we ultimately decide upon."

For that, they could use *Yargus* as a courier. She would be able to jump directly back to Gateway or Earth and save considerable time in getting the message back to the Board.

"Commodore, I know you would like to capture those yard facilities, with all the new construction intact, but, just to point out alternatives," Lieutenant Weaver said quietly, "we could save a lot of lives by simply destroying the ships with missiles. The shipyards have no permanent defenses."

"I'm sure it would save Marine lives," Chowdhury cut in before Brighton could respond, "but I'm equally sure there are Granadan civilian workers on those ships. Warner civilians. The Marines would not be in favor of trading those lives for their own."

"Major, Lieutenant Weaver is not suggesting that your team would not do your duty if asked. He is outlining options, as is his duty as XO," Brighton clarified.

"No offense intended, ma'am," Weaver added quietly but firmly, with a slight nod to the major.

Chowdhury nodded back but said nothing, her face a mask.

"It may be necessary to implement such a bombardment, but I don't see any need to take that measure yet. As things stand, does anyone see any likelihood that we will be forced from the system by the ships the Forrest troops have at their disposal?" He looked around the conference table and then to the two screens that showed the faces of his other two ship commanders. None answered his query. "With that in mind, we should have the time to decide the appropriate method of dealing with all of the issues."

"Commodore," a voice from the comm interrupted, "there is a Colonel Kern calling from the shipyards. I told her you were unavailable and she said to tell you she will start killing civilian workers in one hour if you don't back away from the planet and all orbital facilities. She also said she would begin sooner if you didn't call within fifteen minutes to begin negotiating your surrender."

Chowdhury muttered something under her breath, but Brighton made out the word 'delusional' quite clearly.

"I believe we will continue this meeting later," Brighton said as he stood and moved to the hatch. "Lieutenant Weaver, Major Chowdhury, will you both join me on the bridge?"

"Major Chowdhury, prepare your Marines for an assault," he said over his shoulder as the trio strode through the hatch and onto the bridge. "Wait for the final decision from me, but get everything prepared."

"It will be bloody, sir, going in blind."

"Yes, but our duty is to protect Warner citizens. We cannot abandon civilian hostages to their fates. And we cannot allow the Forresters to dictate terms at the barrel of a weapon, either. They have too many hostages on the surface for us to set that precedent."

"Understood. I'll get things moving at our end." Chowdhury moved to one of the unmanned side consoles to alert Lieutenant Kelley of the change in plans while Brighton and Weaver moved to the comm console.

"Could you tell where the signal originated?" he asked of the comm tech as he strode to his captain's seat.

"Yes, sir. They didn't even try to shield the signal. It originated on the heavy cruiser."

"Very well, open a tight beam link directly to that ship."

The screen lit up immediately and the image of a bulky women in the dark green of Forrester Marines stood with at least eight civilians bound and gagged at her feet. The Warners wore the light blue shipsuits common to the Gateway Interspatial line workers. The woman wore the shoulder pips of a full colonel and she looked haggard and worn. Her blue eyes were bloodshot and there were circles under her eyes, as if she had not slept for several days.

"Colonel," Brighton began firmly before the Forrester could open her mouth, "this is Commodore Brighton, commanding Task Force Ten of the Warner Space Navy. You will surrender your prisoners and answer for these acts of war against the sovereign territory of the Warner Family or you will be destroyed where you stand."

"Ha," she answered feverishly, "you would not dare fire on this station while we hold your citizens. Move off now and we will let them live for a while longer."

"Sir," Weaver, standing directly behind Brighton, said quietly enough to keep the comment from reaching the Forrester, "there are evac pods launching all over the station."

Brighton nodded without turning. His large frame had shielded Weaver from the video pickup as well. He was about to respond to Colonel Kern when the scene behind her exploded with motion. Workers in blue shipsuits flooded the room and began attacking the Marines with whatever lay under their hands. Pipes and wrenches against blasters and rifles. "Grenada Unfettered!" one of them yelled before he was shot down. Kern shot five of the onrushing mob before being overwhelmed by the surging tide of humanity... and then the screen went blank. Brighton turned to the scan monitor as he saw indications of explosions all over the station. All the unfinished ships were destroyed, and explosions were intermittent all along the length of the station.

"How many pods were detected?" he barked at Quèneau, who was frozen at her console.

"Um, uh, sorry, sir. Just over eight hundred at last count."

"What is the civilian complement of that station?" he asked Weaver without taking his eyes from the scan.

"Normally about five thousand," his XO responded in a whisper.

"Helm, move us away from that debris," Brighton called, "All ahead one third."

"Aye-aye, sir. All ahead one third," Warrant Lear said in a stunned voice.

"Sir," Quèneau called urgently from scan, "I'm picking up ships jumping into the outer system."

Brighton spun again to face the scan.

"How many ships? How close are they to *Dagger*?"

"Five so far, sir. They are not near *Dagger* or the JP at all. I can't pinpoint the location, they are pretty far out, but they are on a bearing of 102.88.-33."

"Helm," Brighton called, "come to a heading of 123.88.00 to put us between them and the gate."

"Aye, sir."

"The count is now eleven ships," Quèneau called.

"Orders to *Dagger*," Brighton turned to comm and waited for her nod, "Leave *Peru* at the gate and rendezvous with us at their best speed."

"Sent, sir."

Brighton's stomach turned to ice as he realized the implications of those arriving ships. The Forresters must have discovered another Jump Point and built a gate somewhere in the outer reaches of the system. This piece of missing data answered so many of the nagging questions which had disturbed him. It was just as Samuels had supposed in her earlier message during the battle. He knew, for sure, how the Forresters had been able to take this system without Warner being aware of the increase in traffic. He knew how they were getting the completed warships out of the system. He knew now that the Warner Family was in much greater peril than even he had assumed.

"Eighteen, nineteen… Twenty, sir. Also, the two remaining destroyers are changing course to meet the newcomers."

"Helm, change course," Brighton said with resignation. "Let's head to the gate. Comm, advise *Yargus* to follow our course. Advise *Dagger* to belay my last orders. Have them prepare to transit to Tanner. Have them take all the remaining personnel off the GCP except those needed to activate the gate for their transfer to Tannar. The volunteers are then to evacuate the platform. We will pick up the evac pods when we arrive."

"Twenty-seven ships, sir. Still too far to detect types."

"Very well, let us get back to the gate." Brighton said, his voice firming with resolve. "As soon as *Dagger* and *Peru* are clear and we see the evac pods, we will fire two missiles at the platform to destroy it."

"Aye-aye, sir," Lieutenant Amaya-Garcia called.

"Then we will go home. I want *Yargus* to transfer to the secure yards in Gateway but we have to get word to Earth. There is nothing more we can do here, now."

CHAPTER 49
20 October
WNS *Peru*

Major Tunney turned and looked at Captain Samuels.

"There's no way to fit 48 prisoners into the brig space that we have. There are only four cells and they are only designed to hold three to four prisoners each."

Samuels turned a tired eye to the Marine commander. Now that the fighting on the ship was at an end, he was again in complete control of the Marines on the ship.

The major's left arm was braced and immobilized against his broad chest. Burns showed through the bandaging on his arm and hand. She wondered how he had gotten that much damage through his armor, but decided she didn't want to know the story just yet. She had too many stories going through her head already.

"I'm *completely* familiar with the layout of a security suite on Warner destroyers," she replied dryly.

Tunney's eyebrow went up but he asked no questions.

"Very well, ma'am. I'll find locations to house them all until we can dock somewhere and transfer them."

She gave a tired nod.

"Thank you."

As she and Ensign Roberts began to walk away, she turned to her XO.

"Jherri, let's have a conference with all the department heads. Also, invite Lieutenant Aichele."

Her friend turned to her and nodded. Her eyes were red and she looked like she was barely maintaining control of herself.

"Tell them we'll meet in an hour, that'll give Tunney some time to clean up this mess. And you ought to go rest for a bit after you hand out the messages."

Roberts shook her head, "No, I'm fine."

Samuels started to say more but decided to leave it alone.

* * * * *

Samuels looked around the conference room an hour later. She had asked for the department heads and she was suddenly struck by how humorous the group around her would be on another ship.

Her Executive Officer sat across the table from her. Jheri Roberts, nearly 23 years old and less than a year out of the academy, and the executive officer of a Warner Naval vessel. Such a thing was unheard of. Crystal Giannini, sat at the foot of the table. Samuels looked at her Chief of Engineering. Crystal was not even an officer. She was an electronics tech 1c. She remembered the arguments that Commander Leung had had with Ensign Omundson on *Pathfinder* about him not being able to be the Chief Engineer because he wasn't a lieutenant yet, only an Ensign. *What a sham I've made of all of the rules here.*

Cipi Felix was the next person over, her Bosun of the Ship. He wasn't even in Warner Fleet. She had to smile as she saw his grin, though. She just felt better when he was around. Next to him sat Lieutenant Aichele. She still thought of him as Gunny Aichele, who had rescued her take-over of *Pathfinder* and pointed her in a direction that might have a chance of getting the ship back, all while letting her lead the effort. She wondered if she shouldn't dismiss him to recover in Medbay, then remembered that they did not have an actual doctor, and the medical suite had not actually been stocked yet. The ship hadn't been due to be commissioned for months yet.

She looked at the last two people in the room, Major Tunney and Amber Sullivan. Major Tunney wearing his captain's planets on his shoulder was as solid as ever, even though he had his injured arm resting in his lap. He had a courtesy promotion to major because there could only be one 'Captain' on a ship but had performed every task like a true veteran with the accumulated rank. He took no notice of his injury and so no one else did either. He seemed to be the only one who fit into his appointed place in this group. Amber Sullivan was the last. Samuels was not sure how she fit in any group. How she and Giannini had switched places baffled Samuels also. Sullivan was an engineering tech 2c and Giannini the electronics tech, but when they had come on board and started fixing things, Crystal had ended up in the engine room and Amber had ended up on weapons and targeting. And they both seemed to be very good at the alternate skills. Of course, she had no idea what Amber's total skillset might really be.

And lastly, it came around the table to her chair. She was young, like Roberts. She was just out of the academy, like Roberts, and *commanding* a Fleet ship. She was probably the most out of place of any in this room. And that was just if you went by the record that everyone knew. There was so much more that nobody knew. Well, nobody but Cipi.

She stopped thinking about the people in front of her and started thinking about why they were here. She turned and looked at her Marine commander again.

"Major Tunney, what is the status of our prisoners?"

"Secure," he said flatly.

Here we go again, she thought, but he surprised her by adding details. "They are stuffed into every room that we could find a way to lock, but they are all secured, Captain."

"Very well, and how about your Marines?"

The man grew more somber as he gave a slight nod to his young captain.

"We lost 17 Marines, including Lieutenants Mdembe, Sommers, and Tucker. We also have fourteen more wounded of various degrees. Sergeant Young has a serious chest wound and I'd like your permission to transfer him to *Dagger* for treatment."

"Absolutely. Whatever treatment the corpsmen feel is necessary for any of the wounded is authorized. What about the other Fleet personnel and the Granadans?"

"Most of the Fleet personnel were either in Engineering or in the Bridge, so we didn't lose any of them; but the Grenadans were in the thick of things and they took a heavy toll. We had 35 dead Granadans and 34 wounded."

She looked down at the tabletop for just a moment before coming back up to look into his eyes.

"Do we need any more help in the medbay?"

"No, I think that Thomason has it under control for now."

Samuels felt a strong pull on her emotions as she thought about all of those wounded Marines and Granadans that she had ordered into danger. She wanted to turn the next section of the meeting over to Roberts so she could get herself under control and no one would see that she wasn't strong enough to be a ship captain. She looked at her friend. Roberts was sitting in her chair looking at the wall, her face turned away from Samuels. She could see half of Robert's face and that the eye on her side was red and swollen. Roberts didn't even seem to be paying any attention to the meeting. Turning away any thought of letting her handle the technical part of the meeting, Samuels straightened her shoulders and turned to Giannini. She tightened her voice so no one would hear any weakness and forced herself on.

"Very well, Ms. Giannini, how about the engines? Where are we?"

The dark-haired woman turned her tired eyes to her captain and smiled slightly.

"The Forresters never breached the engineering compartment, so we are still in the same situation as we were before. That is to say that we should still be able to make it move, but there are a lot of things that I would like to be able to fix."

"That's just as well. We should have a little bit of time to get everything straightened out. Commodore Brighton holds the system now, so we should be able to make repairs as we need to. Just don't begin anything major without my approval. Ms. Sullivan, what about the tracking and targeting system? It seemed to work okay during our short battle with the shuttles. Are the problems worked out?"

"No ma'am, we…

Sullivan was interrupted by a tone from the desktop and the intercom coming alive.

"Ma'am, there is an urgent call from the Commodore."

Samuels raised a hand to Sullivan and then reached forward and toggled the switch on the console in front of her.

"This is Captain Samuels, Commodore. I'm in a briefing with my senior officers. Is this something that I need to discuss with you privately?"

The deep voice of the Commodore filled the conference room after she acknowledged the call.

"No, Captain. This is something that they will all need to know. Approximately five minutes ago, ships began pouring through a previously unknown jump point in the depths of this system. There are enough of them coming through that we will not be able to hold the system with the existing ships that we have. You will need to make your way to *Dagger*'s position and prepare to exit this system with them within the next two hours. If your ship is not capable of doing this, you will need to disable it and scuttle her so the incoming enemy cannot use her against us. Do you have any questions?"

Samuels looked around the table at the stunned faces and gritted her teeth.

"No, sir. I will contact Captain Johnson and make arrangements to transit to the jump gate with her and *Dagger*."

"Very well. *Yargus* will be transferring to Gateway to a safely hidden Warner port and I will be transferring directly to Earth with *Pathfinder* to report this incursion to Director Warner. I would assume that a fleet would be on its way here now, due to our earlier reports; but if not, we will ensure that they have this new information about the Forrester invasion. This is not something that can be allowed to stand in any form. If we had the ships to fight with any chance of success, there is no way I would leave this system to them now."

Samuels looked across the table at Cipi Felix. His eyes were hardened and his jaw was firm. She could see that he had pictured GU as being on the edge of success, only to feel them thrown back off of a cliff to fend for themselves once again. She looked straight into Cipi's eyes as she responded to Brighton.

"That is understood, sir. We will do what we need to do to rendezvous with *Dagger*."

"Very well. Brighton clear."

As the comm went dead, Samuels looked around the table at the rest of her leaders.

The table shined into her eyes, making it hard to speak for just a moment as she considered leaving these Granadans unsupported against the brutal Foresters once again.

With the information that they had just received, there was no time for any evacuation. Not only that, they hadn't gotten any of the Forresters off of the planet yet. It was clear from Brighton's comments that there was nothing they could do for them yet. She looked up and ran her eyes across each of them as she began talking.

"Okay, you all need to get your areas ready to go. You know what needs to happen. Get out there and get it done. Keep in contact with Roberts on the bridge. I want everything ready to go in two hours. After the price we paid, we're not losing this ship now. Dismissed."

Each of them nodded as they stood.

She looked at Cipi as she stood and started moving to the hatch. She motioned to the door. He nodded and moved to follow her. She could see the pain in his eyes and she wanted to reach out and hold him but she had to hold back.

"First of all, I want to say that I wanted to follow up this with an attack on the planet as soon as we were able to and remove all Forrest ships from this system and I'm torn that we will not be able to do that. Unfortunately, we don't have time or strength. I'm sorry, but we have to get the word out and deal with the survival of the Warner Family and what to do going forward. We will be back as soon as we possibly can."

"Si, I am aware. We are all well aware of dealing with what must be dealt with."

She nodded, and sighed.

"I wish it weren't so. I need to know how many of your people will want to stay on the ship. Any will be free to stay with us or to stay at the control station for transfer back to the planet."

He stood straighter.

"I don't believe that any of my people will abandon their families or their people and leave until we are able to free the planet. This would not be a right thing to do."

They turned the corner at the end of the cross-corridor and avoided a group of workers who were cutting out the barricades they had used to defend the bridge. They turned aft and started down the starboard corridor.

Samuels turned and looked at him and continued her conversation.

"I will need two or three of your people to stay with the ship; to come to Earth and testify of the Forresters and their attacks and the things done here."

Cipi kept walking and shook his head and gave her a sad look.

"As I said, no one will want to leave their families at this time."

She turned and looked at him.

"I know that this will be difficult, Mr. Felix, but we will need this testimony in order to convince the other Families of what Forrest has done. No one would believe that another Family would do such a thing without your condemnation."

They walked in silence through the damaged walkway, neither saying anything for several moments. Finally, they reached the medbay at the end of the corridor. Samuels turned to walk in and was met with the urgency of people moving at a rush in all directions. She stood for several seconds, just inside the hatch, watching the chaotic motion. Three corpsmen were trying to direct traffic and move between the most urgent patients. After five hours, Samuels had expected that things would have been a little more settled here, as they were at most places in the ship, but that didn't seem to be the case. She stepped in front of CPO Thomason and broke her stride as she had been moving to another patient.

"Thomason, what is our situation with moving most of these Granadans to the Control Station within the next two hours? How many can't be moved?"

She felt Felix stiffen at her side, but she tried to ignore him as he didn't make an attempt to break into the conversation.

The young woman just looked at her for several seconds before answering, "Ma'am, there are several of these people who would die if we move them. Most of the rest have already been moved out of the medbay, in preparation to transfer over to *Dagger*'s larger and better facilities. You should see Siria, back there. She will have a list of all the injured and where they are."

Thomason motioned to the back of the room and she took the opportunity to slip away as Samuels turned to look in that direction.

Samuels shook her head as she noticed the escape and turned to Cipi. He turned his angry face to her.

"You should not be treated with such disrespect. You are the Capitán."

She almost laughed as she thought about their first meeting. "She is not being disrespectful, just busy. Let's go find Siria."

They walked through the beds. Most of the occupants were still unconscious, but a few looked up at the two of them with a smile or a grim nod. One of the faces that she recognized as belonging to one of her Marines, looked up at her as she walked by. She realized that he was one who had been hit while she was delaying her withdrawal into the bridge and she felt a shame as she saw his bandaged shoulder. She had seen the wound that he had received, and she knew it was her fault. She stopped by his bed and he grinned up at her, his dark hair flopping to the far side of his head as he struggled to sit up.

She rested a hand lightly on his good shoulder and said, "No, stay down. I'm so..."

"Don't say it, ma'am. You got us to the bridge and we held off five times our number for far longer than we should have. You have nothing to feel bad about."

"We should have moved faster."

"Maybe," he took a ragged breath, "maybe not. We might have been crushed if we moved faster." Another breath shook his chest with its labor.

He started again before she could start speaking.

"Don't guess with 'what ifs,' ma'am. They'll kill you faster than a heavy blaster. Most of us lived through what could easily have killed us all." Another heavy intake of air. "Learn what lessons you can and don't think about any of the rest of it."

Cipi tapped her softly on the back of her shoulder with his hand and let it rest there.

"I think he is right, my Capitán. This should have ended with us all dead. I have seen many Forrester operations. They would not have taken any prisoners as you have done."

Samuels shook her head and looked at Cipi.

"Oh blast!"

"What is the matter?"

"I just realized that when you and your Granadans leave the ship, we are going to be outnumbered by the Forrester prisoners again."

"Well, I will still be here. You promised me this ship, so I dare not let it sail away without me."

Final Reckoning

CHAPTER 50
21 October
Warner Main Complex – Earth Orbit

Admiral Cosina watched the door close on the heels of the tall officer as Brighton left the office of CEO Gerry Warner. From his position, he looked down toward the owner of the office, who sat at his desk fuming. To all outward appearances, the CEO looked like a sleeping volcano, but Cosina could see the hidden magma below the surface to know the volcano wasn't really asleep. Cosina had known him too long and could see the fury he worked so hard to hide.

"I did not believe it could possibly have gone that far," Warner said, his calm and almost monotone voice giving away none of the anger.

"Nor did I." Cosina sighed, then paced back to the facing chair that Brighton had just vacated. "We were very lucky Brighton was able to close the jump point, at least temporarily."

"Yes," Warner said, tapping his stylus on the heavy hardwood surface of the desk in front of him. "He doesn't seem to be afraid to exceed his orders, does he?"

"Sir, he was doing what looked like the right thing to accomplish the goals of the Family," Cosina began defensively.

Warner waved his hand to cut him off, "I'm not going to second guess him from this distance. I wasn't there, and it's not as if we haven't seen this sort of thing from him in the past. It was one of the reasons you recommended him for this assignment, if I remember correctly."

"Sir, that Humboldt fiasco was a completely different issue."

Cosina stopped as Warner waved his arm again, cutting off the explanation, still angry at the situation. "That is neither here nor there," Warner said. "The pertinent question is: what steps should we be taking now? I assume that he sent *Pathfinder* back to Gateway after it brought him here to report?"

"Yes, that was my understanding. It should be safely in the secure yard with *Yargus* by the end of tomorrow." Cosina began pacing again. "As for our future plans, I will need to find out where that second jump point reconnects to the known systems before we have Forrest warships in our rear areas. With *Victory* gone, we may need to call back more of our heavy cruisers to Gateway. On the political side, you already got the ball rolling with the call for the meeting of the Ruling Council. Maybe you should share some of the information with your allies."

"We can't release any information ahead of time," Warner snapped. "Get me Brighton and Ramirez' official reports by this afternoon; and I want official depositions from each of them and also from your security man. I need legal evidence that I can take to the council."

"Yes, sir," Cosina said quietly, "I'll take care of it. If I may, though..."

"What?"

"It's certain that Amanda Forrest has been gathering support from her allies as soon as the announcement went out that you had exercised your right to adjudication. If you don't contact the Families likely to support us, then those Families will be the only ones blindsided by these events. That means they're going to have to make a decision quickly with little or no time to weigh things out. What we're going to be asking for, even though it's no more than our due, is substantial enough to give anyone pause. I just think a heads-up would give them more time to see that what we're asking of them is the right thing to do."

Warner jumped up and started pacing, trying to burn off some of his excess energy and to dampen his anger. "You're right, Conrad. This is much worse than we believed, or than we could expect anyone else to believe when they hear it cold. They're not trying to get around tariffs, they are actually building fleets and invading territory! Enslaving people — *our* people!"

"Yes, sir, they are," Cosina said with a hardening voice. "And we can't let them get away with killing and injuring our citizens."

Warner stopped near his desk and looked at Cosina, halted in his pacing by the tone in his friend's voice.

"We have overwhelming evidence. The Council will sanction those responsible," Warner finally said with growing confidence.

"And what if Forrest and DaGama don't abide by the ruling. They are building fleets!" Cosina said with venom. "They have committed several acts of war, they have to be ready to deal with the consequences. They will have thought this out very carefully."

Warner looked at the admiral in confusion. "They have to abide by the rulings of the Council," he said in some confusion. "Their fleets can't be large enough to defy the Combined Fleet."

"Gerry, stop thinking like a politician for a moment," Cosina said patiently, but with a hint of exasperation. "They would not have escalated this far if they weren't willing to fight for their position. You mark my words, they will play dirty in the Ruling Council, and they will not abide by any ruling that doesn't favor them. You've dealt with Amanda Forrest in the past. She's a planner. She will have something ready for this contingency. I believe they will not stop, no matter what."

"What choice do they have? They haven't got the strength to defy the Council."

"If it were me," Cosina said, "I'd get the Ruling Council to come out against *us*. They don't have a fleet big enough to take us on, I hope, but Combined Fleet is big enough to take us on. At least that's what they think."

"What do you mean, 'that's what they think?' That is the whole point of the CF."

"Gerry," the exasperation was a bit more evident now, "you're still looking at this like a politician, instead of as the chief executive. What I mean is that you politicians set your treaties and we abide by them, but they don't necessarily work the way you think they will."

"Again, what do you mean by that?"

"Let me ask you a question," Cosina began with a deep breath, trying to assume the tone of an advisor rather than that of a teacher with a dim-witted child. "If an order went out to Combined Fleet in Gateway, ordering the CF ships there to take out the Warner Fleet HQ in orbit. A legal order, from the Ruling Council; would it be carried out?"

"Of course."

"If everything happened the way politicians think the universe worked, then maybe you'd be right, but in reality, I don't think it would work out that way."

"Why not, and what has that got to do with our present problem?"

The 'why not' is because most of the commanding officers of those ships are Warner officers. They have friends, colleagues, and possibly families on that station. They would not fire. The truth is that the CF doesn't really belong to the Ruling Council. It's only loaned to them from us."

"The officers might be ours, but the crews are not. That creates a balance so that no Family can take control of CF."

"Yes, that has been the official line since the Treaty of Dallas, but it's really not true. Everyone has repeated it for so long that it is taken as scripture, but is not exactly accurate. It might be an oversimplification but look at it this way; the officers control the ships, the best that the crew can do is refuse to act. They cannot initiate any actions other than possibly sabotaging their own ships."

"So what has this got to do with us?"

"Warner controls over a third of the ships in CF. With the addition of Sterling, Fermi and Portales, we control over 94% of the total ships, and all the warships. You need to contact those Families and lay out this evidence in advance of the meeting of the Ruling Council. If the non-spacefaring families are making a move, all of *them* are a target as well. Let them know what the stakes are."

Gerry Warner sat quietly looking at his friend. Most of the anger had subsided, though it had not retreated completely. Finally, he sat forward and tapped the comm on his desktop.

"Gina, get me Horace Fermi on the comm. As soon as that call is completed I'll want Amanda Sterling and Anthony Portales."

"Yes, sir."

"Get me those depositions within two hours," he said to Cosina as he switched off the comm. "We are going to need that evidence sooner rather than later, I'm afraid. And… it might be a good idea for our officers in CF ships here in this system to offer 'surprise leave' to any members of their crews who belong to any of the suspect Families."

"Yes, sir, I'll see to it," Cosina said as he moved to the door and exited, pleased to know that even an old dog could be taught new tricks.

"Sir, Horace Fermi is off-planet currently, with most of his Board, and his assistant says he is not responding to calls," Gina called over the comm. "Amanda Sterling is on line one."

CHAPTER 51
21 October
WNS *Dagger*

Captain Fyonna Johnson sat deflated in her rebuilt command chair amid the wreckage of her bridge and tried to clear her head of the fatigue of the last few days. Her scalp bore a bandage wrapped around in circles, making her look more like a mummy than a warship captain.

The brilliant flash of light and energy that allowed her ship to move instantaneously from the Worth system to the Tannar system left her drained and slightly ill, as it usually did. She fought the effects and forced her attention back to the tasks at hand.

"Comm, broadcast a warning to all ships here in Tannar; 'Enemy in pursuit. Activate all defenses'."

She had turned to the vocom console as she began her request and was slightly shaken again to see Warrant Gabriel Davis at the console instead of CPO Hiramoto, who had manned that post during the battle in Worth. Even more than the damage that surrounded her, this brought home the loss and destruction that had occurred on *Dagger*. Hiramoto was one of many casualties of the direct hit to *Dagger's* bridge.

"Scan, did *Peru* come through with us?"

"Yes, ma'am. Still four thousand kilometers astern."

Davis turned to face the captain as scan was reporting, the urgency evident on his face.

"Captain, Admiral Koutsoudas is calling from *Victory*."

Johnson sat instantly erect in her command chair, shocked to hear that the Admiral was here, in the system. She recovered quickly and stood. "I'll take it in my Day Office."

She started moving as she began the statement and reached the hatch almost as she finished. She had to force herself not to run in front of her crew, but her control only lasted until the hatch closed behind her and then she sprinted the twenty steps to her Office. Her head hurt as the hatch closed behind her. What was going on, now?! *Victory* was the 1st Fleet Flagship and Admiral Koutsoudas was the fleet commander. *Victory never* left the Gateway system. That single Battleship represented more firepower than all of the smaller ships of the fleet combined. The fact that it was here was both a relief, that powerful help was so near, and gave her a chill that it was not at home to protect the Family.

Once inside her office, she sealed the hatch, moved to her desk and keyed the console. Admiral Koutsoudas' dapper features filled the screen. She had only met the Admiral once and had liked him, despite the fact that he tended to be something of a martinet. He was stiff and officious with his subordinates but she had discovered that he had a very dry, subtle, wit that she greatly enjoyed, as long as it was not aimed at her.

"Report, Captain," he barked in clipped tones with no signs of humor of any kind, as soon as she had triggered the comm.

"Aye, sir," she began, stalling while trying to sort her thoughts into a coherent report.

"Under the orders of Commodore Brighton, we tracked *Pathfinder* to the Worth system," she began, realizing how much of the story this left out but pushing forward anyway. He would not be here in Tanner if he hadn't been ordered here based on her previous reports, so she didn't bother to backtrack that far. "The system had been taken over by ships calling themselves the Forrest Family Fleet; they engaged our ships to prevent our retaking *Pathfinder*," she began and then proceeded slowly to fill in the events of the past several days to his impassive features. "So," she concluded twenty minutes later, "when the count of incoming ships reached twenty-seven, Commodore Brighton sent us through to report while he destroyed the gate control to keep them from being able to jump through after us."

When she was finished, she waited quietly for him to respond.

"So this oversized destroyer trailing in your wake is one of the Forrest ships?" he asked questioningly.

"Yes, sir. It was originally started in the Caspar yards as a Warner ship, and we took it back from them while it was undergoing its testing. She is named *Peru*. Lieutenant Samuels was placed in command by the Commodore and she only has a skeleton prize crew aboard. The weapon systems were not active when it was taken but some missiles were stolen from the Caspar yards to defend the ship. It was attacked by Marines from the Forrest Family, but they were not able to retake the ship. It took some damage from our attack as well as the Forrest retaliation and it needs some further fitting out."

He glanced up from his monitor screen and said, "I don't see any Lieutenants named Samuels listed among the company of *Dagger* or *Yargus*. Was she a member of the garrison at Granada?"

"No, sir. She was an ensign aboard *Pathfinder* before she eliminated the pirates and took back that ship. She had *Pathfinder* under her control when we arrived and Commodore Brighton gave her a field promotion and the assignment to take the destroyer *Peru* away from the Forresters. When she accomplished that, he left her there, in command."

"So she was one of the mutineers and double crossed them in the end?"

"No, sir," Johnson said with a deep sigh, "She was ordered off *Vanguard* by Commodore Brighton with the orders to delay the pirates if at all possible. She was not able to stop their departure from Antoc, but was subsequently able to take the ship back after arriving in Worth."

"Did the Commodore believe she was sincere in her loyalty? The pirates had to have help from within the crew," he said with no trace on his face as to what his thoughts were on the subject.

"Yes, sir. I believe Commodore Brighton was completely satisfied with her loyalty. His recommendations are appended to my report, sir."

"And you say that these latest Forrest ships were coming from a previously unmapped jump point in the outer reaches of the system?"

"Yes, sir."

"Was there any indication of where that jump point leads to?"

"No, sir. We weren't close enough to get any readings at all. We could only get a general location."

"Could you get a reading on the ships themselves? Do we have a list of type and size?"

"Only very generally, sir. *Dagger's* sensors were damaged in the fighting and our readings were very vague, I'm afraid."

"Very well, Captain," he said, shaking his head slightly, "Send your official report to me and I'll get it on the way to Fleet HQ. I imagine that they will want to send us a few more ships when they find out what has been going on out here."

"Aye, sir. I'll send you my report immediately, but Fleet HQ should already have Commodore Brighton's report."

The Admiral's head snapped up, his dark eyes drilling into her.

"What do you mean?"

Johnson sat very still for a moment. The Admiral had been sent out here to support the rescue of *Pathfinder* and the possible war implications with Forrest but had he not been told about the secrets that *Pathfinder* and *Yargus* held? If so, and it appeared that was the case, because Johnson had not been cleared to release that information, she was not allowed to tell him that specific information directly. How could she convey that information without breaking her oaths?

"Sir," she began, "Commodore Brighton intended to jump *Pathfinder* directly to Earth with the information as soon as he confirmed the destruction of the gate. He also intended for *Yargus* to jump directly to Gateway to be secured in a secure yard."

The Admiral was silent for several seconds. Captain Johnson could feel his black eyes drilling into her and she suddenly felt, again, like the imposter she had felt herself to be at the beginning of this deployment. She felt the need to confess her every shortcoming and literally had to bite her tongue to keep from shouting those shortcomings out to him.

"Captain," he began, his voice dropping to an ominous register, "I believe there are several things that have been left out of your report."

Now came the tricky part of the report, she thought.

"Sir, I left nothing out that was not classified."

"In view of the circumstances," he said in an angry whisper, "I believe that you need to read me in on whatever you have left out. This fleet was dispatched specifically to deal with this issue and I have a need to know all relevant data. I believe my clearance is sufficient to the situation."

She looked at him with her lips compressed and her eyes thinned. She couldn't tell him any more than she already had.

"Sir, I believe that you do need to know everything that has happened. I have reported everything that is not strictly classified."

The Admiral looked at Johnson with his jaw clenched tightly for several seconds, saying nothing. Then he nodded and pointed a thin knobby finger at her.

"Captain Johnson, I understand *your* situation," he said in a slightly softer, more official tone, "therefore, I officially order you to detach your ship to this fleet, until orders arrive to the contrary, and assist in the defense of this system. Now, as your commanding officer, I order you to turn over to me any relevant information that you have in your possession that will aid in that defense."

Johnson snapped up in her seat. He was brilliant! Now she had no choice but to turn over the relevant information in the Project Argos files to him.

"Yes, sir, I do not know why you were not given this information before leaving Earth. I will append all relevant files to my report and I will leave it to your discretion how far to disseminate it. I will allow you to read the files at your convenience but the cogent facts are these; *Pathfinder* and *Yargus* have redesigned engines that allow them to jump without the aid of an established gate. It was this technology that the Forrest Family was attempting to steal with the theft of *Pathfinder*. I believe that is why it was deemed of high enough importance to send *Victory* and your other vessels out here to ensure the recovery of *Pathfinder*."

She continued answering the Admiral's pointed questions until she felt drained and her head was spinning with the remnants of her earlier injury. When he finally released her to move her ship into the fleet dock for repairs she slumped back into her chair and closed her eyes until the world stopped spinning. After a few more moments she reached forward and toggled the switch to the comm suite.

"Yes, Captain?" came the immediate response.

"Get me an open channel to the ship," she asked quietly.

When the light next to her comm turned green, she took a deep breath and began.

"This is the Captain." She took another breath and organized exactly what she wanted to say, "I wanted to take this moment to say how proud I am of what we have been able to accomplish. We stood toe to toe with a Family that wanted to challenge our rights and forced them to back down. Each and every one of you had a hand in that by doing your duty under fire. We have lost some friends and our duty was not without its cost.

"You have all done well, but I believe that this is only the beginning and we will all be called upon to make further sacrifices in the days to come. I know you will continue to make me proud," she said, and toggled the switch to close the connection. She laid her head back onto her headrest and closed her eyes. *I hope I'm up to it,* she thought to herself.

CHAPTER 52
21 October
WNS *Peru*

Samuels watched the bulk of the cruiser *Dagger* as it made its way in front of *Peru*. Abruptly, a sphere of blue and white energy burst into existence, and *Dagger* faded into it. The sphere grew larger as *Peru* crept forward, until it completely filled the main viewer. After a few more seconds, the light extinguished, and the young captain and her ship were not where they once were.

She looked around the Tannar system as her head cleared from the jump transit. Her vision was taking longer to clear than normal, she noted to herself. She must be more tired than she had thought. Not surprising, since she'd only had time for one half-hour nap since she'd boarded *Peru several days before.*

"Are you all right, Captain?"

She turned and found Major Tunney standing next to her command chair. His left arm secured to his chest but his uniform somehow clean and pressed.

"Yes, Major. Just very tired."

The thought seemed funny to her. He addressed her as captain, though she wore Fleet lieutenant's planets on her collar and she called him Major though he wore Marine captain's lightning bars on his collar. Both a tradition of the fleet that struck her as funny just now. She controlled her mirth as she knew it was a product of her lack of sleep. She was Captain because this was her ship, he was called major because there could only be one 'Captain' on the ship. There was nothing humorous in that. She continued to stare forward at the viewscreen.

He turned his craggy features to face the forward viewscreen as well and chuckled slightly.

"I don't know how you could have gotten that way."

He motioned with his head toward the bosun, Felix, seated at the scan station behind them, pulling her attention back into focus. "He seems to have a bad attitude. If he is that upset about leaving Worth, he should have stayed with the rest of his shipmates at the Control Station."

Samuels turned and looked at Cipi.

"No, I don't think he's that upset to leave. He's upset that he couldn't convince me to leave this ship in the Worth system for his fellows to use to help in their counter-revolution. I think he was sure he would be able to pull it off in the end."

Tunney shook his head.

"Against what was coming in that other JP? They wouldn't even have had a chance to hide it in the outer system or the asteroid field, let alone get a crew on it to try to fight."

Samuels nodded her head and blew out a slow breath.

"They've been suffering for so long that I'm not sure they care. They might just have aimed it at the biggest ship and tried to ram it."

Tunney thought about the unarmored Granadans he had led against armored Forrester Marines and just nodded his head, saying nothing.

The silence lingered, though Tunney didn't move away. Samuels watched the monitors at the side of her command chair.

She was finally making her way out of the Worth system after all this time, but she was aboard *Peru* as her commanding officer, instead of a lowly ensign on *Pathfinder*. This was certainly not what she had imagined when Brighton ordered her back. She still wished she were part of *Pathfinder's* crew, in all honesty. With all the havoc of the last few days, it almost made her forget the chaos of the take-over of *Pathfinder*. That part of her life almost felt like a dream, or an old story about someone else, now. What she remembered most vividly were those first months coming to grips with a new assignment and reinforcing friendships with her classmates.

A picture of the corridor, here in *Peru*, after the internal battle flashed through her head, causing to jolt upright. *Had she been dozing off?*

She forced the image, and the drowsiness, away. She'd deal with both of them later. If she thought about it now, she wouldn't be able to function and finish what still needed to happen. It was just another set of memories that she stacked on top of the ones she had left over from the fighting on *Pathfinder*.

As little time as she had spent on *Pathfinder*, she still felt a loss as that ship had gone home to Gateway while she and *Peru* had come here to Tannar.

Samuels turned and looked up at Tunney.

"How are your Marines?"

"We've got the injured taken care of, for now. I've put the first group down to rest and the others are scheduled on quick shifts as soon as possible."

Samuels nodded up to the Marine.

"That's good. Make sure that you and your other officers get some rest, also."

The officer smiled as he continued to look forward to the viewscreen. This thin, inexperienced fleet officer continued to surprise him. She had no time in command, but always seemed to make the 'right' choices, as far as he was concerned. Too many young officers would be more concerned by the fallout from this last major event on their career and would ignore those other subordinates around them to fend for themselves.

"I will, ma'am. And you should be getting some rest yourself. When was the last time you got any sleep?"

Samuels looked up again and chuckled.

"I think, several hours before we left *Pathfinder*. I did lay down for a bit a while back, but I don't know if I actually slept. How about you?"

Tunney grunted with another smile as he started for the hatch.

"Seems about right."

"Comm?"

"Yes, ma'am?"

"Get Tannar Central. Ask them if we could be directed to a dock where we would be able to transfer our wounded and also bring on officers and crew to work as a relief crew for *Peru*."

"Yes, ma'am."

"Very well, I'll be in my quarters when you receive an answer. I don't want to be disturbed for anything that is not urgent. Page Ensign Roberts and have her come to the bridge."

Samuels stood and started for the hatch as well. Her legs almost wouldn't lift her from the command chair. She forced herself to march across the bridge. She couldn't let them see how tired she really was. She hated to call Roberts to the bridge, but she had forced her XO to get some sleep before the engagement, and again after, with a sedative, so she had to be more ready to make decisions than she was right now. She just needed a few hours' sleep and she'd be ready to go again.

"Captain, there is a communication from *Victory*."

Samuels stopped in mid-stride. She looked at the comm tech.

"Is it an answer to our request for additional crew?"

Samuels thought about all of the Forrester Marines and techs that they had locked up in temporary quarters and brig facilities around the ship. After letting the Granadans off at the control gate, they had more prisoners on the ship than they had crew and Marines to guard them. While they had the situation under control right now, it was a disaster waiting to happen.

Based on her experiences on *Pathfinder* and *Peru*, Samuels was of the opinion that disasters always happen if you don't eliminate any possibility that they might kindle themselves.

She needed more crew on this ship. Of course, the likelihood was that any new crew that came to this ship would bring a new commander and she would be replaced. Lieutenants didn't command new destroyers, after all.

"I'm not sure, ma'am. It is encoded with the command codes and labeled for your eyes only."

Samuels stood, all thought of sleep evaporated as she tried to figure out the message. It was completely outside of standard procedures. Had the admiral changed the routine due to the near-war setting they were operating in? She could feel the bridge crew's eyes on her as she stood there.

"Very well, transfer the message to my office. I'll decode it there."

She set her shoulders and walked calmly to the hatch and out into the corridor before she let any of her anxiety show, then she hustled the rest of the way to her office. She knew where it was, adjoining the captain's berth, but she hadn't actually been in either of the two rooms yet.

It took her half an hour to decode the message and for her world to fall apart.

* * * * *

Samuels felt the shuttle settle down onto the deck of the battleship *Victory* and looked at the others on the small ship with her. Lieutenant Aichele sat across from her in his dress black Marine uniform. It was his enlisted uniform, with the rank removed and his new gold Second Lieutenant planet clipped to the collar. All the crew had moved their personal storage from their previous ships to *Peru* before the transfer to Tannar. With *Yargus* and *Pathfinder* heading directly to Gateway, their gear would have been inaccessible otherwise. Luckily, that made the switch to their Dress Blacks possible. When Samuels had seen the list of the group ordered to the flagship, she knew it was not just for an update of the actions in Worth. When the replacement crew had arrived, she had indeed been replaced. A short lieutenant commander named Monroe had read the orders to her nearly as soon as his feet had touched the deck, taking command of *Peru* from her just as suddenly. He had then ordered her, Aichele, Sullivan, Burton and Giannini to board his shuttle to transfer back to the flagship in order to confer with the admiral. Samuels had seen this in the orders that had come from *Victory* and had ordered all of them to clean up and to get into their best uniforms. She had a feeling that bad things were coming, and she wanted them all to present the best image possible.

With this group, the topic had to be the takeover of *Pathfinder*. With Brighton gone, the admiral needed those who had the most contact with the issue to present him with their reports. Samuels *hoped* that was what he needed. If he was doing any further investigation of the mutiny or the takeover, her own family peculiarities might come into question. They had been hidden when she went to the academy. But the academy investigation for entry would not be nearly as extensive as a general investigation into a shipboard mutiny and Marine recapture of a major R & D investment, if Admiral Koutsoudas decided that was what he wanted to do.

Samuels hoped that was not what they were headed for.

The transit to the Flagship passed without a sound as the two armed Marines watched them from the front of the shuttle. Samuels felt like a prisoner and didn't feel like talking. Apparently neither did any of the others.

The landing was smooth and Samuels realized that she had been drowsing again. She cursed herself as she thought of all of the plans she should have been making.

As the hatch finally started to unseal, she rose to exit, the rest of the crew following her to the rear of the shuttle. She stopped so short that Aichele nearly ran into her before he could stop. She started moving again before anyone else could notice, trying to keep the embarrassment from her face. She had come from the academy and served on *Pathfinder*, a *Risea* class ship that displaces 32 kilotons and moved from that to *Peru*, that had been built from the plans of the *Brazil*-class destroyers which displaced 42 k-tons. And she had just walked into the boatbay of one of only two battleships ever built by humanity. They had both been constructed during the Vector Rebellion as command vessels, and *Victory* was nearly ten times the size of *Pathfinder*, displacing nearly 312 kilotons.

Samuels had been momentarily overwhelmed by the old ship. She thought she was used to being in the Fleet, but she had just discovered a new and very different type of Fleet than she had been sailing in. She was pulled out of her thoughts by a troop of Marines standing to the front of the shuttle. They stood to arms, with weapons in hand, as she turned to them and the captain at their front stepped forward.

"Ensign Monica Samuels, Gunnery Sergeant Eric Aichele, Staff Sergeant Jill Burton, Technician 1c Amber Sullivan, Technician 1c Crystal Giannini; you are all under arrest for mutiny and treason to the Warner Family. You will submit yourselves to answer for these crimes."

Samuels heard mumbling begin as soon as her rank was changed at the beginning of the statement and Crystal was ready to revolt by the end. Aichele grabbed Giannini's arm to keep her from trying to assault six armed Marines. He was the first to find his words. He waved an arm to hold back the others, though no one else had moved.

"Everyone hold on a minute. They will have the statements of all of those involved. Let's not let things get out of hand here before we know what is going on."

Samuels could not begin to form any structured thoughts, but she had no plans for trying to fight what was happening, physically. The Marines were huge and already had weapons at the ready, while the five of them had already been through a wringer. Still, the fear of an investigation nearly sent her into a panic.

She had gotten so close to what she wanted, and then her life goals had been derailed by a group of idiot opportunist pirates. And the truth was, she had found that she was good at what she did in the Fleet. She had thought about staying in Warner Fleet after everything was over. Now it might all be ruins if she couldn't make this investigation go away, and she couldn't even think of anything to say. What a waste!

The Marine captain didn't give them any time to think or to make any resistance. She motioned to three of her troops and they holstered their weapons and moved forward to begin restraining the prisoners, starting with Giannini.

She made another move to resist, but stopped at a small headshake from Aichele. He turned back to face Samuels, and when she didn't react, turned to the captain, giving her the shipboard promotion, "Major, there is obviously some small misunderstanding going on here. I understand that you are doing your duty, but could you please inform your superiors that there are records from Commodore Brighton that stipulate our clearance from all of these charges and ask them to review those documents?"

The officer nodded a small nod at Aichele as her troops continued to bind all of the prisoners.

"I believe the admiral is aware of all documentation on the mutiny and was aware before filing these charges, but I'll pass on all comments and actions that have taken place here to my superiors."

She looked at all the prisoners as she continued, "Your representatives will be along soon to confer with you about your defense."

The five shipmates were then escorted forward to the exit hatch out of the boatbay. As soon as they passed into the corridor beyond, they took a ladderway down to M Deck and started marching forward. Samuels had gained enough control to notice that the Marines were not acting angry or scared or emotional in any way. They were just doing their job. After the last several months, where every action that she took could mean her life, people just doing their jobs was something that came across as strange to her now. These people didn't really have a clue as to what was going on yet. She followed the group as they marched through the passageways, two Marines out front, one on each side, and two in the back with the commander. She watched the few non-Marines here on M-deck look on in curiosity at a group going by under guard, but no one ever stopped to watch or ask questions. Finally, they arrived at the security suite and the brig.

She had hoped that they would be put into some kind of stateroom or chambers where they would be kept until this was all resolved. It appeared they would be locked away instead. The exhaustion of the last few days started to settle itself on her again. She couldn't think of what to do. There had to be a way out of this.

They marched into the security station and passed the monitoring consoles and stopped at the first brig cell. It was a solid white door, glistening with a cleanliness that nothing on *Pathfinder* or *Peru* could match at this point. Another example, to Samuels, of the difference between this world and hers. She had gotten used to functioning in the warrior world of making things work in the the most efficient possible way, no matter how rough. She needed to shift back to the clean world that she had used to start taking back *Pathfinder*. The clean, precision planning. She needed to think clearly, but she was *so* tired. It was hard to think.

She was forced out of her thoughts as one of the guards lightly pushed her into the opening cell doorway. He turned her around and quickly removed her bindings and released her as he closed the door with a solid locking clack. She took a few steps into the small room. There was a single small bed, a shining sink, and an open toilet against the wall. The room was slightly cold. She looked around, trying to think about a plan as she sat down on the edge of the bed. She laid her head on the pillow and before she could come up with another thought, she dropped into a welcome oblivion.

CHAPTER 53
21 October
Forrest Main Complex – Earth

"This meeting will come to order," Amanda Forrest intoned, many hours before the sun arose along the eastern coast of North America. She knew that none of the other Families adhered to Roberts' Rules nearly so precisely as Forrest did, and the exactness of the opening was a calculated move to emphasize who was running this conference.

It took nearly a full minute for each of the virtual presence avatars to seat themselves and for the side conversations to quiet down. These, too, were calculated gestures, intended to underscore that each of them was completely independent, and were coming to order only on their own terms; because they were being courteous, not taking orders.

None of the other Family leaders were physically in the room with her, preferring to remain in their own enclaves. Given the rapidity with which this conference had been arranged, and the very early hour, Amanda really couldn't blame them for choosing to meet virtually. It fitted with her needs, too, since there were too many eyes watching the movements of such powerful figures.

The conferencing software had seated Jill-Andra Norcross to Amanda's immediate left. The Norcross president had held that post for longer than many in the meeting had even been alive. Her body was actually showing some signs of its age: wrinkles, gray hairs, liver spots; which, given her unopposed access to every age-defying therapy in existence, meant she was far older even than she appeared.

Horace Seligman held the next position at the table. Horace, like most in the Seligman Family, avoided any modern genetic therapy, and proclaimed it proudly by his mostly bald head and not-quite-straight teeth. Of all the Family heads Amanda had invited, Horace was easily the most genial and easy-going. He was no pushover, though. You couldn't run a Family for even a day if you were. Amanda made a mental note not to underestimate him, as many had done in the past.

Directly across from Amanda was Timothy Walton, who had only taken over the pharmaceutical giant two years before. Timothy was as inscrutable as his Family was always reputed to be. Every Family paid close attention to internal information security, but Walton put all the others to shame. Rumor had it that each of their enclaves was built with eight concentric rings, with increasing layers of security at each. No one knew for sure if this were true, because no one but a full Walton citizen was allowed inside the outermost ring, enforced by a full-body genetic ID scan. Amanda had spoken to Timothy dozens of times, but she did not know even the most basic of personal facts about him.

Paola DaGama was to Amanda's right. She represented the only one for whom Forrest was confident on which side of this issue she would come down.

Hyrum Weigant, taking the last open seat between DaGama and Walton, looked barely awake. He was conferencing in from his Family's main enclave in Dallas, which made it an hour earlier for him. Norcross was in Boston, Walton in Havana, and Seligman in Caracas; all three in the same time zone as Forrest. DaGama, located two hours ahead in Sao Paolo, was the only one for whom this was a decent hour.

"Thank you all for joining me this morning, especially on such short notice," Amanda began, once the others had settled.

"There is only one item of business on the agenda, and I grant the floor to Paola to open the question."

Paola rose promptly to her feet. "I move that the six Families represented here form an alliance directed toward removing the monopoly on interstellar travel and extrasolar territory held by the Warner, Fermi, Portales, and Sterling Families."

"Those are a lot of big words, Paola," Norcross said acidly. "Are you sure you know what all of them mean?"

"Of course I do, Jill," DaGama said sweetly. "*I'm* not the one with senility problems."

"Then tell me how a *mono*poly can be held by four separate Families? Wouldn't that make it a quadropoly?" the old woman fired back.

"A tetrapoly, actually," Horace supplied helpfully. "Greek roots. Although," he continued after a pause, "oligopoly is the more common phrase, if much less precise."

"Oh, stop nitpicking," Paola directed at Jill-Andra, ignoring Seligman. "You understand the intent of the motion, and the exact wording can be ironed out if it gets as far as a treaty."

Norcross looked ready to continue the argument, but a rap from the gavel held her tongue. "There is a motion on the floor. Is there a second?" Amanda said into the ensuing break in the storm.

The silence held for longer than was comfortable. Amanda was about to second the motion herself, procedural gray area or not, when Timothy spoke up. "Second."

"It has been properly moved and seconded that this group form an alliance with the aim of removing control of interstellar travel, and ownership of extrasolar territories from being held exclusively by the four Families named." Amanda very judiciously avoided repeating the disputed word. "Is there any debate? The chair recognizes the author of the motion."

Paola once again rose to her feet. "Business conditions for the last few decades have been getting tighter and tighter. In the past twenty years, there have been nine new worlds settled, and populations are up 11%. That should translate into larger markets, and better cost structures as economies of scale come into play. However, delivery expenses over that same period have gone up an average of 164%; with Warner being the worst gouger at a 210% increase.

"The result has been a marked difference between what we can sell on Earth, and what is economically feasible to ship off-world. There has been an even more marked difference between the growth experienced by our Families, as well as the others tied to this world's economy, and the four space-faring Families. Essentially, our ability to grow our Families has been halted. Market growth on Earth and the other habitats in the Sol System has been practically non-existent for fifteen years, while market size outside this system has more than doubled."

"Do you have anything to say that we don't already know?" Norcross asked. "If not, I'm going back to bed."

Paola glared at the other woman, then dropped the remainder of her prepared statement. "DaGama has laid claim to off-world territory and begun building a fleet of ships to defend it. We want to know if any of you other Families are interested in joining us and expanding your growth opportunities," she summarized and sat back down.

Three of the other corporate heads voiced questions and exclamations at once. As usual, Walton showed no outward change, as if the statement was not news to him. The din from the other three was incomprehensible, and Amanda again had to tap, then pound, the gavel to restore order. "One at a time! Quiet unless you have the floor!" Once everyone had settled down, Amanda asked, "Paola, were you done?"

She smiled sweetly. "I have plenty of details to go with that statement, but I know how cranky Jill-Andra gets without a nap, so I'll just leave it at that."

"All right, further debate, anyone?"

Four hands shot up, requesting the floor. "The chair recognizes Seligman," Amanda announced, fielding another of Norcross' glares.

Horace did not stand as Paola had, which was not strictly proper, but he did address his questions to the chair, which was. "Madame Chair, could you please have Miss DaGama elaborate on precisely what we are being asked to sign onto? As things stand, the motion on the floor could be interpreted a number of ways. I, for one, would appreciate a delineation of the terms being proposed."

"Paola?" Amanda nodded to her.

DaGama stood once again, and shot a look at Norcross, daring her to interrupt again. "Okay, let's lay all the card out on the table. One: we all know that the rules are slanted to keep any of us from claiming other systems. 'Whoever gets there first can claim the system.' Seems fair, until you realize that those four Families control all the jump points and gates, so no one can go anywhere they don't want you to."

Norcross looked like she was going to point out, again, that everyone in the room already knew this, but a warning look from Amanda stopped her.

"I know this is all old news to you," Paola continued, aware of the byplay to her left, "but it is the root of the problem each of us is facing. Without expanding to other worlds ourselves, other Families control how much we are able to grow. If that state is allowed to continue, we will steadily lose power and influence to Sterling, Warner, Fermi, and Portales, until we'll have no options but to take whatever crumbs they deign to leave us.

"What none of you were aware of was that new technology has been developed that allows a ship to jump between points without using either a jump point or jump gate."

Jill-Andra sat up straight at that, and her jaw fell slack. Even Timothy seemed surprised this time. Hyrum Weigant was wide awake now, his sharp mind instantly processing what that would mean for his company.

"Who developed this technology, and when will it be available to license?"

"Warner, and never," Paola responded, before Amanda could tell him he was out of order. "This is simply one more tool they can use to expand their influence without sharing anything with the rest of us. Both Forrest and DaGama made separate attempts to acquire this technology," she gave a slight emphasis to the word 'separate,' a little jab at Forrest for the double-cross of their joint efforts, "but were either unable to seize control of a test ship, or, since the test ship described was spotted jumping into the Sol System earlier today, unable to keep Warner from retrieving their stolen property."

This news had an even more profound effect on everyone than the last pronouncement had; everyone except Timothy Walton, once again his inscrutable self, who simply looked back and forth between DaGama and Forrest, his tanned face and brown eyes giving nothing away.

"Are you *insane*?" Norcross squeaked. "That's clearly provocation to enact the Treaty of Dallas against both of your Families! And you want *us* to ally ourselves with *you*? What makes you think that any of us are that stupid?!"

"That is a valid question," Horace pointed out mildly.

"Hold your horses, there, you two. I'm sure that the lady was about to explain the whole situation," Weigant said, then turned back to Paola and tapped the brim of his Stetson so it rested higher on his head, "weren't you?"

"Yes, I was," Paola said calmly. "But please wait to hear the whole story before you decide anything, especially what our plan is for moving forward." She turned to the head of the table, "Do you want to tell your story first?"

"No, thank you, Paola," Amanda said with a smile. "You're doing an admirable job. Why don't you go ahead, and I will fill in anything that gets missed."

The DaGama leader had evidently hoped to let Amanda take over, which was not surprising, since she was about to reveal information that could lead to the legal disincorporation of her Family, but she nodded anyway. She paused to accept a glass that was handed to her from outside the pickup range of the 3-

D scanner, and took a drink before she continued. "Nearly twenty years ago, the DaGama board met to address the very projections I just brought up with all of you. Several options were considered, most of which amounted to 'wait and see.' The plan we eventually decided to implement led us to place agents in various positions within the space-faring Families as a long-term investment in the possibility of laying claim to extrasolar worlds."

Paola stopped to take another drink before continuing. Amanda suspected there was something a bit more potent than water in it. Her Family, even more than Forrest, needed to gather allies to her side, and signs of the weight of that knowledge, and the uncertainty of the outcome, threatened to peek through her mask.

"All told, we were able to get two dozen or so of our own people past the security screenings and into sensitive jobs," Paola continued, "and about the same number that we were able to bribe or coerce to provide us with information. One of this latter group was the captain of a Sterling exploration ship. The ship's course led her exploring out past Cambridge for nine months and mapping out systems where planets within the ability of terraforming to transform could be found, and the process of expanding begun. This captain came across a system containing a world that needed no terraforming, but could be colonized almost at once. She took steps, then, after leaving the system, to alter the records so that Sterling saw nothing of value there, while providing us with a place to plant our own flag.

"Of course, that was the smallest hurdle we had to overcome. Sterling still controlled the only access to that area, and it wasn't exactly on a high-traffic route, where no one would notice an extra ship coming or going. Plus, there were no permanent gate generators established in any of the systems beyond Cambridge. Some problems had engineering solutions, some could be solved by contracting services from minor families, and some by the liberal application of bribes. All of these roadblocks, in their turn, we were able to overcome, one way or another, though the cost was high. We were willing to pay it because we knew that the alternative was a slow, lingering death for the Family."

Paola took another swallow and gauged her audience. It seemed that everyone was willing to hear her out to the end, as she had requested, at least so far.

"Another of our plants was a junior officer in the Warner Navy, and it was through him that we learned of Warner's project to create an on-ship gate generator, what they're calling a 'jump drive.' This breakthrough could not have been better suited to meet our needs. Our board felt that we needed to keep a continuous presence on our newly-claimed planet, DaGama, for five years before we revealed its existence to the Ruling Council. That would have given more legitimacy to our claims of ownership. However, due to our circumstances at the time, our new colony had a limit on the materials we could provide them at the outset, and so they were in need of constant resupply. That was difficult to arrange, and every shipment increased the chances that Sterling would notice what was happening. If we had Warner's new jump drive, however, we could bypass all of Sterling's systems and build up our colony without limitations.

"It was at this point that we decided to contact Forrest to propose a joint venture." Paola nodded toward Amanda, but kept her features bland. Showing animosity would work against her, since the others would be less likely to join an alliance that was already on shaky ground. "Once we had access to the designs, Forrest would be better positioned to do the manufacturing work of building ships with the new jump drive, since their heavy equipment production facilities were large enough to mask what they were doing while constructing ships. We would have needed to build such large-scale plants, and that might have raised too many eyebrows.

"To make a long story short, there were two test ships which contained jump engines, *Vanguard* and *Pathfinder*. It was decided that our two Families would independently pursue one of the two: Forrest took *Pathfinder*, while we went after *Vanguard*. Unfortunately, neither of us was successful." Which was true, as far as it went. That the choice had been forced upon DaGama by Forrest's back-stabbing could be bypassed. No need to complicate things with too many details.

"I'm still not seeing anything to convince me to throw in with you," Jill-Andra practically spat. Paola had been sure Norcross wouldn't have the patience to wait until the whole story was done. She'd held off longer than Paola had thought she would, though.

Paola was about to snap back and Amanda was about to rap the gavel, but Weigant got there first.

"Simmer down there, Jill. Paola's not done yet, and she did say you'd need to hear it all before you could decide. Go on, Paola."

"Thank you, Hyrum," Paola acknowledged, nodding her head in his direction. "So, now you know what's happened in the past, at least from my perspective. Amanda can fill you in on her side of things in a few minutes. As for the current situation, Jill's summary is pretty accurate." Jill was, as Paola knew she would be, surprised at the admission. Paola took advantage by pressing on quickly. "Both Forrest and DaGama have broken the law and at least one treaty in our actions over the past few years, and it is likely that, if something drastic is not done, the full weight of the Ruling Council will come crashing down on us. As Jill said, there is little reason in what I have already brought up for any of you to join us."

Paola let that statement hang for several moments, knowing that everyone expected more, and she waited until the moment was right to continue.

"Little reason, except that, first, if you do nothing to stop the stranglehold the space-faring Families have, your Families will wither and die, and second, it is the Ruling Council which will have to decide whose version of events to accept, ours or Warner's, and between those of us in this conference, and those who owe us allegiance, we can control the outcome of such a vote."

All eyes turned to scan the assembled faces then, trying to judge how each of the others was taking this last statement. It was, clearly, a violation of yet another major treaty even to be discussing such vote tampering, but after a few moments, it was clear that no one was going to bring that up.

Walton raised his hand and waited for the chair to acknowledge him.

"That's an interesting statement," Timothy said drily, still giving no indication of his feelings, either favorable or negative. "But there are still some pieces missing that I hope you are planning to address. What has Forrest done that needs covering up? What alternate reality are we supposed to vote to believe over the actual one? Just how much support are you asking of us? And finally, what do we get out of it?"

Paola nodded at each of the questions, and did not look at all uneasy.

"Yes, Tim, those are all questions we are planning to address. Since the first of them can best be answered by Amanda, I will yield the floor to her." Paola sat down, and took another long drink.

Amanda rose and looked at each of them in turn before beginning.

"Let me provide the shortest answers first, if I may. For the story, we'd like you to support, Warner will claim that we have violated their property. In the last few days, we've been floating stories of improper searches and seizures at some of their jump points. When the Ruling Council meets later today, we'll have evidence to support that. We'd like you to agree with us that's what's been happening, and even bring your own stories and evidence to back that up.

"Now, the proposal that Paola and I are making is for a full partnership in all matters relating to off-world activities. If we can acquire the jump drive technology, we will share it with all of you. If we can gain concessions allowing us to inhabit other worlds, those too would be shared equally."

Walton nodded, apparently accepting the promise at face value. The Forrest CEO went on, "Back to the first question, here's what we've done. Like DaGama, my Family has been concerned with the growing power and influence of the space-faring Families for many years now; even before DaGama began taking action on the issue. Twenty-two years ago, shortly before I took on my current position, the Forrest board voted to pursue an aggressive program to force our way into the ranks of those with a planet to call their own. One of the branches of this program was the same as Paola described; to infiltrate those other Families and use those connections to occupy another planet.

"Our contacts were not the same, of course, and we wound up receiving information and support from an unlikely source. The governor of the Margin System, which was annexed by Fermi after the Vector Rebellion, found records of another jump point in the system, which no one knew anything about. The Parkinson Family had known, of course, since it was their records he had come across, but they must have taken the information with them to the grave at the end of the war. In any event, in exchange for an exorbitant amount of money, Governor Gururaja allowed us to build our own jump gate and ship unimpeded through his system, while he kept the information from being reported back to Fermi.

"We've been in the Sherwood System for twelve years now, and we have built up a considerable infrastructure there. The heavy manufacturing that Paola was concerned about we were able to implement out in the open, including building our own warships and exploration vessels. The main planet is still undergoing terraforming, but there is a permanent population above 800,000 in the system, almost all in orbital facilities. Asteroids have been providing an abundance of raw materials, and have even lowered some of the costs for our Earth-based production. In addition to these natural resources, the system also boasted three jump points, and we immediately added permanent gate generators to our list of construction projects. The first gate was the one to Margin, one went to an unclaimed system, and one connected to Worth, which belonged to Warner.

"About two and a half years ago, our board voted to take things one step further. It was clear that we could not move forward to legitimize our claim on that system without publishing the story of how we came to be there. Once the facts were out, Fermi was certain to dispute the claim, most likely with force if we wouldn't back down, which we cannot do and remain a viable Family in the long run. We could see where things were headed, and armed conflict seemed inevitable."

Many of her audience were shifting in their seats uncomfortably, but Amanda was determined that these four needed the whole truth before they signed on; actually, all five. What she was about to reveal, even Paola knew nothing about. The board's decision to double-cross DaGama had been a mistake, one which most likely led to neither of them getting what they needed. This time, she had convinced all of the board members that they had to play it straight; no secrets that would come out later and destroy their alliance. Besides, it wouldn't be long now before everyone knew everything.

"We chose to make the first moves, before anyone knew what was happening.

"Worth was our first target. Because the second jump point had never been detected from the Warner side, they still considered it a cul-de-sac system, and Worth had infrequent contact with the rest of the galaxy. But the Worth System had something which we really wanted; a high-capacity shipyard.

"So, we took it."

"The shipyard?" Horace asked.

"The whole system," Amanda clarified. By now, the others had received one shock too many. Only Paola even raised an eyebrow at this one.

"We went in hard and fast, removed Warner's military presence, and sealed off the jump point so no one got far enough in-system to see anything before leaving again. Those that we couldn't keep at a distance, we didn't allow to leave, sending back word that they were delayed due to equipment failures. We had managed to keep anyone on Earth from discovering what was going on out at the end of explored space, but all that has changed now. *Pathfinder* jumped from the Worth system into the home system a few hours ago, which means that Warner discovered its location and was able to retake it."

"Now, just hold your horses a minute, Amanda," Hyrum broke in. "You started a war with Warner, and *now* you want us not only to absolve you, but lie in court to protect you? I feel the same way you do about being locked out of market expansion opportunities, but *this*...this is going too far. I'm sorry, but count me out." Weigant's finger stabbed at the table in front of him, and his holographic image disappeared.

There was a pervasive stillness that lasted an uncomfortably long time. Finally, Amanda asked calmly, "Anyone else?" There were plenty of glances exchanged, but no one spoke. "Very well, what Hyrum said is correct, we started a war, even though Warner has only recently discovered that fact. Most of you are probably thinking that I'm insane, along with the rest of my Family. After all, Warner has a larger navy than any other Family, so the outcome of any armed conflict is a foregone conclusion, right?

"And it probably would be, if it were just Warner against Forrest, or even Warner against Forrest and DaGama. In actuality, though, if we have enough backing to control a vote in the Ruling Council, it would be Warner against the entire Combined Fleet, and that matchup is a foregone conclusion much more to my liking," she said with a predatory smile, one that quickly found an echo in the Norcross leader's face.

Amanda Forrest let that notion settle into the minds of those gathered for just a while, then said, "If there is no further debate on the topic, we'll put the question to a vote —"

"I do have something relevant that I should add before everyone votes," Timothy cut in.

"The floor is yours," Amanda said, retaking her seat.

"The Walton Family has also seen the writing on the walls for many years now. Like Forrest and DaGama, we knew that if we wanted to expand, we were going to need to force our way out into space, and defend whatever territory we were able to claim. We had not yet been able to actually acquire anything outside this system, but we do have a fleet of 48 destroyers and light cruisers which have been built and crewed. I am in favor of an alliance, and I pledge those ships to our common defense."

This time it was the Forrest CEO who was shocked. Before she could say anything more, Jill-Andra said, "We'll join."

"You can count on Seligman, as well," Horace added.

Pleased, but still off-balance, Amanda asked Timothy, "Where did you build nearly fifty ships without anyone getting the slightest notion of what you were doing?"

Walton looked pensive, and for a moment, Amanda thought he would decline to answer. At last, he shrugged.

"They're on the floor of the Caribbean."

CHAPTER 54
22 October
Ruling Council Main Complex, Geneva, Earth

Gerald Warner strode purposefully up the steps of Council Hall, doing his best to ignore the shouts of the inevitable picketers, paparazzi, and pushy journalists looking for a quote. The task was made considerably easier with four aides, four lawyers, two generals, three admirals, and a squad of serious-faced Marines surrounding him. The incessant pressure eased once they passed through the barrier of the massive cherrywood doors and left the throng behind. Once inside, all of them had to pass between the scan boards that verified their identity as well as checking for weapons. They then joined the line which had bottlenecked at the main ramp.

The group took the conveyor ramp up another level and proceeded to the center of the building, entering the enormous rotunda, where the broad granite dome was visible from all twelve levels. Here Warner left the majority of his retinue. Seating was limited inside the audience chamber, so Gerry was bringing in only Admiral Cosina, Captain Brighton, Jon Nabeyev, his chief counsel, and a single aide.

The rest of the group would wait in one of the anterooms, where they could monitor events on the council floor and send notes and comment in, if needed. Warner had to admit that his last discussion with Admiral Cosina had him evaluating possibilities much more pessimistically. Even though, by law, none of the Marines could be armed inside these walls, he still felt better knowing there were more options available to him if the situation deteriorated rapidly. After his thoughts following Cosina's comments, however, he wished he could have them closer.

Taking in a lungful of air, Gerald Warner reached out and swung the double doors wide. A low murmur rippled its way through the expansive meeting hall as all the Family heads and their attachés shuffled in and found seats. There was very little of the banter that normally accompanied these meetings, and none of the joviality that sometimes occurred. As the chrono toned the top of the hour, there was a single gavel rap and Felix Rial called the Ruling Council to order. The traditional opening statement followed, then Rial turned to Gerald Warner.

"Since this is a special meeting, as provided for in Article VII, old business will not be addressed today. There is only one item of new business specified. The floor is now yours, CEO Warner," he said calmly before moving back to his seat.

"Thank you, Mr. Chairman," Warner said, as he stood to his full height. He looked around the room and mentally counted the votes before he began. He would better know where and how to focus his statements when he knew who would be undecided.

His count came up short.

"A point of information, if you would indulge me, Mr. Chairman. I see that Horace Fermi is not here to represent his Family. Are we to expect him?"

Rial rose and turned to that area of the room, clearly not noticing before that the man was absent. He again moved behind the podium and spoke into the pickup. "Could the Fermi delegation respond, please?"

An attractive young woman rose and said, "My name is Marie Fermi, and, as the nearest relation on Earth at the time of a Council meeting, I will exercise my proxy rights for the Family."

She hadn't made it back into her seat before Amanda Forrest shot up and said, "Point of order, Mr. Chairman."

Warner cringed, knowing what was coming, and not having any legal counter to it.

"State your point," Rial directed.

"What Miss Fermi has quoted from section eight of Article V applies only to regularly scheduled meetings of the Council. In Article VII, proxy votes are specifically disallowed for specially called meetings."

"Your point is well taken," Rial told her. "Miss Fermi, you and your contingent may remain for the meeting, but without the head of Family present, Fermi will not be allowed to cast a vote today. Mr. Warner, you retain the floor."

Warner had spent the last three and a half days poring over all the evidence they had gathered. He proceeded to lay all of it out for the Ruling Council now, trying to maintain his trademark calm, not letting the anger that he deeply felt seep out. He walked through all the reports from Warner Navy and Marine officers, calling up their affidavits to the shared display. He detailed the confessions of the POWs who had spoken, and the names, ranks and citizenship of every prisoner that the WSN had captured. He paused and took a moment to look every CEO there in the eyes. Some averted their gaze. Some had looks of incredulity on their faces, and two in particular, a sneering disbelief.

"In conclusion," Warner said, "I charge both the Forrest and DaGama Families with acts of war and acts of piracy as proscribed by Articles IV, IX and XVII of the Families Bylaws. Further, I charge that their most egregious offense is that they have taken over an entire planet and enslaved the population – citizens of my Family." At this there were some vocal objections from various parties at the table in the Forrest and DaGama delegations, but Gerry plowed on with steely resolve, "and I move that these unlawful acts be redressed immediately, and that the Ruling Council resolve to enforce these Articles and their requirements!"

CEO Norcross was acknowledged by the chair for a clarifying question and asked, "How are we supposed to know that the so-called evidence you are presenting us is not falsified? How can we know that this isn't some elaborate ploy to gouge further reparations from these two competitive Families?"

Gerry Warner glared directly at Jill-Andra Norcross. His indignation had climbed to a level he didn't know possible.

"Madame Norcross, are you calling me a liar?" he shouted back, half rising from his seat.

Amanda Forrest stood and shouted, "Warner, I deny your absurd allegations and counter-charge you with willfully imprisoning innocent free citizens of my Family in order to support your asinine claims!"

Even though Conrad had warned him the opposition would try something like this, Gerry still could not believe the bald-faced guile of this woman. It took him a moment before he could make any sort of coherent reply. "My evidence is clear and ready to be tested at anyone's request. My Family has done nothing wrong of any kind! Every one of these claims is absolutely true, as hard as they are to believe. You and yours will pay for the suffering you have caused!" he shouted back, the fury and menace clear to read on his face. Warner knew that he needed to remain calm; to project a face of reason and fairness in order to keep his claims from being dismissed out of hand, but he could not put the genie back in the bottle. His fury, kept so firmly in check during the preparations for this meeting, had escaped, and tranquility eluded him like a will-o'-the-wisp.

The once orderly meeting, which had already been deteriorating, fell completely into chaos as more than half the CEOs in the room were on their feet shouting, pointing and deriding one another. Felix Rial once again banged his gavel, but the sound had no apparent effect on the unruly mob. He banged it again, and then repeated it four more times in escalating furor while he called for order. He signaled to the Sergeant at Arms, who toned the claxon once, which finally brought everyone up short. After a few last ditch insults were thrown out, the room once again became silent. Rial glared every CEO back into his or her seat. All but Warner took it.

Gerry Warner stated calmly, "Mr. Chairman, I move the previous question."

Rial, grateful to be back in parliamentary waters, called for a vote of the previous question. It passed. He then proceeded to take a roll-call vote on the main motion. When all sixteen CEOs had responded, Fermi's name being skipped from the roll, he looked back at Gerry Warner.

He took a moment, and rather quietly stated, "There were six in favor. There were five abstentions, including one absent, and there were six opposed. The motion fails for lack of a majority, Mr. Warner."

Warner, who had taken his seat as soon as the previous question had been called for, stood once again, and addressed the Chair without waiting to be recognized. He shook his head, but the anger was still roaring on his flushed face.

"It is a sad day for humanity when the purportedly rational men and women who have been called on to lead the human race cannot or will not see the facts that stare them in the face. I will not tolerate your inconceivable lack of fundamental human reason. We have not sought out a conflict with any of you, but some among you have plotted violence against my Family. I believe this was done for no other reason than pure unadulterated greed. Rather than working for mutual prosperity as we have done, you seek only to steal the fruits of our labors like a common thief in the night. And just as for any thief who is discovered, a final reckoning must come."

Warner's voice softened now, though his eyes still blazed. "I am aware that many of you feel threatened by Warner's success. Some of you hate me simply because you feel I have more than my fair share. I will not debate that today with you, since it is unlikely that any of us could agree on what is 'fair.' But I will state two facts that cannot be disputed: First, Warner has nothing that it has not earned through its own labors. And second, in all the years of you all whining about how the spacefaring Families have an unfair hold on the galaxy, not once did any of you approach me with a proposal that would have allowed me to help you expand beyond this system. Instead of extending a friendly hand and looking for an ally, you have extended instead the naked sword of an enemy, and tried to take by force what we might have shared. And that, I will not abide.

"Therefore, I hereby declare that a state of war exists between the Warner Family and all other Families which will not support it in maintaining its guaranteed rights of life, liberty, and property. The Forrest and DaGama Families have violated those rights without provocation, and I will see them punished, so help me, God!"

With that, he kicked his chair out of his way and stormed out of the room, followed by Cosina, Captain Brighton and the rest of the Warner contingent.

Seconds later, all five of the other Families which had voted in favor of Warner's motion also took to their feet and followed Warner out.

Hey, Reader.

So, you got to the end of our book. We hope that means you enjoyed it. Whether or not you did, we would just like to thank you for giving us your valuable time to let us try to entertain you. We are truly blessed to have such a fulfilling occupation, but we only have that job because of people like you; people kind enough to give our books a chance and to spend their hard-earned money buying them. For that we are eternally grateful.

If you would like to find out more about our other books, then please visit our website for full details. You can find it at:

www.7csbooks.com.

Also feel free to contact us on Facebook, Twitter, Goodreads, or email (all of the details are available on the website), as we would love to hear from you.

If you enjoyed this book and would like to help, then you could think about leaving a review on Amazon, Goodreads, or anywhere else that readers visit. The most important part of how well a book sells is how many positive reviews it has, so if you leave us one then you are directly helping us to continue on our journey as writers. Thanks in advance to anyone who does this. It means a lot.

ABOUT THE AUTHORS

Jeffery L. Cheney

Jeff is the second of the seven Cheney brothers. He has worked as a civilian contract mechanic for the US Army, a heavy equipment mechanic, a High School teacher, and currently works in high technology computer chip manufacturing.

Jeff has been writing science fiction and fantasy stories for enjoyment for over thirty-five years and has published two SF novels with his brothers; <u>Dead Reckoning</u> and <u>Day of Reckoning</u>. <u>Force of Reckoning, and Final Reckoning</u> is his fourth novel with his brothers. He is also completing his first solo novel, <u>Forged by Betrayal</u>.

He enjoys coaching youth basketball, working on cars and doing woodworking when the time allows.

He has three grown children and he lives in a small town in NW Oregon with his wife of 29 years.

Craig J. Cheney

Craig is the fourth of the Cheney sons. He holds degrees in Accounting, Business Administration, Computer Engineering, and Electrical Engineering. He has worked as a disk jockey, put on trade shows, organized a circus, taught classes on Shakespeare, Math, Debate, and Parliamentary Procedure, and is currently dabbling in rocket science.

Craig was the runner-up for the 2009 Next Mark Twain Award. He, his wife, and their children live on Utah's Wasatch Front.

Jared L. Cheney

Jared is the youngest of the brothers. He has worked for many years as the director of Information Technology for a global cloud services company.

He loves to travel and has lived and worked all over the US and in over 10 different countries.

Jared and his wife live in the Portland, Oregon area with their children.

The authors all graduated at or near the top of their respective classes at the same high school on the Oregon Coast. All three are Eagle Scouts and volunteer their time to support The Boy Scouts of America.